The Beginning and the End

NAGUIB MAHFOUZ

The Beginning and the End

Translated by
Ramses Awad
Edited by
Mason Rossiter Smith

Anchor Books
Doubleday
New York London Toronto Sydney Auckland

AN ANCHOR BOOK
PUBLISHED BY DOUBLEDAY
A division of Bantam Doubleday Dell Publishing Group, Inc.
666 Fifth Avenue, New York, New York 10103

ANCHOR BOOKS, DOUBLEDAY, and the portrayal of an anchor
are trademarks of Doubleday, a division of Bantam Doubleday
Dell Publishing Group, Inc.

This English translation was first published by
The American University in Cairo Press in 1985.
First published in Arabic as *Bidayah wa-Nihayah* in 1949.
Protected under the Berne Convention.
The Anchor Books edition is published by arrangement
with The American University in Cairo Press.

Library of Congress Cataloging-in-Publication Data
Maḥfūz, Najīb, 1911–
[Bidāyah wa-nihāyah.   English]
The beginning and the end
Naguib Mahfouz; translated by Ramses Awad;
edited by Mason Rossiter Smith.
1st Doubleday ed.
   p.   cm.
Translation of: Bidāyah wa-nihāyah.
1. Smith, Mason Rossiter, 1909–   . I. Title.
[PJ7846.A46B513   1989]   89-33116
892'.736—dc20   CIP

ISBN 0-385-26457-7   ISBN 0-385-26458-5 (pbk.)
Copyright © 1985 by The American University in Cairo Press
ALL RIGHTS RESERVED
PRINTED IN THE UNITED STATES OF AMERICA
FIRST ANCHOR BOOKS EDITION: 1989

INTRODUCTION

Naguib Mahfouz was born in 1911 in Gamaliyya, an old quarter of Cairo, which was the setting for several of his novels, to a family which earned its living from trade. When he was six years old his family moved to Abbasiyya, then at the outskirts of the capital.

Mahfouz's writings clearly reflect the deep concern of the Egyptian petite bourgeoisie with material security, its worry about the morrow, its conformity to the system, and its disinclination to challenge the authorities or the powers that be. The sole preoccupation of this class was, and perhaps still is, security.

In 1930 Mahfouz entered the Secular University in Cairo, where he studied philosophy. It was his desire to give up this field to study the Arabic language, with which he was infatuated, but since this proved to be impossible, he accepted his academic lot and obtained a B.A. in philosophy in 1934. Then he registered for the master's program in philosophy, the proposed title of his thesis being "The Concept of Beauty in Islamic Philosophy."

Almost all of his readings as a graduate student were in philosophy. His readings in literature were meager. This early concern with philosophy led him to contribute a number of essays to the field, such as "The Evolution of Social Phenomena," "What Is Philosophy?," "Bergson's Philosophy," "Perception and the Senses," "The Decline of Some Beliefs and the Emergence of Others," "Pragmatism," and "Old and New Trends in Psychology." Slim as his readings in literature at that time were, the choice of aesthetics as the topic for his unfinished thesis (perhaps never embarked on) is evidence of his long-standing love for the arts.

With his awakening to literature in the late thirties, Mahfouz turned to Arab as well as Western literary masterpieces. He was greatly influenced by the works of Taha Hussein, Abbas al-Akkad, and Salama Mousa, and openly acknowledges this influence. Mahfouz says that he learned the meaning of intellectual revolt from Taha Hussein, and acquired a belief in the value of the arts, democracy, and individual liberty from Akkad. In Akkad's *Sarah,* he also found an Arabic prototype of the psychological novel. From Salama Mousa, Mahfouz gained an awareness of the value of science, socialism, and intellectual tolerance, and the opportunity to publish many of his articles in *The New Magazine.*

When Mahfouz appeared on the literary scene, the Arabic novel was still a new genre, received from his predecessors in a crude form that only vaguely foretold the changes it would undergo as Mahfouz and his contemporaries transformed it into a highly developed art form. In order to develop their talents, however, he and the other novelists of his generation felt they needed to become acquainted with the fictional heritage and techniques of the West.

Mahfouz read widely in the literature of the West, reading world literature either in English or in Arabic translations. On the whole, he found it much easier to read the moderns—the difficulties of the foreign languages of earlier periods stood between him and the classics. He is conscious of this limitation and the resulting gap in his readings: as he ruefully points out, instead of going directly to the masters, he has learned at the hands of their disciples. He regrets that he has never read Dickens or Balzac, both precursors of the realistic novel for which Mahfouz himself is noted; instead, he discovered realism in the works of such authors as Huxley, Lawrence, Galsworthy, and Flaubert.

His favorites in Russian literature were Tolstoy, Dostoyevsky, Turgenev, and Chekhov; in German literature, Thomas Mann, Goethe, and Kafka. Of French literature he read Anatole

France, Flaubert, Proust, Malraux, Mauriac, Sartre, and Camus; of English, Shakespeare, Wells, Shaw, Joyce, Huxley, and Lawrence; of American, Hemingway, Faulkner, Dos Passos, O'Neill, Tennessee Williams, and Arthur Miller. Much as he has gained from the work of these authors, none of them has visibly affected his own fiction, which remains unmistakably Egyptian, a clear testimony to his uniqueness and originality.

When Mahfouz started his novelistic career Egypt was undergoing a period of political unrest, suppression, and despotism. In June 1930 the notorious despot Ismail Sidki became Prime Minister. He suspended the 1923 constitution under the pretext that Egypt was not yet ready for a Western-style democracy. Silencing all opposition, he brutally crushed any attempt at questioning his authority. A ferocious and merciless attack was launched against Taha Hussein for daring to voice and publish some skeptical views about pre-Islamic poetry, and he was accused of being a heretic and a disciple of the devil. The tumult ended with his expulsion as dean of the Faculty of Arts. Akkad's fate was no better: he landed in prison on the charge that he had abused the royal family.

In this repressive atmosphere, Mahfouz acquired a serpentine wisdom which he has never lost. Realizing, like his predecessor Tawfik al-Hakim, the futility of open rebellion against the autocracy of the ruler, he managed to devise a narrative method that would imply criticism of the system without jeopardizing his interests or running the risk of antagonizing the authorities. As the painful lessons of the early thirties sank into his mind, the wary Mahfouz veiled in his historical fiction his criticism of contemporary Egypt, whose plight he blamed on three sources: despotic monarchy, imperialism, and the servants of imperialism. In three historical novels set in ancient Egypt, *The Mockery of Fate* (1939), *Radobais* (1943), and *The Struggle of Thebes* (1944), he mixed history with symbols, projecting his political sentiments into the events of pharaonic history.

In the later forties and fifties, Mahfouz began employing a

more realistic style, with modern Egypt as his setting. Between 1956 and 1957, he produced his famous trilogy, consisting of *Bayn al-Qasrayn*, *Qasr al-Shawq*, and *al-Sukkariyya*, in which he depicted the vicissitudes of fate which swept up three generations of a Cairene family from the 1920s up to the Second World War. To this phase also belong *The Beginning and the End* (written in 1942–43 and published in 1949), *The New Cairo* (1945), *Khan el-Khalili* (1946), and *Midaq Alley* (1947). *The Beginning and the End* is a masterpiece of human compassion. So striking is its humanitarianism and sensitivity to human suffering that its tragic vision of life transcends the Egyptian locale and assumes universal significance. It reflects with sympathy and well-balanced pathos the material, moral, and spiritual problems of an Egyptian petit bourgeois family confronted with poverty during the Second World War.

A versatile and prolific writer, Mahfouz published a number of other novels, including *Awlad Haritna* (1959, published in English as *The Children of Gebelawi*), an allegorical novel with metaphysical implications that deals with man's quest and thirst for religious faith. In the 1960s, Mahfouz returned to his fictional preserve, the social novel, experimenting now with more impressionistic, psychological styles. In 1961 he published *The Thief and the Dogs*, this time mixing social and political realism with the stream-of-consciousness technique, new to the Arabic novel. Again, the quest for the mystical and spiritual is to be found in his novels *The Beggar* (1965) and *Chitchat on the Nile* (1966).

The importance of Mahfouz's work as social and political commentary is well described by M. M. Badawi in an article written for *The Egyptian Bulletin* in June 1982:

The destinies of the individual characters are the microcosm, but the macrocosm is the destiny of modern Egypt. The tragedies, the poignant sufferings, the conflicts of the numerous men and women who people these novels reflect the larger social, intellectual, and political changes in one significant part of the modern Arab world. The struggle of the younger generation of men and women to attain their domestic freedom to shape their own lives mirrors or parallels the nation's struggle to achieve political independence and to free itself from the shackles of outworn and debilitating, almost medieval, conventions and world outlook in a gigantic endeavor to belong to the modern world.

On the whole, this is a valid description of Mahfouz's fictional world. But it is not this which inflamed my imagination and so much stirred my feelings that I was eager to translate *The Beginning and the End*. More often than not, critics focus their attention on the social, political, and documentary aspects of Mahfouz's work, reducing him to a mere producer of sociopolitical commentary. They very regrettably ignore his powerfully tragic vision of life. There is something Shakespearean about the unfortunate lot of the miserable family which unfolds in *The Beginning and the End,* just as there is something Shakespearean about the tragic fate of the family in Thomas Hardy's *Tess of the D'Urbervilles*. Nevertheless, a gleam of the hope for regeneration penetrates the almost overwhelming gloom of both novels.

RAMSES AWAD

The Beginning
and the End

ONE

The master in charge of school discipline cast a gloomy look down the long corridor which overlooked the upper school classes. The Tawfikiyah School was enveloped in deep silence. He went to one of the junior classes, knocked apologetically, and approached the teacher, whispering a few words to him. The teacher looked intently at a pupil in the second row and called out, "Hassanein Kamel Ali."

At the sound of his name, the pupil arose, casting his eyes in suspense and anxiety from his teacher to the school proctor. "Yes, sir," he murmured.

"Go with the proctor," said the teacher.

The boy left his desk and followed the proctor, who walked slowly out of the classroom. Uneasy about the reason for this summons, Hassanein kept asking himself: Could it be those recent demonstrations? He had taken part in them, shouting together with the others, "Down with Hor. Down with Hor, son of a bull!" He thought he had escaped the bullets, the canes, and school punishments altogether. Had he been optimistic? Thoughtfully, he followed the proctor along the long corridor, expecting him to turn around at any moment and confront him with whatever charges he had against him. This train of thought was interrupted when the man halted in front of one of the senior classes and excused himself before entering. He heard the teacher calling out, "Hussein Kamel Ali." He wondered: My brother, too! But how can he be charged with anything of the sort when he never participated in any demonstrations? The proctor returned, followed by the dumbfounded boy. As soon as he saw his brother, Hassanein murmured in astonishment, "You, too! What's wrong?"

They exchanged puzzled glances, then followed the proctor as he strode off in the direction of the headmaster's office. "Why," Hussein asked him gently and politely, "have we been called out of class?"

"You're to see the headmaster," the proctor answered hesitantly.

Silently, they continued along the remaining part of the corridor. The two brothers looked very much alike. Both had long faces, large hazel eyes, and deep, dark complexions. Yet the nineteen-year-old Hussein, the elder by two years, was shorter than his brother. Hassanein had fine features, which made him look more radiantly handsome than his brother. Nearing the headmaster's office, they became more alarmed. In awe and apprehension, they saw his stern countenance in their mind's eyes. The proctor buttoned his jacket, knocked on the door, gently opened it, and entered, nodding to the boys to follow. They went in, staring at the man, who was bent over his desk facing the door. He was carefully reading a letter; as if he were unaware of their presence, he did not raise his eyes to the newcomers. The proctor greeted the headmaster with extreme courtesy.

"Here are the two pupils, Hussein and Hassanein Kamel Ali," he said.

Folding the letter in his hands, the headmaster lifted his head. He extinguished a cigarette butt in an ashtray, and glanced steadily from one brother to the other.

"Which class are you in?" he asked.

"Four D," answered Hussein, his voice trembling.

"Three C," said Hassanein.

"I hope you can take what I have to tell you as brave young men should," he said, looking at them intently. "Your elder brother has informed me that your father is dead. My condolences."

They were stunned and deeply perturbed. Hassanein was unable to comprehend the news.

"Dead!" he exclaimed. "My father dead! Impossible!"

"But how?" Hussein murmured as if to himself. "Only two hours ago we left him in good health, getting ready to go to the Ministry."

For a moment, the headmaster was silent. "What does your elder brother do for a living?" he asked them gently. "Nothing," Hussein absently replied. "Don't you have another brother?" the man continued. "A public servant, perhaps, or something of that sort?" Hussein shook his head. "No," he answered.

"I hope you can bear up under the shock like men," said the headmaster. "Now, go home. May God help you."

TWO

They left the school and walked along Shubra Street, groping their way through their tears. Hassanein was the first to weep. Nervous, Hussein wanted to scold him, but his own tears gushed forth, his voice was choked with sobs, and he kept silent. They crossed to the other side of the street and quickened their pace toward the blind alley, Nasr Allah, a few minutes' walk from the school.

"How did he die?" Hassanein asked his brother as if he were looking to him for help. Stunned, Hussein shook his head. "I don't know," he murmured. "I can't imagine how it could have happened. He had his breakfast with us and we left him in good health. I don't know how it happened . . ."

Hassanein tried to recall the details of this morning's events. The first time he saw his father, he remembered, was when he came out of the bathroom. As usual, he said good morning to his father. Smiling, his father replied, "Good morning. Isn't your brother up yet?" Then they gathered around the breakfast table. His father asked their mother to share their meal; saying that she didn't feel like eating, she excused herself. "Join us and you'll have an appetite," the man said, but she insisted. Shelling an egg, he said indifferently, "Do as you like." Hassanein couldn't recall having heard him again, except for a brief cough. His last sight of his father was the man's back as he went into his bedroom, wiping his hands with his towel. Now he was gone! Dead! What a horrible word. Secretly casting a fearful glance, Hassanein saw his brother's sad, grief-stricken face, set hard as though he had suddenly grown old. Memories returned to him in painful anguish. *I don't believe he's dead. I can't believe it! What is death? No, I can't believe it! Gone! Had I known that this would be his last day on earth, I would never have left the house. But how could I have known? Does a man die while he's eating and laughing? I don't believe it. I can't believe it.* Hassanein was recalled from his thoughts as his brother pulled him by the arm toward Nasr Allah, which in his distraction he had almost passed by. They walked along the narrow alley, lined on both sides with old houses and small shops and cluttered with paraffin oil and vegetable and fruit carts. Their eyes sought their three-storied house with its huge dusty yard. Then they heard the wailings and screams. Distinguishing the voices of their mother and elder sister, they were so deeply moved that they burst out crying. They ran on heedlessly, climbing the stairs two at a time until they reached the second floor. They found the door of their flat open and rushed in, crossed the hall to their father's bedroom at the far end, and entered it, panting. Their eyes fixed on the bed, the form of a dead body apparent under the coverlet. They approached the edge of the bed and, weeping hysterically, flung themselves upon it. Their mother and sister ceased their wailing and two strange women in the room departed. Their mother, dressed in black, her eyes red with weeping, her nose and cheeks swollen, composed herself to help her sons in their pent-up grief. Their sister threw herself on the sofa, hiding her face in its back. Her body was shaking with sobs. Hussein was weeping, mechanically reciting short verses from the Koran asking for God's mercy to fall on his dead father. Fear-stricken, distracted, and incredulous, Hassanein was crying, too. He stood in the presence of death, protesting and rebellious, yet helpless and frightened. *This cannot be my father. My father would never have heard all this crying without stirring. Oh, my God, why is he so still? They are wailing, as resigned, helpless people do. I had never conceived of this; and I still don't. Didn't I see him only two hours ago walking in this very room? No, this is not my father, this is not life.* Waiting seemed endless. Then, Samira, the mother of the two young men, moved toward them. "That's enough. Hussein," she said, leaning forward. "Get up and take your brother outside."

She kept repeating the same words until Hussein got up and pulled his brother to his feet. But they did not leave the room; instead they stood there, staring through misty, streaming eyes at the body laid out upon the bed. Hussein couldn't resist a mysterious inner urge. He bent over the body and lifted the cover from the face, not heeding the movement which his mother made. He looked upon the strange countenance, frightfully blue, mute evidence of the extinction of every living thing. An unearthly stillness hovered over it, as deep and infinite as nothingness itself. His limbs shuddered. Neither brother had seen a dead man before. They were frightened as well as sad. Deep within them, they experienced a piercing, all-conquering sorrow which they had never known before. Bending over the dead body, Hussein kissed the forehead; and once more he shuddered. Hassanein also bent over it, and, almost in a trance, kissed it. The mother pulled the bedcover back over the dead face; standing between them and the bed, she firmly said to her sons, "Go out."

They took two steps backward. Suddenly obstinate, Hassanein stopped. Emboldened by his brother, Hussein did the same. In a semi-trance, their eyes roved about the room, as if expecting a mysterious transformation to change it all. Yet they found it exactly the same. At the right of the entrance stood the bed; the wardrobe in front, the peg next to it. At the left was the sofa upon which their sister had flung herself. A lute lay against the edge of the sofa, the quill in place between the strings. Surprised and disturbed, their eyes focused on the lute. Their father's fingers had often played upon those very strings; often delighted friends had gathered around him, begging him to repeat the same tune—as he always did. How thin is the line between joy and sorrow, even thinner than the strings of the lute! Their wandering eyes fell upon the dead man's watch, still softly ticking as it lay on a table near the bed. On its face, the dead man might have read the date of his departure from this world and of his sons' initiation as orphans. Perspiration stains on the collar, his shirt still hung on its peg. They looked at it with profound tenderness. At that moment, it seemed to them that a man's sweat was more lasting than his life, however great. The mother watched them in silence, uninterested in the thoughts crossing their minds, for she realized the full impact of the catastrophe which had befallen them—and that her sons were not yet completely aware of all that it would mean. A deep sigh escaped from Hassanein, catching his brother's attention. Hussein placed his hand upon his brother's shoulder.

"Let's go," he whispered. The two young men cast farewell glances at the dead body, sharing the traditional belief that, even in death, their father's eyes could still see them. Lest they hurt his feelings, they avoided turning their backs to him. With a warm parting greeting, they retreated backward to the door and left the room. Hassanein noted the profound sadness on his brother's face, and his heart quivered in compassion and a pressing need for mutual sympathy.

THREE

The two brothers left the flat and went downstairs to the entrance of the house, where some chairs had been placed in rows. There sat Hassan, their eldest brother, silent and gloomy. They sat down beside him, sharing his quiet melancholy. What to do now? They had no idea. Hassan, however, was an experienced man of the world. He closely resembled his two brothers, yet the look in his eyes was very different from theirs—daring and devil-may-care. Moreover, his ostentatious manner of styling his bushy hair and the way he wore his suit implied, on the one hand, that he took good care of himself and, on the other, that he possessed great cheapness of character. Hassan always knew just what to do. Yet he remained there sitting in his place, doing nothing, for he was expecting an important person to arrive.

"How did our father die?" Hussein inquired, deeply agitated.

"He died suddenly, to our amazement," he answered with a frown. "He was putting on his clothes, and I was sitting in the hall. All of a sudden I heard our mother calling me in such a terrified voice that I rushed into the room to find him flung on the sofa, his breast heaving up and down. He was motioning, in pain, to his heart and breast. So we carried him to bed. We offered him a glass of water, but he couldn't drink. I hurried out of the room to call a doctor; but no sooner did I reach the yard than sharp wails struck my ears. When I came back, terrified, it was all over."

Watching his brothers' faces as they twisted in pain, Hassan's own countenance became even gloomier than before. He was afraid his brothers might think he was not really sad. Obviously, they knew about the differences and quarrels he had had with his parents over his recklessly irresponsible life; and he feared they might think him less grief-stricken than themselves. For he really was sad. In fact, despite their strained relations, he had never hated his father. If his sorrow differed from theirs, this was because, at twenty-five, he was older and more experienced in life, with its pleasures and frustrations; indeed, the latter made death seem less bitter. True enough, his heart kept telling him, never after today would he hear anyone yell at him, "I can't support a failure like you forever. As long as you've chosen to leave school, you'll have to make your own living and stop being a burden to me." Indeed, nobody would say such words to him again. But it was also true that, whenever he was in desperate straits, as was often the case, he could never find anyone else who would give him shelter. He could better understand the catastrophe which had befallen them than those two big infants. How, then, should he be lacking in sorrow and grief? With glistening eyes, Hassan stealthily cast a glance at the distressed faces of his two younger brothers and bit his lips. He loved them both, regardless of all the circumstances which might have provoked his spite—in particular, despite their success at school and their father's love for them. He did not think that school was an enviable privilege, and he was convinced that his father loved him as much as he loved Hussein and Hassanein, although in his case paternal love was tainted with anger and resentment. Above all, thanks especially to their mother, the Kamels' family ties had always been very strong.

Hassan broke off his thoughts as he saw a man and a woman approaching in peasant clothes. The brothers recognized them as their aunt and her husband, Amm Farag Soliman. The man offered his condolences and sat down with them; their aunt rushed into the house screaming, "Oh, my poor sister! Your home has fallen apart!" Her words had a resounding, tragic effect, and the two younger boys, Hussein and Hassanein, burst into tears again. While they sat absorbed in their thoughts, Amm Farag Soliman conversed with Hassan. Unaware of each other's thoughts, the younger boys' minds both turned to their father's fate after death. Hussein's strong faith, based partly in tradition, developed partly from some of his readings, left him with no doubts about the hereafter. In his heart he was praying to God to grant him and his father eternal bliss when they met in the hereafter. Hassanein, baffled by the anguish of death, banished all contemplation of it. His faith was completely imitative and traditional; his intellect had no part in it. His mother had once forced him to perform the Commandments of God, and he did them automatically. Then, a little hesitantly, he had stopped performing the Commandments without denying them heretically. The religious creed never dominated his mind; he never gave it much thought. Nevertheless, he was never skeptical about its truth. Death made him think, but not for long, and under these circumstances a strong personal emotion confirmed his faith. *Is death the end? Would nothing of my father survive but a handful of dust? Would nothing else remain? God forbid! This will never be. The word of God never lies.*

Only Hassan was unconcerned by religious thoughts. As though he was instinctively pagan, even death itself could not cause them to enter his mind. In fact, he was not influenced by education or any other kind of discipline. By nature he was a tramp, just as his father used to call him when he was angry. His disposition was so frivolous that there was no room in his heart for any creed; rather, religion was often the object of his ridicule and the butt of his jokes. Even the slight religious influence which his heart had once absorbed from his mother had been dissipated by the pains of practical life. Thus his thoughts rambled away from eternity to center on terrestrial existence and on the prospects life presented to himself and his family. But he did not long remain with his two brothers and his aunt's husband, for in the distance a man appeared, hurrying toward them. No sooner had Hassan seen him than he exclaimed with relief, as if he had been waiting for him, "Farid Effendi Mohammed!"

Although the autumn weather was mild, the newcomer was wiping perspiration from his forehead with a handkerchief. He was extremely fat, with an enormous belly and a round, full face with fine, delicate features. His obesity, old age, and elegant dress gave him an air of dignity of the sort which made government officials, particularly clerks, so proud. The brothers fixed their eyes hopefully on the new arrival, with the reverence to be accorded such a neighbor and old friend of their father's. The man came up to them offering his condolences.

"Today I took leave from the Ministry," he said, addressing Hassan. "Let's go to your late father's office at the Ministry and cash the funeral expenses. Then we can buy the necessary things."

He asked Hassan about plans for the funeral and told him to carry them out. Then he took Hassan's arm and both departed for the Ministry.

FOUR

When it was nearly time for the funeral, Hassanein became very depressed. Deeply disturbed, he forgot his grief. He had hoped for a magnificent funeral, appropriate to his father's position and prestige. His brothers were not of a type to be much concerned about such a matter, but to Hassanein a degrading funeral seemed as much of a catastrophe as death itself. As much for the sake of his beloved father as for himself, he dreaded the prospect.

He cast his eyes about him, searching the crowd of mourners for a man of stature but found none except Farid Effendi Mohammed, their good friend and neighbor. There was his aunt's husband, not much more than a laborer; and Amm Gaber Soliman, the grocer, could offer little more. Present also were the barber, even lower in station than these two, and several people whose absence would have been less disgraceful than their presence. He felt disheartened and deeply depressed that no one else should attend his father's funeral. But he was too impatient: no sooner had the hour struck four than large groups of government employees filled the blind alley until they blocked it. His heart felt lighter and free from worry, and he returned to his grief. Then something unexpected happened. A splendid car suggestive of wealth and luxury drove up and stopped near the house. An attendant stepped out and opened the door for a man whose appearance indicated position and title. He stepped forward, his large body and his fifty years contributing to an air of dignity. The three brothers hurried politely to receive him. Farid Effendi Mohammed accompanied them to have the honor of receiving this great personage, whom he, as a government employee, esteemed more than any other person.

"Is this the house of the late Kamel Effendi Ali?" the new-comer inquired in low voice.

"Yes, sir," Farid Effendi answered respectfully.

They could offer him nothing but a bamboo chair in the middle of the street, and they were more than a little embarrassed. Hassanein felt relieved by his arrival, yet it annoyed him that the man should ask about the house, for this showed that he did not know where it was. He stepped closer to his brother Hassan.

"Who is that man?" he asked.

"Ahmad Bey Yousri," said Hassan, "a great inspector in the Ministry of Interior and a good friend of our father."

"But why, then, did he ask the way to the house as though he didn't know it?" Hassanein asked, astonished.

Hassan gave him a strange look.

"Our father visited him often, but he . . . well, you see, he's a great man!" came the answer.

The young man was silent for a moment; then, correcting himself, Hassan went on: "Our father loved him and regarded him as his best friend."

Hassanein, not wanting to have his pride deflated, ignored this unpleasant aspect of the situation. He wished that all the people there could see the great inspector. The painful moment came when the bier was carried out of the house. Wailing reached their ears, coming from the balcony and windows. The people lined up to follow the bier, while the two younger brothers, amazed and unbelieving, fixed their eyes upon it. They wept all the way to the mosque. Once there, they turned to thank the people for the trouble they had taken and bade them farewell. When a few offered to accompany the bier to its last resting place, Hassanein whispered to his elder brother, "Don't allow anyone to come with us!"

He did not want anybody to see the family's humble burial place. They succeeded in getting the crowd to depart and climbed into the hearse, accompanied only by their aunt's husband and Farid Effendi Mohammed, who flatly refused to leave.

The car carried them swiftly to Bab el-Nasr and stopped at a place where the graves were situated in the open. Here the dead body of Kamel Effendi was buried in something not much more than a pauper's grave, not very far from the twisting path that led across the burial ground. Drowned in grief, Hassanein was crying. Despite his grief, from time to time he looked furtively at Farid Effendi Mohammed in shame and resentment; he kept thinking: *Had the other pupils known about my father's death, they would surely have come to offer me their condolences. Some would have accompanied me to this graveyard. Thank God they did not come. No decent burial place! Nothing! Why didn't my father provide a suitable one for our family?*

FIVE

It was almost midnight. When everybody else was gone, the family, the aunt, and her husband sat in the hall. For the twentieth time on that same sad day, their mother was relating how their father had died. Hussein and Hassanein were listening intently, while Hassan, with gloom on his face, was absorbed in his own thoughts.

Hassanein spoke about Ahmad Bey Yousri. As much for the presence of his aunt and her husband as for his own preference not to remember it, he did not mention the inspector's apparent ignorance of where the family lived. Compassion for his dead father filled his heart, and he kept looking sadly toward the closed bedroom door, in his sorrow and incredulity imagining the empty bed. The mother turned to her children and told them to go to bed.

As they had spent a painful and arduous day, they obeyed her without objection, and went to their room, in which there were three small beds. They left one for their aunt's husband, who joined them presently, and Hassanein shared Hussein's bed. They could not sleep. Tenderly and mournfully they kept talking about their father, recalling his last days on earth and his sudden death.

"His funeral was really appropriately dignified," said Hassanein.

"God be merciful to him. He was a great man; no wonder his funeral was great, too," Amm Farag Soliman agreed. "The alley was full of people; they crowded the area from the house to Shubra Street."

Hassanein disliked the man's voice; he was annoyed by his presence. Then, remembering that the man had seen the bare grave, he said indignantly, "It's surprising that our father, who spent so much, never thought of providing a burial place becoming to the family."

Once more came the voice which Hassanein disliked: "How could he have ever thought of dying at this age? Your father was only fifty. In this country, lots of people marry at this age for the second or third time." The man was silent for a while. Then he spoke again: "Don't forget, Master Hassanein, that your father left Damietta with his grandmother for Cairo when he was your age. That's why yours isn't one of those Cairene families that have tombs for generations."

"It's true," Hassanein retorted; "we don't originally come from Cairo. But all ties with our relations in Damietta have been severed."

Sadly, he remembered that his aunt was the only relative he knew. The obscure grave in the open would always remain a symbol of his family's being shamefully lost in the big city. The presence of this uncle of his, occupying his bed, increased his annoyance, and to stop him from talking, Hassanein fell silent until sleep overcame them all.

The widow, her sister, and her daughter did not stir from their places in the hall. They never tired of talking about the departed loved one. Here, grief was deeper than in the other room. Its marks appeared on Samira's thin oval face and burning eyes. With her short nose, pointed chin, and short slim body, she gave the impression of one who had given the best part of herself to her family. Of her old vitality nothing now remained except a firm look which bespoke patience and determination.

So deep was the change which had overtaken her with the years that it was hard to imagine how she might have looked in her youth. Nefisa, her daughter, however, who resembled her closely, was an adequate replica of what she once had been. Nefisa, too, had the same thin oval face, short, coarse nose and pointed chin. She was pale, and a little hunchbacked. She differed from her mother only in her height; she was as tall as her brother Hassanein. She was far from handsome, indeed almost ugly. It was her misfortune to resemble her mother, whereas the boys resembled their father. In grief she was completely undone, and she looked extremely ugly. Her mind was preoccupied with memories of her beloved father.

Her mother, despite her deep sorrow, was thinking of other things. She felt uneasy with her sister. She could not forget that her sister had often made her life miserable, and that she frequently enjoyed comparing their lives—declaring, in envy, that her sister had married a government employee, whereas her own husband was just a laborer working in a ginning factory; that her sister lived in Cairo, whereas she was doomed to the confinement of the country; that her sister's sons were schoolboys, whereas her own sons were destined for laborers' lives; that her sister's larder was always full, whereas she had plenty in hers only at feast times. Maybe now, the widow thought, she won't find any reason to envy me. But with her grief came resentfulness. More than anyone else, she was aware of the sad consequences of this catastrophe. Her husband was gone. She realized that she knew no one but this hopeless, useless sister. She had no relations or in-laws. The deceased had left nothing behind him. His entire salary had been consumed by the needs of the family. She did not even hope for a suitable pension. In the dead man's wallet she had found only two pounds and seventy piasters, and that was all the money she had until matters could be straightened out.

Absentmindedly, she glanced in the direction of her sons' room. True, two of them attended school and were exempted from fees; still, that was nothing. The third son was something of a tramp. She sighed deeply. Then she turned her eyes to Nefisa, agonizing over her condition; a girl of twenty-three, without beauty, money, or father. This was the family for whom she had now become responsible, without help from anyone. She was not the type of woman to resort to tears for relief. Her past life, now a happy bygone dream, had not always been easy, especially in the beginning when her husband had been a junior employee with a small salary. Life had taught her to struggle, but also to be patient and stoical. She was the main pillar of the home. Her attitude toward her children was probably more fatherly than motherly, while her husband possessed the tenderness and frailty of a mother. The sons themselves provided a living example of the contrast between the characters of their parents. Hassan was miserable evidence of his father's laxity and tendency to spoil his children; while Hussein and Hassanein attested to their mother's firmness and discipline in bringing them up. Certainly, she told herself, she would be strong as a widow, too. But at this hour of the night, she had nothing to live on but grief and worry.

SIX

Next evening no outsider remained in the house, and the family was left to itself. The furniture in the dead man's room was piled in a corner, and the door was closed. The children gathered around their mother awaiting her comments. Samira knew that she must say something. What she had to say was clear enough to her, for she had thought about it for a long time. Perhaps nothing perplexed her more than her contradictory character with its outward firmness and strength, while her inner self held nothing but mercy and compassion for her poor afflicted family. Avoiding the waiting glances, she lowered her eyes. "Our calamity is great," she said. "We have no one to resort to but God, who never forgets His creatures."

She was unable to ask them: *What are we to do?*, for she would never get an answer to it from any of those around her, not even from her eldest son, Hassan. There was not a soul in the world to whom she could appeal for help and share her worries with. She felt the void engulfing her, but she wouldn't surrender.

"We have no relatives to depend on," she went on. "Our dear one is dead, leaving us nothing except his pension, which will undoubtedly be far less than his salary, and that was hardly enough. Life seems to be grim, but God never forgets His creatures. Many families in the same circumstances as ours have been patient until God has led them by the hand to security."

Nefisa's voice was choked with tears. "No one dies of hunger in this world," she said. "God will surely lead us by the hand. The only catastrophe for which we can never be comforted is his death. Oh, my dear father!"

But her tears had no great effect upon the boys, for their

mother's speech foreshadowed the graver things to come, upon which they were now concentrating. Their eyes were fixed on their mother. "We must never despair of God's mercy," she continued. "However, we must know exactly where we stand, or else we perish. We must also school ourselves to endure our lot with patience and dignity. God be with us."

She felt there was nothing more she could say to them as a group. Now she must speak to each of her children about the things which concerned them individually. She found it wiser to start with the less serious problems, to pave the way for the more difficult ones. Glancing at Hussein and Hassanein, she tried to conceal her concern. "I cannot afford to give you pocket money anymore," she said calmly. "Fortunately, this is usually spent on trivial things . . ."

Trivial things! Were membership in the football club, the movies, and novels trivial? Hussein heard this verdict in mute dejection. Trying to picture what life would be like without his pocket money, his mind rambled off; yet he uttered not a word. As for Hassanein, he appeared to be struck with a thunderbolt. Almost unconsciously, he raised an immediate objection: "All our pocket money! Not a millieme?"

Samira stared at him for a long time. "Not a single millieme," she said firmly.

His objection troubled her. Yet she welcomed it since it gave her an opportunity to reaffirm what she had already said, and to make Hassan, whom she feared would be more troublesome than his two brothers, hear her words. Hassanein opened his lips and muttered something indistinctly. "We'll be the only pupils in school who get no pocket money," he said in a low voice.

"You imagine things," his mother replied sharply. "The calamities of life are many, and plenty of other pupils lack money. If you search the pockets of all the pupils at school, you'll find that most of them are penniless. Even supposing that you were the only ones who were poor, there would be nothing to be ashamed of. Besides, I am not responsible for what happened."

Remembering that he was addressing his mother, Hassanein kept silent. He had always found his father more tolerant and understanding, for his father loved him as dearly as he loved his daughter, Nefisa. But his mother's firmness never relaxed. By way of reply, she added, "I also warn you both not to skip your school lunch as you usually do."

The two brothers ate very little of their school lunch since they preferred to wait for dinner at home. The pupils who ate their fill of lunch at school were the subject of their mates' ridicule.

"Why shouldn't we eat at home as usual?" Hassanein asked gently.

"Who knows? Maybe, you won't find the kind of food you like at home!" his mother replied sharply.

There was a shadow of a smile on Hassan's lips as he listened in deep silence to all that was said. He tried to hide it under a frown, but Samira had already noticed it. She was determined to face him with the truth if he still needed it after that long preamble. She asked him sadly, "What about you, Hassan?"

He was her eldest, her firstborn and her first darling! Yet he was tangible evidence that motherly love may be influenced by factors which have nothing to do with instinct. Of course, this did not mean that she hated him; far from it. She merely dropped him from her accounts, and to her great distress, he no longer fulfilled her once rosy hopes. Now, he simply occupied an obscure corner of her heart, and whenever she recalled her love for him, it was tainted with deep sorrow and pitch-black memories. He had always been and still was the black sheep of the family. At first he was the victim of his father's poverty and favoritism; he was sent to school later in years than other boys. Soon it had become evident that he revolted against school life. He ran away frequently from school; year after year he failed in his examinations; finally he left school when he was only in his junior year. His relations with his father, strained by rows and quarrels, finally degenerated into genuine enmity. Sometimes, his father would kick him out of the house, leaving him to roam the streets for days; he came back home after associating with delinquents and plunging deep into sin and addiction, though he was just in his teens. When his father despaired of reforming him, he sent him to work in a grocery. There he remained for a month, until, following a quarrel in which the grocery was almost wrecked, he was fired. He worked for an automobile manufacturer, and was fired again after another quarrel. He became indifferent to his father's anger and his mother's firmness; but he imposed himself upon them, accepting their indignation either lightly and playfully or quarrelsomely. He never left home, nor did he search seriously for a job. He seemed to have no consideration whatsoever for the future, persisting in his recklessness until he was suddenly confronted with his father's death. He knew how serious the situation was, for he alone knew what his father's salary was, and he made a calculation of his approximate pension. He quite understood what his mother meant when she asked, "What about you, Hassan?" *Well,* he thought, *you say that God never forgets His creatures, and I am one of these creatures. Let's see how He remembers us! Why did He take away our father? Why should He manifest His wisdom at the expense of victims like us?*

Yet in his courteous, compassionate smile at his mother, there was a sense of responsibility. "I understand everything," he said.

"What's the use of mere understanding?" Samira replied irritably.

"Something has to be done."

"This is what we often hear from you." She was vexed.

"Everything is changed now."

"Isn't there any hope that you will change, too?"

"A man of my type will never get lost in this life," he retorted. "I can manage and hack my way through. There are lots of opportunities, and I have countless weapons in my hands. Listen, Mother, all I ask of you is shelter and some morsels of bread."

That had always been his method! He started as though he were yielding, and ended by making fresh demands. A shelter and some morsels of bread! What else was there? She eyed him resentfully. "This is no time for joking," she said.

"But who's joking?" he asked.

"We need someone to feed us; how, then, can we afford your food? Why do you force me to be blunt with you?"

"It's only for a while, till things get better," he said with a faint smile. "You won't find me a burden. Or would you like to kick me out? I shall do my best to earn my living. But suppose it takes me several days to find a job, would it make you happy to see me die of hunger? Anyway, I'll share your loaf until I find a job."

She sighed in despair. She was encountering a real problem and did not know what to do about it. The worst that she dreaded was that he would persist in a life of idleness, laziness, and wandering, especially once the effect of his father's death upon his feelings diminished.

"I hope you'll earnestly and sincerely look for a job," she said beseechingly.

He said, quite sincerely, "I promise you. I swear it on my father's grave."

His oath reawakened their sorrow and his mention of their father's grave moved them deeply. Nefisa burst into tears and Hassanein's heart sank, while Hussein eyed Hassan with a puzzled look of reproof. Their mother kept silent, feeling her deep wound. But even then she did not forget that she had not finished what she wanted to say. She kept turning her red and swollen eyes toward her children.

"Nefisa is good at sewing," she said. "Out of friendship and courtesy, she often makes dresses for our neighbors. I see no harm in her asking for some compensation."

"That's a good idea," cried Hassan enthusiastically.

But Hassanein, his face white with anger, cried, "A dressmaker?"

"Why not? There's nothing to be ashamed of," answered Hassan.

Hassanein retorted sharply, "No, my sister will never be a dressmaker. I refuse to be a brother to a dressmaker."

Samira frowned and shouted angrily, "You're just a bull that eats and sleeps, and you know nothing about life! Your foolish mind will never understand how bad our situation is."

He opened his mouth to object.

"Shut up!" she shouted. He snorted and did not utter another word.

Seeing that she had done with his objection, Samira turned to Hussein. Their eyes met for a moment; then he lowered his and murmured reluctantly, "If it can't be helped, let God's will be done . . ."

Samira was deeply moved. She said, "As Hassan has said, there's nothing to be ashamed of. I don't like to see any of you humiliated; but there are things that cannot be helped. I can do nothing about it."

There was a painful silence. Hussein was more like his mother than the rest of her children. He had her patience, sagacity, and loyalty to the family. He was greatly pained by the plans for his sister. Yet he felt it was stupid to object to the dictates of necessity. In his suffering he began to think that in these two days he had learned more than he had in the rest of his life. Nefisa remained helplessly silent. It wasn't the first time that she heard that proposal, for her mother had already convinced her that it was inevitable. For her, dressmaking was an entertaining hobby. She had only to accustom herself to receive fees for it. Now her feeling of worthlessness doubled the grief she felt from her father's death. It was no use.

Interrupting the silence, Hassan said in a tone of regret, "It's a real pity that my late father forbade Nefisa to continue her school education. Imagine how things would be now if our sister had become a teacher."

When they stared at him curiously, he understood that he had blundered. He hadn't realized that what he said sounded like a joke. Would it not have been better if he had himself understood the value of education and continued his schooling? Frowning irritably, he said, "Education is good for those helpless ones like her."

SEVEN

The next morning, Hassan, the eldest son, accompanied Samira to the Ministry of Education. When it became known at the Ministry that she was the widow of Kamel Effendi Ali, many of his colleagues offered to put themselves at her service. She asked for whatever part of his salary might be due and was advised about the procedure for getting the required inheritance papers. She inquired about her husband's pension, and one of the dead man's colleagues accompanied her to the Personnel Department. They were told that since he had worked for the government for about thirty years at a salary of seventeen pounds a month, his heirs would receive a pension of five pounds per month. She had never imagined this, nor did she know anything about the government's share of the pension. What really terrified her was the description of the months-long procedure required before she would receive the pension. She was so shocked that she could not help saying, "But how can we wait that long?"

"We've nothing to live on except this pension," said Hassan in an attempt to explain his mother's concern. But no sooner did he utter these words than he regretted them, for they sounded strange coming from a man as tall and strong as himself. The official, however, paid no attention to these remarks.

"Madam," he said, "I promise you that we will not waste a single moment. But we can do nothing about the formalities of the Ministry of Finance."

What use were those nice words! But what would she gain by grumbling and complaining? Worried and despairing, they left the Ministry.

"How," she cried, "can we face life during these months, and afterward how can we live on five pounds a month?"

The young man lowered his eyes in gloom and consternation. Desperate though she was, a gleam of hope appeared before her fatigued eyes. "I'll visit Ahmad Bey Yousri," she said. "He is a great, influential inspector. Besides, he was a good friend of your father's."

"Right," said Hassan hopefully. "A word from him can speed up the government formalities."

She looked at him earnestly. "Don't waste your time with me," she said. "Perhaps now you realize our real situation. Go and find a job for yourself."

She returned to Shubra Street alone and remained at home until afternoon. Then she went to Taher Street, the so-called Quarter of the Wealthy. It was three blocks north of Nasr Allah alley; a side street with elegant villas and modern buildings on both sides. She asked some passersby the way to the Bey's villa. It was a beautiful two-storied building surrounded by a blossoming garden. She gave her name to the porter as "widow of the late Kamel Effendi Ali." He returned quickly and led her to a magnificent sitting room overlooking a wide terrace. The Bey, he told her, was dressing and would come soon. It seemed to her that she was kept waiting for a long time, but she stayed where she was, without removing her black veil, her mind too preoccupied with troubled thoughts to observe her luxurious surroundings. She had great faith in this great friend of her husband's, of whom he often spoke with love and pride. She had herself witnessed the fruits of that friendship, manifested in the baskets of grapes and mangoes presented to them in their respective seasons. Her husband had spent most of his evenings in this villa, perhaps in the very same place where she now sat, playing on the strings of his lute far into the night. It was possible, then, that she might leave the villa comforted and recompensed. While she was thus absorbed in her thoughts, the inner door of the hall opened and in came the Bey, his body broad and tall, his plaited mustache carefully groomed. Courteously, the woman stood up. The Bey greeted her.

"Have a seat, please, madam," he said gently. "You have honored us with your visit. God be merciful to your husband. He was a dear friend of mine and his loss distresses me, now and for the rest of my life."

The woman saw this reception as a good omen and thanked him for his kindness. The Bey continued talking to her about her late husband until her eyes were filled with tears. She was even more moved by the situation itself and, motivated by an instinctive desire to stir up his sympathy, made no attempt to check her tears. Silence prevailed for some time. Despite her grief, she noticed that his mustache and whiskers were dyed, that he was overcareful about his appearance, and that he exuded a strong, fragrant smell of perfume. He inquired kindly about the purpose of her visit.

"Your Excellency," she replied, "I came to seek your help in expediting the formalities for receiving my late husband's pension. I'm told this may take months to settle."

The man pondered. Then he said, "I will do my best. I'll discuss the matter with the Under Secretary of State for the Ministry of Finance."

Relieved, she thanked him. Hesitating for a moment, she said, "Your Excellency, our condition, and only God knows what it really is, requires quick action."

"Yes, of course. I understand," he said earnestly. "Do you need any help?"

What a question! She had nothing but those two pounds left over from the money she had found in her husband's wallet. She wouldn't have anything else till she received what was due of his salary. But how could she tell him that? She had never been in such a position before. One had to be shrewd and get used to it. Shyness kept her silent for a while. Then she said in a low voice, "Thank God, He has protected us. I can wait a little longer."

The Bey was quite relieved by her answer. He had asked the question out of embarrassment and courtesy. His feeling of relief resulted from no inherent stinginess in his character, nor was it due to any resentment toward the idea of helping his friend's widow. It was just that he was not in a position to help. In spite of his wealth, he usually spent all his money on himself and his family; so much so that nothing was left. Yet he was ready to help her, but only if she asked him for assistance. The woman was not aware that her husband had not been a friend of the Bey's in the sense that the Bey understood the term. He might have been a friend of the third order. The Bey liked him and enjoyed his company and entertaining art, but had not considered him an equal or a friend like the rest of his friends among Beys and Pashas. But he was sincere in his desire to help the woman get her pension, in memory of the deceased, and to avoid any further obligation to help her. She stood up to take her leave and he saw her off respectfully. When she reached the street, she sighed hopefully. But she said to herself rather regretfully, "Had I been more courageous I'd not have lost that chance of help which I desperately need!"

EIGHT

Nefisa disappeared into the kitchen. Nobody knew where Hassan was. Their mother had gone to the Ministry of Education to find a solution to her problems. Thus Hussein and Hassanein were left to themselves for the first time since their father's death. Hussein squatted cross-legged on the bed while his brother sat at his desk in a corner of the room twirling a pen between his fingers.

"Life no longer seems to be bearable!" he complained.

He expected an answer from Hussein, but the latter ignored his remark. Indignantly, Hassanein raised his eyes to him. As the youngest, it was not surprising that Hassanein should expect the others to solve his problems. He was annoyed with his brother's silence.

"What do you think?" he asked.

"About what?" Hussein replied, pretending to miss the point.

"About what she said, of course! Do you think that our situation is really that bad?"

Hussein shrugged his shoulders. "Why should she lie?" he answered.

His brother's eyes glistened with a gleam of hope. "To restrain us, of course!" he replied. "To frighten us and make us be careful! No wonder, for she has a harsh disposition. Had it not been for our father, we'd never have known any joy!"

"I wish we never had known it," said Hussein sadly.

"What?" exclaimed Hassanein.

"If we'd never been pampered before, this new life to which we are doomed would be much easier for us!"

Overcome by fright, Hassanein answered, "Then you believe what she said? Is it true that our father has left us nothing? Wouldn't the pension be enough to cover our expenses?"

"I believe everything she said. It's the truth," sighed Hussein.

"How are we to endure such a life?" Hassanein wondered anxiously. A sad smile hovered over Hussein's lips. He shared his brother's sorrow and anxiety but found it wiser to oppose him.

"We shall bear it as lots of others do," he declared. "Do you think that everybody lives in prosperity, with a generous father to provide for him? Yet all human beings survive and don't commit suicide!"

Hassanein became exasperated. He stared at his brother and exclaimed, "Your sangfroid is amazing!"

"If I agreed with you, you would renounce hope and burst out crying," Hussein replied with a smile.

"Whoever yields to fate encourages it to impose further tyranny!"

The other boy smiled sarcastically. "Let's revolt against fate," he said teasingly, "and shout, 'Down with Fate,' just as we shouted, 'Down with Hor.' Didn't 'Down with Hor' do us some good? But the other shout would not do us any good whatsoever."

Distressed, Hassanein frowned and wondered, "Who can we appeal to now?"

Hassanein's broad smile flattened his nose and it appeared at that moment as coarse as his mother's.

"Only to God," he answered curtly.

This answer added fuel to his anger. He did not doubt it, but he did not consider it enough. It is true that God is the resort of all people. Yet how numerous on earth are the hungry and distressed! He had never renounced his creed, but in his dread he was eagerly searching for a tangible means of security. He imagined that his brother was putting him off in the hope that he would leave him alone. But this only made him more obstinate.

"God has taken our father from us," he said, "and left us without support."

"He is our support," said Hussein, as if he were deliberately trying to provoke his brother.

Hassanein burst out, "I'm not taken in by your pretended calmness. Do you really feel secure?"

Hussein listened to him with resentment and pain. Then, perhaps to hide his feelings, he said, "The believer would never feel anything but serenity."

"I believe, but I am still worried!"

"Then your faith is weak," said Hussein, not really believing his own words.

"Oh, let it be so!" Hassanein exclaimed indignantly. "I know some students who don't hesitate to proclaim their doubts."

"I know."

"They are intelligent and well read."

"Would you like to do the same?"

"No, I am not so much interested in reading," he answered in fright. "You read too much yourself!"

"That's right," said Hussein with a smile, "yet I have never driven God out of my heart. To tell you the truth, we overdo it when we hold God responsible for our many calamities. Don't you see, if God is responsible for our father's death, he is not responsible for the small pension he left us."

Hassanein felt that the conversation had drifted away from his true worries. He said, disturbed, "Tell me how we are going to live without our pocket money. Without movies or football. I was about to take up boxing!"

"Avoid whatever may cause our mother pain," Hussein said with a frown. "If we cannot help her, let's at least spare her unnecessary troubles. Remember, she is all alone. We have no uncles on either side of the family."

"No uncles on either side! Indeed! However, this would have

been much less humiliating if our sister had not become a dress-maker. Oh, my God! What will people say about us!"

Hussein became depressed. The word "dressmaker" was very painful to him, and he said angrily, "We can go on living without caring for what people say." Then, to cut the conversation short, he stood up and left the room.

NINE

They were embarrassed as they entered the school yard for the first time after their father's death. They could never resume their old life and everything would be changed. Nothing could be hidden from the rest of the students. That was so obviously painful to both of them. Only a few friends knew what had happened but soon the news spread around and their friends came to express their condolences. One of the students warned them: "Your family should choose the right guardian for you, for I never realized what a catastrophe my father's death was until my uncle's guardianship was inflicted upon me!"

A guardian! Hussein pretended to be listening to some pupils talking about the last demonstrations and the endeavors to present a united front, but he heard Hassanein's answer to his friend: "We are quite sure of our guardian."

"How lucky you are," said his friend. "But it all depends on the sort of inheritance you got. In the case of land, it will be easy to cheat you. But if it is buildings, it wouldn't be that easy for the guardian. That's what my mother says."

"Fortunately, our inheritance consists only of buildings," Hassanein calmly replied.

Hussein listened, infuriated. He was not only vexed by these lies, but also feared their consequences. *How could we face our new situation if the boys thought that we were wealthy?* he wondered. *What are we going to do, and what are we going to say? He is lying irresponsibly. Damn him!* He gave a warning look to his brother, but, annoyed, the boy avoided his eyes. One of the pupils asked how their father had died. Hassanein replied, deeply moved, "We are told that he died suddenly. Amazingly enough, on the day of his death, in the morning when he saw me going out to school, just one hour before his death, he patted my shoulder tenderly and said, for no obvious reason, 'Goodbye. Goodbye.' How could I have known that he was bidding me farewell?'" Nothing of that sort had really taken place and he did not know why he said it. It was still more curious that his words rang with true emotion, as though all of this had actually happened. What he said was impromptu, motivated by a mysterious urge to venerate his father. So surprised was Hussein by his brother's description and show of emotion that he almost smiled. Averting his face, he saw the captain of the football team standing some distance away. He wanted to give vent to his pent-up feelings. He walked up to the captain and greeted him.

"Please," he said, "release my brother and me from membership in the Shubra Club."

The captain looked astonished. He was particularly troubled because Hassanein was the right wing on the team. "What's troubling you?" he protested.

Hussein was touched. "Our father is dead," he said.

The captain fell into deep silence, then gently expressed his sorrow. After several speechless moments, he inquired, "Need this really mean that the club should be deprived of two skillful members like you?"

"Mourning dictates it," Hussein quickly replied.

"Mourning is not incompatible with sports," said the captain with compassion.

"Our circumstances warrant this. I'm sorry," said Hussein amiably.

He made his farewells and walked away, avoiding his eyes. Joining his friends, he found them discussing politics. One was saying, "God be merciful to the martyrs of the Faculties of Art, Agriculture, and Dar el-Ulum!"

"Sacrifices must be made," said another, "for blood is the only language the British understand."

"The pure blood of the martyrs has never been shed in vain."

"Don't you hear the call for unity now?" said a third.

"And here is *The Times* hinting at negotiations."

The bell rang and, still arguing, they went to their classes.

TEN

Carrying their books, they silently crossed the courtyard of the house. "The Shubra Club football team will soon be starting its training for the next match!" said Hassanein as they went upstairs. Hussein did not answer. He kept imagining the playground and the players, and he mentally heard the voice of the captain telling the others of their withdrawal from the team "on account of the recent family circumstances." There would be no play, no joy, and no escape from Hassanein's continuous complaints. They knocked and were let in. Inside they stopped in astonishment at the strange, unexpected sight that met their eyes. They saw all the furniture of the house piled into the hall in complete disorder, the chairs on the sofa, the carpets rolled up, and the wardrobes undone. There stood Samira and Nefisa, their sleeves rolled up, covered with dust and sweating in spite of the mild weather.

"What's the matter?" cried Hassanein.

"We are leaving this flat," their mother answered.

"But where to?"

"Downstairs. We shall exchange flats with the landlady."

A ground-floor flat, on the same level with the dusty courtyard and with no balconies! Its windows, which overlooked a side blind alley, all but exposed the rooms to the people passing by; no sunlight, no fresh air.

"But why?" asked Hassanein discontentedly, although he had already guessed the answer.

"Because the rent is only one pound and fifty piasters," their mother replied in a clear voice.

"The difference in the rent is less than fifty piasters. It doesn't match the difference between the two flats!" the young man complained.

"Would you undertake to pay that little difference?" the mother asked indignantly.

"Why, then, did we allow Nefisa to become a dressmaker?"

His mother gave him a fiery look. "So that we can eat!" she cried. "To keep you from dying of hunger!"

Trying to keep his face pleasant and not show any resentment, Hussein asked his mother, without a trace of objection, "When did all this take place, Mother?"

"I suggested it to the landlady, and did not hide anything from her," the woman replied as she wiped her forehead with the sleeve of her black dress. "She was good enough to agree without hesitation."

"If she were really good, she would let us stay in our flat without asking for the difference in the rent!" Hassanein grumbled.

"People have other things to attend to than your welfare!" His mother answered sharply.

"How are we going to sleep tonight?"

In a downcast voice, which indicated that she had not yet recovered from the shock of her father's death, Nefisa answered, "We shall sleep in the new flat."

At that moment Hassan emerged from his dead father's bedroom carrying the peg, the last piece of furniture. "Stop bickering," he said quickly, "and let's take the furniture downstairs. We have only two hours before dark."

Wishing them to follow his lead, he lifted one side of a sofa, saying to his brother Hussein, "Lift the other end."

Nefisa opened the door wide, and the two brothers passed through with their load. Going carefully downstairs, Hussein wondered if anyone in the family of their good neighbor Farid Effendi Mohammed, who lived on the third floor, would see them.

Separation, he thought, *is not the worst part of death. It is only secure people who experience sadness on account of their separation from the ones they have lost. But as for us, our troubles succeed one another so fast that they leave us no time to be sad. How our condition deteriorates! But we have to be patient or at least to pretend that we are. The worst thing we can do is increase, through our anxiety, the misery of our mother. I shall speak more firmly to Hassanein!* Their mother and sister followed with whatever pieces they could carry. Hassanein could not bear to stand there as a spectator, so he joined them. The members of the family climbed up and down the stairs, moving in. The landlady had emptied her flat and all her furniture was lying in the courtyard. Her porters were standing nearby awaiting their turn to start working. All the members of the family, whether or not they showed their emotions, shared the same feelings of sorrow and pain. Samira's face was not easy to decipher, but Nefisa's eyes were filled with tears. Hassan was working hard as if to ingratiate himself with his mother through his labor, lest she criticize him for his idleness. Being used to a vagabond's life, it was natural that, of the three brothers, he should be the least affected by the radical change that had been visited upon the family. Panting with exertion, Hassanein whispered to Hussein, "Don't you see that we will never make up for the loss of our father?" Two tears rolled down his cheeks.

ELEVEN

Hassan left early in the morning immediately after his brothers' departure for school. There was no need for him to go out so early, but he wanted to avoid friction with his mother so as to spare her a quarrel which, in her grim and unfortunate circumstances, she could very well do without. He left Nasr Allah behind, and walked on aimlessly and hopelessly. *"Find yourself a job." That's what she is telling me all the time. Where am I to find that job? As an apprentice in a grocery? But that will end in a quarrel, an ambulance, and the police.* Yet, he did not feel as hopeless as he should have. He was too self-confident and optimistic for that. He could not, however, ignore his precarious position and he kept talking to himself: *Your father (God be merciful to him) is dead now. You've lost your shelter. True, you've always made your living through quarrels and rows, and you had to put up with insults and abuse, but, anyhow, that was a sure living. Even this suit you're wearing, which makes you look not too bad an Effendi, comes with his money. Yes, at first he refused to buy it for you, but you threatened him that you would walk along the streets in your underwear, and burst almost naked into the palace of Ahmad Bey Yousri, where he usually spent his time, and so he gave in and instructed the tailor to make this suit. Now, if you go around completely naked, nobody will mind except the police!*

The suit was nice, though slightly stained at the knees. He put on a bow tie, which showed off his dilapidated shirt. His hair was the most peculiar feature of his appearance, for he had let it grow so long, thick, and frizzy that it looked almost like a second head set upon his real one. His face was as handsome as the faces of his brothers, and besides, his body was tall and muscular with broad bones. He went on his way with these thoughts until suddenly he regained his self-confidence and said to himself: *Don't worry; only fools worry. You will live long and experience life, be it sweet or bitter. I've never heard of any man who died of hunger. There is always plenty of food, and you're not greedy; all that you need are some morsels of bread, clothing, a few glasses of cognac, some hashish to smoke, and a few women to sleep with. And all these are available in more abundance than one can ever conceive of. Well, my boy, depend on God and stop worrying.* He wasn't penniless, for he had managed his father's funeral and in the process garnered forty piasters which no one knew about. He wondered whether to give the money to his mother. *Oh no! Mother will not make much use of it, whereas there is no doubt that losing this money would be a great setback to me. I don't know when I shall ever find so much money again.* With his sharp eyes, he saw the Al Gamal café and he hurried to reach it. It was a café of no distinction, but it overlooked the street. At that early hour, there were only two people there, sitting at a table placed on the pavement, basking in the sun and drinking coffee. Inside, in a corner, sat three youths whose appearance and bemused looks indicated idleness and desperation. It was not strange, then, that the young man should walk up to them and join their group. Presently, one of them asked for a pack of cards, and they all got ready to play. Each one of them hoped to win his bread for the day from his friends; five piasters would be more than enough. Hassan was often the winner, for he was clever at cards and quick with his hands and eyes. Thus before they started to deal, one of them said, "No cheating."

"Of course not," answered Hassan.

The young man said, "Let's recite the opening Exordium of the Koran."

They all recited Al Fatihat audibly; it was possible that Hassan had learned it at that gambling table. They played for an hour. After paying half a piaster for his cup of coffee, Hassan's net profit was four and a half piasters. One of the players suggested that they continue. But just then a young man entered the coffeehouse. No sooner had Hassan seen him than he stood up and approached him, addressing him with warmth and respect.

"Good morning, Master Sabri!"

The newcomer self-importantly stretched forth his hand. "Good morning."

They sat face to face at a table. Hassan succumbed to a sudden generous impulse. He summoned the waiter and ordered coffee for Master Ali Sabri. Before the waiter went away, Master Ali Sabri added, "And bring a nargileh, too."

Hassan's heart sank. He was afraid he would also have to pay for the nargileh and lose all that he had won at cards with his luck and quick hands and eyes. But soon he forgot his worries and watched his visitor's face. Ali Sabri was about twenty-five, of medium height, slim, and with delicate features. His hair was very much like Hassan's, with whiskers that crept down to the middle of his cheeks. His general appearance showed how bad his condition was, but he covered it up with unlimited false pomp and self-conceit. Searching his face, Hassan said with regret, "We haven't heard your voice for a long time."

On several occasions he had broadcast songs for private companies, and it had seemed as though fortune was beginning to smile upon him. But when these private stations were closed down and an official national broadcasting station established, his performances came to a standstill, and his attempts to renew them failed. Hassan was a member of his unemployed band. Naturally, he earned no more than a few piasters from that kind of work; but he loved it and preferred it to a serious job, which, from his point of view, was hard, degrading labor, in which he had never achieved much success.

"I'll be starting new work very soon," said the master.

Hassan's heart beat hard. "We are your men," he replied, "always at your service."

The master nodded with satisfaction, for he was never treated with dignity except when he was addressed by one of the tramps who constituted his band—especially the fierce and tyrannical Hassan, who turned into a gentle flatterer when he was speaking to him.

"Of course, of course. You're good at singing refrains, and your voice is not bad," came the answer.

Hassan's face lit up. "I have memorized a lot of popular songs," he said.

"Such as what?"

"Such as 'He Who Loved You,' 'Why Are You Unjust to Me?' and 'When I Was Burnt with the Fire of Love.'"

Belittlingly, the master shrugged his shoulders. "Chanting and Laiali are the cornerstone of true art," he replied. "But what do we hear on the wireless nowadays? Nothing of value. Just yelling, not singing. If the station were really aware of art, I should stand next to Um Kalthum and Abdul Wahab. Even Abdul Wahab himself is often afraid that his voice might fail him. So he avoids the kind of singing that requires long breath, and, under the guise of innovation, divides up what he is singing into short parts. Then he uses musical instruments to camouflage the weaknesses of his voice. Here is how he sang 'Ya Lil' in his last performance."

He coughed before he started to imitate Abdul Wahab's singing of "Ya Lil." When the waiter came with the nargileh and coffee, he was busy singing. So he held the sucking pipe of the nargileh, and did not stop singing until he was done.

When he finished, Hassan's companions cheered. He inhaled a puff of smoke from the nargileh without paying attention to them. Then he whispered to Hassan, "They admire my voice and not my art. Now, listen to the same Laiali as it should be sung."

His singing filled the small café. The proprietor raised his head from the till, half smiling, half objecting. Master Ali Sabri finished singing and returned to his nargileh. This time he intended to thank the company for admiring his singing. But silence prevailed, interrupted only by the gurgling water in the phial of the nargileh. The master frowned.

"This," he said confidently, "is the way of true art."

"No doubt about that," said Hassan enthusiastically.

"Train your voice and continue practicing. Sing more Laiali and never stop sucking candy," was the man's advice.

"You don't say!"

"That's very useful. It is also advisable that you wake up at dawn and chant the summons to prayers. This is the best practice for the throat. It's what the great singer Salama Hijazi used to do."

Hassan laughed and said, "But usually I sleep just before dawn."

"Then do Al Aza'n before you sleep."

"In a mosque?"

"It does not matter where; in a mosque or a tavern. What matters is Al Aza'n itself at this early hour."

"Excuse me. But if one is under the effect of alcohol or hashish?"

"So much the better, for when you become sober you can make sure that you will do much better than when you are unconscious."

"We must occasionally meet so that God will help us to earn our living."

He turned to the three comrades and asked them, "What were you doing?"

"Playing cards—a game of *komi.*"

The master Ali Sabri said with interest, "Let's try our luck."

The company got up and moved toward them without any

hesitation. They sat around the table; their hearts filled with greed. However, Hassan was worried and uneasy about the possible consequences of such a game. He thought: *What can I do with this son of a bitch! If I win, I shall antagonize him, and if I lose, then my day has been wasted.*

TWELVE

"I will not pay one millieme more than three pounds," said the furniture dealer, casting a last look on the bed of the deceased. Samira's bargaining became futile. She had decided to sell the bed and its accessories because of the grief its presence provoked and because she was desperately in need of money. She had hoped for a higher price, which would meet her urgent needs; however, she had no choice but to accept the price the man offered. She said to the dealer, "You have been too sharp; God forgive you. But I have to accept." Swearing that it was she who had been too clever, the dealer paid her the three pounds and ordered two of his men to carry away the bed.

The family assembled in the hall to cast a farewell look on the bed of their beloved father. The deceased vividly appeared before their eyes, and Nefisa was overcome by grief and burst into tears. Samira tightened her lips, subduing her pain, controlling her tears before her children lest their own grief be revived. As the only person in this world the whole family could rely upon, she had to behave stoically. Had there been another person to depend upon, she could have found refuge in tears, as other women do. She felt it was incumbent upon her to be solid and patient. Besides, the worries and burdens of their new life allowed her no opportunity to give vent to her grief. She found that for the most part she had to forget her own anguish to combat the menace of poverty that confronted the family. *My dear dead husband and master,* she thought, *it grieves me that I don't have even the time to mourn for you. But what is to be done? To us poor folk grief is a luxury we cannot afford.* It had never occurred to Hassanein that they would dispose of his father's belongings, but he did not think of objecting. In fact, the family's difficult condition had become known to everybody. The dealer left, taking the bed with him, and the door was closed behind him. An unspoken sadness fell upon them. Hoping to dispel this hovering sorrow, Samira told her two younger sons, "Go to your room and study your lessons."

Before they could make a move to depart, Nefisa was overcome by emotion. "Never," she said, "will I let anyone touch my father's clothes."

Hassan agreed. "Selling them would be of no use."

They were silent for a while. He continued as though there had been no quiet interval of silence. "Furthermore, it won't be long before we need these clothes!"

"Is it possible," Nefisa asked in fright, "that you would wear my father's clothes?"

No one dared to object. Samira's heart softened and she spoke tenderly. "There is no harm in that . . . nothing to offend the memory of the deceased. He himself would approve of it. But I shall keep these clothes myself until they are really needed."

Encouraged by her words, Hassan said with relief, "You spoke wisely. May I remind you that I am the only one who is almost exactly my father's height and breadth."

His two brothers forgot their grief. Hassanein protested, "Sure, I'm taller than you, but the trouser hems can be unfolded and extended."

"Or they can be folded again to make them shorter," Hussein said.

The mother was annoyed. "No need to wrangle," she said. "There is more than one suit in good condition, and I shall distribute them according to need."

A knock at the door interrupted their conversation. Nefisa hurried to open it. The servant of Farid Effendi Mohammed entered carrying a basket with a white cover and placed it on the table.

"My mistress sends you her regards, madam," she said, "and she sends you mourning pastry."

The mother accepted the basket from the servant and sent her back to her mistress with greetings and thanks. Hassan went up to the basket and uncovered it. The pastry appeared in its rosy colors, its delicious aroma filling their nostrils. Because of the mother's caution and determination to economize, the family had not tasted such delicious food for the past two weeks. Temptation was reflected in the brothers' eyes, but grim thoughts crossed their mother's mind. In fact, these days had nothing good in store for her. Even the little good that came to her was not free from disappointments. Thoughts formed wrinkles on her face.

"We are most thankful for this present," she said, "but we have to return its equivalent when we come back from our visit to the graveyard. What are we to do, then?"

The brothers felt disappointed. Hussein wanted to comfort his mother. "Let's thank them and send it back to them," he suggested.

Their mother was perplexed. "Such an act," she said, "would be considered disgraceful and unfriendly."

"It might even be considered an act of hostility," said Hassan, enthusiastically supporting his mother.

He took a pie, smelled it, and then said lightly, "Don't worry. This kind of present is to be returned on certain occasions. When, after a long life, Farid Effendi passes away, we can present his family with a basket of pastries. We shall be able to afford to do so, by God's will."

Hassan started to devour the pie. Exchanging a look, his two brothers stretched their hands to the basket. Even Nefisa, hearing them chewing, could no longer resist.

THIRTEEN

Bent over the sewing machine, Nefisa sat on the sofa in the room in which she slept with her mother, the floor littered with scattered scraps of cloth. Her mother was working in the kitchen, the two younger brothers were in school, and nobody knew where Hassan was. In her innermost heart, the girl bitterly blamed her elder brother; had he taken a job she would have been spared this situation. Nobody believed that he was serious in his protestations that he was searching for a job. He was away from home all day long, returning at midnight as penniless as ever. Now only misfortunes were to be expected. Today her mother had been forced to dispense with the servant to economize on her wages. Under the circumstances, two daily duties devolved upon Nefisa: to do the shopping for the house in the absence of the servant and, then, to devote most of the daylight hours to her work at the sewing machine. Two days earlier Samira had personally seen to it that her daughter was provided with work. Addressing the landlady, who came to her with a piece of cloth to be tailored, she said, "Do you mind paying Nefisa for her work?"

Without hesitation the woman replied, "Not in the least, Umm Hassan; to be fair, this is her due. We cannot possibly repay our debt to Miss Nefisa."

The echo of these two sentences still resounded in her ears. Never before in all her life had she found herself in such a situation. Her pallid face turned red as blood gushed to it, and she felt as though she were tumbling down from great heights, and that she had become a different person. The demarcation line between dignity and humiliation is easily crossed. She had been a respectable girl but now she had become a dressmaker.

Curiously enough, there was nothing new in the work she performed. She had made dresses on many occasions for the landlady, for Farid Effendi's wife and her daughter, and for other
neighbors as well. Dressmaking to her was a hobby in which
she distinguished herself, so much so that her neighbors and
friends often asked her to make dresses for them. But now how
tremendously her feelings changed! She was overcome by
shame, humiliation, and degradation. Her sorrow over the death
of her father doubled. She wept bitterly for him and in so doing
she was actually weeping for herself. Now her dear father was
dead, and with his death the dearest part of her ceased to be.

Depression overwhelmed her while she sewed, and she neither laughed nor sang as she had in the past. Now she awaited
the landlady, who would arrive at any moment. She would
make her some underwear with the cloth she had received that
morning. The cloth had reached her only two days after her
mother's conversation with the landlady. This made Nefisa think
that the landlady sent it out of charity. She confided her
thoughts to her mother, who chidingly silenced her. "Do not
allow such fancies to clutter your mind; otherwise all that we
are striving for will be frustrated."

She dared not object to her mother, for lately she had begun
to feel an inward pity for her. *How stupid I am,* she thought, *to
imagine that my mother is pleased about my condition. She is undergoing a murderous kind of bewilderment, and, of all of us, she is the one
who really deserves pity. Misery pierces our flesh as a needle pierces a
piece of cloth. Had my father been alive, he would not have allowed
anything like this to happen. But where is he now? My sorrow over his
death increases day after day, not only because of its injury to us but
also because this injury fell on the heads of those he loved and wished
well. I feel his pain. He must be suffering for us now. To think how
much he loved me, as if he anticipated intuitively the misery in store for
me. He used to say to me whenever he heard my ringing laughter,
"Laugh, my girl! How dear your laugh is to my heart!" He also told
me that a sweet temper was more precious than beauty, as though he*

sought to console me for my ugliness. Oh God! How nice, how sweet he was, and he among men was powerless. Alas! Now he is dead, dead. Until I die I shall never forget him motioning to his chest as he lay on the sofa. Poor father, asking for help, and nobody there to help him. Let mountains fall and destroy the earth. What an abhorrent and tragic thing life is. Father dead and I a dressmaker! Soon the landlady will arrive, not a guest as she used to be, but a customer. How should I receive her? Enough. Enough. My head spins!

She heard her mother speaking to someone in the hall. Her hand stopped working on the machine and she listened intently. The endless bargaining of the furniture dealer resounded roughly in her ears, while her mother, in a voice both solicitous and reproachful, was doing her best to defend herself against his haggling. *Mother is not a fool,* she thought. *Nobody in any similar situation could have taken her in. But it is merciless need which weighs so heavily upon her. When will we get the pension? I don't know. Nor does Ahmad Yousri know. How inadequate the pension is! Only five pounds! What a catastrophe! The man has come to carry away the big mirror in the sitting room. Only two weeks before, my beloved father's bedclothes were sold. The man will come tomorrow and the day after tomorrow until he leaves the flat utterly bare. Why are we brought into this world only to become obsequious slaves of food, clothing, and shelter? This is the root of our trouble.*

She hurried to the door of the room and opened it. Through the open door of the sitting room, she saw her mother standing at the threshold and the merchant with his men carrying the long mirror outside. The man carrying one end of the mirror was shorter than the other; thus the mirror was being carried in a slanting position. On the surface of it, she could see a reflection of a corner of the hall ceiling, swinging, as the legs of the carriers moved, as though the house were shaken by an earthquake. Unconsciously, the memory of her father's bier struck her again. As she cast a last look on the mirror which she had known ever since her birth, she became even more depressed than before. She went back to her sitting place, thinking: *The mirror should be the last thing I should feel sorry for. It will not reflect a pleasant face for me. "A sweet temper is more precious than beauty." You are the only person to say so, Father. But for me, you would have never said it. I have no beauty, no money, and no father. There were only two hearts that were concerned over my future. One is dead and the other is engrossed in its worries, and I am terribly lonely, desperate, and suffering. I am twenty-three years old. How dreadful! When our circumstances were much better, no husband put in an appearance. How is it possible, then, that a husband will turn up today or tomorrow?! Suppose that such a husband agrees to be married to a dressmaker, who will pay my marriage expenses? Why should I think of a husband and marriage? No use. No use. I shall remain as I am as long as I live.*

There was a knock on the door, and the landlady came in as merry as ever. She embraced Nefisa and kissed her. They sat side by side. The woman spoke to the girl tenderly and affectionately. Perhaps she made a point of being more tender and affectionate than was her custom. To hide her shyness and confusion, Nefisa pretended to be pleased and at ease, but actually the woman's exaggerated show of affection not only hurt her deeply but also doubled her shyness and confusion. The woman tried on the dress and the underwear Nefisa had finished. Then she sat close to Nefisa and placed silver coins in her hand.

"It is impossible for me," she said, "to pay off my past debts to you."

After remaining with her for some time, the woman said goodbye and departed. Nefisa unfolded the palm of her hand to find two ten-piaster pieces. With storm and agitation in her heart, she stared at the coins. Overwhelmed by shame and humiliation, she thought: *This is painful, but I should not think of it. What use is there in breaking my heart over it? I have to train myself to accept the inevitable. This is my life, and there is no alternative to it.*

Her mother came in while she was still staring at the money and took it from Nefisa's hand.

"Is this money for all the clothes or only for the dress?"

"I don't know."

The mother swallowed with difficulty. "They are good wages anyhow," she said, taking care that the expression on her face should not betray her feelings.

FOURTEEN

Some weeks passed. The curtain of the night fell; melancholy and a kind of silence permeated the flat. The two brothers sat at the desk facing each other, busy studying their lessons. To economize, Nefisa and her mother sat in the hall in semi-darkness, seeing only with the aid of whatever light emerged from the boys' room. Mother and daughter, as was their habit every evening, spoke quietly. Most of their conversation revolved about the troubles of life. Since poverty was still their major preoccupation, the older woman was fear-stricken. She viewed the future with profound worry and sadness. However, they were getting accustomed to their circumstances. Austerity in food was no longer as disturbing as it had been at the beginning. Nefisa began to adapt herself to her new occupation, yearning, with some humiliation and a great deal of hope, for new customers. Hussein and Hassanein had gotten used to relying on the school meal as a substitute for dinner and, stoically, went to bed as a substitute for supper. The force of habit overcame their initial humiliation, and Samira's dominating firmness helped to keep the nerves of her afflicted family in check.

That evening Farid Effendi and his wife came to visit them. Samira and Nefisa welcomed the visitors and led them to the sitting room. The two felt quite at home as they entered, Farid Effendi wearing an overcoat over his gown, and his wife a dressing gown. To accommodate his obesity, the man sat on the sofa. He spoke softly, affectionately, and entertainingly. Um Bahia, his wife, was rather short and as plump as he; yet because of her blue eyes and pale complexion, she was considered the most beautiful woman in the building. Gently reproaching

Samira, she asked her, "Why do you stay at home the way you do? Why don't you get some relief by visiting us as you used to?"

"The cold of the winter assails us," the mother replied. "In the evening, we grow lazy, and in the course of the day the burdens of managing the house never leave us an hour's rest."

"We are one family," said Farid Effendi, "so we ought to spend most of our leisure time together."

Farid Effendi was the type of man who never left his home except in cases of emergency. He spent his leisure time squatting on the sofa, surrounded by his wife, his daughter Bahia, and his younger son Salem. They told stories, chewed sugarcane, and roasted chestnuts. Samira felt genuine affection for his kind and generous heart. She never forgot his care and thoughtful assistance on the day of her husband's death. In addition, he had lent her some money until she received her husband's pension. He never failed to go to the Ministry of Finance to inquire about the pension and give the papers a push. But contrary to her flattering notion of his position, he was just a minor official, promoted only recently to the sixth grade when he reached the age of fifty. His neighborly relations with the dead man's family went far back, and ties of friendship between the two families were strengthened by their mutual good-naturedness and similar standards of living. Theirs was not a bad life, nor was it devoid of entertainment. The family of the late Kamel Effendi had enjoyed new prosperity when he had been promoted to the sixth grade, five years before his death. Farid Effendi had entered on a new era two years earlier when he inherited a house in El Saida Zeinab, which brought a monthly rental of ten pounds. Thus his income had amounted to twenty-eight pounds a month, which was considered very substantial in 1933. Farid Effendi became master of Nasr Allah alley, grew fatter than ever, and if not for his wife's insistence on saving for the future of their daughter and young son, he would have satisfied his desire to move into a flat on Shubra Street.

Their conversation ranged widely, and then Farid Effendi expressed a wish which was probably the chief reason for his visit.

"Madam, I ask you to do me a favor."

"Anything you wish, sir," Samira replied.

"My son Salem, who is in the third year of primary school, is weak in English and arithmetic. Teachers being greedy, as you know, I have thought, with a view to economizing, of asking Hussein and Hassanein to undertake the job of tutoring him for an hour a day or every other day. This is the favor I am asking, Um Hassan."

Samira realized what the man was offering: a face-saving means of assisting her sons by providing them with a monthly supply of pocket money. This was as clear as broad daylight, and in keeping with the man's gentle, kindly character. "Hussein and Hassanein are your sons, and both are at your disposal," she said softly and shyly.

"They will really be helping me out. I hope they can start next Friday," he replied happily.

They went back to their conversation, and the man and his wife left at about nine o'clock.

Nefisa hurried to her brothers' room with this happy piece of news. Regaining some of her former disposition, she told them merrily, "There's a surprise for you!"

They raised their heads inquiringly.

"Farid Effendi," she continued, "wants to choose a tutor for Salem."

"What has this got to do with us?"

"He will choose from you."

"For what subject?"

"English."

"He will choose me, of course," Hassanein cried.

"And arithmetic, too," she said with a smile.

"Me." Hussein heaved a sigh.

"He wants to employ both of you, gratis, of course," she added slyly.

Understanding her insinuations, both shouted with delight, "Of course!"

FIFTEEN

Since they felt no need to put on their suits when they visited a flat in the same building, they merely pulled on their coats over their pajamas and went out. Furthermore, to avoid unnecessary wear, their mother forbade them to dress in their suits except in cases of extreme emergency. The shining forenoon sun tempered the cold weather. Filled with hope and delight, the two young men climbed up the stairs. On their way, they passed the door of their old flat, casting silent looks at it, then continued to climb until they reached the top flat. Finding its door partly open, they hesitated for a few moments. Hassanein approached and raised his hand to knock on the door, but it stopped in midair as, in spite of himself, he stared inside the house. There he saw a girl, her back to the door, her head bent over something she held in her hands; perhaps she was looking for something in a drawer of the sideboard. Her shapely buttocks protruded and her dress, slightly raised, exposed her naked legs and the backs of her knees. The color of her legs was sparkling white, and the eye could almost sense their softness. The sight so attracted Hassanein that he stood entranced, and Hussein began to wonder at the cause. He came near his brother, craned his neck to cast a look over his shoulder, and was overcome with astonishment. But like an escaping fugitive, he quickly retreated, pulling his brother by the arm away from the door and looking sharply at him, as if to say: Are you mad? They stood for a while, overcome by a vague sense of guilt, for the spectacle made their blood run hot. Hassanein leaned toward Hussein and whispered, "Bahia!" in his ear.

His brother pretended to be indifferent. "Perhaps," he murmured.

Hassanein hesitated, a diabolic smile in his eyes. "Shouldn't we steal another glance?" he said.

Striking him on the shoulder, his brother pushed him aside, then knocked on the door. They heard footsteps approaching, and when the door opened, a beautiful round face appeared, chubby, white and slightly pale, adorned with eyes of pure blue. As soon as she saw the two newcomers, she retreated shyly. Then from afar came the voice of Farid Effendi, shouting, "Please come in, great masters!"

They entered the hall, which also served as a dining room. Farid Effendi sat on a sofa facing the sideboard; his loose garment made him look like a balloon. As they shook hands, he welcomed them warmly and closely studied their faces. Then he called Salem. The boy came in to stand before them, embarrassed and uncertain. "Shake hands with your masters," Farid Effendi told him. "You know them, of course. But from now on, they are different people. They are your masters. So you must behave in their presence as you would with your teachers in school."

The boy approached politely, doing his best to conceal a smile at the two young men, for whom he had not yet developed the habit of respect. His father pointed to a room to the left of the entrance.

"The sitting room," he said, "is the most suitable place for your lessons. There is a balcony, too, if you want to be in the sun."

The two instructors proceeded to the room, with their pupil leading the way. The boy hurried to the balcony and opened its French windows, then closed the door. Since Farid Effendi had no son of their own age with whom they might have exchanged visits, this was the first time the pair had entered the flat. They discovered that the sitting room was much like their own. It contained an old set of seats, two European sofas, half a dozen chairs, and a huge mirror whose lower section was a basin filled with artificial flowers. But whereas their own sitting room had looked much the same for years, here the carpenter's hand had renovated the interior and its coverings for Farid Effendi.

Hussein sat on the sofa, and Salem brought a chair to sit facing him across a table lined with texts and notebooks. Meanwhile, Hassanein went out onto the balcony to await his turn. Hussein went through the boy's books. "I shall repeat the lessons from the beginning," he told him, "and explain whatever is not clear to you. And when we start the next lesson, I shall check to see that you've studied the first one."

They then got down to serious work.

Hassanein leaned on his elbow on the edge of the balcony, as he had when they had had a balcony themselves. The exciting scene was still vivid in his mind: her superb legs, her full, shining face, her blue eyes, her solemn, quiet glance suggesting steadfastness, no frivolity. Although there was something disagreeable about her enchanting beauty, her impression upon him had lost none of its force. His blood was still running hot in his veins, and his heart continued to flutter from the excitement of the scene. His mind churned up images and dreams. His heated imagination made him see everything behind a feverish veil: the roofs of the surrounding houses, Nasr Allah below, multitudes of people coming and going. When would his peace of mind be restored? He remembered Bahia as he used to see her often when she was a young girl hopping about in the yard of the house. At the age of twelve, she had disappeared from the yard and for some time stopped going to school, before entering secondary school. Perhaps now she was fifteen years old. He felt as if he were seeing her for the first time.

I need such a girl, he thought, *to accompany me to the cinema, to play and talk with me. There'd be no harm in kissing and embracing her. My barren life has no pretty face to attract me. I have had enough of the boys' friendships at school and the Shubra Club. I want a girl. I want this girl! In Europe and America boys and girls grow up together, as we see in films. This is true life. But this girl, no sooner did she set her eyes on us than she fled from us as though we were monsters who*

*would devour her. Our forefathers kept concubines. Had I grown up in
a house full of concubines, I would have experienced another life, in spite
of my mother's admonitions. Even the servant we employed was dismissed because we are poor. What does the future hold in store for us?
The greatest sin we shall answer for in the hereafter is that we have left
this world without enjoying it.*

*Really, the most beautiful sight was the back of her knee, in the center
a tense, delicate muscle, and blue veins beneath the whiteness of her skin.
If her dress had revealed just a little more, we could have seen the
beginning of her thigh . . . the most beautiful sight in the whole world
is that of a woman undressing. It is more fascinating than the sight of
a naked woman.*

*They say our history teacher is a great lover of women. When shall
I become a free man? Tomorrow, we have a history period, and this
evening I have to study the Germanic tribes. God bids us to marry as
many women as we please. But this country no longer respects the
ordinances of Islam.* He absorbed himself in his reverie until the
voice of Hussein reached him, asking him to start the English
lesson.

On their way out, they saw the girl sitting in the room facing
theirs. Hussein, with his usual dignity, lowered his eyes, while
his brother cast a penetrating glance. Shyly, she lowered her
eyes.

SIXTEEN

"What fees will we be paid?"

Hussein pretended indifference. "Don't be a disgreeable beggar!" he replied.

"We have been teaching Salem day in and day out," Hassanein said hopefully, "and a long time has passed. Perhaps we'll be paid at the beginning of the month. Mother thinks each of us might receive fifty piasters. That would be wonderful! We'll be able to play ball, go to the movies, and buy chocolate from the canteen during breaks again."

The two brothers climbed up the stairs. The short winter day disappeared into the early darkness of evening. Cherishing the hope that revived in their breasts every evening but which had so far been unfulfilled, they knocked at the door as usual and waited for someone to come and open it for them. The servant came and led them to the sitting room. The hall was empty, and a light, at its end, emerged from the parents' bedroom. Hassanein walked ahead, searching the place from the corners of his eyes; Salem came and closed the door behind him, sat in front of Hussein, and began his lesson. Disappointed and bored, Hassanein took out a book he had brought with him to study while he awaited his turn. He looked at it distractedly, indignantly raising his eyes at the closed door. Cunningly, he inquired, "Wouldn't it be better to close the balcony window to protect ourselves from the cold, and open the door instead?"

Salem was on the point of rising from his place, but Hussein signaled him to stay where he was.

"Close the French window of the balcony if you like," he said, "but the door of that room must remain closed."

He gave his brother a meaningful look, which Hassanein received with suppressed indignation. He felt so restless that he went out onto the balcony, forgetting that only a few moments earlier he had suggested closing the window. Facing the dark, he felt as melancholy as the murky clouds of the sky, which made the darkness outside more profound and desolate. Not a single star shone on the horizon. The light of the lamps was dimly perceptible under a thick envelope of mist. A silence, as heavy as lead, fell on the universe, and a mute coldness almost suffocated him. *A puritan. A puritan,* he thought. *He wishes prematurely to be a dignified man. He does not want to help me. Who knows! Perhaps if she had a sister, he might have behaved differently. He is as serious and as stern as our mother. I must solve this problem in my favor.* He kept pondering until he heard Salem calling him, then he entered the room.

"Have a cup of tea," the boy said.

He saw two cups on the table, and as he took one of them, he felt his tension relax. Before a minute passed, they heard the doorknob grating. They looked toward the door. It opened a little and Bahia appeared. She was carrying the sugar bowl, which she gave to Salem. "Take this," she said. "Perhaps there's not enough sugar in the tea."

She wore a brown dress, the hem almost touching the upper part of her ankle. The length of the dress lent charm to her rather short figure. The two brothers stared at her face, but her eyes remained on the boy. Stunned, Hussein lowered his eyes, but Hassanein kept staring at her face, as though he had lost the power to turn his eyes away from it. He watched the boy bring the sugar bowl. His beating heart was filled with consternation when he saw the girl shut the door. It was painful for him to see her disappear while his astonishment was still unyielding, all-absorbing, and from his depths sprang an irresistible desire to express himself. "Thank you," he said, hurriedly. "There is enough sugar in the tea."

Her eyes turned to him in embarrassment, then she disappeared without uttering a word. Perhaps her eyes revealed a suppressed smile. He avoided looking at his brother and fixed his eyes on the cup of tea. *This is a surprise which I did not expect,* he thought. *A happy dream. In spite of the closed door!*

He took a big sip of the hot liquid. It burned his tongue and palate, and made him gasp. But temptation soon made him forget the burning effect of the hot tea, and his mind contemplated her again. *What a soft body, and what fascinating eyes. Even that long dress could not hide the image of her legs, particularly her knees. Neither the long dress, closed door, nor darkness can conceal such an image. One's greatest duty in this world is to flirt with a beautiful girl whom one loves. I wonder how a shy girl, who dares not look into the face of her lover, can one day carelessly take off her clothes in his arms!*

Such a girl is apt to infuse delightful hopes even in dead souls. Perhaps this is due to the force of habit. Yes. The force of habit, which has rendered supperless nights quite a familiar thing to us. What right do I have to think of love under the present circumstances of our life! "Thank you. There is enough sugar in the tea!" I did well when I thanked her! My disposition dislikes cowardice and hesitation. Thus I can seize upon the opportunities of love in the midst of the desolation of poverty. If poverty were a man, I would kill him. But poverty is a woman. It kills us all and we do not resent it. Does my father suffer for our condition? What shape does he assume now? Alas! My father! True, life is a big lie. But she came in person, carrying the sugar bowl. In fact, she came especially for me. I wish I were the Charlemagne of my age. If one day I returned to Nasr Allah in the full majesty of knighthood, she would unconditionally surrender to me. He recovered from his reverie only when he heard Hussein speaking.

"Come. It is your turn."

Ah yes. The English language. He took his brother's place. He gave a lesson replete with kindness and affection for the boy in whose veins ran the same blood as that of his sister . . . the blood which he detected in the delicate back of her knee. At last he finished. But he was so absorbed that he was unaware of the passage of time. Then the two young men left the flat and climbed down the dark stairs. He was no longer able to contain his feeling.

"Her appearance today was a wonderful surprise," he said.

Hussein spoke in a suspiciously critical tone. "Take care. Don't be insolent. This is a respectable house."

"What did I do to deserve that reproof?"

"Do not do anything you would not dare to do if Farid Effendi was with us."

So delighted was Hassanein that he said as if to himself, "She came in person! Oh God! How nice she is!"

"She did nothing wrong by coming."

"Do you think that her father asked her to bring the sugar bowl?"

"How could I possibly know?" Hussein answered, sounding bored.

"Did she come of her own accord?"

"What difference does it make?"

"If she came of her own accord, did her father know about it?"

There was no answer from his brother, who nevertheless paid close attention to his words.

"Did she come surreptitiously?" Hassanein persisted.

"Surreptitiously?!"

Hassanein pressed his brother's arm. "Do they not say in proverbs, 'Between lovers there is discreet communion'?" he said as they reached the last stair.

SEVENTEEN

"Now I have come by myself, and Hussein will come after me, so that our time will not be wasted unnecessarily."

"That is better," Salem answered politely.

Each took his place. Before starting the lesson, Hassanein suggested, "It will be better if we close the balcony window and open the door."

Salem rose and carried out the wish of his teacher, who noted that the silent hall was completely dark. But he did not lose hope. There was still time for tea and sugar. In his desire to be good to his teacher, Salem confided his thoughts to him. "Father and Mother," he said, "have gone out to visit my grandmother."

Hassanein's heart shook violently. He gave the boy a long look. "When did they go out?" he asked.

"In the afternoon."

Anxiously, he sought to learn whether the girl had gone with them. "How could you stay alone in the house?"

"My sister Bahia is staying with me," the boy replied.

This answer gave Hassanein relief, delight, and hope. Thoughts came to his mind: *Tea and sugar, especially sugar. Not sugar, but the sugar bowl. I shall find out today whether she deliberately appeared that other time.* He asked the boy to read, and the lesson was in progress. He listened to his pupil for a few minutes, but then his thoughts again rambled off. *Should I ask for tea? That would be too forward. But if they are late in bringing the tea, I must ask for it. I am too agitated. She and I are alone in the flat. Neither Salem's presence nor that of the servant will make any difference. She and I are alone. Let me enjoy being alone with her for a while, in my imagination. If life were as lusciously simple as it used to be in early times, I would take her in my arms and ask her with no hesitation to*

78

uncover her legs. What stops me from doing so? It is the folly of the world, which killed my father and caused the sufferings we have been undergoing. He became aware of Salem only when the boy asked him the meaning of a word. He explained it to him and ordered him to proceed with his reading. Before the youngster's voice faded away, he heard the sound of approaching footsteps. He turned his eyes in the direction of the open door. He saw the tea tray before he could distinguish who was carrying it. His eyes fell on her arms holding the tray. His heart beat violently and he rose like a man obsessed. While he was moving toward the door, he heard her soft voice, speaking almost in a whisper: "Salem."

Hassanein appeared before her, his eyes ravaging her.

"Thanks a lot," he whispered.

Her almost pale complexion flushed. Perhaps she did not expect to see him. She lowered her eyes in confusion. Hassanein stretched his hands to take the tray from her. In so doing, his right hand clutched the fingers of her left hand. At once, something akin to an electric current flowed through his hand, arm, body, and soul. His daring had no limit. He pressed her fingers in a manner that could not be mistaken. Resentfully she withdrew her hand, and a frown darkened her face. Very angrily, she walked away from the door. He was extremely perturbed when he returned to the table carrying the tray. Confused, he addressed the boy. "Continue," he said.

His thoughts rambled: *Was I too hasty, not waiting for things to develop naturally? How impatient I am! I am always like that. What a frown came upon her face! She frowned and went away. If shyness is the reason, nothing will be dearer to my heart. But if it's indignation, then it is the end of everything. Never shall I retreat. Never shall I know hesitation. Why did she come in person? Why didn't she ask the servant to carry the tray? She came particularly for me. This is obvious. There is nothing to fear.*

He was intermittently aware of Salem, asked him some questions, then fell into worry and distraction, wavering between apprehension and pleasure. When the lesson was over, an idea occurred to him. He rose up, determined and unflinching, to put it into effect. Salem left the room to make way for his teacher. In this interval he took a handkerchief from the pocket of his coat, dropped it on the seat, and left the flat. But he did not budge after the door had been closed. Before knocking at the door, he listened attentively until the boy's footsteps died away. His heart was pounding with extreme agitation. *If the servant opens the door for me, my plan will be foiled. But probably she will come. I have to be resigned to whatever happens.* The light in the hall was turned on, approaching footsteps were heard, and the door was opened. It was she. He did not like the astonishment that appeared on her face. But he wasted no time.

"I am afraid I have angered you," he said tenderly and sympathetically. She withdrew a step without uttering a word, and he said hurriedly, "I can never bear to see you angry."

As though she could not endure being spoken to, she whispered resentfully, "No, no, no. That is too much!"

He could not answer, because Salem appeared on the threshold of the room on the left to inquire, "Is Mummy back?"

"I forgot my handkerchief in the room," Hassanein said aloud.

Salem ran into the room, and the girl hastened inside the house. The boy brought him the handkerchief. He took it and went away. He forgot to thank him.

EIGHTEEN

Hussein raised his head from the desk. Scrutinizing his brother's face, he said, "What is the matter with you?"

Hassanein answered with only a short laugh. In a meaningful tone, his brother asked, "Did you give your lesson?"

Hassanein threw himself on the bed. "Do I look changed?" he inquired.

"Certainly."

Hassanein sighed. "I have to thank God that our mother is sitting in semi-darkness," he said.

"What happened?"

Would he tell him what happened? But what would he get from him but reproof? "Nothing happened," he replied.

"But you look confused! And when you are confused, your nostrils twitch like a donkey's."

After saying this, Hussein paused to ask himself if the nostrils of a donkey actually twitched. How did such a smile come to his mind? His brother laughed.

"Just a bit of excitement. That is all," he said.

"So what?"

"Nothing."

Then Hussein said in earnest, "I want to understand your intentions."

"I don't know what you mean."

"Don't feign ignorance. You understand everything. Why don't you leave her alone? Aren't you afraid that Farid Effendi will discover your forwardness, or that the girl herself will tell him about it? That will put us in a difficult situation."

"My brother," Hassanein said, smiling, "if they place the sun on my right hand and the moon on my left and ask me to leave her, I won't. I'd rather perish."

Hussein laughed in spite of himself. Reassuming his seriousness and solemnity, he inquired, "What do you want from her?"

What a question. Too simple, yet unanswerable. Had he asked himself that question, he would have found no answer. He was motivated by his impulses and instincts, without need for thinking. He said in bewilderment, "In my case there is no distinction between cause and effect."

"I don't understand what you mean."

"Neither do I."

"So leave her alone, as I told you."

"I shall keep chasing her until . . ."

Hussein pressed on. "Until what?"

"Until she falls in love with me as I have with her."

"Then?"

The young man replied, perplexed, "That's enough."

Hussein shook his head angrily. "You are mistaken," he said. "She is a decent girl of a good family, and your conduct will displease her."

"She is that and even more; but I shall never give up hope."

He stood up and went to the desk. He put his books on the sill of the closed window immediately adjacent to his bed. He sat cross-legged before the sill, as though he were sitting at a desk.

"Why don't you sit at the desk?" his brother asked.

"I want to sit cross-legged to warm my legs."

He was preoccupied with an important matter. He opened a copybook, cut out a page from it, and took up a pen. Intense with love and deep distress, he thought: *I shall write to her. There is no alternative. I shall not have another opportunity to speak to her again. But what should I write?*

The silence in the room, punctuated only by the sound of Hussein turning pages in his copybook, helped Hassanein to concentrate. His ears began to distinguish the sound of a wireless stealthily murmuring through the closed window from one of the houses in the alley. He knit his brows, pretending to be annoyed, but he actually felt relieved to hear it since this helped him to escape his perplexity. He listened to the melody of "Happy Nights Are Here Again," which completely swept him away. Tenderness gushed into his breast. His heart overflowed with affection, yearning, ecstasy, love, and life. Engulfed in his enthusiasm, he was filled with energy, he wanted to go free into the open air, concealed by the dark. He gradually became oblivious to the song, once it had opened up before his soul the gates of a paradise full of visions and dreams. *I must write a few words,* he thought, *just two sentences on a small piece of paper that nobody will detect if I throw it at her feet.* He started to write: *"Dear Bahia, I am extremely sorry for making you angry." Is it not better to say, "Do not be angry, my dear"? Both are the same. What, then? I should confess my love to her? I want to write a decent sentence. Oh, God! Help me.*

Hussein interrupted his thoughts, inquiring, "What are you writing?"

"A composition subject."

"What is it about?"

"The influence of music on the renaissance of countries," he replied without hesitation.

"Dear Bahia. I am awfully sorry for making you angry. Do you have the right to get angry because I love you?" That is enough, as there is nothing better than to be brief and significant. No, that is not enough. Something is missing. Shall I quote a line of verse? No, it usually sounds ridiculous when people do that, and if she laughs once, the whole letter will misfire. Let me write another touching sentence. Oh, God! I implore you to help.

A fairly good sentence suddenly came to his mind. He started to write: *"I swear by God that I have done what I have done . . ."*

But once more he was interrupted by Hussein. "Did you finish the points you plan to tackle in the subject?"

Hassanein was disturbed and in suppressed anger he said, "Almost. Excuse me for a second."

He returned to the letter, determined to complete it.

"I swear by God," he wrote, *"that I have done what I have done only because I love you, and shall go on loving you as long as I live. To please you gives me reason to live."*

He carefully reread the message and heaved a deep sigh of relief. He folded the paper, tucked in its edges, and put it in his pocket. *When she comes near the door, or passes by me in the hall, I shall seize the opportunity to throw this paper at her feet, come what may.*

NINETEEN

Nefisa found herself in a medium-sized room. There were two big sofas, a few chairs on either side of the room, and an Assiut carpet on the floor. The wall facing the entrance led to a balcony on the fourth story overlooking Shubra Street. The furniture was old, and judging by the placement of the wireless close to the door, the room was arranged so that the members of the family could sit there in their leisure time. The moment Nefisa entered, it was readily apparent to her that the family occupying it was quite prosperous. This was evident from the small hall, furnished as an entry to the house, as well as from the large, luxurious hall used as a dining room. After all, she was right to believe the words of her landlady in Nasr Allah, who had said, "I have brought a rich customer to you, a bride from a good family. I hope you will take great care in making her dresses, for this might encourage other well-to-do people to come to you." Nefisa was excited to enter a strange house for the first time. She sat on a chair close to the door, and waited. She was dressed in mourning, her black hair falling down her back in a short plait. Thus her face, free as it was from makeup and beauty, looked pale and despairing. She thought about her situation: *A strange house and strange people. A new step in the practice of my job. I am just a dressmaker. Oh, Father, I am not sorry for my humiliation so much as I am sorry for the loss of your dignity.* She did not have to wait long, for soon a twenty-year-old girl, both beautiful and graceful, entered the room. Nefisa rose to greet the girl, who cast a scrutinizing glance as she shook Nefisa's hand.

"Welcome," she said. "You are Miss Nefisa, whom Mrs. Zeinab asked to come?"

"Yes, madam," Nefisa shyly replied. "Are you the bride?"

The lady smilingly nodded yes and sat down.

"Mrs. Zeinab praises you highly," she said. "You strike me as being a good dressmaker."

A faint smile appeared on Nefisa's face. Her lips opened without uttering a word, and she thought: *Perhaps she told you that I was a skillful dressmaker. Well, is that praise or disparagement? I don't know. I wonder if she told you about the situation of our family. I had a father like yours, and I was as much of a lady as you are. I had waited long for a bridegroom to come. But he never did and he never will.*

The bride asked her tenderly, already knowing the answer, "Why are you in mourning?"

"My father died two months ago," she answered sadly. "He was, may the mercy of God be upon him, an official in the Ministry of Education."

"Mrs. Zeinab told us about it. My condolences."

"Thank you. We come from Benha. My aunt lives there with her husband, who owns a ginning factory."

At that moment a servant entered carrying a bundle, which she placed beside her mistress and departed. The bride untied the bundle, which contained a pile of silk cloths of different colors. Nefisa realized immediately that it was material to be made into underwear. Perhaps she had sent the dresses to another, more capable dressmaker. This made her feel relieved, because she was afraid of harming her professional reputation by putting it to such a difficult test. She was content to undertake what lay within her abilities in return for a fair price. She moved to the place where the bride sat, examined the cloth, and felt it with her hand.

"Congratulations," she said. "How precious this silk is."

A happy smile appeared on the bride's lips. "Now," she said, "we start by taking measurements. By the way, do you mind coming to work here in our house? We have all the things you need for your work. There are no children in the house to dis-

turb you. Besides, you do not live far away. So it will be easy
for you to come every day."

"As you wish, madam," Nefisa found herself obliged to reply.

The girl rose and stood before her, and Nefisa started to take
her measurements. The smell of new silk filled her deprived
nostrils, and when she touched the fabric, she experienced a
strange feeling of both desire and pain as it glided between her
fingers. Surrendering to her confidence in the skill of her hands
gave her a sense of mastery and the hope of consolation, but
hope very soon died and gave way to dark despair. She thought:
*A bride and silk. Am I really making these clothes for the bride? In fact,
I am making this underwear for the bridegroom more than the bride!
His fingertips will playfully touch its relaxed fringes, its softness. So I
am taking part in the preparation of this marriage, and I shall also
participate in so many marriages, without getting married myself, to be
left to my burning dreams. What a beautiful and happy girl she is!
Happiness almost radiates from her eyes. Today the silk is prepared,
and tomorrow the lover is awaited. A waft of warm maternity blows on
her from a rosy horizon. I have been dreaming of that for so long; and
my father used to tell me that a sweet temper was more precious than
beauty. Time passed between solicitude and hope until I reached the age
of twenty-three. Why was I born ugly? Why wasn't I created like my
brothers? How handsome Hassanein and Hussein are! Even Hassan! I
am as dead as my father. He lies dead in Bab el-Nasr, and I lie dead
in Shubra.*

Then the voice of the bride came to her. "Would you like to
receive part of your fees in advance?"

"No need at all," she hastened to reply.

She regretted this injudicious reply, which doubled her resentment and despondency. She heard the creak of approaching shoes and raised her head in the direction of the door to
see a young man merrily enter the room. He quickly came to
the bride, their hands clasped, and they exchanged a happy
smile.

"Where is your mother?" he asked.

"In her room."

He turned to Nefisa, and the girl introduced the young man. "Hassan, my fiancé."

Bending her head toward him, she said, "Miss Nefisa, the dressmaker."

TWENTY

Nefisa was tired when she left the bride's house, just before sunset. Nasr Allah was only a few steps from the house, so she wended her way through the passersby leisurely and relaxed. The cold air refreshed her, and she quickened her pace. Memories of what took place in the bride's house rushed to her mind in a mixture of pain and pleasure. She was sitting on a sofa, and the couple was sitting on one opposite her. They sat close to each other, speaking sometimes audibly and sometimes so quietly that their voices became lovers' whispers. How great was her desire, then, to raise her head from the sewing machine and have a look at them. But fear and shyness stopped her from meeting their eyes.

Once, when she raised her eyes, she saw their legs touching. So absorbing was that sight to her that she regained her awareness only when the bride slapped the bridegroom on the hand, saying to him half coyly, half threateningly, "Be careful!"

Nefisa was so absorbed in her fancies that she almost collided with the others who were walking in the street. A burning desire for love overcame her. Throughout her life she had not found a single heart with love and compassion for her. Her strained nerves found vent only in laughter, mocking herself, her brothers, and others. Thus she became known for her light-hearted laughter, although it concealed a profound bitterness. She could not avoid such feelings. In fact, her female instinct was the only part of her that was free from blemish; it was ripe and warm. A captive urge, imprisoned by her upbringing, by dignity and family, tortured her. But the scene she witnessed in the bride's house was enough to shake her violently and cruelly. When she thought of Nasr Allah, a fresh, tantalizing hope revived in her breast. There she saw Amm Gaber Soliman's grocery, which lay a short distance from her house. There also was Soliman Gaber Soliman, Gaber's son and apprentice. Since her family had dismissed their servant, Nefisa frequently went to the grocery to buy what they needed. Thus began her acquaintance with the young man, and it became closer as time went on. She conjured up before her the image of the young man, tall and stout, rather dark, with an oval face and narrow eyes. She asked herself: Did he really show interest in her or did she imagine it? It seemed that he had smiled at her hesitantly many times. Perhaps he could not forget, despite their circumstances, that she was the daughter of the late Kamel Effendi. Although she wasn't pretty, she still looked like a respectable girl, while Soliman was only the son of a simple grocer, and he was only an apprentice in his father's shop. She was aware of all this, but she could not afford to reject any man, whoever he might be, who seemed interested in her. She couldn't afford not to love anyone who loved her. All of a sudden, resentment and a kind of lukewarmness returned to her, and her old despair engulfed her. Her heart said: *Don't deceive yourself and allow false hope to make you lose your head. Be contented with despondency. It will give you relief, which is the sole consolation for a girl like you, without money, beauty, or a father.*

But she knew that she would not listen to her heart or obey the voice of her fears. The closer she approached the blind alley where she lived, the greater became her surrender to hope and tenderness. She thought: *God is omnipotent. Inasmuch as He ordains my sorrow, He can, be it His will, grant me hope and comfort. He is my sole hope and He will never let me down. I have not done anything wrong to deserve humiliation. Neither has our family. So this anguish is bound to be dispelled. But Soliman is an obscure person. Will Hassanein accept him? My brothers are all proud, and I do not think our poverty will diminish their pride. Hassan behaves like an outsider. Oh! To think of Hassan. I wish he could change his attitude and save us from our distress. My father's pension and my work are not enough. And what has Hassan done? Nothing. None of them will accept Soliman, and nobody better than Soliman will ever come to me. How can I make sure that he is really interested in me?* With her eyes fixed on Amm Gaber Soliman's grocery store, she continued until she reached the alley. She thought of going to the grocery to buy something . . . anything. Without hesitation, she went to it. The old Amm Gaber Soliman was sitting at his small desk, busy working on his ledger, while his young son Soliman Gaber Soliman stood behind the counter at the entrance. As soon as the girl stood before him, the young man became aware of her; he looked at her with a jubilant face, and his narrow eyes brightened. His features betrayed foolishness, bestiality, and cowardice. The only part of his face that could be described as handsome was his short mustache. He spoke first. "Anything I can do for you, Miss Nefisa?"

Blinking in confusion, she replied, "Give me one piaster's worth of Tahania sweets."

He took a knife, cut an ample portion, and, slicing a little extra piece, he said to her in a low voice, "This slice is for you alone, Miss Nefisa."

He wrapped up the sweet in a paper and handed it to her, then took the piaster, watching his father out of the corner of his eye. Noting that his father was busy working on his ledger, he became encouraged.

"I shall keep your piaster for good luck."

She smiled faintly and went away. She had smiled deliberately as if she wanted to encourage him. That cost her a great effort. *He is no longer content with the language of the eyes, and he did well when he spoke*, she thought, and in spite of his humble position and appearance, her heart beat with delight and she was overcome with excitement. Before it actually happened, she had played the scene over in her mind while she was engaged in her work for the bride. Reality turned out to be only slightly different from her imagination. She had imagined herself standing before him to buy Tahania sweets, and he, devouring her with his eyes, had said to her, as he was taking the piaster, "You are sweeter than sweet." He hadn't actually said that, but he'd said something similar. She sighed with relief and her imagination flew to the memories of her past loves! Her first was a minister whose picture she had seen in *Al Musawar* magazine, and she had embroidered around his picture some rosy day-dreams in which she imagined herself begetting a unique child by him. The second was Farid Effendi Mohammed himself, and because of her love for him, she quarreled with his wife and family. As for Soliman, he was the worst of the lot. Yet he was the only one who actually existed.

When she reached the middle of the courtyard, she began to fear that her mother would scold her for spending the whole day outside the house. This aroused her resentment and she imagined herself replying: *"Stop scolding me, I can no longer bear it. What I am suffering from is enough."*

Her voice rose, ringing in the staircase. Cautiously, she looked around her, and with her fingers suppressed a laugh that almost escaped her lips.

TWENTY-ONE

Hassanein left Farid Effendi Muhammed's flat and closed the door behind him. He was extremely depressed. He walked toward the stairs, suffering with despair and frustration. But he stopped, putting his hand on the banister. He raised his head to follow the rustle of a dress. He saw the hem as the wearer climbed the last flight of stairs leading to the roof of the house. Who was it? He knew all the occupants of the house very well. Which of them was it, dressed in that red color? His heart beat violently, and he felt some power urging him to climb upward. He cast a wary look at the closed door and listened with attention and anxiety. On tiptoe, he crossed the corridor in front of the flat and walked toward the last flight of stairs leading to the roof. Perhaps it was she. He had seen her no more, either in the room or in the hall, since he threw his folded letter at her feet. She had disappeared in anger, and was, undoubtedly, indifferent to his letter and emotions. Thus the teaching hours became tedious and a torture to him. Noiselessly he climbed up the stairs until he reached the last flight. He saw the slanting rays of the setting sun level with his eyes. Waves of gentle breezes blew on his forehead. He looked all over the roof, from its front ledge overlooking the alley to its back ledge; but he found no trace of a human being. There was nothing on the roof but two wooden chicken houses. One of them faced the door to the roof, and the other, which belonged to Farid Effendi's family, stood in a corner beside the back ledge. He silently approached the second chicken house and stood near the door, pricking his ears. At first, he heard only the cackle of chickens. Then he heard a voice clucking to the chickens. He could not tell whose voice it was.

Afraid that the girl's mother might be inside, he retreated a step. He was about to flee. But the door opened, and on its threshold appeared Bahia in a red overcoat. Her blue eyes widened in amazement, and they were fixed dumbfounded on him. She blushed so intensely that her face resembled the red velvet of her overcoat, but her blush lasted only for a few moments. Then, controlling her feelings, she crossed the threshold and closed the door. She went away from him, walking toward the door of the roof. But he did not allow her to escape, leaping to block her way. She gave him an angry look and indignantly straightened her head.

"This is too much!" she exclaimed.

In a mixture of daring and tenderness, he replied, "Always angry! I wonder at my bad luck, always finding you angry."

She looked annoyed. "Let me pass, please," she said.

He stretched out his arms as if to block her way altogether. "This is an opportunity I couldn't dream of," he said. "So I can't allow it to slip from my hands. After your deliberate disappearance which caused me the most painful torture, I have the right to keep you for a while. Why do you disappear? Let me ask you: How did you like my letter?"

She frowned. "You mention that paper!" she said sharply. "How brazen of you! I don't approve of it."

His look at her wavered between hope and fear, and he thought: *Should I believe this anger? My heart tells me that it is exaggerated. Perhaps it is a symptom of shyness. Surely it is. If she had really wanted to force her way, I couldn't have stopped her. I don't want to believe it. But why did she insist on disappearing?*

"My brazenness is the result of exhausted patience!" he said to her beseechingly.

She shook her head with annoyance. "Patience," she muttered. "Do not play with such words, and let me go, please!"

"I have told you nothing but the truth," he said with warmth and sincerity, "and it was my true feeling alone which urged me to write that short letter. Every word in it is true. So I am terribly offended to find that you recoil so angrily at my feelings."

Panting, he swallowed hard, then corrected himself. "Yes," he said with a sob. "I love you."

She turned her head away, still frowning, her brows closely knit and her lips tight. But when she kept silent for a while, a fresh gleam of hope revived in him. Then she said in a voice that was softer than before, "Let me go. Aren't you afraid someone may come up to the roof and find us?"

Oh God! Is she annoyed only that someone may come up to the roof?! He was filled with ecstasy; his shining brown eyes radiated with delight.

"Let me express my feelings to you," he exclaimed. "I love you. I love you more than life itself. Not only that. The only good in life is that I love you. This is what I wrote, what I am saying, and what I will repeat. Believe me, and don't keep silent, because I can't bear it."

He could read seriousness and solemnity on her pure face as she turned it to him. But he thought he could perceive in her some sort of tender feeling which, perhaps, she found it hard to suppress.

Then he heard her say in a whispering voice, "That is enough! Now, allow me to go!"

She was adamant in wearing that mask. How easily she yields to shyness. He heaved an audible sigh. "I do not want to go back to my tortures without a gleam of hope," he said quietly. "I have opened up the secrets of my heart to you. And I do not hope to get from you more than one word to infuse life into my dead soul."

But she seemed unable to utter that word. In her extreme confusion she said only, "Oh, God! How can I leave this place?"

He was touched. But hope rendered him more stubborn and persistent. "Don't be so scared," he said warmly. "I love you. Does this confession only arouse annoyance in you? I won't go back to desperate torture. Never. Never."

"So what?"

Observing her flushed face in the quiet and the waning light of the dusk, he was swept by an uncontrollable upsurge of loving emotion, and he felt that to perish was less painful than to retreat. He implored her from the depths of his soul.

"Say just one word! If you can't, only give a nod. Again, if you can't even do that, then your silence—if I can perceive contentment in it—is enough for me."

Her lips moved without uttering a word; then they closed. Her face flushed more deeply, and she turned away from him. His desire mounting, his heart leapt ecstatically inside his breast. "Is that the silence I want? I love you. I give you my word that I shall be yours unto death."

She inclined her face more without breaking her beloved silence. A sweeping ecstasy overcame his body until his eyes were intoxicated. Unconsciously, desire made him move toward her, but she shrank away as if she were awakened from a profound dream by a sudden shake; she almost leapt away from him. Then she fled. He remained transfixed, looking with mad love at her back until she disappeared behind the door. He sighed heartily. Looking far away into the dusk at the embroidered phantoms of the horizon, he felt that his soul was dissolving into the universe and singing in its splendor. Then he moved slowly, drunk and glowing, until he almost reached the door. As he passed the other chicken house, a magnetic power seemed to attract him to it. Looking to his left, he saw his brother Hussein standing behind the wall of the chicken house.

TWENTY-TWO

"Hussein," he said with surprise.

Hassanein observed a change in the color of Hussein's face, who, though livid with anger, was exerting his utmost effort to control himself and keep his anger in check. Hassanein wondered why his brother had come up to the roof. Probably Hussein had followed him. On his way to give his lesson, he may have seen Hassanein warily climbing up the stairs to the roof and become suspicious. This was the only rational explanation. However, it was out of character for Hussein to hide himself, to eavesdrop and spy. It did not occur to Hassanein to ask his brother why he had done it. On the contrary, he was overcome by shyness and confusion. Despite his anger, Hussein's shyness and confusion were no less. Perhaps Hussein sought to conceal his own feelings by exaggerated anger.

"I have seen certain things that offend me very much," he said. "How dare you chase the girl in this rude manner? Your behavior is disgraceful and is not becoming of a neighbor, who respects the obligations of neighborliness!"

Hassanein found relief in his brother's cruel tone, as it saved him from shyness and confusion. He answered angrily, "I have not committed anything shameful. Perhaps you heard what I said."

Ignoring this last remark, Hussein said, more angrily than before, "You think there is nothing shameful in blocking the girl's way in that disgraceful manner?"

"I do not think she considers it so."

"She will tell her father," Hussein said.

"She won't."

Overcome by his anger, Hussein retorted sharply, "I was

very much afraid you would attack her. Had you done so, I would have punished you cruelly."

Hassanein was surprised at this belated threat. Anger was about to make him lose his head. Cruel words jumped to the tip of his tongue. But, miraculously, he managed to keep them under control. He fell into deep silence until the intensity of anger diminished.

"You shouldn't be afraid that I would do anything of that sort," he said.

Hussein thought a little. Then he retracted. "Anyhow, I am delighted to hear you say so. And if I have the right to give you counsel, I advise you always to maintain honor."

Coldly, Hassanein replied, "I don't need such advice."

He left his place. Hussein followed him. They went down together in silence. Hussein did not go to Farid Effendi's flat. Hassanein noticed that, but he did not comment.

"What made you come back so quickly?" Samira asked Hussein.

"Salem has not studied his last lesson, and I shall see him tomorrow," Hussein answered.

They went to their room. Hussein sat on his chair at the desk. Hassanein went on to the window, opened it, and sat on the edge of the bed. He thought: *The worst end for the best beginning. How foolish of him! How did he allow himself to spy on me. He spoiled the poetry of this happy situation. No. Nothing could ever spoil it. Everything will disappear; but she will remain shining, happy, and fascinating. Never shall I forget the moment of her silence, which said far more than words. She said everything without uttering a word.*

"Close the window. Are you mad?"

He was frightened by Hussein's cry. Then anger and obstinacy filled his heart.

"The weather is gentle and comfortable," he said.

"Don't be stubborn; close the window!" Hussein shouted at him.

His brother's tone only made him more obstinate. "Move to

the other chair to keep away from the draft, if you think there is one!"

Hussein snorted angrily. He went to the window and violently slammed it shut with a disturbing bang that ripped the silence to shreds, and broke a windowpane. Fear and a dreadful silence prevailed. Soon Hussein became blinded by fury and, slapping Hassanein, he shouted, "It's your fault!"

Hassanein went out of his mind and struck his brother's head with his fist. They started to fight; Samira and Nefisa rushed into the room. In their mother's presence, each muttering and mumbling, the boys stopped railing at each other. The mother, standing between them, eyed both angrily; then her eyes fixed on the broken glass. She inquired in a quietness that portended an approaching tempest, "What is the matter with you?"

Hassanein said hurriedly, "He slammed the window closed and broke the windowpane. Then he slapped me."

"He opened the window in this cold weather," Hussein said with a sob. "I asked him to close it but he was rude and refused. I got up to close it myself, and here is the result."

Samira sighed and said, "Oh, God, your mercy be upon me. Don't I have trouble enough?"

She gripped both of them by the shoulders and pushed them to the middle of the room. She shouted in Hussein's face, "Aren't you ashamed of yourself? You're supposed to be an adult!" and punched him twice in the chest, then slapped him.

She also fell upon Hassanein, who withdrew, crying, "It was he who started beating me, and it was he who broke the windowpane."

But she slapped him hard on the mouth and kept hitting his head and face until Nefisa intervened.

"I don't want to hear another sound from you," Samira shouted. "As for the window, it will remain broken until you repair it yourselves."

Downcast and filled with unhappiness, she left the room. Nefisa stood between them for a while in distress.

"The time for quarreling is over," she said. "You are men now!"

Then, smiling, she said to Hussein, "You couldn't bear the draft for a little while. What are you going to do now that it is permanently open? Fill the hole with a newspaper. If you don't, you are both good for nothing."

Finding that her words did not have the effect she expected, she left the room. Hussein silently went back to his chair. Meanwhile, Hassanein excitedly threw himself on the bed. Often the quarrels between them ended with such intervention on their mother's part. Despite their close friendship, their life was not free from arguments and quarrels and occasional jealousy. Yet they always remained loving and brotherly companions, indispensable to each other. Of the two, Hussein was the wiser, Hassanein the stronger. Hussein undertook the task of guiding and directing in whatever problems presented themselves; the bulk of these being related to play and minor questions about money. Hassanein bore the larger burden of defense in any fight they had with outsiders. In fights with other schoolboys, they never asked their elder brother Hassan for help when they felt they might be overcome by their adversaries, or even if a quarrel threatened to become a really bloody scrap. Anyhow, the two brothers had seldom quarreled in recent years, and consequently their mother rarely punished them with a beating. A long period of peace, about a year, had preceded this latest quarrel. However, no quarrel estranged them from each other for more than a day, and thereafter they always became reconciled. Then the aggressor, a little confused, began to speak to his brother, and both soon forgot all about their scrap. Their mother suffered from it more than they did. Their quarrels distressed her and left a piercing and profound pain in her heart. To punish them, she found no means better than beating, hoping that it would rectify the ill effects of their father's tendency to spoil his children. Nothing was more repulsive to her than seeing one of her sons trespass beyond the limits and show any sign of transgression against the sacred unity of the family. She saw in Hassan's life a bad example; she would rather die than see it repeated in the others. Hassan himself was not exempt from her blows, but these came too late. She never ceased to blame herself and her husband for spoiling him, and she was bitterly tortured by the fact that her son was a victim of lenience as well as poverty.

A part of the night passed, but the two brothers were still silent and alienated. The silence became more oppressive after Samira and Nefisa went to sleep. Hussein started to read a book, in an attempt to concentrate his scattered thoughts. Hassanein was secretly watching him, wondering how he should feel toward his brother. Hassanein cherished happy, consoling, and reassuring memories. Soon a smile appeared on his lips, and he thought: *All is well. Bahia kept silent, which means that she loves me. Really! How I yearn to hear it uttered by her luscious lips. Be patient. All this will come in time. Silence is only a beginning. But the end . . . ?* Suddenly, he turned to his brother and the smile returned to his lips. *What harm would I have suffered if I had closed the window? He seems unable to follow what he is reading. Had he been endowed with my good fortune, he would not have found it difficult to forget all that happened.* He felt a kind of sympathy for his brother.

TWENTY-THREE

Nefisa returned to Nasr Allah at sunset, as was her habit in those days. She seemed to have started paying attention to her appearance, which she had neglected for so long in mourning the death of her father. She applied kohl to her eyes, and colored her cheeks and lips with light lipstick. Something is better than nothing. His persistence in flirting with her and treating her nicely gave her a measure of self-confidence, reassurance, and hope. She no longer cared that he was the son of a grocer, and she the daughter of an official. That he was interested in her made her think very highly of him. Motivated by her inhibited impulses and passions, her suffocating despair and the zest for life which only death can extinguish, she responded and continued to encourage him. As time went on, his image became familiar, even lovable, and in the midst of the barrenness of life, it cultivated a fragrant flower of hope. She no longer lived her days in listlessness, waiting for something to break the monotony. Now, walking in Nasr Allah after a full day's work, she quivered with a warm delight that overflowed her heart, her nerves, her whole body. Once he said to her, "You want sweets. You are nothing but sweets." His words invaded her heart, and she smiled with happiness and delight. She felt an urge to say to him, "Don't tell lies. There is nothing sweet about me!" But, doubtful and perplexed, she kept silent. She reminded herself of the proverb that says, "After all, every girl will find her admirer." Who knows? Perhaps she was not as ugly as she thought. She continued to walk along the road with her eyes turned to the shop, until she stood before him face to face. Delight shone in Soliman's face.

"You're welcome," he said. "I was wondering when you would come."

Casting a look at his father's seat, she found it empty. She could see him praying behind the column, laden with cans and pots, in the middle of the shop. Reassured, she said coyly, "Why do you wonder?"

He screwed up his narrow eyes. "Guess. Ask my heart," he replied with a smile.

She raised her painted eyebrows. "Ask your heart? Oh! His heart! What are you keeping inside?"

The young man whispered, "My heart says it is delighted to see you, and it most eagerly waits for you!"

"Really?"

"And it also says that it desires to meet you now in the street to confide to you something of importance."

He turned toward his father and heard him uttering the Salutations marking the end of his prayers. So he said in a hurry, "I can leave the shop for a few minutes. Go on out ahead of me to the main street!"

Baffled, she looked at him with excitement. She felt an urge to meet him. But she refused to acquiesce so easily, without persistence on his part and professed objection on her own.

"I am afraid of being late," she said.

Nodding warningly toward his father, he said anxiously, "A few minutes. Go on out ahead before he finishes his prayers."

Realizing that there was no time to be coy or coquettish, she changed her mind. After a moment of hesitation, she turned with a beating heart toward Shubra Street. She was overpowered by excitement, anxiety, and fear. But she continued to walk, with no thought of retreat. Her long-cherished dreams lightened the weight of the new step she was taking. Soon she overcame her fears, thinking only of the sweet hope that she could see at the end of the road. When she reached the street, she looked behind her, to see him approaching at a quick pace, wearing a jacket over his gown. She turned to the right and walked quickly away from her quarter. In long strides, he caught up with her. Pleased, he said, "I excused myself from my father for a few minutes."

She cast a significant glance at his apparel, and he understood. "I cannot put on my suit except in my free hours," he said apologetically.

He looked merry and delighted. His amorous eyes were not so blind as to see her as beautiful. But deprived and oppressed as he was by his tyrannical father, he welcomed this opportunity to enjoy whatever love was available to him, even from a girl so ugly, helpless, and deep in despair. In any case, she was a member of the beloved female sex, otherwise beyond his reach. He was afraid to let the minutes pass without saying what he wanted to say. So he spoke hurriedly.

"The shop is usually closed on Friday in the afternoon. Meet me then. We could go together to Rod el-Farag."

"Go together? I don't like the idea. I'm not one of those girls."

"What if we do? What is wrong in it?"

"God forbid!"

"We'll find a place safe for conversation."

"I am afraid one of my brothers may see us."

"We can avoid that easily."

She shook her head and said, a bit bewildered, "I don't like this life, so full of fears."

"But we must meet!"

She pondered. "Why?"

He looked at her in astonishment. "So as to meet," he said.

Worried, she answered, "No. No, I'm not that type."

"Don't we have anything to say to each other?"

"I don't know."

"I have much to say."

"What is it you want to say?"

"You will know it in due time. There is no time to say it now."

As doubts assailed her, her face reddened. "I've told you, I am not one of those girls!"

The young man exclaimed in a sorrowful tone, "How could I possibly think so, Miss Nefisa! I'm a man of the world, and I can judge people."

She felt relieved. But she wondered why he failed to ease her heart by uttering the very words she was yearning to hear. Once more he asked, "Shall we meet, then, next Friday?"

She hesitated a bit, then murmured, "By God's will."

Deeply preoccupied, she returned home. This was the beginning of the love she was so eager to experience. Her heart shook off the dust of frustration, and it became full of life, ecstasy, warmth, and hope. That was true. Yet she was at once baffled and worried, not knowing how the affair would end, and how her family would react to it.

TWENTY-FOUR

Hassanein reached the door of the roof and sighed audibly. She heard him, but, ignoring him, she walked slowly toward the chicken house. He coughed. The sun was emitting its last rays as he boldly rushed toward her. She turned on her heels, confronting him with a stony face, revealing neither anger nor pleasure.

"Is there no end to this?"

He said with a short laugh, "You're giving me an unforgettable lesson."

Preserving the reticence in her face, she replied, "I wish you would learn a lesson."

He cracked his fingers, shouting, "Never!"

He sighed aloud. He was extremely jubilant in the discovery that she wanted to converse with him.

"Never shall I stop loving you," he continued.

Her face flushed. "Don't utter those words again," she said, frowning.

He spoke obstinately, quietly, and emphatically. "I love you!"

"You want to tease me?"

"I want nothing but your love."

"I shall deafen my ears," she said sharply.

Slightly raising his voice, he repeated, "I love you. I love you. I love you!"

She kept silent with longing and conflicting emotions; he continued to devour her with his eyes. Unable to bear the weight of his glances, she turned her back and walked away. He rushed after her. She turned to him with a frown. "Please. Leave me and go away."

He said in astonishment, "There is no reason to say that now. It's past history. We are now in the stage of 'I love you.'"

"And what do you want?"

"To love you."

She was about to scold him, but she was overcome by a smile she had long been suppressing. Then she gave a short stifled laugh that came out of her nose as a pleasant snort. She couldn't help lowering her head in shyness. So moved was he by her gesture that his overpowering passions rose still higher; encouraged and desiring more, he went up to her, stretching his hand to hold hers. But she looked almost horrified, and withdrew.

"Don't touch me," she said with serious finality.

The smile of triumph appearing on his lips faded away. But she did not care. In the same serious tone, she went on, "Never try to touch me. I won't allow it. I won't even think of it."

He was dumbfounded. "I am sorry," he said in astonishment. "I didn't mean any harm. I love you, truly and honestly."

She looked at her feet. Her appearance showed the gravity of what she was about to utter. "Thank you for saying it," she said seriously. "But this matter is not for me to decide."

He was astonished at her words. So swept away by emotion was he that he had never paused to think of anything beyond it. He loved and saw nothing but love. Yet what she said brought him back to his senses. Now he understood what he had overlooked; he realized that the matter was serious, that it was no trifle. He was not sorry about that and his delight increased, but he was pervaded by a feeling of fear and anxiety, and unaware of the reasons for it. In an attempt to overcome his perplexity, he said, "I see your point of view and approve of it. But this is not everything. I ask your heart first."

Her features softened, but without losing control of her will, she replied, "Please, don't entrap me in talk which I don't like."

"Talk which you don't like!"

She did not mean exactly what she said. But she found herself forced to mutter a feeble "Yes."

"This is a bleeding stab into my heart," Hassanein said fearfully.

Shy, perplexed, and confused, she replied, "I don't like to be secretive about what I do and say."

He couldn't help smiling, saying, "But this is inevitably part of the whole thing, and there is nothing wrong in it."

His words and his smile made her ill at ease. The redness in her face increased, and she said rather sharply, "No! I don't like flirtation!"

"But my love for you is genuine."

"Oh! Don't force me to hear what is unbearable to me!"

Smiling, he inquired, "Should I kill myself, then?"

She smiled inwardly, but no sign of that appeared on her face. "There is no need whatsoever to kill yourself," she said. "I have told you everything."

The last sentence brought him back to fear and perplexity. "I am just a young man of seventeen," he said, after some hesitation, "and a pupil in the third year of secondary school. How, then, can I broach this subject?"

She turned her face away.

"Wait until you become a man!" she replied coldly.

"Bahia," he said in astonishment mixed with resentment.

"There is no other way," she answered quietly.

He was irritated and upset by the firmness of her attitude. But meanwhile, he felt his love overpowering him, obliterating his fears and worries. Surrendering, he said, "Have things your own way. I shall talk to those who have a say in the matter."

She raised her eyes to him for a moment, then lowered them. For a while she seemed about to speak but she kept silent.

"I shall speak to Farid Effendi," he said.

"You!"

"Yes."

A silent objection appeared on her face.

"Is it necessary that my mother should do it?" he asked.

She hesitated briefly. Blushing, she said with difficulty, "I think so!"

He was upset by the frankness of her reply, which deepened his worry. He imagined his sad mother sitting with her head bent in the dark hall, unlighted to save expenses. He became agitated. "I shall talk to him," he said in a low voice, "and convince him to approach my mother about it."

The girl asked, surprised, "Why don't you talk to her yourself?"

He was about to say "I can't," but then he closed his lips. He ignored her question.

"I am very much afraid that he might scoff at me," he said, "or that he would keep you waiting until I finish all the long years of education which lie ahead of me."

Impatiently and almost unconsciously, she replied, "He will approve waiting, as long as I consent to it."

She bit her lips in shyness and pain. Very eagerly, he looked at her, and with a heart quaking with love, he stretched out his arms to reach her. But she withdrew, frowning to hide her emotion.

"No, no," she said. "Have you forgotten what I told you?"

TWENTY-FIVE

Hussein and Hassanein were sitting at the desk in the evening as usual. Hassanein, supporting his face with his hand, was absorbed in his thoughts. His looks, and the fact that he kept biting his fingernails from time to time, indicated that he was worried and tense. Hussein himself did not seem to be attracted much by the book that lay open before him. He could not help smiling, and his heart was swayed by different, alternating emotions. Annoyed by the silence, he said, "They have been negotiating for a long time."

Fearfully, Hassanein became attentive. Then, sighing, he said, "An hour has passed. Even more. I wish I knew what is going on out there."

"The order of things is now reversed," Hussein replied sarcastically. "The ordinary procedure is for the young man to ask for the hand of his girl. But in your case the girl's father comes to ask for the hand of the young man!"

Indignantly and irritably, Hassanein said, "As long as you are not involved, you have the right to mock me. I wish I knew what is being said in the sitting room. What is Mother saying?"

"Soon," Hussein said calmly, "you'll know everything."

"Do you think she will turn down the petition of a man like Farid Effendi?"

"Who knows? What I am sure of is that we shall lose our heaven-sent monthly pay if she rejects it."

Hassanein eyed him in perplexity. "How long will this painful waiting last?" he asked.

Having thoroughly thought the matter over, they returned to silence. They had discussed it intermittently over a long period

THE BEGINNING AND THE END

of time, ever since Hassanein had told his brother about his conversation with Farid Effendi. To Hassanein's surprise, the man had warmly welcomed his proposal. Farid Effendi promised to broach the subject to his mother and to remove whatever obstacles stood in the way. In explanation of the man's attitude, Hussein slyly suggested that the good nature of Farid Effendi and his known attachment to their family were the cause. The two young men could do nothing but await the outcome of the present negotiations. As time went on, Hassanein's worry increased. *I shall know everything after a few minutes,* he thought. *Will Bahia be mine? Or shall I burn this newborn hope? This is the only means of having the girl. I want her and I can't do without her. What is she thinking of right now? Isn't she worried about our fate? There is no doubt that she loves me. For all the world, that is enough for me. Damn Hussein. He just keeps reading so calmly, and since he has no love or anxiety at the mercy of this meeting, he enjoys observing the battle with detachment. What a torture tyrannical passion is. Who says that it resides in the heart? Is it not more likely that it nestles in the mind? This is the secret of insanity.*

He was awakened from his reverie by Hussein saying, "They are coming out."

Hassanein pricked up his ears and overheard his mother exchanging compliments with Farid Effendi and his wife. They proceeded to the door, while Nefisa came to her brothers' room and stood looking curiously at Hassanein.

Then she said, "Sometimes malice is hidden under apparently innocent silence! Do you really want to get married?!"

Hussein murmured, "This is the first drop of the oncoming shower."

In instinctive self-defense, Hassanein moved from his chair to the bed in a remote corner of the room, close to the window, whose broken glass had been replaced with sheets of newspaper. Then they heard their mother approaching. Her features hard and stern, she walked heavily into the room. Searching for Hassanein, her eyes wandered until they rested on him at the farthest end of the room. She stared at him for some time, then proceeded to the chair he had left vacant and sat down, somewhat exhausted. An intense silence, which no one dared to interrupt, prevailed until she looked at Hussein and asked him calmly, "Don't you know what Farid Effendi and his wife came to discuss with me?"

The question was totally unexpected, and Hussein was confused. Considering himself no more than a spectator to the whole business, he kept silent. "Answer!" she demanded.

Perplexed, he turned his eyes to Hassanein, seeking help. Regarding the movement as an answer, Samira proceeded to question him further.

"When did you know?"

Frightened, he answered, "The day before yesterday."

"Why did you hide it from me?"

He took refuge in silence, cursing both his bad luck and his brother; the two had combined, despite his innocence, to get him into this mess. Then she sighed sorrowfully. "I am resigned to God's will. The misery you have caused me surpasses my suffering at the hands of my dark fate."

Nefisa, who detested this quarrelsome atmosphere, felt she had to fight its hold over them. However, she had no intention of encouraging her brother to persist in his desires. She was perhaps even angrier with him than her mother was. She even considered the whole matter a mean plot aimed at kidnapping her brother. But she still hoped to avoid useless friction, and so she said to her mother, "Don't excite yourself. What's done can't be undone. Have mercy upon us and stop giving us all a headache."

Her mother scolded her sharply. "Shut up!" she said.

Then she turned to Hassanein and spoke to him contemptuously. "Perhaps you are eager to know the outcome of your underhanded planning."

Sorrowfully, she shook her head. "One may well envy the

heart you possess, for despite our catastrophe and misery, it can love, and in pursuit of its happiness it is indifferent to us all. I was actually amazed when Farid Effendi spoke to me about your great hopes and curious love. But in my turn I spoke to him about our struggle and misery. I spoke to him about our furniture, which we are selling piece by piece to provide for our basic needs, and about the misery of your sister, who must work as a dressmaker, spending her days moving from one house to another. Then I told him frankly that none of my sons would marry until he helped his collapsing family to get back on its feet."

The woman was silent. She fixed her eyes on the hopeless and depressed face of her son, who could not look his mother in the face. Then she added bitterly, "However, I have to congratulate you on your affection and human feelings!"

The woman departed from the room, leaving a heavy silence behind her. She was so furious and sad that she could hardly see her way. Nefisa was so disturbed that she forgot her deep anger. She spoke to Hassanein, feigning merriment.

"Mother didn't tell you everything," she said. "I assure you that, really, there is no reason for you to be so despondent. She couldn't possibly ignore Farid Effendi's friendship or his affection for us. Who could ever forget his help and magnanimity? Mother told him that she considered his approval of your proposal a great honor. But she did tell him about our condition, which he knows quite well, and requested him to wait until our stumbling family could get back on its feet. She asked him to be content for the time being with her verbal agreement to the engagement until it is officially announced, when you become a responsible man. She also told him that she would be delighted to have Bahia as her daughter-in-law. So there is absolutely no need for you to be sad."

The girl looked at her brother's face, which started to shine once more. A sudden indignation seized her, but she managed to conceal it and said, with a touch of sharpness in her voice, "Forgive Mother. She is poor and sad. Certainly, it consoles her to share her troubles. But if she finds that we . . . well, I don't want to return to the subject. It's enough for me to tell you that things will go the way you like." Then she added laughingly, "Damn both you and your love."

TWENTY-SIX

Soliman Gaber Soliman spoke. "Don't have any doubts about it. We shall marry as I have told you. I make this promise before God."

Nefisa listened to him attentively, her heart beating hard. There was no longer anything new in her taking his arm and walking by his side in one of the back streets of Shubra, where darkness prevailed and the passersby were few. Ugly and of mean appearance though he was, she always looked upon him as a wonderful beau because of his warm emotion and great interest in her. Thus she developed a profound, even mad love for him.

She believed that he was her first and last lover. Hope and despair made her cling to him passionately, and love him with her nerves and flesh and blood. Her turbulent instincts saw him as her savior from despair and frustration.

He was the first man to restore her self-confidence. He reassured her that she was a woman like other women. She was born anew each time he confessed his love for her; and in spite of the engulfing gloom of the world, she perceived its illuminating splendor. However, words of love were not enough for her. She was eager for something more that was no less important than love itself; or, perhaps, to her, the two were identical. She kept urging him until he promised to marry her. Encouraged by the enveloping darkness, she asked him, "So what do you intend to do?"

He answered without hesitation, "It would be natural for me to tell my father and then we would go together to your mother to ask for your hand."

"I think so, too."

He sighed audibly and said, "I wish it could be. But right now, it's a remote hope."

She became depressed. "Why?" she inquired anxiously.

"My father," he said angrily, "damn him. He's a foolish, obstinate old man. He wants me to marry the daughter of Amm Gobran el-Tuni, the grocer, whose shop is located on the corner of Shubra Street and Al Walid Street. I don't need to tell you that I refused and will continue to refuse. But I can't suggest to him at present that I have proposed to another girl. If I do, he will dismiss me."

She felt her throat becoming dry. Looking at him with disdain, she inquired worriedly, "What is to be done, then?"

"We have to be very patient. No force in the whole world could deflect me from my goal. But we must be on our guard lest he become aware of our relationship."

"Till when must we remain patient?"

He hesitated, perplexed. "Until he dies," he murmured.

"Until he dies!" she exclaimed with anxiety. "Suppose we die before him?"

Confused, he gave a dry laugh. "Leave this matter to me and to time," he said. "We are not completely helpless."

His words struck her as equivocal and most ungratifying. *I can't tell him that I am afraid that in the interval of waiting someone else may step in and propose to marry me,* she thought. *This would be a good tactic for a girl of wealth and beauty. But as for me, who will ask for my hand in such hard times as these, when men are avoiding marriage? I have degraded myself by accepting the worst, but the worst does not accept me. He is just a son of a grocer! Even the suit on his body appears odd and ill-fitting.* She felt an oppressive hand pressing her neck. Her fear made her cling to him more and more. At that moment, he was worth all the world to her. It was not clear to her how she could marry him, even if he removed the obstacles standing in their way. Her mother could not possibly offer her anything by way of help. Besides, her family could not do without the few piasters she earned. But she desired him; desired him from the depths of her soul, at whatever cost.

Her face grew grim, and she opened her mouth to speak. Suddenly, she saw someone coming along the road, and the blood congealed in her veins. She uttered a terrified groan and was about to take to her heels. But she stopped when she distinguished the face of the newcomer as he passed under the light of a lamppost. Her terror disappeared, and she gave a sigh of relief. Wondering, Soliman inquired, "What is wrong with you?"

She answered breathlessly, "I thought it was my brother Hassan."

The young man seized this opportunity to express a long-cherished desire. "We shall always be subject to fear," he said to her, "as long as we roam about in the streets. Listen to me. Why don't we go to my home and stay for a while, where no one could see us?"

"Your home!" she exclaimed in astonishment.

"Yes. My father spends Friday evening with the Sheikh of the Al Shazliah sect, and he remains there until midnight. My mother is also away in Zagazig on a visit to my sister, who is expecting a baby. So there is no one at home."

Astounded by his suggestion, she said with a palpitating heart, "How can I possibly go home with you? Are you mad?"

"We need a safe place," he entreated her. "My home is safe, and my invitation to you is innocent. I want to be safely alone with you so we can discuss our troubles quietly, far away from fears and watchful eyes."

As he spoke, she listened with a frown on her face. In spite of herself, fearfully and anxiously she was forming a mental picture of his empty home. To no avail, she tried to use anger to obliterate this mental picture; but it persisted in her mind's eye. She said sharply, "No, not at your home!"

Pressing the palm of her hand, he said beseechingly, "Why

not? I thought you would welcome my invitation. I want to be alone with you so that I can talk to you about my love for you, my hopes and plans. There is nothing wrong with what I am asking you to do, and nobody will ever know about us."

She obstinately shook her head, and her heart kept throbbing violently. She wished to be left alone, to have time to think this matter over. She felt a desire to escape, but she remained motionless. She walked on by his side, with the palm of her hand in his. She tried in vain to banish the picture of the presumably empty house from her imagination. Then she felt her insides turning upside down, as if she was sinking into a bottomless abyss. Overcome by more worry and confusion, she said, her tension obvious in her voice, "Not at your home."

His quivering hand pressed hers.

"Yes, in my home," he said. "Think it over a little. What are you afraid of? I love you and you love me. We want to talk in a safe place, away from watchful eyes, about our love and our future. It is a rare opportunity to have the whole house to ourselves and we should not miss it. I'm surprised at your hesitation!"

She also wondered why she was hesitant, but for different reasons. Had she really wanted to refuse his invitation categorically, she would have done so quite easily and clearly. But it seemed to her that she was persisting in her hesitant refusal so as not to frighten him away. Probably she was afraid and shy, but she could not ignore the radical transformation that had occurred inside her. She was overcome by confusion, anxiety, and tension. She said feebly, "It's better to continue walking."

Temptingly, he pulled her to him, saying, "You never can tell. Your brother Hassan might appear at any moment."

She found herself responding to his fears and surrendering to him, saying, "I'm afraid of what would happen if he did."

Sighing with relief, he exhaled a fiery breath. "Let's go home."

She resisted his hand feebly. "No, I won't go."

"Just for a few minutes. Our alley is dark and nobody will see us." He walked on, and she followed him with heavy steps, saying, "No."

Her heart was throbbing so violently that her ribs seemed to crack.

TWENTY-SEVEN

Opening the door with a key, he whispered, "Please, come in."

"Let's go back," she entreated him.

He pushed her gently inside.

"You must honor our home."

He entered behind her and closed the door. She found herself enveloped in pitch-darkness. She raised her face toward the ceiling, waiting for him to turn on the light. She felt his hand touching her shoulder, and a quiver passed down her spine.

"Turn on the light," she whispered in fear.

"The light in the hall is out of order," he answered apologetically.

"Then light another lamp to get rid of the dark."

Encircling her waist with one arm, he pushed her, saying, "I know the way to my room."

She tried to wrest herself from his arm, but he tightened his grip on her waist and clung to her. He pushed her gently, walking slowly beside her. A feeling of suffocation weighed heavily upon her chest, and she kept wondering what she had done with herself.

Gradually she became accustomed to the darkness and in the obscurity she perceived the shapes of several chairs, a cupboard, and a few other things which she could not identify. Slowly and cautiously they crossed the hall. Then, as he stretched out his free hand to open a door, it creaked, breaking the dreadful silence. Holding her on both sides of her waist, he pushed her inside, and shut the door with his foot. Quickly, she escaped from his hands.

"Light the lamp! I can't bear the darkness!" she said sharply.

His voice reached out to her, gentle, cautious, and apologetic.

"I am sorry, my darling. My uncle's flat is next to ours. So I'm afraid some member of his family might see the light and come to knock on our door."

"Are we going to remain in the dark?" she asked him, astonished and angry.

"The light of your beauty is enough," he answered in a cajoling tone.

"Let me leave," she entreated him.

He kept groping for her hand in the dark until he found it. Then he lifted it to his mouth and kissed it, twice.

"No, you sit down and rest. Once you're used to the darkness, it will not disturb you," he said, somewhat agitated.

Leaning toward her, almost leaping upon her, he lifted her in his arms and carried her to the end of the room. He seated her on a sofa and sat very close to her. She was too astonished to resist him. Then he said, "Let's stop arguing. We should be sitting and chatting calmly. We've gone to a lot of trouble to get here, and it makes no difference whether we are in the dark or the light. It doesn't matter where we stay and it shouldn't disturb our peace of mind," he said.

He took her arm. She was quivering, trying in vain to collect her scattered thoughts as he covered her arm with kisses from his coarse lips. She moved away from him to catch her breath, and he leaned toward her; but she stopped him with her hands.

"Leave me alone. I'm tired," she said breathlessly.

He drew in his breath.

"Have no fear. Why are you so frightened? You're quivering. You're in your own home—your husband's home," he said laughingly.

She heard her throbbing heart beating in her ears, all through her head. She drew in a deep breath. She felt his hand taking hers, and was about to withdraw it, but as though realizing her own foolishness, she changed her mind. So he kept her hand between his.

"Everything is nice and quiet. I can see your beauty even in the dark." His tone changed.

"I'm not beautiful," she said almost unconsciously.

"Leave it for me to judge. I am not mad about you for no reason," he said as he stroked her hand with his palm.

In the deep silence she focused her attention unconsciously on her palm, as if he were devouring it with his hands.

A feeling of numbness crept into her palm, spreading to her arms and breast. "That's enough," she whispered, trembling.

"Give me your lips so I can kiss them. I shall press so many kisses on them, a hundred or even a thousand kisses. I shall keep kissing them until I die," he said, sobbing.

He thrust himself greedily upon her, planting a long and passionate kiss on her lips, pressing her head into the back of the sofa.

He lifted his face and moved it away from her.

"Kiss me. I want to feel your lips devouring mine!" he whispered excitedly.

She was too tired to disobey him. Raising her face a little, she kissed him.

"We didn't come here to do this," she murmured.

"To do what, then?"

"To sit and talk."

He pressed his lips very hard on hers. Then he turned his face and placed his cheek against her mouth, and whispered into her ear, "That's better. We have talked much. I am telling you once more that you are my wife; my wife even if the whole world ostracizes me. It's only a matter of time; it won't be long."

Perhaps he believes that I am anxious and in a hurry to marry him, she thought. *Let him keep this illusion. My family's circumstances being what they are, maybe waiting is better. Right now, my family neither welcomes my marriage nor is prepared for it. There is no harm in waiting.* She kept these thoughts to herself, however.

"It's only a matter of time. But in the meantime, how much we need to have a little fun," Soliman said again.

Stretching his left hand around her back, he grasped her breast with his right hand, feeling her firm, large, blossoming bosom under her arm. The blood boiling up in his veins, he embraced her savagely, and his hot breath streamed down her cheek and neck. She felt amazed and numb, and her desire and fear returned to her. She felt at once a mixture of anxiety, pleasure, and despair. The surrounding darkness became thicker than ever. It was as if this profound and eerie darkness stretched its wings in an infinite void, free from the limitations of time and space.

"You're unusually late," her mother said to her.

"I wanted to finish my day's work, and I did," she answered grimly. Putting seventy-five piasters in her mother's hand, she continued, "They gave me all my wages. I shall keep the rest of the pound for myself."

Samira kept silent. Nefisa entered her room and began to undress. In the utter silence of the place the voice of Hassanein, reading aloud, struck her ears and left a curious impression; whether it was fear or unmitigated sadness that flowed over her, she could not tell.

TWENTY-EIGHT

"To me, the splendor of Bahia and the splendor of the sunset are the same," Hassanein told her as he pointed to the setting sun, and gazed upon her shining, moonlike face.

Opening her mouth, with her teeth sparkling in the sun like gems, she said, "You'll keep following me to this roof until someone sees us together."

"I'm your fiancé and have my rights!" he said proudly.

"No. You have no rights at all."

Incredulous, he laughed cheerfully from the bottom of his heart. He feasted his amorous eyes on her body, wrapped in a red overcoat, its opening at the neck revealing a gray dress underneath, and two thick plaits of hair flowing down the back. The intense red color of the overcoat made her white complexion and blue eyes appear still purer and increased their splendor. *She is so small,* he thought. *If I came very close to her, the crown of her head would touch my chin. But she is fresh and plump and her skin is delicate. Damn this overcoat; it hides her exquisite body, all its outlines and features. She is careful and conservative, and she appeals to me as much as she irritates me.*

"I have no rights at all!" he said, surprised.

"Of course not," she answered with a calm that showed strength.

Does she really mean what she says? he wondered. *How beautiful she looks! When she stands on this roof it lifts her above the whole world, and turns the horizon into a mere frame for her own beautiful image. Nothing becomes her more than this frame, so serene, pure, and remote. Nefisa says her disposition is unattractive. It's true she doesn't have a sweet temper. But that doesn't detract from her beauty. I love her with both my heart and my mind. Perhaps I am overpowered by my senses. Does she really mean that I have no rights? How strange. I thought my engagement to her would entitle me to so many rights!*

"Sometimes it seems to me that you are heartless," he said with astonishment.

Her face flushed, and she lowered her eyes shyly. Then, raising them again, she challenged him, "What should I do to prove to you that I have a heart?"

"Declare that you love me," he said enthusiastically, "and—"

"And?"

"Let's exchange a kiss."

"Then I really don't have a heart," she said sharply.

"I wonder! Don't you love me, Bahia?"

Confused and annoyed, she took refuge in silence. "If not, why did I agree to the proposal?" she finally said with a sigh.

His burning chest was relieved. "I want to hear it with my own ears," he cried hopefully.

"Don't ask me to do what I cannot."

Half desperate, he sighed in his turn. "If you can't bring yourself to speak of it, a kiss won't bother you."

"How horrible!"

"How rosy and honey-sweet. Without this kiss, I shall die in misery."

"Then may God have mercy on your soul."

"You can't even bear a kiss? It will be no trouble to you. Stay where you are. Then I'll take a step toward you and put my lips on yours. It will animate my soul!"

"Or cause our final separation!"

"Bahia!"

"Yes," she said firmly.

"You don't mean what you say."

"I mean every word of it."

"But it's a kiss, not a crime!"

"It's a crime to me."

"I've never heard such a thing!"

She pondered a little. "But I've heard it frequently," she said.

"Where?"

She pondered again. Clearly hesitating, she proceeded to speak with candor and naiveté. "Don't you read what *Al Sabah* magazine publishes about girls who are deserted because of their recklessness? Don't you listen to the wireless?"

His mouth fell open. "Who says that a kiss is recklessness? Haven't you read what Al Manfaluti, though he was a turban-headed sheikh, said about a kiss?! You forbid what pure love licenses. *Al Sabah,* the wireless! What nonsense!" he shouted, laughing.

She watched him warily and suspiciously. "Don't laugh at me. It's true. My mother told me once that any girl who imitates lovers in films is a hopeless prostitute."

That bitch, that daughter of a bitch, he fumed, silently cursing her mother. *Then it was she who told you this. That short, cunning woman. She is turning the girl against me and spoiling our life.* The anger almost suffocated him. *What use is this engagement for which I was bitterly scolded?! No use at all! My fiancée is hopelessly obstinate, and all because of this woman, this daughter of a bitch, this contemptible carrier of dry sticks!*

"Are you really so puritanical?" he asked her in desperation.

"Of course."

"Then your love is only a name."

"Let it be so."

Casting a long scrutinizing look at her, he saw that she was as obstinate and unyielding as ever. His eyes roved up and down her delicate neck, imagining how it looked beneath her dress. He went further, and imagined her naked shoulders and blossoming bosom. Overcome by his heated, uncontrollable passion, he leapt upon her, stretching his mouth toward her lips. Surprised by his sudden assault, she retreated in terror, stopping him with the palms of her hands.

"Hassanein, stop it!" she shouted breathlessly.

As he saw the burning anger in her eyes, his passion subsided, and he withdrew in shame and confusion.

"Be careful. I might change my opinion of you," she said, and added, "I think it is time for you to leave."

"All right, on condition that you won't be angry," he murmured, hiding his confusion with a short laugh.

She remained silent for a while.

"And also on condition that you don't do that again," she said gently.

He turned away in heavy steps, obviously desperate and confused. Her heart softened and, without thinking, she said to him, "My happiness lies in preserving for you—"

Catching the word before it slipped from her tongue, she bit her lips and fell silent.

TWENTY-NINE

The arrival of the great feast day of the year, the Bairam celebrating God's intervention in the sacrifice of Abraham's son, focused the family's thoughts and sentiments on their shared memories. On the eve of the feast day, the members of the family, Hassan included, assembled in the hall. A burning desire to celebrate the feast surged up in their breasts as nostalgic recollections of former feasts passed unspoken through their minds. On such an eve in the past, the sheep bought for the occasion was tied to the balcony of their former flat, craning its neck between the bars and bleating, thus announcing to the alley the family's celebration of the feast. Hussein and Hassanein never left the sheep, giving it fodder to eat and water to drink, playing with its horns, or excitedly dreaming of the delights of the forthcoming day.

After slaughtering the sheep in the morning, the family hurried to roast and devour it. Samira busily distributed alms to poor folk such as the street sweeper and the baker's apprentice, while her husband, after eating some of the roast meat on the table, retired happily to his room to take up his lute and play on its strings. In addition, they all received presents of money and new clothes. On the feast day, they went out for a walk in the open air in the morning and to a cinema in the evening. During the interval between the morning outing and the evening film, they enjoyed sweetmeats, games, and fireworks.

Today, however, the family assembly was fatherless, and given their circumstances, they saw no prospect of celebrating the feast. Nor were they delighted by its arrival. With anxious and solicitous eyes, they sneaked furtive glances at their mother, still dressed all in black. No. There was no sign of the feast, no prospect of celebrating it. *Is it possible,* Hassanein thought, *that the feast day will pass like any ordinary day?! There will be no feast. I know it. It is finished. Finished.*

Hassan was the only member of the family who still had hope. Perhaps his frequent absence from home estranged him somewhat from the kind of life his family was leading. Furthermore, like the rest of his brothers, he thought that his mother was omnipotent. In his laziness and dissipation, he found consolation in telling himself that his family had the pension and Nefisa's earnings. It was his habit, on returning home, to approach Nefisa alone and ask her, "How are things going with you?" Her answer was always one of bitter complaint; but her heart could never ignore him when he stretched out his hand to ask for a few piasters. He was hopeful in spite of his grim circumstances. He hoped for a large share of meat that would compensate him for his long days of deprivation. Annoyed with the prevailing gloomy silence, Hassan leaned toward Nefisa and asked her in a whisper, "What have you prepared for the feast?"

The mother understood the purpose of his whisper. Instantly, she attacked him with this question: "As the head of the family, what have *you* prepared for the feast?"

"We have an admirable mother, nice, witty, and charming. What should I say, Mother? God has not yet ordained that I should have earnings. However, it is enough that I have relieved you of the burden of sustaining me. You can count the number of times I've eaten at your place since my father's death," he said with a laugh.

Realizing the futility of blaming him or giving him advice, she sighed mutely.

Hassanein was encouraged, and pursued the subject, inquiring, "What shall we eat on the day of the feast?"

"Meat, of course. This is God's commandment and it cannot be ignored," Hassan replied.

Nefisa gave a laugh, but quickly stifled it lest she be accused of encouraging him. "It's God's commandment, indeed, but how can we fulfill it?"

Flattering his mother, Hassan said, "We depend on your extraordinary merits to fulfill it. You are a blessing to our home. Your firmness and judiciousness can always be counted on. Besides, you are the greatest cook in the world. How is it possible for the feast to pass without our filling our bellies with all sorts of meat, with roasted meat, boiled meat, fried meat, cutlets, sausages, and shin? How sumptuous the table of Lady Umm Hassan always was, filled with delicious foods!"

His words released a pleasant breeze of merriment into the atmosphere of pervasive gloom. A faint smile appeared on his mother's stern face. But she said sorrowfully, "A good cook whose hands are cut off!"

Nefisa cast a meaningful look at her mother. "Listen. We have learned that Farid Effendi will present us with half a sheep," she said to her brothers.

Stunned, they all looked at her. Finding it impossible to keep silent, Samira described how Farid Effendi had discreetly suggested it, and how she had thanked him but declined his present. Farid Effendi had been upset, even angry, and reminded her, among other things, that they were one family. A somber look appeared in Hussein's eyes and Hassanein seemed to find it difficult to swallow, but Hassan was pleased, and praised his virtue and faithfulness.

"It's impossible. We cannot allow this to happen!" Hassanein shouted, pained and suffocated. "It doesn't detract from our dignity. It's just observance of tradition. Anyhow, Farid Effendi is no stranger to us," Hassan replied, and Nefisa began to fear that her revelation might cause an argument.

"There is no need for you to quarrel. If you decline the present, we shall buy some mutton," she said.

"How much?" Hassan asked sharply.

"As much as we can afford. Let's say ten pounds of mutton."

"Only ten pounds for the four days of the feast! You cannot decline the present. Remember, our Prophet accepted presents. Besides, do you want to anger a family that wishes their daughter to marry into ours?" Hassan cried in alarm.

"This is begging!" Hassanein shouted at him.

"No. Begging is something else; I can tell you all about it. This is definitely a present," Hassan said with assurance.

"A present such as those we used to give to the street sweeper and the baker's apprentice on feast days," Hussein replied, unable to keep silent any longer.

This retort angered Hassan, who had hoped to win Hussein over to his side, or at least prevent his opposition.

"Don't confuse presents with alms. What you give to the street sweeper is alms, but what you give to a friend is a present," he said indignantly.

Hassanein knew that Hassan's argument was specious, and objected. "It is the duty of a fiancé to give presents to his future bride," he said, lowering his eyes with pain and shyness.

"True enough, if he has asked for her hand, but not if she has asked for his," Hassan sarcastically replied. "Spare us your philosophy, which does nothing to fill a hungry stomach. I assure you there is nothing shameful in accepting this present. Ahmad Bey Yousri used to bring presents to us in the seasons. And why has that son of a bitch forgotten us this year? He is not a faithful man. But Farid Effendi is, and we should accept his present if we want to be courteous. I assure you that if there had been anything undignified about it, I would have been the first to decline his present."

"Imagine what they'll say about us!" Hussein said gloomily.

"Imagine the meat roasting on the fire, the delicious odor permeating the house."

Hassanein turned to his mother. "What do you intend to do?"

"I have no choice but to accept," she answered without looking at him.

Silence prevailed, not only because none of them dared to object but also because accepting saved them from the conflict raging within themselves between their sense of wounded pride and their desire to enjoy the delights and pleasures of the feast day. Besides, they had great confidence in their mother's judgment, as though she were infallible, and they told themselves that if she accepted the present, that meant there must be no harm in accepting it. Or so they told themselves as a way out of their quandary. Samira felt particularly upset. The only possible consolation to her came from the fact that Farid Effendi, with his persistence and warmth of friendship, had obliged her to accept the present. She was glad that Nefisa had brought up the subject, and had hoped that her sons' approval would give her solace. But when her two important sons objected, it only increased her pain, and so her declaration that she had accepted the present amounted to a confession of her own guilt. It pained her more and more to see her children enjoying food only on feast days, like the poor folk who used to come to them and others asking for charity. Their condition was progressively deteriorating, and God only knew where that deterioration would take them!

Reassured, Hassan saw no harm in philosophizing. "Once the Prophet accepted a present from a Jew. So, can Farid Effendi be worse than a Jew?" he sermonized.

"Who said that?" Hussein asked in astonishment.

"History."

"Which history?!"

"I thought they taught you everything at school," Hassan shouted.

"Tell us about the history you have learned in the streets," Hassanein retorted sharply.

Hassan pretended to be angry. "I swear by the majesty of God, if you had not been the cause of the present, I would have broken your head. However," he added, "they should have presented us with a whole sheep, and not just half a one." Then he turned to Nefisa and said, "Be careful not to accept the present unless it contains half the sheep's liver, too."

THIRTY

They stood face to face waiting for the tram to arrive. She was dressed in her old overcoat, which she wanted to replace with a better one, even if she had to get it secondhand. He was wearing a suit which obviously didn't fit him very well, and he was visibly nervous as he tried to screw up the courage to say something that had been weighing heavily on him. He was afraid the tramcar might come before he was able to speak his mind.

"Nefisa, I am very ashamed to tell you something," he said.

"What is it?" she asked.

"My father ordered me to accompany him today on his visit to the Sheikh of the Al Shazliah sect. I refused, and he got angry," he whispered.

She felt inexplicably fearful, perhaps because of the mention of his father. Expecting to hear unpleasant news, she looked at him, silent and inquiring.

"He got angry at my obstinacy and refused to pay me my wages for the day." He was whispering again.

Astonishment overcame her fear, and she asked him, "Don't you have any money?"

"No. My father is a tyrant. May God take his life."

She said "Amen" to herself. "I have some money."

Anxiously, he remained silent for a few moments.

"Are you going to pay the tram fare for both of us in front of the other passengers?" he asked her in embarrassment.

She understood what he was hinting at, and, her heart softening, she opened her handbag and took out five piasters for him. Carefully watching the people standing nearby, he took the money.

"Thank you. I will pay it back the next time we meet," he said. "Or," he added after some hesitation, "you can take the equivalent in sweets or cheese."

"Aren't you afraid your father might notice that I'm not paying for what I'm buying?" she inquired.

"He doesn't see further than his nose," he said, laughing.

The tramcar to Rod el-Farag arrived. They got on board and sat near each other.

How can I squander money like this, she thought, *when our home is badly in need of every millieme that I earn? My mother is still selling some of the furniture. Even my brother Hassan needs these piasters more than this hard-up young man. What am I doing with myself? I also squander my money on powders and lipstick. Oh! He is not a man. If he were, he would never be tied to his father's apron strings in this ridiculous fashion, and he would not fear him so much. The old man is treating him like a child, depriving him of his pocket money. But I love and want him. I am body and soul to him. I have no one else in this world. Why should I have such a self-torturing soul?*

She heard him whisper in her ear, "It's a real pity that my mother has returned from her visit to my sister. So the flat is no longer empty."

She knew this perfectly well, and needed no one to remind her of it. However, she felt pleased that he had brought up the subject. Her flesh experienced a wakefulness, and her imagination became active. She remembered their lovemaking, the total darkness and whispering voices. She remembered all this in a heat of passion mixed with fear. She did not like to comment on what he said, and so, shyly, she ignored it, but her face flushed, her makeup standing out. She remembered his words: "My mother returned and my father does not approve!" *When will all this come to an end?* she thought. *When shall I have him without fear, and according to God's law?!* Sometimes she felt so stricken with fear that she yearned for the peace of death.

"But I shall find other opportunities, and once more we'll have the flat to ourselves," his whispering voice said to her.

"No. No. There is no need for that," she said coldly.

"God forgive you. Have you forgotten? Have you really forgotten? We shouldn't burn with unsatiated desire while we are waiting. I hate waiting."

Wouldn't it have been better for me to wait? Nefisa wondered, and she kept wavering back and forth, unable to decide, thinking first yes, then no, then reversing herself, over and over again. As she sighed, perplexed at it all, her familiar feelings of despair returned.

"I don't like waiting, either," she said. "But I also don't like what we have done."

"That's a lie. You do like it. Have you forgotten? You couldn't have," he said slyly.

"I remember nothing."

"I shall never forget it as long as I live. You were very passionate and lively, and I still feel your heat scorching me."

"Hush. You must be mad."

"However, we shall manage to find some empty dark back street."

"Beware. Your sight is as weak as your father's. You may think the road is empty, when the policeman is right before your eyes."

"Then let us depend on your eyes." He hesitated a moment, and sighed, "When will we be able to marry?"

She was at once pained, irritated, and embarrassed by his query, and her emotions cooled and her face remained sullen for the rest of the journey.

THIRTY-ONE

It was midnight. There were only a few customers at the Al Gamal café, which was now almost empty. Hassan's companions had left and he was sitting alone at a table. The piasters he had managed to gain from them were safely tucked in his pocket. As though deep in thought, he cast a languid look about the café with his tired eyes. The owner of the café began to check his daily accounts, heaping the metal counters on a large tin plate, while the waiter stood leaning against one of the door panels, his hand in the pocket of his apron, temptingly jingling the coins inside it. Hassan's thoughts rambled off. *My father, may the mercy of God be on you. How much I have suffered since your death! We never ceased to quarrel and sometimes I felt I hated you. But your days are gone! Since your death, I haven't taken a meal at home except on the feast days. And what do they eat at home? I eat nothing but beans. Beans. Always beans. Even donkeys get a change in diet. Maybe I really should seriously search for a job.*

He remembered that he had tried his luck twice and that each time had ended in a quarrel that almost sent him to jail. No. Such trivial jobs were not his aim. He still preferred the life of a vagabond and mean gambler. In fact, he lived by stealing. He and his coterie knew this perfectly well. They would ensnare the new customers at the café and give them the illusion that they were playing a fair game of cards. But the truth was that they were stealing from them. It was a hard, risky life for the sake of a few piasters. How could he be satisfied with this kind of life? He was neither happy nor contented. He seemed to be waiting for a miracle to save him from the depths his life had reached and take him to a land of dreams. On the whole, his life was as violent and as savage as the murderous drug he was taking. Jobless though he was, he remained a leader among his company, because he could strike awe and fear in their hearts. Thus, he found it unbearable to start a new life as a simple and obedient worker, even though he was fully aware of how much his mother needed him to develop a serious attitude toward life. He still heard her afflicted and complaining voice humming in his ears, never ceasing to chase him whenever he came out of the stupor of drugs. He loved his mother and family. But he did not exert the slightest effort; he kept waiting inertly for something to happen, and remained at the bottom of the ladder, doing this donkey work for the sake of a few piasters. To him, this seemed a folly even worse than . . .

"Good evening, Mr. Hassan," came a voice in greeting.

Emerging from the mist of his thoughts, he raised his head to see Master Ali Sabri sitting in front of him, calm and proud.

"Good evening, Master," Hassan cried, his heart full of delight.

The so-called master summoned the waiter and ordered a nargileh. Then he turned to Hassan.

"I have decided that we should work together. I want you to join my band," he said at once.

Hassan's eyes, opening wide, suddenly glistened. Working for the master's music band was the only thing he liked, not because he was aesthetically disposed to this kind of work, but because it was light, pleasurable, and usually associated with the fragrance of liquor, drugs, and women's perfume. Though he never expected much from Ali Sabri, he thought the offer was better than nothing. Perhaps it would lead to other things. Who could tell?

"Do you mean it, Master?" Hassan said.

"Sure."

"Will we be working in a music hall or a café?"

"Maybe one day soon we'll have a place at the broadcasting station. But for the time being, we'll be playing at weddings," the master said, passing his long, lean fingers through his unruly hair.

Hassan's enthusiasm died. Had he been dealing with anybody other than Ali Sabri, on whom he still pinned some hope, he would have given him a stunning blow and sent him flying head over heels. He had actually worked with him at a few family parties in return for supper and a twenty-piaster piece, but only a few times a year. There was nothing new in this. Yet he felt a hidden motive behind this offer, and new hope stirred in his breast. He feigned delight.

"There is no doubt," he said, "that you will one day occupy the place you deserve. Your voice is superior to that of Abdul Wahab himself."

Ali Sabri grinned. "Which of the instruments of the band do you want to play?" he asked. "You told me that your late father was an excellent lute player."

"I haven't learned to play any instrument at all."

"Not even the tambourine?"

"You tried me out as a Sannid, chanting refrains for you, and I think I'm the right man for the job."

The master shook his head as he said, "As you like. Do you know many songs?"

"Yes. Mawawil, songs, and *takatiqs*."

"How about a solo right now?"

At bottom, Hassan felt disdain for the pomposity of his companion, but he was determined to go along with him to the end. He was dreaming of one day becoming an independent singer, even in low popular coffeehouses. He waited until the waiter came back with the nargileh and the master enjoyed his first puffs.

"What would you say to my singing the Mawal 'My Eyes, Why Are You Weeping?' for you?" Hassan asked with a cough.

"Excellent."

As best as he could, Hassan began to chant the Mawal in a

low voice, while the other man kept moving his head forward and backward, pretending to be absorbed in the song. When Hassan finished he said, "For a Sannid, that's more than enough, but I should like to hear you singing Hank, too. Do you know the song 'How I Waited When I Lost Your Love'?"

Hassan coughed again, clearing his throat, his enthusiasm grew, and he began to sing with more zest. He sang without a pause to the end.

"Excellent. Excellent. Do you know the basic tunes, Sica, Biati, Hijaz, and so on?" the master asked.

Sure of the master's ignorance of those tunes, Hassan answered, with extraordinary daring that others rarely exhibited. "Of course."

"Chant the Laiali 'Rast' for me."

He chanted the first Laiali that came to his mind.

"Bravo. Chant another—a Nahawound," Ali Sabri said, shaking his head.

Hassan continued to sing, suppressing a feeling of inward sarcasm. The other man was following him, feigning attention. Suddenly, he looked meditative and seemed to have something important to say. Instinctively, Hassan was waiting for this moment. Perplexed, he wondered whether Ali Sabri wanted to appoint him to lead a fight. What did he want precisely?

"Your voice is good enough. But working for the band requires other talents and skills. Here we must be in complete agreement. For instance, you should know all about propaganda methods, too," the master said.

"Propaganda!"

"Yes. You should, for example, speak highly of my art whenever an occasion arises. You should also persuade people to ask me to sing at their marriage ceremonies. You will get your reward, of course. When you are at a songfest held by another singer, you should criticize his voice and tell everyone around you how wonderful Ali Sabri would have been if he had been singing instead, and so on."

"That's easy. You can expect even more," Hassan said with a smile on his face.

Ali Sabri paused for a moment, and then said, "You are a strong and daring young man, and you should exploit your talents to the utmost. But let me ask you one more question. Which narcotic most appeals to you?"

Hassan wondered what made him ask such a question. Did he want to offer him a present? Impossible. He was always ready to accept presents, and generosity was certainly not part of his personality. Or was he seeking his collaboration on an important task? His heart fluttered at such a thought. He had long dreamt of trafficking in narcotics. Yet, he decided to be wary and on his guard.

"I think narcotics harm the throat," he said slyly.

Ali Sabri laughed. With a thunderous and powerful voice, he started to sing a Laiali.

"What do you think of that singing?" he asked when he finished.

"Peerless."

Ali Sabri went on to say, "This is what comes of fifteen years of addiction to hashish, opium, and *manzoul*,* and five years of taking cocaine as well."

"You don't say!"

"Narcotics are the very lifeblood of vocalizing. Any singer worthy of the name is as much addicted to drugs as he is to such basic foods as *molokhiva* and *fool mudammis*."

Hassan laughed. "Only if those drugs are available," he said, surrendering.

"You are right. And it is as I thought. You don't hate narcotics, but you have no access to them. Let me tell you, it is easy to turn rivers of water into rivers of wine, and mountains into mountains of hashish. You are both daring and strong. But I will be frank with you; I was very much afraid!"

* A cheap mixed drug.

"Of what?"

Ali Sabri gave a short laugh that revealed his yellow teeth. "Of all people," he said, "I hate most those who say, 'My morals won't allow me to do this' or 'I have fear of God' or those who fearfully ask, 'What about the police?' Now, are you one of them?"

Hassan smiled, feeling that he would be well rewarded for his long patience.

"I live in this world, assuming that there is no morality, God, or police," he said.

Ali Sabri erupted in a powerful laugh that shook the café as much as his singing, and said, "Let's spend the rest of the night at my place and continue our talk."

Hassan agreed, hoping some profitable scheme would come of all this. His confidence never failed him for a single moment, but he had little faith in his interlocutor. However, he had not quite given up hope in him. Deep down, he felt that he would have to wait a long time before the earth, shaking underneath his feet, became stable once more.

THIRTY-TWO

Content with the light that shone from Hussein and Hassanein's room, Nefisa and her mother were sitting in the hall when their friend and landlady paid them a visit. As befitted someone who had done such important services for Nefisa, they welcomed her warmly. She installed herself on the sofa between the two women and insisted that they need not turn on the hall light. She and Samira entertained themselves with conversation while Nefisa went to the kitchen to make some coffee for their guest.

Always expecting profitable work for Nefisa from Mrs. Zeinab's visits, Samira was seldom disappointed. Her mind was never free from the worries of life, even after the passage of almost a year. She was particularly worried now about the approaching summer holidays, when she could expect to shoulder the additional task of providing her two younger sons with food at home in place of the meals they took at school. And so she was complaining to Mrs. Zeinab of her troubles during the last months, and the landlady was consoling and encouraging her, when Nefisa came back with the coffee. Wanting to explain her reasons for paying this visit, Mrs. Zeinab smiled sweetly and good-naturedly and said, "I've brought you a new bride."

"Then I'm entitled to call myself the bride's dressmaker," Nefisa replied, laughing with pleasure.

"I pray to God that you will soon be making your own wedding dress."

"Amen," Samira murmured.

Nefisa's gloomy memories were stirred by her mother's invocation, and she said "Amen" to it in her innermost heart. *When shall I become a bride?* she wondered. *Not before Amm Gaber Soliman dies. How ironical! To cherish such a hope has cost me both body and soul. It is possible for Mother to conceive of what has happened? She thinks of the worries of everyday life as the greatest calamity. But how ignorant and miserable of her to think so!*

"Who is this new customer?" the mother inquired.

"The new bride is the daughter of Amm Gobran el-Tuni, the grocer."

At the sound of this unforgettable name, Nefisa's senses were jolted. "Does his shop lie at the intersection of Shubra and Al Walid streets?" she asked, her heart beating violently.

"Exactly."

"Nefisa, I see you've become as well-informed as a roving detective," her mother said, laughing.

The girl laughed mechanically. *Surely it is she,* she thought. *The girl whom Amm Gaber wanted his son Soliman to marry, as Soliman himself has told me. Her marriage will clear the way for me; it will remove the nightmarish thoughts of her that weigh so heavily upon me.*

"Is Gobran el-Tuni well off?" the mother inquired.

"He is rich enough."

"Who's the bridegroom?"

"He is nearer than you may imagine him to be," the woman said, laughing. "It is Soliman, the son of Amm Gaber Soliman, the grocer."

"Soliman!"

Nefisa uttered the name as one would utter a cry. The two women looked at her in astonishment. Thinking that she was surprised to learn that such a girl would accept marriage to a trifling young man like Soliman, the landlady said, "Yes, Soliman. It seems the bride's father didn't object, since he is a friend of Amm Gaber. As you see, God bestows the goods of life on whomever He pleases."

Despite the magnitude of the shock, Nefisa realized that she had almost given away her scandalous secret. With a strenuous effort, she composed herself to counteract the bleeding cry which had burst out of her breast and escaped her lips. She no longer felt able to follow the conversation and an overpowering feeling of death quickly overtook her. The surrounding darkness seeped in to conceal her features, but she had to press her fingers together painfully to prevent herself from letting out another cry. What did the man say? She could not believe her senses, but she knew she was not demented or tormented by a mere nightmare. Undoubtedly this was the bare truth. Surely the bridegroom was Soliman Gaber Soliman, and nobody else. Memories of old fears, which she had experienced from time to time in her solitary hours, returned to her. Sometimes these were mysterious, like a gnawing worry that dug its fingernails into the flesh of her breast; sometimes they were tangible fears, assuming hideous shapes that caused her to shudder. In her agony she was for a moment under the illusion that she was merely having a nightmare. But this hallucination lasted no more than a moment, after which she was invaded once more by the heavy, dreadful feeling that she was dying. Together with her family, she had already experienced life's cruelty, but it had never occurred to her that life could be so cruel. She bit her lips, not knowing how to resist the sense of disintegration that was overtaking her body and soul. It was not just frustration in love. It was the sense of the futility of human existence itself. However, she knew she must control herself. Their guest might speak to her at any moment, and her answers must not betray any tremor or tearfulness in her voice. Perhaps it would be safer to flee for a while. Without hesitation she picked up her cup of coffee and retired to the kitchen. There, a deep breath emerged from the depths of her soul; she pulled at her braids, and gazed at the kitchen ceiling, smudged with smoke, its corners covered with cobwebs. Like a person possessed, she remained transfixed. *Then it was not a hope I have been cherishing*, she thought, *but a fraud, a terrible fraud, a fatal blow, a robbery, a stain, a wound that will never heal. I am done for; undoubtedly done for. It is impossible for my mother, let alone for Hussein and Hassanein, to conceive of what has happened.*

Oh, God! How was it possible for him to deceive her to that extent?! They were together only last Friday! What a criminal! And how heinous his crime! But what use was her anger? She felt a merciless, poisonous detestation for him. But she recognized the great need to think the matter over and prepare herself for what was to come. She was eager to escape from her surroundings, her big living circle, for which she had developed so much abhorrence, to a remote, solitary place where she could ask herself this question: *Nefisa, how did you fall into the abyss so easily, so readily, so degradingly?*

On hearing her mother call, she shook with terror. At that moment she was extremely angry with her mother, and she came near even to hating her. She remained motionless. Her mother called her again. Clenching her teeth, she moved away. She saw their guest getting ready to leave, her mother seeing the woman off at the front door.

"Come to me the day after tomorrow," the landlady said as she shook hands with Nefisa. "We shall go together to the bride's house."

Without a word, Nefisa nodded her approval. When the door was closed, her mother said, "Soliman! By God, he doesn't deserve such good luck!"

Nefisa felt a dagger stabbing her heart. She uttered not a word of comment. Sick of the place and its surrounding atmosphere, she realized that she could not bear to stay with her mother. Acting on a sudden impulse as scorching as a flame, she walked steadily to her room and returned wearing her overcoat.

"Are you going out?" her mother asked in surprise.

"Yes. To buy something for supper," Nefisa replied as she went toward the door. "Perhaps I'll spend an hour in Farid Effendi's flat."

THIRTY-THREE

Breathing heavily and with difficulty, Nefisa reached the court-yard of the house. The clear sky was studded with stars and the cool weather was punctuated by the gentle breezes of budding spring. She walked up to the gate, then dauntlessly proceeded to Amm Gaber's shop. The old man was busy toting up the day's accounts, while his son Soliman stood with an elbow on the counter, staring absently between his fingers. Drawing near, she cast a sharp, fiery glance at him. He raised his two tiny eyes toward her. A look of confusion and alarm suddenly appeared in them.

"Can I help you, Miss Nefisa?" he asked warily.

She answered with steadiness and determination, "Follow me at once!"

He nodded affirmatively, pretending to give her something from the shop. She went out to the street and stood waiting at the top of the alley, carefully inspecting her surroundings. She felt relieved at what she was doing. She could not possibly wait until the next morning. She kept looking about the alley until she saw him hurrying toward her with confused steps, wearing a jacket over his gallabiya.*

How mean and cheap, she thought. *Disgusting. How disgusting!* A deceiver, an impostor, and a liar. What would she do? Would she lie prostrate at his feet, wailing and begging? Would she plead with him to remain hers alone? This seemed to her at once monstrous and detestable. Yet it provoked in her profound, inexpressible feelings. Only one hour before, she had considered him her man, and herself his wife. She had even thought that to

---

* A long, robelike garment typically worn by members of the lower classes in Egypt.

perish was more tolerable than to see herself separated from him. Once a worthwhile human being, she had now become worthless ... absolutely worthless. How dreadful was the void ahead of her, how murderous her despair! Soliman approached her warily and, without turning to her, inquired, "What's wrong?"

His voice drove her to exasperation, but she suppressed it. "Follow me to Al Alfi Street," she said, still walking on.

She went by way of a back street to avoid the inquisitive eyes watching her. She slowed her steps until he caught up with her. Losing patience, she suddenly addressed him.

"Don't you have any news for me?"

"What news?" he inquired anxiously and fearfully.

His equivocating attitude enraged her. With biting sharpness, she snapped, "Don't you really know what I am asking about? Stop deceiving me!"

Fear-stricken and sighing with resignation, he muttered, "You mean the business of the marriage ..."

"Of course. Don't you think that's worth asking about?" she answered with bitter sarcasm.

"It's my father," he said, complaining.

"Always 'my father'!" she cried, her body convulsing with fury and agitation. "Are you a man or a woman?"

"A man who can't prove his worth," he said submissively, with sheepish resignation.

"You mean a woman."

"God forgive you. The only thing I hear from you or from him is scolding and reproof. What can I do?"

She cast a fiery glance at him; her breast overflowing with disgust. *A woman! A coward! Pitiful! How could I have loved him? How could I have degraded myself so much as to yield to him?* To her, the worst of the world's miseries and tortures was the fact that it was she who made advances to him, desperately clutching at him and making obsequious attempts to get him back.

"What a mean, complaining, bewailing person you are! How

149

could you betray me after what had happened? How could you hide this news from me? Answer me!" she shouted at him.

"My father did what he wanted, against my will. He disregarded my wishes, and I had two alternatives: either submit to his will or die of hunger," he said with a snort.

"Why don't you look for a job in another shop?"

"I can't. I can't," he muttered in a desperate tone.

"What a mean coward! Don't you know what this means to me?" she said.

"I know. It's a pity," he answered in a voice dripping with sorrow. "God only knows how distressed and sorry I am . . ."

She threw a sharp look at him. His sorrowful tone drove her to the point of murderous detestation.

"Distressed and sorry!" she said in a quivering voice. "What use is your distress and sorrow to me? Distress alone cannot undo mistakes. What use is your sadness to me? You brought me to a fatal predicament. So you shouldn't let me down like this. Don't you know that?"

He seemed perplexed and tongue-tied. Looking at her in fear, he gave no answer. She was provoked by his silence as much as by what she felt sure was a pretense of sorrow.

"What am I to do now?" she said.

Swallowing hard, he said in a low, disconnected voice, "I am very sorry. I realize how difficult this is for you. How painful it is to me! But . . . I mean . . . What can I do?"

"Reject this marriage! That's the only way to save me!" She spoke with rancor, barely able to suppress her upsurging passion.

"Reject it? It's too late now!" he answered. His reply increased her exasperation.

"You must reject it, and it's not too late. You must think of me. Your rejection of this marriage is my only hope of salvation."

He was frightened. "I can't do that," he said in a hopeless tone.

Overcome by despair, she realized that she could expect nothing from this unmanly weakling.

"You were able to do what you have already done. You were able to accept marriage to that girl. But you can't repair the mistake. You won't extend a hand to save me," she cried passionately.

"How distressed I am! My sorrow for you knows no bounds!"

"What use is this sorrow to me?" Encountering only silence, she shouted in his face, "What use is your sorrow?"

"What can I do?" he murmured.

Seized by a demon of furious despair, she turned on him. As swift as lightning she leapt upon him and, not knowing what she was doing, gripped him by his clothes.

"You ask me what you can do!" she cried. "Do you take me for a plaything that you can throw away whenever you like?!"

"Nefisa! Behave reasonably! We're in the street," he said, trying in vain to snatch his jacket from her grip.

"A coward, a scoundrel, mean and treacherous!" she cried.

She withdrew her hand quickly, and with all her might, she struck him twice in the face with her fist. She saw blood streaming from his nose. She was out of breath, her agitated heart beating violently and irregularly. Soliman felt his nose with his hand, then stretched it out to protect his eyes. Taking a handkerchief from his pocket, he pressed it to his mouth and nose. Contrary to what she expected, he appeared calm and silent. In the beginning he was frightened. But now his fear was superseded by a curious sense of relief, as though he had passed the danger point and there was nothing more to fear. Thus for him the crisis was resolved, the danger over, and after this spilled blood, her moral claim upon him dropped away.

Quietly and patiently he said, "May God forgive you, Nefisa. I excuse you."

She was incensed by his words. Once more she was driven by an insane impulse. Without thinking, she leapt upon him again, and seized him by his clothes, as if to keep him from escaping. Terror-stricken, he lost his composure. Suddenly he snatched at his jacket, freeing it from her grip.

"Don't touch me!" he cried, stepping backward. "Go away! Go away! You have no claims on me."

She continued her assault; he pushed her, shouting in frightened agitation, "Don't touch me! I didn't force you! You came home with me of your own accord. If you touch me I'll call the police!"

He continued to step backward until he was some distance away from her, then turned on his heels and fled.

She was transfixed, her body shaking violently. She lost control of herself. The whole thing seemed to her a dream, or the hallucination of an overheated mind, in no way related to reality. She was not quite sure that the physical objects around her, the street, the tree, the lamppost, and the passersby, actually existed. Everything seemed remote from the world of reality. She regained her bearings only when she burst out weeping, burning tears overflowing from the depths of her heart.

THIRTY-FOUR

Soliman was wiping the counter. He saw the shadow of some-one reflected on it. Raising his head, he found Hassan standing before him. His body shivered with horror as though he were struck by a thunderbolt. There before him stood Hassan, tall, his hair bristling, the color of his suit faded with wear, his eyes emitting a sharp light, violent and daring.

I'm done for, Soliman thought. *My hour is drawing near if Nefisa has confided her secret to him.* He cast a silent glance at Hassan, like a mouse watching a cat.

"Peace be upon you," was Hassan's salutation, his resonant voice echoing painfully in Soliman's fearful ears.

"May the peace of God, His mercy and blessing, be upon you." Amm Gaber's answer came from behind his desk. "How are you, Master Hassan?"

Soliman was too terrified to reply to the salutation. *This is no greeting,* he thought. *It's an evil omen. Oh, God! How did I allow myself to have an affair with a girl who has such a brother!*

"Thanks be to God," Hassan said. "I've come to speak to you about an important matter."

He knows about the affair, Soliman thought. *Now my father will know of the scandal. The devilish man is drawing near.* Raising the ledge of the counter, he quickly slipped into the shop. *I'm just a few inches from the devil's grip. How foolish of me to have an affair with Nefisa! I wish Hassan would give me a chance to renounce this forthcoming marriage and undo my mistake.*

Hassan leaned over the desk, supporting his hands on the edge. He kept turning his eyes from father to son. Expecting to receive a terrifying blow, Soliman lowered his head.

"I've learned that Soliman is to be married," Hassan said.

"By God's will," Amm Gaber answered. "We hope your marriage, too, will soon occur."

"When will the wedding ceremony be held?"

"In the very near future, by God's will."

"Amm Gaber, we are neighbors, and I think I am the right singer for the occasion," Hassan said, rapping his fingers on the desk.

Soliman's small eyes opened wide. He could not believe his ears. So this was the purpose of his visit! How could he forget that Nefisa would die rather than tell her secret to this tyrannical brother! He laughed twice, then burst out into uncontrollable, hysterical laughter. Surprised, his father and Hassan looked at him scoldingly. He stopped laughing at once.

"Without your singing, the wedding party will be nothing," he said to Hassan genially.

Hassan smiled in satisfaction.

Afraid of the consequences of this foolish promise, Soliman's father added, "With the greatest pleasure, Master Hassan. Personally I don't object. But I'm afraid the bride's father may have a different idea."

Hassan looked at him suspiciously. "The bridegroom has the final say in this matter," he said.

"We prefer to have you, Master Hassan," Amm Gaber said gently, "but give me time to consult with Amm Gobran el-Tuni."

Hassan pondered this. "Thank you, Amm Gaber," he replied, "but I would like to remind you of the advantages of having me sing at the wedding party. The most important, in my view, is that nobody, however strong and evil-intentioned, would dare to break into the party, as often happens."

The old man's face betrayed interest. He quickly realized the threat that lay behind this polite talk. He smiled at the fearsome face of the young man. He spoke gently. His son's mouth was open as he listened to his father.

"Not all wedding parties suffer from such attacks."

"There are many wild hoodlums out there," Hassan replied. "They rarely pass up an opportunity to invade a wedding party and rob the guests."

"That used to happen in the past," the old man said warily. "But now there are the police to fear."

Hassan smiled and shook his head. "They think nothing of the police," he said, "and they usually do their dirty work before the police arrive. How simple it is to begin by destroying the lamps! In the darkness, fear strikes the hearts of the guests, who are unable to see where they are walking. Decorations are torn down, chairs are overturned, food is spilled, clothes are stolen, and members of the bride's and bridegroom's families are seriously injured. When the criminal activities are over, people find themselves more in need of first aid than of the police. And to put it in official jargon, the perpetrator always remains unknown in such cases. Even if it occurs to somebody to lead the police to the evildoer, he merely exposes himself to a greater danger. So the case, instead of being a minor one tried before a misdemeanor court, turns into a case for a criminal court. And it is simple common sense to notice that, even if the evildoer is punished, this hardly compensates for the loss of life and money."

Amm Gaber listened, attentive and most pessimistic. He felt helpless. He could think of no way to avoid this threat. So he tried to console himself with the belief that Hassan was not a bad singer after all. The old man smiled faintly.

"However evil these wrongdoers are," he said, "they dare not invade us if you're the singer at our party."

"Amm Gaber," he replied, "you're a generous man. Perhaps one day I shall be lucky enough to sing at your own wedding party, if you ever think of marrying again!"

Relieved, Soliman laughed like a man suddenly safe after exposure to certain danger.

His father smiled wryly. "May God forgive you," he murmured.

Hassan feigned a cough. He said in a fresh tone, "I don't want to take up more of your time. It's time for me to leave, after picking up the advance payment."

"Now?" the old man asked in terror.

"The sooner, the better. You know, I'm just a modest singer; I only charge five pounds for myself and the members of my band. And for the time being, I'll be satisfied with only one pound."

Perplexed, the old man was silent for a time.

This is the will of God, and I have to be resigned to it, he thought. He opened the drawer of his desk, took out a one-pound note, and placed it on the desk. Hassan picked it up.

"My best wishes," he said, and went away.

THIRTY-FIVE

The tramcar arrived. Nefisa climbed on board, followed by her landlady, Mrs. Zeinab, who accompanied her to the home of Amm Gobran el-Tuni to introduce her to his family. Her makeup applied, Nefisa's face was as presentable as possible. She put on her best dress. Nefisa had felt all along that there was something peculiar about her journey. She had said to herself many times that it was mad to go to this particular house, but she was at a loss as to how to relinquish such a fortunate opportunity, which her mother regarded with great happiness. Undoubtedly, her soliloquy did not express her real wishes. She was aware that she was trying to hide her true desires from herself. She wished to see the bride at whatever cost. Her desire to do so was too strong and persistent to be resisted. She had no intention or desire to compare her beauty with that of the bride. To start with, she knew that the bride was more beautiful; there was nothing new in that. But though this was obvious enough to her, she could not resist a chance to see the girl. Somehow she felt attached to the bride by strong ties, felt that her own fate was bound up with hers. She had not yet recovered from the violent shock which had crushed her body and soul. But the passage of time managed to calm her boiling revolt, and replace it with a poisonous bitterness, a fatal despair, and a tortured sense of loneliness that made her feel alienated from her own family and abnormal among the creatures of the earth. She experienced an overwhelming sense of oppression that aroused in her two opposed, persistently alternating desires: uncontrollable revolt coupled with further self-torture and self-laceration. Such was her state when she boarded the tramcar in anticipation of the coming meeting. Nefisa and Mrs. Zeinab got off at the fourth stop. They headed for Al Walid Street, then turned into a large building, on the ground floor of which was Amm Gobran el-Tuni's grocery. They climbed the stairs and entered a flat on the second floor, and were received by a very fat lady, in her fifties, with a white complexion. They all entered the sitting room.

As soon as they sat down Mrs. Zeinab said, "This is Miss Nefisa. You will see for yourself that she possesses skill and taste."

"Mrs. Zeinab has told me much about you. You are welcome," the lady remarked.

Nefisa felt pained by this commendation, as though it were satirical invective. For no obvious reason, it irritated her, and her confidence in her ability to control herself was shaken. Turning to the door of the room, the lady called out, "Adillah!" Nefisa's heart was pounding. She guessed that the lady was calling the bride. It was as if she heard Soliman calling out her name. She imagined him taking her to his breast and in the distraction of heated emotion saying to her with a sobbing voice, "Adillah, I love you. I love you more than this world and the next together."

This is what he usually said when passion overcame him. It was a lie, or at least it was a lie insofar as her affair with him was concerned. Probably life itself was a big fraud. Overcome by pain, despair, and anger, she turned to face the door. She was frightened at the sound of approaching footsteps; she wished she could vanish into the air. Possibly it was a casual, surface feeling. A girl came into the room. She was in the prime of her youth and, like her mother, of medium height and white complexion. She had an oval face, with large, well-proportioned features. But she looked too fat. Thinking of her obesity, Nefisa wondered what she would become after marriage! A tense, sarcastic laugh, to which she could not give vent, was surging up inside her. Her casual fear evaporating, she experienced a feeling of great excitement, which she tried hard to control. She was introduced to the bride, and the girls exchanged greetings. Nefisa kept silent, lest the tone of her voice betray her.

All of a sudden she felt stung by a heartrending jealousy. She was envious of this girl, who had robbed her of her man; certainly he was hers after what had happened between them. No other woman could have a similar claim upon him. She wondered how he could marry such a buffalo, and how she could be the very dressmaker to make the bride's wedding clothes! A world in which such things happened deserved to be destroyed by fire. At any rate, the flames of this fire would burn less than that which was consuming her jealous heart. *Oh, God!* she thought. *How can I make any dresses in this strained, nervous condition?!* The two women went out of the room, leaving the two girls together, and a servant came in carrying some pieces of cloth and placed them on the sofa beside Nefisa, thus helping her to escape her thoughts. Nefisa examined the cloth with apparent interest, while her downcast eyes darted furtive glances at the bride's feet.

"Have you ever made dresses for brides?" the girl asked.

Raising her eyes, Nefisa looked at her in astonishment, as if she did not expect to be spoken to.

"Very frequently," she answered in a crisp voice.

"That should make the job easier for you."

"I find no difficulty in my work."

Her answer was an expression of the revolt fuming inside her, regardless of the reality of her circumstances. For a while the bride remained silent. Then she asked again, "Do you live in Mrs. Zeinab's house?"

"Yes," she said, urged on by the same rebellious impulse. "For many years. My late father was an official in the Ministry of Education."

"Mrs. Zeinab told us about it. Do you know that my bridegroom's grocery is near your house?"

Nefisa felt a stab piercing her heart. She lowered her eyes so that the other girl would not detect any signs of it in them.

"You mean Amm Gaber Soliman?" she murmured.

"Himself. The bridegroom is his son. Don't you know him?"

I know him better than you do, she thought. *It will take you months, as it did me, to know what kind of person he really is. You'll find out that he is a beast and a scoundrel.*

"We know him very well," she replied. "Have you never seen him?"

"Only once, in this house."

"Did you like him?" Nefisa could not help asking her.

With a laugh that made Nefisa detest her even more, the girl said, "The room was full of guests. And you know, of course, how embarrassing that kind of situation is."

"No, I don't," she answered coldly.

"Since you know him well, let me ask you what *you* think of him," the bride said with a laugh.

Not expecting such a question, Nefisa was taken aback. All of a sudden, her self-control vanished, and she was overwhelmed by insane passions.

"His type doesn't appeal to me," she said in a strange voice.

The bride's laughing eyes darkened. They opened wide in astonishment and disapproval. As though she did not believe her own ears, she stared at Nefisa absentmindedly and sullenly.

"Really? What type, then, does appeal to you?" she asked.

"Forget it," Nefisa said coldly, still driven by a mad urge. "What matters is that he appeals to you. Isn't that so?"

"I think so," the girl said, not yet recovered from her astonishment.

"Congratulations."

But the bride did not want the conversation to end at that point. Her pride wounded by Nefisa's words, she grew angry.

"What about the other brides you've worked for? Did they marry the type of husband that appealed to you?" Adillah asked sarcastically.

Realizing the challenging implications of the girl's words, Nefisa persisted in her mischief. She felt an urge to relieve herself of the burden which weighed heavily upon her heart.

"Actually, all of them deserve admiration. They are respectable employees," she hastened to say.

The bride resented this unexpected insolence. "Do you think that a man is not respectable," she inquired angrily, "unless he is an employee?"

"I do," Nefisa said in a quavering voice, which she was unable to control.

"And what about the status of a dressmaker?" the bride cried.

"It doesn't matter that I am a dressmaker," Nefisa answered angrily. "My brothers are educated students, and my father was a respectable employee."

"I assure you, not all poor folk deserve mercy when some of them are as insolent as you are."

"I'm not surprised that this invective comes from the daughter of a grocer."

Shaking with anger, the bride stood up and shouted, "How criminal! How insolent! Go away before I call the servants to throw you out of this house!"

Out of her mind, Nefisa rose and threw the bundle of cloth in the girl's face. The bundle came undone, and the pieces of silk, scattering on the bride's shoulders, fell to the floor, twisting in their bright colors at her feet. Nefisa hurried out of the room, followed by the screams of the girl, who directed the worst kind of abuse at her.

Nefisa quickly fled the flat. Outside she felt relaxed, and strangely relieved. She was almost overcome by a desire to laugh, but only for a moment. Soon she became meditative and dejected. Recollecting her behavior, she saw it in its proper perspective.

What have I done? she wondered. *They'll tell Mrs. Zeinab everything and she, in turn, will tell my mother. Mother will get angry, and be extremely upset about the profit I have lost on account of my folly.*

But I shall justify myself by telling her that the bride spoke arrogantly to me, insulted me for no reason, and that I had to defend my wounded dignity. And if she does not accept my excuse, I shall make a point of complaining loudly so that Hassanein will hear me. His pride wounded, he will get angry and take my side, and thus put an end to the episode. But how could I have been so rash as to act as I did? How mad of me! I did not mean to behave like that. So how did it all happen? I have lost a profitable job. But I should not feel too sorry about it. I have another rather good job on the same street. I don't regret what happened.

She walked up to Shubra Street. The beams of the setting sun almost disappeared, save for a few faint rays still visible at the top of the houses. She walked along the pavement in the direction of the tram stop, passing on her way a mechanic's garage. She was so absorbed in her thoughts that at first she failed to notice that someone, blocking her way, was saying to her, "You are welcome here."

Raising her head, she saw a young man in khaki trousers and shirt, his sleeves rolled up. He looked like one of the garage workers. She eyed him askance and moved off, but once more he blocked her way.

"Be patient, my lady," he said. "Look to your left and you will find a car owned by my humble person. Old though it is, it can carry us to any place you like. I am your servant, Mohammed al-Ful. I don't mean to boast, but I own this garage!"

"If you don't go away," she cried, "I shall call the police!"

"No need to do so," he said. "I love women but I don't love the police."

THIRTY-SIX

Some weeks later, the two brothers sat for the promotion examination at the end of the scholastic year, and both passed. Hussein was promoted to the fifth year, and Hassanein to the fourth. Failure in their case was not possible; success was their only alternative. Working hard and with great determination, the two boys achieved their goal. But their success confronted their mother with a new problem related to their dinner meals. Usually Samira and her daughter were content with the cheapest food. They often depended on ready-made food from the market to save the expense of meat, fat, and paraffin oil. Now, despite her frugality, the mother found herself obliged to change this rigorous regime, and thus the boys' success brought the family little pleasure. With the passage of time, its life seemed grimmer and gloomier than ever.

One evening Hassan arrived after being gone for three weeks. He came home laughing as usual; he frequently resorted to laughter to conceal his embarrassment and confusion.

"Good evening, Mother. Good evening, children. I have missed you so much," he said.

Looking at him with astonishment, his brothers greeted him. Samira kept staring through her fingers, making her resentment felt by remaining deliberately silent and ignoring his presence. However, she had given up her former habit of scolding him, settling accounts with him, or persuading him to search for a job; she had realized how futile it was. She felt the same sadness that usually overcame her whenever she thought of him or laid eyes on him. She knew his standard answers. He would tell her in a touching voice that he had left home to relieve her of the expense of feeding him, and that he had never stopped searching for a job, on and on. As for his brothers, they were genuinely pleased to see him after his long absence. They loved him as much as he loved them.

"*Bonne arrivée.* Where have you been all these weeks?" Nefisa asked him.

Hassan took off his coat, tossed it on the desk, and sat on the bed.

"One has to toil to earn one's living." Turning to his mother, he said, "Rejoice, Umm Hassan. Our troubles are coming to an end."

Raising her head, Samira looked at him with suspicious interest.

"Is this true?" she said quietly, somewhat hopefully.

He laughed, delighted to have aroused her interest, especially after she had ignored him. "I've already told you that Mr. Ali Sabri has enlisted me in his band," he said.

"I don't believe this is a serious job," Samira sighed.

"A week ago, Ali Sabri was asked to sing at a wedding party in Bulaq. I took part in it in return for twenty piasters, plus my supper of course. I know that this is a trivial sum of money. But earning a living is always difficult in the beginning."

"For the thousandth time, I beg you to look for a serious job," his mother said with irritation. "For your own good, if not for ours. What should I say to you, Hassan? Don't you realize that we never get enough to eat?"

Hassan lowered his eyes in confusion. His love for his family was the only noble feeling still alive in his heart. Perhaps it was his mother's sole influence in the formation of his character.

"Be patient," he murmured. "I haven't yet finished what I want to say ..."

But Hassanein interrupted, inquiring, "Do you think that the so-called Ali Sabri will ever be a worthwhile singer?"

Hassan raised his thick eyebrows in disapproval. Hoping to wipe out the effect of his mother's words, he said merrily, "Damn this country which doesn't appreciate talent! Ali Sabri

is a great artist. There is healing and therapy in his singing of
'Ya Lil.' Have you ever heard him shift his tune from Biati to
Hijaz and return again to Biati? Only the great singers, Abdu
al-Hamoli and Salama Hijazi, were able to achieve this feat once
or twice. As for Mohammed Abdul Wahab, once he uses Biati,
he finds himself unable to sustain it in the same performance,
and if he ever does, it will be in his next performance. It does
not degrade Ali Sabri that he charges only a few pounds for his
performance, for he is still at the beginning of his career. History tells us about several great artists who took the first humble
steps in their careers singing for a few loaves of bread."

His brothers laughed at his frivolity. But their mother sighed.

"In everything connected with you, I am resigned to God,"
she said.

Casting a superior look at his mother, he replied, "Let's stop
talking about art. The important thing for you to know is that
I shall be singing at a wedding party tomorrow."

"As a member of Ali Sabri's band?"

"No. I shall sing alone."

His mother looked at him with disapproval.

"Have you really become a singer?" Nefisa asked him.

"It happens sometimes that a distinguished member of a band
is chosen to sing at a party, which is the first step he takes on
the way to success."

"Who asked you to sing at his party?" his mother asked in a
rather sarcastic tone.

"Amm Gaber Soliman asked me to sing at the wedding party
of his son, Soliman."

Nefisa lowered her eyes, her enthusiasm extinguished. She
underwent a feeling of suffocating anguish.

Samira was astonished. Nodding at Nefisa, she asked, "Did
he ask you after what happened?"

Hassan laughed. "We had agreed to it before Lady Nefisa's
fight at the bride's house, and the man dared not break our
agreement."

For a while silence prevailed. Everyone gazed at him incredulously. It was true that there was a touch of sweetness in his
voice, but it was not enough to make him a singer.

Perplexed, his mother at last asked him, "Do you really mean
what you say?"

"Yes. I swear by God's mercy upon my dead father."

"How much would you charge?"

"Five pounds. Of these five pounds I shall give you one
whole pound."

He kept silent to allow the effect of his words to sink in.

"What do you think of joining my band as Sannids, to sing
choruses? Your voices are good enough," he asked, looking at
his brothers.

The two burst into laughter.

"You're fools!" Hassan exclaimed. "This is a rare opportunity
for you to feast on the sumptuous food and drink at the buffet."

The two brothers continued to laugh sarcastically; yet in their
minds they saw the table loaded with appetizing food. Various
delicious plates promptly and most temptingly presented themselves to their hungry imaginations. Sensing the strong temptation swaying their minds, Nefisa cried with indignation,
"What shame! Do you want to reduce your brothers to beggars
in the grocers' houses?"

Hassan laughed. "Lady Nefisa," he said, "I understand the
reason for your anger. Your attack on the bride made it impossible for you to be invited to the party. But what have these
two poor chaps done to be deprived of it? This party will be a
real event. There will be meat, pastries, fruits and vegetables,
and desserts. You'd better think twice about it."

Finding that his words had no effect, Hassan shrugged his
shoulders and dropped the matter. His offer was well-inten-
tioned, in thoughtful consideration for his brothers. But because
of their own folly, he thought with sorrow, they would lose the
good he intended for them. Though his two brothers did not
share his sorrow, their hearts fluttered at the mention of all the

food—the meat, pastries, fruits and vegetables, and desserts. They were pained at the thought of missing such delicious things, and their regret increased as the time for supper approached. Since Samira considered this meal superfluous, the family usually went to bed without it. They concealed their hunger so as not to increase her misery and discontent. And so, without uttering a word, the two young men imagined the delicious meals. Meanwhile, Nefisa was engrossed in her own thoughts, which rambled away from the pleasures of life in general and food in particular. Hassan's talk evoked her sorrows, despair, and fears. In surprise she wondered whether it was really true that her brother Hassan would sing at the wedding party.

THIRTY-SEVEN

At about nine o'clock on the morning after the wedding, Hassan was crossing Al Khazindar Square on his way to Clot Bey Street, where Ali Sabri had asked to meet him. He was tired after the previous night's party, the memories of which were still fresh in his mind. What a night it had been! He was peerless in his daring. With steady steps, he had cut his way through the crowd to the pavilion constructed on the roof of Amm Gaber Soliman's house, until he reached the dais amidst applause and shouts of welcome for the new singer. Solemnly greeting his audience, he took a seat in the middle of his band, which consisted of a lute player, a *kanum* player, and a violinist, who also repeated the refrains. He sang a song entitled "I Am Angry with You as Much as I Love You." After a while he observed that his audience had become indifferent. Nevertheless, without a care, he continued to sing. He drank a great deal of liquor. At the beginning of the second set many people clamored for a song entitled "In the Forlorn Night." Since he did not know the song, he began instead to sing another, called "The Garden of Your Beauty." Very soon, any relationship between the singer and his audience was severed, the singer straining his voice with useless vocalizing, his audience busy with drink and laughter. This embarrassing situation reached its climax when a drunken man stood and addressed the singer, his speech thick from the effects of alcohol.

"I swear by God," he said, "that if you weren't a bully I'd ask you to shut up."

Hassan recognized the man. He was a blacksmith whose shop stood at the opening of Nasr Allah alley. Under his breath Has-

san swore to punish him. However, he continued to sing "Gone
are the days; the days are gone."

Quickening his pace, he remembered all that had happened
and laughed. *What is done cannot be undone,* he thought. *There's
no reason for me to regret it since I've managed to grab the five pounds.*

Besides, recollections of the buffet were still lingering in his
mind. He proved invincible in the battle over the buffet. He was
at his greatest when he swallowed an entire pigeon, bones and
all. He was not eating, but devouring, snatching, looting, and
quarreling. The battle reached its zenith when the plate of beef
was emptied. Seizing the hand of the guest next to him, Hassan
forced him to relinquish the meat he had in his hand. But his
real feat came after the party was over. Surrounded by the members of his band, who were claiming their pay, he said to them
simply, "The food you have eaten is enough."

When they asked him, "What about the money due to us?"
he answered brutally, "Take it by force if you can."

They went away discontented, angry, and desperate. Only
one thing made him very sorry—the fact that his family had
not shared the delicious food with him. He wanted to help his
mother more than he actually did. But his protracted vagabondage had taught him to be careful, at least as long as his circumstances were bad. He was going toward Clot Bey, the
courtesans' quarter, specifically toward a very narrow path
called Darb Tiab, where Ali Sabri was waiting for him. Ali Sabri
had opened before him prospects of a life that suited his taste
and inflamed his imagination. They had agreed to meet in a
coffeehouse in the middle of the *darb,* across from the house of
a courtesan named Zeinab al-Khanfa, called the Twanger because she spoke with a nasal twang.

He climbed the stairs leading to the *darb.* He quickened his
pace between two rows of closed houses, their occupants still
asleep. The *darb* looked deserted. In the small cafés the workers
were cleaning up the litter left over from the previous night.

Hassan reached the middle of the *darb*. He saw Ali Sabri sitting before the entrance of the café and walked up to him, greeted him, and sat in a chair by his side. It was no longer the same old café: it looked much newer to him. A few workers were whitewashing the walls, in an attempt to renovate it.

"Here, in this café, where we are sitting, we shall inaugurate a new project, and start a new life," Ali Sabri said proudly.

Hassan was astonished, because, accustomed though he was to Ali Sabri's many projects, it was the first time he had heard of this new undertaking, the management of a coffeehouse.

"And what is to become of the band and wedding parties?" he inquired.

Ali Sabri spat with so much force that his spittle reached the walls of Zeinab the Twanger's house on the other side of the *darb*.

"The band will be working in this coffeehouse," he continued. "As for wedding parties, may God convert them into mourning assemblies. The days of true wedding parties are over. Instead of such parties, we now hear of small family gatherings to celebrate the occasion. And the wireless is monopolized by Umm Kalthum, Abdul Wahab, and a bunch of singers who specialize in producing discordant sounds. So it's impossible for us to earn a decent living in this country."

Hassan pretended to be dissatisfied with this state of affairs and said, "You are right, Master." He paused, then asked, "What will the band be doing here?"

Ali Sabri stretched out his legs, which reached the middle of the *darb*. He pointed to the coffeehouse. "It will be a café during the day," he said, "and a tavern by night, in which Madam Zeinab's women will dance. By the way, she is my partner. I, too, shall sing from time to time, and as you see, this is an excellent opportunity to make a good living. If you are interested in working with us, you will have to study the songs of Abdul Wahab."

"I know almost nothing about them."

"You will have to learn them, and you will have to study the *takatiqs* of Umm Kalthum, too. That's the way things are, and we have to make the best of it."

"May God be with us," said Hassan, laughing.

"I'm optimistic," Ali Sabri added. "This place is blessed. It is to this place that Mohammed al-Arabi is indebted for his wealth,"

Hassan wondered how Ali Sabri had obtained the money to start this new life. Had he gotten it from Zeinab the Twanger? At best, she was over forty. Except for her bovine body, her beauty was gone. But she was a godsend, and her arms were encircled with heavy gold. There was no need to envy Ali Sabri, since Hassan would have his share of the wealth. Now prospects were good, and perhaps the days of vagabondage and hunger would be gone forever.

"But your work as a repeater of refrains is secondary to what you're expected to do," Hassan heard his companion say.

"And what am I expected to do?"

Hassan approached this matter with the confidence and pride of a man who really knows what is expected of him.

"You're thoroughly acquainted with this district. On every corner there is a thug, a man who is up to no good, or a debauched drunkard. And who is the right person to deal with them? You. There is also the important traffic in narcotics, which requires skill, strength, and daring. And who's the right person to deal with it? You again," Ali Sabri said.

A broad smile appeared on Hassan's face, and remained there for a long time. He felt proud, pleased, and enthusiastic. This was real life, pulsing under breathtaking perils in the obscure *ghoraz*, the hidden shelters of hashish addicts, where cudgels and overturned chairs fell on the heads of brawlers. Here gold dropped from the sky, and the way of a man was strewn with thorns, leading either to pleasure and glory or to danger and death. Here, in the twisting *darb,* where the balconies of neighboring houses were intimately close to each other, coquettish cries mixed with debauched screams, the smell of perfume with the odor of liquor, and the blows of combatants with the vomit of drunkards, here Hassan felt quite at home. Added to all this were singing, instrumental music, and just plain frolic. In such an atmosphere he could live indefinitely without growing bored, eating, drinking, earning money, taking hashish, singing. His face beamed with the light of hope. He cast a look around him. He heard the footsteps of newcomers dispelling the silence, and his ears were struck by the prolonged laughter characteristic of courtesans. He watched their swaying buttocks and the glaring, lascivious glances in their eyes. The doors of the houses opened, incense burned in the *darb,* chairs lined the coffeehouses, and lewd giggles and cackles were heard, marking the beginning of the morning's activities.

THIRTY-EIGHT

"Thank you, Summer," Hassanein said with feeling.

Not knowing what he meant, she asked shyly, "Why do you thank the summer?"

"Because it has made you take off your thick overcoat, and put on a dress that reveals your charm and beauty."

Her face flushed. To hide the sparkling pleasure evoked by his compliments, she frowned. "Didn't I ask you to stop it? You keep doing things that annoy me," she said.

With a perplexed smile on his face, he listened to her. His eyes were devouring her plump body with pleasure. She was wearing a decent, almost prudish dress which revealed her arms, the lower parts of her legs, her delicate white neck, and the outlines of her soft, plump body. His eyes remained fixed on the round, minutely latticed parts of her dress above the chest, designed by the dressmaker to fit her blossoming bosom that seemed almost on the point of bursting out. As he imagined that he was softly stroking her breasts with his fingers, his body shook with a quiver of desire. He imagined that he was squeezing them, but their stiffness resisted him. Thirsty with desire, he swallowed. But he knew she would neither respond to him nor allow him to come too close to her body, and that she would persist in her adamant attitude of refusal. He had hoped that with the passage of time he would reach her, but he finally realized the futility of his hope.

"Bahia," he said in dejection, "you speak with the cruelty of a person whose heart has never throbbed with love."

A contradictory look appeared in her eyes. "I do not approve of the kind of love you want; you deliberately misunderstand me," she said.

"But love is love, and you cannot possibly divide it up into different kinds."

"No, no, no. I don't agree with that at all," she replied.

Defeated, he sighed, casting a look at the distant horizon. The sun had already disappeared, leaving behind it an expansive red halo, its remote purple fringes becoming lighter in the center, almost the color of rose juice, and gradually fading away at its edges until the red was finally superseded by a pure, deep blue interspersed with delicate clouds, as tender as soft sighs. His eyes returned to her face.

"I love you and I am your fiancé," he said hopefully, "and I only want us to enjoy our love in all its purity and innocence."

A confused look appeared in her eyes. For a while she seemed to be in pain. "I can't," she said. "And I don't want that."

His smile was without meaning.

"You thrust me into the lap of a strange loneliness," he replied. "And I can't bear it. I have a burning desire to press a kiss on your lips and embrace you to my heart. This is my right and the rightful privilege of our love."

"No, no. You scare me."

"Don't you love me?"

"Don't ask me about what you already know."

"I wonder! Wouldn't you really like me to put my lips on yours?"

"Surely," she said, snorting, "you must enjoy making me angry."

"And to have you lie on my breast, hear the pulses of my heart, while I tightly encircle your waist with my arms?"

Angrily, she shrank from him.

"If this is not love, then what is it?" he said with annoyance.

"Let our relationship remain as it has been up to now," she murmured entreatingly.

"You mean we meet, talk, and burn with desire."

"No. I only mean meet and talk."

"You're lying to yourself."

"God forgive you."

"Is your love so heartless?"

"God forgive you."

He stamped the floor with indignation. Frowning and baffled, he walked back and forth in front of her. Signs of anxiety appeared on her face.

"I thought you had forgotten your upsetting demands and were satisfied with our life, gentle and amiable as it is," she said. "I wonder what now makes you return to the same old fearsome persistence. Be a decent boy and stop all this nonsense. Real love knows no such frivolity."

He shook his head, defeated, desperate and wondering. What did she know about real love?! What an enigma she was! Did she really love him? He could not doubt her love for him. But hers was a kind of love beyond his understanding. Rather, her character itself was beyond his understanding. What a calm, solemn girl she was, with her blue eyes, cold and serene, entirely devoid of mischief, frivolity, and warmth. *How,* he wondered, *could anybody with such a fascinating body possess such calm and frigid eyes? The fire of love can be extinguished only by another fire similar to it, or even stronger.* He felt he was wasting his days in hopeless monotony. It occurred to him frequently that it always perturbed her whenever he spoke to her about love, and that she recovered her self-assurance only when both of them were silent or when she spoke of her distant hopes, which she never tired of repeating. When she talked about these things, she forgot herself and transcended time and space; her eyes beamed delightfully and her limbs were animated with a fresh vivacity. At that moment he would love her with all his heart. But this was love tainted by anguish, sometimes even by anger and resentment. Then he would wonder why her heart failed to respond in the same way to the feeling of love itself. Why was she afraid of it? Why did she shrink from the mere mention or hint of this emotion? He wondered, too, how long this barrier

would separate them! Rather angrily, he looked intently at her face for a long time.

"Shall I suffer this deprivation forever?" he asked.

In spite of herself, she smiled, and his anger increased in response.

"Not forever," she said.

His heart quivered. He kept his eyes fixed on her.

"Till we marry," he answered curtly.

She looked down. He could see only her closed eyelids and rosy cheeks. At that moment, he was overcome by a vindictive impulse, a desire to injure, if only by words.

"After marriage, you will give me willingly whatever you deny me now," he said. "You will give me your lips, your breast, and your body, and you will take off your clothes and appear in crystal-like nakedness before me."

She did not hear these last words, for she had left him, taking to her heels. She quickened her pace toward the door leading from the roof. Words erupted from his mouth, heated, angry, and vindictive.

THIRTY-NINE

Ali Sabri's coffeehouse became a small nightclub, featuring songs, dances, and liquor. Above the entrance was a large sign bearing Ali Sabri's name in big letters. There was a dais for the band at the farthest end of the interior, and tables and chairs were arranged at the entrance and along the two sides. Having finished his singing for the first performance, Ali Sabri sat down among his drinking customers to entertain them. Then a tall, glistening, muscular black man entered, his eyes portending evil. Standing on the threshold of the coffeehouse, the newcomer shouted in a loud, insolent voice, "Where's the owner of this café?"

Hiding his astonishment with a faint smile, Ali Sabri walked up to him.

"Yes, sir?" he said.

"I've heard you've got the filthiest kind of liquor to be found in this district. Since good liquor no longer has any effect on me, I've come here to get drunk," he said defiantly. Pushing Ali Sabri roughly aside, he went toward a table at which a number of relatively dignified men were sitting. Casting a savage look at them, he said authoritatively, "Clear this table!"

They all stood up and silently left the café. Examining the faces around him with insolent defiance, the intruder sat in a chair and stretched his legs onto another.

Approaching Ali Sabri, the café apprentice whispered in his ear, "This is Mahrous the Negro, a bully; everybody in the whole district is afraid of him."

Worried, Ali Sabri asked, "Is he likely to stay long?"

"He frequents any café he likes, eats and drinks, and nobody dares ask him to pay. Perhaps he's come to introduce himself to you. Or perhaps ..."

The boy hesitated a little.

"Speak," Ali Sabri urged him.

"Perhaps one of the café owners in the *darb* has incited him to destroy our coffeehouse!"

Casting a furtive look at the Negro, Ali Sabri observed that he was half asleep, apparently feeling secure and at home, and that the customers had deserted the nearby tables. His heart filled with fear and depression. He retreated silently to the dais, where Hassan was sitting with the rest of the band. He nodded to Hassan, and they both withdrew behind the buffet, where he confided to Hassan what the boy had told him.

"Maybe it would be better for us to ask Mistress Zeinab the Twanger to use her tact in this dire situation," Ali Sabri suggested.

Inspecting Mahrous from a distance, Hassan replied, "I don't approve of asking a woman for help. In this *darb* such a policy won't do. Leave it to me."

"They say that he is a terrible bully."

"They say the same thing about me, too," Hassan said with a smile, "though the people here don't know it. Leave this matter to me." Then he thought, sarcastically: *My mother is not the only one who endures misery just to live.*

"It will be a fierce fight," he told Ali Sabri, "and unless we win, it'll be impossible for us to make a living in this place."

"Suppose we don't win?"

"Trust God and me."

Whatever the consequences, he would not avoid the forthcoming fight. After all, this was the only means by which he could enhance his own prestige in the eyes of Ali Sabri and throughout the whole district.

Perhaps Ali Sabri is right in worrying about the safety of his coffee-

house and his money, he thought. *But my own future depends on the outcome of this fight. So let Ali Sabri himself go to hell. Besides, I should not forget that sooner or later a victory of this sort is my only means of gaining access to the girls of Zeinab the Twanger. My fortunes in life, and perhaps those of my family*—this occurred to him as an afterthought—*depend on the outcome of this fight.*

Mahrous the Negro stirred. Stretching his limbs, he yawned and belched. "Where's the filthy cognac we've heard so much about?" he bellowed.

Calmly and steadily, Hassan left his place. He walked up to the Negro and stood before him.

"Peace be upon you," he said quietly.

Arrogantly the Negro raised his fiery eyes. He examined Hassan's solid body and glistening eyes with malice and suspicion. He frowned angrily and his face assumed an inhuman glow.

"The curse of God be upon you and your mother! What do you want?" he shouted at Hassan.

"I heard you shouting for cognac, and I saw it was my duty to tell you that here we require payment in advance," Hassan said in clear tones, preserving his veneer of calm.

Pulling his legs from the chair before him, Mahrous burst out into a long, affected laugh, beating his knees in excitement. Then he calmed himself and stopped, casting a disparaging look at Hassan.

"Are you the bouncer of the café?" he asked mockingly.

Hassan said quietly, "I should also like to tell you that your behavior is not proper."

In the next few moments the nearby customers jostled their way out of the coffeehouse. The path facing the entrance was crowded with people of all ages. The workers at the buffet quickly concealed the bottles, glasses, and musical instruments —anything that could be broken. Mahrous still had a sarcastic smile on his thick lips.

Then, suddenly, he gave Hassan's left leg a violent kick.

Hassan staggered backward. Though he had been vigilant and wary, watching his rival, Hassan had been focusing his attention on Mahrous's hands, expecting him to throw something or thrust a dagger at him; thus he hadn't seen the kick coming until it actually hit him. Hassan staggered under the force of the kick, but he summoned sufficient strength to avoid falling down. Staggering backward, enraged at the pain, he clenched his teeth to overcome it. The Negro allowed him not a second's rest. He jumped at him like a man diving into the water. Afraid lest he become an easy victim for his adversary, Hassan made no attempt to control his staggering. Instead, he jumped backward, crashing against the wall of the café, and thus evaded his powerful enemy. Mahrous gave Hassan no time to regain his balance. He attacked him with a blow to the abdomen, which Hassan blocked with his hands. With this punch, Mahrous had expected his adversary to expose his neck; as swift as lightning he seized Hassan's throat in his iron hands, pressing them together brutally to strangle him. The fight seemed to be over. Ali Sabri's head swam. The faces of the café workers and members of the band turned white. They exchanged worried looks, hoping someone would act to save their dying friend but remaining transfixed in their places. Expecting Hassan's corpse to fall to the floor, the girls began to wail. As he began to lose consciousness, Hassan was suddenly aware that he could not escape the deadly grip of his rival, who held his neck in a vise. Realizing that the end was very near unless he did something to avert it, Hassan clenched his teeth and stretched the muscles of his neck, concentrating all his strength in it. Then, with all the force he could muster, he bent his right leg and drove his knee into his adversary's groin. The Negro's firm hold on his neck immediately relaxed. Shaking with anger as he regained his breath, Hassan gave his rival a second blow; all of this occurred in the first thirty seconds after the Negro's attempt to strangle him. Finally Mahrous's hands were lifted from Hassan's neck and the Negro retreated with dazed, gloomy, blood-shot eyes, his face contorted with rage. Realizing that he was now master of the situation, Hassan wasted no time. He attacked his rival, who was now striving fiercely to shake off his pain. Using his forehead like a pile driver, Hassan butted his rival on the forehead. The two heads snapped dreadfully as they collided. The Negro dealt Hassan several terrible blows but these failed to weaken Hassan's determination. Blood gushed from the Negro's head, streaming over his face like flames on burning tar. He seemed to be struggling. Hassan recovered from the pain in his leg, neck, and chest, and with the side of his palm he delivered a blow to his adversary's head as cutting as the sharp edge of a knife. The Negro groaned and fell unconscious to the floor. Thrilled with his victory, Hassan stood over his rival, his chest heaving. But with the danger passed, the pain began to mount. Had no one been watching him, Hassan would gladly have flung himself down beside his enemy. But the eager eyes of the onlookers forced him to compose himself. The screams, commotion, and shouts of the mob struck his ears. He sensed a strange movement throughout the café, and at the touch of a hand on his shoulder, he turned to see Ali Sabri smiling at him, his face deathly pale.

"Come with me," Hassan heard him whisper in his ear. "I want to offer you a glass of cognac."

He went with him in silence to the dais. He sat on a chair, and Ali Sabri brought him a full glass of cognac; Hassan drank it down and when he asked for another, Ali Sabri brought him one, and said, "You must be very tired."

"The fight was inevitable," Hassan murmured with confidence.

The waiter came. "They are calling you the Head* be-

---

* In colloquial Arabic, this is a play on words, associating the expression which means "Russian" (a complimentary reference to a strong man) with "*russiat*," which means "butting with the head."

cause you knocked him down with your head," he said, laughing.

Hoping to avoid people's glances, Hassan said to Ali Sabri, "Let's wipe out all traces of the fight. Start the second singing performance!"

FORTY

His strength, vitality, and fighting experience had enabled Hassan to regain his composure. It was an hour or more past midnight when the last intoxicated customer staggered out of Ali Sabri's café. The *darb* was almost completely dark once the lights outside were turned off. Houses were closing their doors so that the parties inside could begin, usually to last until dawn. Two policemen were passing by, and the street resounded with their heavy footsteps. Hassan was sitting with Ali Sabri at the back of the café discussing the night's take when a boy who worked as a waiter in the house of Zeinab the Twanger walked up and greeted them.

"Someone wants you," he whispered in Hassan's ear.

When Ali Sabri overheard the boy's whisper, an interested look appeared on his face. "A woman?" he murmured.

"I think so," Hassan answered indifferently.

"Don't you prefer transitory love, as I do?"

Hassan gave a meaningful smile. "But this kind of love doesn't amount to much," he replied.

"Wait and see."

Hassan bade his companion goodbye and followed the boy to the house opposite the café. The boy knocked on the door; it opened warily to a narrow slit. The boy slipped inside; Hassan followed. The door closed. Just at the front entrance, a blind man sat in a chair playing a flute, while Mistress Zeinab the Twanger, wearing a black cloak and a veil with a big gold clasp in the center to hide her decaying nose, sat on a raised divan. Casting a scrutinizing look around him, Hassan saw that all the girls were engaged. Leaning toward the drawn curtain at the threshold of the stairs, the boy pulled it aside and entered. Hassan followed. They climbed the stairs together in silence.

"Who is it?" Hassan asked, breaking the silence.

"Lady Sana'a."

Hassan remembered her. She was a woman of dark complexion, curly hair, fleshy body, coarse lips, and large black eyes. She spent most of the day sitting at the entrance to the house, her crossed legs exposing her thigh all the way up to her white silk panties. They climbed to the second floor and passed through a long corridor leading to a small hall with three doors. The boy went to the middle door and knocked three times. A brassy, resonant voice shouted, "Come in!"

The boy pushed the door open slightly and stepped aside. Hassan entered the room. Before closing the door behind him, he felt the boy's hand stroking his back. As he turned, the boy laughed.

"Recite the Exordium of the Koran for us," he said as he departed.

Hassan closed the door. The room was pitch-dark. It occurred to him to grope for the switch to turn on the light, but he soon changed his mind. He stood leaning against the door, waiting for his eyes to become accustomed to the surrounding darkness. For a while, the silence seemed complete. Then he became aware of someone breathing, and he listened, smiling. He expected something to be said or done, but nothing happened. He walked slowly to his left, toward the sound of breathing, until his knee bumped against something solid. Groping with his hands, he recognized it as the edge of a wooden bed. He stood looking down with glistening eyes until he could distinguish in the darkness an obscure, featureless mass stretched out on the bed. He lowered his thumb little by little until it pressed into the soft flesh of a body that quivered at the touch. A suppressed laugh emerged from the dark.

Afterward, turning on the light, he started to put on his clothes. He took ten piasters from his pocket and put the money on the bed while the woman watched him with laughing eyes. She jumped to the floor and walked naked to the table. She opened a drawer and returned with a fifty-piaster note, which she silently placed on top of his ten piasters.

"Are you bringing me the change?" he asked with a laugh.

"This is your fee," she said calmly.

Pretending indifference, he casually finished dressing, controlling his features lest they betray his delight. He picked up the money and put it in his pocket.

She cast a deep glance at him. "Would you be my lover?" she asked.

"I have a mistress," he lied.

Her glistening eyes betrayed her. "In this *darb*?"

"No, in another."

"Is she a foreigner?"

"No, an Arab."

Silence prevailed for a moment.

"Do you still desire her?" she asked.

He decided to keep silent and replied only with a smile.

"Where do you live?" she inquired, laughing.

"In Shubra."

"It's too far from your work. Do you have to sleep there?"

"No."

"I live nearby, in Gandab alley in Clot Bey. Do you know where it is?"

"From now on I shall know where it is."

FORTY-ONE

At about sunset Nefisa left the house of one of her customers on Al Walid Street. She looked annoyed. She always felt miserable when she was alone. The fact that her meager earnings from her work were swallowed up by the family's urgent needs increased her misery, for she was unable to keep any of her earnings. Besides, a serious change had come over her. Now she paid close attention to her appearance. Her orange dress, decorated with violets, revealed her tall, slim body. She applied makeup flamboyantly. She continued walking along Al Walid Street until she reached Shubra Street. At the corner she turned, casting a distant look toward the garage, which infused her heart with vitality and watchfulness. The sight of the garage and its proprietor, Mohammed al-Ful, brought back to her memory a violent conflict that had torn her heart throughout the past weeks. She neither stepped forward nor backward, but came to a complete stop. Fear paralyzed her legs. Although her tortured wavering had been resolved, yet, as she took the last step, she was stricken by fear.

Isn't it better for me to think the matter over? she thought. *No, no. Thinking will only cause me headaches. He'll block my way as he does every evening. I can't deny that I smiled at his pleasantries. What will happen next? Now it is too late to retreat. He doesn't conceal his motives or intentions. Nor am I ignorant of them. I understand everything. I understand why he invites me to ride in his car. He doesn't try to deceive me as someone else did. What he wants is perfectly clear. Shall I do it? Why is he interested in me? I'm not pretty, and it's impossible that this makeup will make me so. But in the market of lechery even ugliness itself is a salable commodity, and pleasure seekers, at least some of them, are not fastidious in their demands. This is the truth. Marriage is a different matter. But where seeking pleasure is concerned, people are all the same. Should I allow myself to fall? Why not? I wouldn't be losing anything I haven't already lost. But isn't it better to think this over carefully?*

Bitter memories of her old despair galled her and besieged her mind, and she remembered how bitterly hopeless her condition had become. However, in addition to the feeling of despair, an intense desire boiled in her veins, clamoring for gratification; she felt helpless before it. Whenever she surrendered to despair, this fierce desire stung her to the depths of her being. This desire alone would get in her way, were she ever to think of hiding herself away from people. It was so strong that she came to detest it as much as she detested her life itself, but consciously she denied its existence. Shutting it out of her mind, she would persuade herself that she could accept humiliation for the sake of the money which her family so badly needed. Her family's condition being what it was, she was not lying when she thought in this fashion. But it was only half the truth, the half she admitted while she ignored the other. She found pleasure, if we might call it that, in looking upon herself as a martyr and a victim of despondency and poverty.

At that moment, the young man appeared from the garage. He was speaking to some workers. Her heart fluttered, and her eyes remained fixed on him. Instinctively, she realized she would not retreat. Turning her back and standing at a distance from him, she mentally surrendered to him, and her surrender was complete. It was at this moment that the violent, distressing conflict which had torn her heart for weeks was finally resolved. In despair and heated emotion, she sighed, and with slow steps approached him, pretending to ignore him until she felt him, with his usual daring, somehow blocking her way.

"My lady, why are you so hard-hearted? My entreaties would soften even a rock. My car is waiting at the turn of the road. For ages it has been waiting for you," he said.

Encouraged by her smile, he walked by her side. "Stop being

so coy. Even if I had the patience of Job, it would run out ..." he pleaded.

How delicious flirtation was, even if it was false! Though it was a pity to feel this way, his flirtation restored her long-humiliated sense of female dignity. She wished he knew who she was and who her father had been. She heard him speak to her in a menacing tone: "Here is the car. If you don't get in, I'll pick you up in my arms in front of everyone."

They reached the car, parked in the next blind alley. With one hand he seized hers, and opened the door of the car with the other. Swallowing, she nervously entered the car and sat down. He closed the door behind her. Walking around the car, he got in through the other door. She was almost unaware of his presence. She leaned far back to avoid the window looking out on the road. At that moment she experienced a feeling of alienation. Everything seemed to her eerie and phantasmagorical: the road on which the curtain of night was falling, the figures of the people passing by, the old dilapidated car, herself, people's voices, and the rumbling sound of the wheels of tramcars. Determined, she forced herself to regain her composure. She gave him a furtive look. He was sitting erect before the steering wheel, veins bulging from his solid face with its big, rocky nose, protruding cheeks, and broad, bulldoglike mouth.

The sight of him brought her back to the real world, the world of consciousness, nerves, blood, and fear. Cautiously looking about, the man took a bottle from under the seat and uncorked it. Raising it to his mouth, he took huge gulps. He turned to her, his face contracting convulsively. "Would you like a little wine?" he asked.

"No. I don't drink," she said hurriedly.

Smacking his lips, he raised his eyelids in surprise. He returned the bottle to its place and the car started to move.

"It's better to drink now so that I'll be in the right frame of mind when we reach our destination," he said.

He drove the car recklessly at high speed. Nefisa wondered at his bravado. He seemed to her strong and daring, but at the same time dishonorable and untrustworthy. What need did she have for an honorable man! She was not worthy of such a man, who had ceased to be the object of her dreams. A scandal was the only thing in life she feared. She heard him laugh and say proudly, "You've been coy for so long! But I always thought that one day you would fall into the trap, and here you are!"

She welcomed his conversation; it helped her escape from her thoughts and confusion. A smile appeared on her lips.

"Who told you that I'd fallen?"

"We'll see what happens in the Almaza Desert," he said with a laugh.

"The Almaza Desert? Will we be there long?" she inquired, worried.

"Until midnight."

Terrified, she visualized the faces of her mother and two brothers.

"What a disaster! I must return home before supper. For God's mercy, stop the car!" she entreated.

"Really? Don't be frightened. We'll return before supper. But what are you afraid of?" he asked halfheartedly, in astonishment.

"My family."

He watched her with pretended suspicion.

"Your family! Don't they know?" he asked her in a meaningful tone.

His painful words stabbed her in the heart. Her family know! What did he take her for?!

"How could my family know? My brothers are university students and my father was an official," she said quickly.

Pretending belief, he shook his head.

My mother is only a washerwoman, and my brothers are just vagabonds, he mentally mimicked her, full of sarcasm. *But I have to be resigned to God's will.* He doubled the car's speed to reach his destination as soon as possible. The wine was taking effect, and he felt pleased.

"What's your name?" he asked her.

"Nefisa."

Unimpressed, he asked her, "Why didn't you choose a sweeter name?"

Not catching his meaning, she misunderstood him. "I like it," she said resentfully.

"Excuse me, Lady Nefisa. Long live your name!"

At length, turning to the desert road, the car dived into total darkness. At a distance the city lights seemed like a powerful giant with innumerable fiery eyes. He started to slow down, then finally stopped and turned off the headlights. Stretching out his arm, he suddenly encircled her waist, pulling her toward him with unexpected violence. Sighing, she fell upon him. Opening his broad mouth, he thrust it upon hers, reaching the middle of her chin. He pulled her brutally to his breast, breathing hard through his nose with a rattling kind of snort. At first she felt pained and worried. But her uneasiness vanished in a strange, mysterious inner darkness. Their two shapes dissolved in the total darkness which engulfed them. She felt grateful for it; it not only made her bold, it concealed her defects. Impelled by an instinctive urge, she did her best to gratify him. In addition to fear and worry, she felt shy at first. But soon she was overcome by an insane passion that thawed these feelings that held her back.

"Let's wait for a second go," he said seductively.

Wiping the perspiration that streamed from her forehead, she beseechingly replied, "I can't. Please, let's return at once."

Taking the bottle, he quenched his thirst in successive gulps. His face long and rigid, he drove the car in silence until they reached Ramses Square.

"I feel like doing it again. Shall we go back?" he said.

"No, no, I can't," she begged him fearfully.

Suddenly he frowned indignantly. Then he spoke with un-expected roughness. "Damn you! This trip wasn't worth the gasoline it took to get there!"

His words fell like lashes upon her soul. She was speechless. Her heart overflowed with disappointment. Stunned, she stared at him, but, indifferent, he drove on. Perhaps his ungratified desire for more was an excuse. All the same, would it not have been better to treat her kindly, or at least to say a tender word to erase the ill effects of his roughness? He continued to drive in silence. Turning into a back street to let the girl get out unseen, he stopped the car near the pavement. Considering the insult as she left the car, she wondered whether to accept or reject another appointment to meet him. She was too perplexed to know how to face this inevitable question. But she saw him stretching out his hand, offering her a ten-piaster piece.

"This is enough for one time," he said.

As she stood motionless before him, he threw the silver coin at her feet and drove off in a trail of choking smoke, the car roaring and gurgling. Blind with fury, she remained transfixed, her body shaking all over. Biting her teeth, she continued to quake. She kept sucking in her breath rapidly as if from a burst-ing chest. He did not care to ask her for another appointment. Just a transient relationship as though she were ... Oh, God! Just a transient relationship! Then she remembered how he threw the ten-piaster piece at her! An idea occurred to her, ex-tinguishing her anger and replacing it with embarrassment and a sense of failure. No. Wasn't it possible that she failed to appeal to him and satisfy him? This was quite possible, even probable. It was certain! She was overwhelmed with a profound feeling of sorrow and degradation. She suddenly realized that she was still standing on the pavement. On the point of leaving, she remembered the coin lying at her feet. Not knowing what to do, she gave it a furious glance. Memories rushed to her mind. She immediately recalled the five-piaster piece which Soliman had borrowed one day at the tram stop, the day he had taken her to his home, the total darkness of the place, her quarrel with him in the street, and her dead father's words about her sweet temper. Then once more she focused her attention on the silver coin at her feet. She gazed at it for a long time. Seeing no reason to leave it there, she picked it up.

FORTY-TWO

After a rather long absence, Hassan paid his family an unexpected visit. The members of the family were gathered in the two brothers' room, their favorite sitting room during the summer months. This time he arrived with a basket in his hand. Putting it behind the door, he stepped forward with laughter in his greeting. They welcomed him as usual. His sister and brothers' reception was unreserved while the mother cast an inquisitive glance at the basket.

"What on earth may a mother expect from a worthless son?" she murmured sarcastically.

Taking a seat in their midst, he assured her with a laugh, "Don't be in a hurry. Patience has its rewards."

But none of them paid any attention to the basket, for they were not accustomed to expect anything good from him.

"You come to see us only as a visitor!" Nefisa remarked.

"I roam God's vast land, arduously making my living. Don't be surprised if you see me only as a visitor. The reason is that I've found myself a dwelling!"

All eyes focused on him with interest.

"Has God guided you? And have you found a job at last?"

"With Ali Sabri's band and nobody else. But now God has provided us with earnings enough."

"I shall never be convinced that this is a job in the true sense of the word," the mother remarked.

"Why not, Mother? With the band I sing, while in other occupations I quarrel, as you know," Hassan replied.

"Have you really found a dwelling of your own? Where?" Hussein asked.

For a while, Hassan kept his thoughts to himself.

"Why do you want to know?" he asked.

"So we can return your visits."

"Don't. My dwelling is not properly furnished to receive people. Besides, it isn't a private place; it's occupied by all the members of the band. Let's forget about it. Tell me, when did you last eat meat?"

"To tell you the truth, we've forgotten. Give me a moment to try to remember," Hussein said sarcastically. "If I draw on obscure memories, I'm able to visualize the last slice of meat I've eaten. But I don't remember when or where. We're a philosophical family. Following the principles of Al Maarri," he added with a laugh.

"Who is this Maarri? One of our forefathers?" Hassan inquired.

"A merciful philosopher. So merciful toward animals that he abstained from eating their flesh."

"Now I understand why the government opens schools. It does this to make you hate eating meat so as to have all the meat for itself."

Hassan rose and went to get the basket. Returning, he placed it before his mother and removed the paper cover. Underneath was a fleshy leg of mutton, the red surface of the meat blending with the white fat. Beside it lay a medium-size tin box.

"I can't believe my eyes," Hassanein exclaimed. "What's inside the box?"

"Shortening."

The spirits of Hassan's brothers and sister rose high and their eyes glistened. Their mother's heart was touched by the atmosphere of contagious merriment.

"Now we're sure of a sumptuous dinner for tomorrow," she muttered, smiling.

"No! You mean a sumptuous supper right now!" shouted many voices.

"Have you any idea of how long it will take to prepare this supper?"

"Never mind. We're ready to wait until the break of dawn!"

Nefisa rose and carried the basket into the kitchen.

Without further objection Samira rose, too, nodding to Hassan to follow her as she left the room. With a knowing smile, Hassan traipsed after her. She took him aside in a corner of the hall.

"Is it true," she asked eagerly, "that you're really making enough money?"

"To some extent! But my future is uncertain."

"Can I trust you to help us?"

"Yes, whenever I've enough. I hope so."

"Where do you live?" she inquired after a moment's silence.

Knowing that she understood him inside out, he realized the futility of telling her lies. "Number seventeen Gandab alley in Clot Bey," he answered.

"With a woman?" she asked, hesitantly.

"Yes," he said, giving a short laugh.

"Is it marriage?"

"No," he muttered, laughing again.

In the darkness, he could not see the signs of disapproval in her face. Having long since despaired of reforming him, she did not take the trouble now to scold him or give him advice. Yet she asked him with interest and warmth, "I suppose you get your earnings by decent means?"

"Yes," he reassured her. "Have no doubt about this. We are requested to give so many marriage feasts, and we sing in coffeehouses and music halls," he added emphatically.

FORTY-THREE

Another year passed, and life continued its usual course. The members of the family followed their normal routines of everyday life. Had their dead father come back to life, he would have been shocked by the tremendous change which had come over the souls, bodies, health, even the looks of his family. But he would certainly have recognized them. His wife and children had not changed that much. But his house had become so completely transformed that, no matter how hard he tried, he would have failed to remember it. The furniture had almost disappeared. The sitting room contained only a sofa and a pale thin carpet which had formerly covered the floor of Samira's bedroom. Now it replaced the sitting-room carpet, which had been sold. Most of the furniture had been bartered away, and nothing remained in Samira's bedroom but two sofas, used as seats during the day and as beds at night. Once the sideboard, table, and chairs were sold, the hall, which served in former times as a dining room, became bare. Hassan's bed had been sold. So degraded was the family's condition that they took their meals from a tray laid on the floor. Hussein and Hassanein's beds would have been sold, too, were they not indispensable. The family's life was hard and arduous. Without Samira's determination and frugality, the father's pension and Nefisa's meager earnings would together have been insufficient to meet the essential expenses of food and shelter. As for Hassan's assistance, it was scanty and unreliable, extended only on his rare visits, when he brought them hope and delicious food. From time to time he bought his mother a garment, a handkerchief, or some pieces of underwear. Apart from these rare visits, nobody know where he was.

Apologetically, he spoke to his mother about his strenuous struggles and slim earnings. This being usually the case, he was not always exaggerating. In fact, he had found life harder than he had expected.

He sang with Ali Sabri's band, took part in brawls whenever occasion arose, trafficked in narcotics on a small scale, and possessed the body and money of a rather beautiful woman. But his earnings fell short of his aspirations. Furthermore, his mode of life made it necessary to be extravagant and spend money lavishly, to keep up a dignified appearance and hold his assistants. He was constantly torn by a conflict between his personal needs and selfishness on one hand and love for his family on the other. Sometimes love for family gained the ascendant. But self-love being almost always predominant, he allowed himself to be carried away by the strong current of his reckless life. Then, remembering his family, he would act generously toward them as far as his means would allow. Under this generous impulse, he would wish very much to restore his family to the relative prosperity of the past. But, again, his adventurous life would make him oblivious to it; then, once more overcome with remorse and pain, he would remember, and the cycle would continue indefinitely. Though Hassan's visits afforded the family relief and entertainment, they could not look upon him as the man of the house whose substantial assistance would help them stand on their feet. Samira alone was the cornerstone of the family. Sacrificing herself for the sake of the others, she almost went to pieces; two years of this life had aged her quickly, telling on her more than the previous fifty. She became thin and pale, a mere skeleton. Yet she did not surrender to the ordeal. Never complaining, she steadfastly adhered to her ingrained virtues of fortitude, determination, and strength. She worked throughout the day cooking, washing, cleaning up, sweeping, patching, darning, and attending particularly to her two sons, watching their play, urging them to study, settling their trifling disputes, and checking their impulses, especially those of the whimsical Hassanein. Busy though she was, she kept thinking of the family's present and future, absorbed in her pain at seeing her daughter, Nefisa, moving incessantly from one house to another, working hard but earning little, in her laborious and desperate endeavors. With supreme stoicism she endured her pains, drawing upon an unshakable faith and clinging to a firm hope, which she believed was bound to be rewarded no matter how long it might remain unfulfilled. By her efforts, her two sons were able to make steady progress without swerving from their goal, and despite their austerity and deprivation, to continue their progress with admirable persistence.

Hassanein was more pained by his deprivation in love than by life's humiliation. His beloved was no less stubbornly adamant than his mother. She forced him to be content with an ascetic, platonic relationship that was unsuitable to his passionate temper. Engrossed in the troubles of their private lives, the two brothers were almost oblivious to the drastic changes their country was undergoing at this time. In fact, Hussein paid very little attention to politics and public affairs. Perhaps Hassanein was more interested in politics than his brother, but not sufficiently so to be considered a political-minded student. His interest was confined almost entirely to partisan discussions or participation in peaceful demonstrations.

Their mother objected to their participation in political life. Entirely ignorant of politics, she was so absorbed in her feelings for her family that she had no room for national sentiment. Hearing the distressing news of student deaths and injuries in demonstrations, she became alarmed.

"Poor boys!" she was saying to her sons. "What use are demonstrations and politics when these boys have lost their lives?! Their families are afflicted, their homes are ruined, and their death serves no purpose."

Conscious that he lagged behind his fellow revolutionaries, Hassanein gave vent to his suppressed feelings.

"Countries live by the death of their heroes," he said.

She gave him a stern look. Lowering his eyes, he changed his mind and desisted from his inflammatory speech. Later, when the Home Front was formed and the nationalists entered into negotiations with the British which led to the conclusion of an agreement, a general sense of relief pervaded the whole country. Hassanein resumed his political conversations, with more daring than his brother when speaking to their mother.

"Now do you realize," he said, "that the sacrifices made by the martyrs have not been in vain?"

This time she did not get angry, feeling that the danger was now past and that peace had returned. But she did not give up her former opinions.

"Nothing in the world can make up for the death of a young soul," she said.

"Mother, you've lived for half a century under occupation," Hassanein said. "Let's pray to God"—he laughed—"that you'll live for another half century under independence!"

"Occupation! Independence!" the mother replied, in disapproval. "I don't see the difference between them. It's better for us to pray to God to relieve our distress and make life easier for us."

Hassanein spoke with enthusiasm and faith. "But for the occupation, our family would never have been left in the lurch after Father's death. Isn't it so?" he asked, turning to Hussein.

"I believe so," Hussein said hopefully.

Very skeptical, the mother looked from one to the other. She did not care for general conversations such as these which occasionally cropped up, whence God only knew. For only one purpose was she ready to forget the external world, and it weighed heavily upon her mind. This was to steer these two young men, whom she loved more than her own life, out of troubled waters to secure harbors, and to see them become two happy, successful men, immune from the evils of life, providing the family serenity and peace.

FORTY-FOUR

At the end of the scholastic year, Hussein obtained the bacca-laureate. During the interval of waiting for the results of the examination to appear, the family suffered bitter doubts and fears. Nobody dared to predict how things might develop if Hussein should fail to pass or lose his exemption from fees. After her prolonged patience, it was impossible for Samira to conceive of such an outcome, or to see all her hopes in ruin.

Surrounded by his brother, his sister, and his mother, their quivering hearts palpitating with hope and fear, Hussein took the newspaper from the newsboy, cast dazed looks at it, search-ing its pages for his successful number. It was a dreadful mo-ment, indelibly imprinted on their memories. But now it was a happy day, the first happy day after two gloomy years. Their souls filled with joy, they offered their thanks to God. Their happy mood sometimes manifested itself in their gentle conver-sations, and occasionally in the prevalence of a glowing silence of reassurance. This gave them hope for tomorrow. But as they thought about the future, both near and distant, their happiness evaporated almost without their realizing it. Once more they imagined the difficulties confronting their lives. Thus these tran-sient moments of serene happiness gave way to worry and deep pensiveness.

For the first time in his life, Hassanein discovered the truth that happiness is short-lived and that sorrow and pain outlive it. Hussein used to think of his future. Of course, he had his ambitions and dreams. Yet he was aware of the unpleasant facts of life. As if probing their reaction to his success, he inquired, "What do you think my next step should be?"

The mother's greatest desire was that their miserable condition of life be terminated at any cost. All the worthwhile pieces of furniture in the flat having been sold, she knew that it was impossible for her family to continue this sort of life much longer. But she was reluctant to impose her opinions on him and control his career the way she controlled his life. He was no longer an infant. If on his own accord he agreed with her views, all well and good. But if he did not, let him choose whatever course of action he judged best for himself. In that event, the family was bound to continue as before in stoicism, fortitude, and even hunger, until God would ordain plenty and abundance for them.

"Let's think it over carefully," she said curtly.

Moved as usual by his passions, Hassanein was thinking fast, disguising his egocentricity behind what he believed to be the common good. "Life has become intolerable," he said. "We're ill-nourished and almost always hungry, our clothes torn, darned, or threadbare, and our house is empty. We shouldn't prolong our suffering. We've no choice but to become practical about our lives," he said.

Understanding his brother well, Hussein realized at once what he was driving at. Convinced though he was of the substance of his brother's argument, he was irritated at his cunning. "Why do you say 'we' when I'm the only person involved in this matter?" Hussein asked.

Realizing that his brother usually divined his ulterior motives, Hassanein became disturbed. "I'm laying down a general principle that applies to you right now and to me in the future," he said.

"You mean to say that I should find a job?"

Hassanein avoided an answer. "What do you think?" he asked.

Hussein turned to his mother. "What do you think, Mother?" he asked with a smile.

His smile affected her profoundly. She realized that he was placing his career in her hands, and that he was transferring responsibility for his future to her shoulders alone. But she would never persuade him to do anything against his will. Never, even if that meant that they must endure further humiliation for another four years. Of her three sons he was the only one who obeyed her without resentment or hesitation. So how could she permit him to become the family's sacrificial goat?

"Hussein, your opinion will be mine, too," she said unequivocally.

Hussein smiled mysteriously. Impelled by an irresponsible desire to annoy Hassanein, he said, "I'm thinking of continuing my higher education."

"You've chosen the right thing." Nefisa was pleased.

"This means four more lean years," Hassanein said hesitantly.

"No, just one more year, and at the end of it, by God's will, you'll become an employee," Hussein said with a grin.

Defeated, Hassanein laughed. "Perhaps," he said apologetically, "you think that I want you to find a job to give me a chance to continue my higher education in peace and security. But, in fact, I want to relieve our suffering family. Besides, granting that to be employed on the baccalaureate is a sacrifice, you should be the one to make this sacrifice, not because I wish to deny you something which I want to get for myself, but because our family can make use of your sacrifice right now, while it has to wait another year to make use of mine."

"This is false logic. I'm sure that you won't agree to make any sacrifices, neither this year nor the next," Hussein said, laughing.

The mother intervened to decide the matter once and for all. "Do what you like, Hussein. We've no objection," she said.

Smiling at her serenely, he remarked, "I didn't mean a word of what I said. I just wanted to make it clear to him that I understand him well enough. I don't even blame him for the way he thinks; he has his reasons. Now, one of us two has to make sacrifices and accept a job. As the elder brother and having obtained the baccalaureate, it's my duty to do so. I know how bad our circumstances are, and how wicked and cruel it would be of me to think of continuing my education. I must be content with my lot. Let's all pray to God to help us get what we want."

Despite their expressions of regret, Hussein could see relief in all their eyes. Sorry though he was, he experienced feelings of peace and pleasure. *Our family,* he thought, *has almost forgotten all sense of relief and security. I should be glad to restore some such feelings to them. Why should I regret my sacrifice? To be a teacher or a clerk is all the same to me. Had our dreams been down-to-earth, we wouldn't have subjected ourselves to sorrow and frustration.*

FORTY-FIVE

"There is Ahmad Bey Yousri, your late father's friend," Samira said to her son. "He can find a job for you overnight."

She remained for a while absorbed in her thoughts. "My overcoat is too shabby for me to put in an appearance before respectable people," she continued. "I can't go in person to him. So you go to him and take your brother along to give you courage. Only mention to the porter that you're the late Kamel Effendi's sons."

In the afternoon the two brothers went to Taher Street. Arriving at the villa, as instructed by their mother they told the porter they wished to see the Bey. After a few minutes, the porter returned to lead them to the sitting room. Walking along a path through the center of the garden, they cast astonished glances at the variety of flowers, their delightful colors enlivening the place. They climbed a flight of stairs leading to a grand reception hall. Confused, the two brothers sat close to the door in the same place their mother had chosen on her visit to the Bey two years earlier. They glanced quickly at the thick carpet covering the vast floor of the room, the many elegant seats, cushions, rich hanging rugs, gigantic curtains on the walls, and a chandelier with electric lamps suspended in a halo of dazzling light from a high ceiling.

Pointing to the chandelier, Hassanein said, "It's like the chandelier in the mosque of Saidna al-Hussein."

Hussein was preoccupied with other matters. "Yes," he said. "But forget about the chandelier. What should we say to him? You must use your tongue to help me!"

"Do you think that you'll be addressing the devil?" Hassanein said sarcastically. "Speak boldly, and I'll speak too. Damn him!"

His curse, free from resentment, was intended to encourage his brother as well as himself. He was stunned by the luxurious surroundings.

"Do you think Ahmad Bey's heirs will be sorry when he dies?" he asked in a low voice.

"Wouldn't we be sorry for our father's death if he were rich?" Hussein said.

Pondering, Hassanein knit his eyebrows. "I think we would," he said. "But perhaps sorrow has different shades and gradations. Oh! Why wasn't our father a rich man?"

"This is another question."

"But it's an all-important one. Tell me, how did this Bey get rich?"

"Perhaps he was born wealthy."

Hassanein's hazel eyes glistened. "We must all be rich," he said.

"And if this is impossible?"

"Then we must all be poor."

"And if this is impossible, too?"

"In that case we must revolt, murder, and steal," he replied angrily.

"This is exactly what mankind has been doing for thousands of years," Hussein remarked with a smile.

"It pains me to think of spending our lives in toil and squalor until we die."

"God forbid." Hussein smiled.

Before Hassanein could open his mouth again, they heard footsteps approaching from the veranda. Then the Bey entered, his tall, broad body garbed in a white silk suit. As he shook their hands in welcome, his laughing eyes scrutinized their faces. He said to them as he sat down, "Welcome to the sons of the dear departed. How is your mother?"

The two young men thanked him simultaneously. The man's warm welcome thawed Hassanein's resentment, but Hussein's confusion returned. Ahmad Bey was afraid this meeting might involve demands for his assistance. He took it for granted that, if a request was made, he would have to comply with it. Though he was not a miser, his generosity was not voluntary. He would be upset and annoyed to be asked for help but would act generously, unable to turn down any such request.

Overcoming his confusion, Hussein spoke in a soft, courteous voice, so full of supplication and entreaty that his words seemed superfluous. "Sir, I have obtained the baccalaureate. Our family circumstances force me to look for a job. My mother has sent me to Your Excellency, and we all have great hope that you would kindly extend a helping hand to us."

The Bey ran his fingers through his thick dyed mustache.

"A job?!" he said. "Chances of government employment are very slim nowadays. But I shall do my best, my son. I don't think I'll be able to find a job for you at the Ministry of Interior, but the Under Secretary of State for Education is my friend, and so is that of the Ministry of War. Fill out an application form, and I'll write a strong letter of recommendation for you."

Thanking him for his kind generosity, they made their farewells and departed. As they moved away, Hassanein gave the villa a last glance. Turning his eyes to his brother's face, he found him absorbed in a contented reverie. Hassanein wondered if today his brother was rejoicing over what he had considered sacrifice the day before.

"After breathing the fragrant breeze of the full life which blows from this villa, I'm sure we can hardly count ourselves among the living," he said.

Hussein was too preoccupied with thoughts of his employment application and the letter of recommendation to pay attention to his brother, who resentfully said, "I wonder at your calm contentment! But the pretense doesn't deceive me."

"What use is discontent?! It won't change the world," Hussein replied with a smile.

"But the world must change. There can be no doubt that we

have a right to live in a clean house, eat healthy food, and enjoy a proper social status. As I look back over our life, I see that it has been no good at all."

Hussein gazed curiously at his brother, who failed to comprehend the significance of his glance.

"Yet you enjoy love and will continue your education. Isn't this good enough for you?" Hussein asked.

Hassanein cast a glance at his brother. He wondered what Hussein had meant by these words. He felt ill at ease and his annoyance redoubled. He gave vent to his pent-up feelings. "Hasn't our misery driven you to sacrifice yourself?" he inquired. "We've elementary rights, none of which should be put aside. But where are we? How do we live? Through what sufferings our mother goes! What is Hassan's status? And how is it possible that our sister has become a dressmaker?"

His peace of mind disturbed, Hussein frowned. Ignoring the essential point of his brother's argument, he cried reproachfully in his brother's face, "A dressmaker!"

Filled with excitement and agitation, Hassanein replied, "Yes. A dressmaker! Do you sincerely hate this? Do you really wish she was married like other girls?! That's a lie. If she had married, or even if she hadn't worked as a dressmaker, both of us would have stopped going to school and been forced to take any menial jobs we could find. This is the truth."

Hussein's anger increased, not because his brother's words had failed to convince him, but because, in his heart, he believed them to be true. He knew that he wouldn't have welcomed his sister's marriage and consequent happiness. *We devour one another*, he thought. *We should be pleased with Hassan's buffoonery and frivolity as long as he visits us every month and brings along a leg of mutton. We should also be pleased with our sister the dressmaker as long as she provides us with our dry morsels of bread. And this rebellious young man should be pleased that I am discontinuing my education so that he can continue his own. We devour one another. What a brutal life this is! Perhaps my only consolation is that a superior power grinds and devours us all. But we struggle and fight back.* This last thought brought him calm and peace.

No. We do not devour one another, he told his brother silently. *Say no such thing* (he was unaware that his brother had not, in fact, said any such thing). *Never say such a thing. We're a miserable family and countless other families are in the same boat. It's the duty of each one of us to make every sacrifice.*

Then, as they reached the doorstep, in a firm voice he asked his brother to stop arguing.

FORTY-SIX

Hussein realized that his job, for which he was willing to sacrifice so much, was not easily obtainable. He had already spent three whole months in anguish and despair, paying frequent visits to Ahmad Bey Yousri's villa and to the Ministries of War and Education. At length the Bey informed him that he had managed to appoint him as a clerk at the secondary school in Tanta, and persuaded him to appear before the Medical Commission and prepare himself to leave for Tanta to start work on the first of October.

The young man was pleased, as was his family, but their pleasure was tinged with bitterness. Samira had been looking forward impatiently to this appointment, hoping that it would rescue the family from its misery. But his appointment in a distant town frustrated these hopes. As she wavered between joy and regret, Samira realized in her perplexity that the job would offer the family very little relief. Her son's travel and living expenses in Cairo and Tanta were bound to exhaust his income from the job. Besides, on the horizon there appeared the dreadful shadow of a new separation, for which the family was not yet prepared and which was a source of pain to them. Samira wondered at her luck, grim even while it smiled at her, which caused her to be separated from the only son who never gave her trouble, and in whom she saw an image of herself, her calm and her patience. From Hussein's company she derived comfort and solace which she could not find in any of her other children. He was not her favorite son; the naughty Hassanein was her darling. But at this particular moment Hussein seemed the most precious element in her existence. He had never been away from his family for a single day, and so his sorrow at the parting was great. His feeling was accentuated both by his deep attachment to his family and by his crushed hope that, living among them, he would bring some relief. He had frequently looked forward to restoring Nefisa to her former station, a respectable mistress in the house, as soon as he cashed his first salary check from the government. But he saw his dream vanishing into thin air. Tomorrow he would leave his dear family, leaving them in almost the same unfortunate condition.

This, perhaps, was the reason why he went once more to Ahmad Bey Yousri, begging him to use his influence to keep him in Cairo. But now the Bey was fed up with him; he told him that his wish was too difficult to fulfill at present. With no money to live on in Tanta until he cashed his first salary check at the beginning of the month, Hussein was confronted by a new problem. How could he obtain these initial funds? He turned to his sister, Nefisa, but she always gave her mother the bulk of her limited earnings, keeping almost nothing for herself except some money for essential clothes. Even if the rest of the furniture was sold, the proceeds would be too meager to meet his requirements.

Thus he thought of Hassan as the only possible source. He confided his thoughts to his mother, who agreed. She had no doubt that her eldest son would come to their rescue if it was at all possible for him to do so. She gave Hussein his brother's address. He set out at once for Clot Bey Street, and there started to search for Gandab alley. At the beginning of his journey, his heart was filled with great hopes. Gradually hope gave way to anxiety, until he finally wondered whether Hassan would really give him what he needed, and whether he might lose the job just because of his inability to obtain a few pounds.

By the time he had found his way to the alley at last, his mood was one of painful pessimism. It was a narrow, zigzagging alley, with dilapidated houses on both sides, its polluted air permeated by the smell of fried fish, crowded with people and cluttering handcarts, and the echoes of hawkers advertising their wares was interspersed with abusive language, rattling coughs, and the sound of people gathering spittle in their throats and spewing it into the street. The ground, covered with dust, vegetable litter, and animal dung, was a gradual incline, so that the alley appeared to be constructed on top of a hill. Hussein went to number seventeen, an ancient two-story house. So strikingly narrow was it that it seemed more like a huge pillar than a dwelling. Not far from its entrance sat a woman selling pips, peanuts, and *dome,* the fruit of palm trees. Hesitantly he entered the house. As he climbed the spiral stairs, which had no banister, his nostrils were filled with a putrefying odor. When he reached the second floor, he knocked at the door. He was extremely afraid he might not find his brother at home, and his fear was intensified when nobody opened the door for him. Violently and desperately, he kept knocking until his hands ached. In his despondency he stood there, not knowing what to do. He was about to move away when he heard a rough voice inside, shouting angrily, "Who is this son of a bitch knocking at the door at such an early hour?"

Hussein's heart pounded with delight. Answering the voice, which he well recognized as that of his brother, he said, "Hassan! It's me, Hussein."

"Hussein!" The voice sounded astonished. Then Hussein heard the rattle of the bolt being lifted. As the door was opened, he saw Hassan, his hair unruly and disorderly, his eyes swollen and bloodshot. Extending a hand to greet his brother, Hassan shouted in surprise, "Hussein! You're welcome. Come in. I hope no calamity has brought you here. What's the matter?"

Rather confused, Hussein entered. Soon his nose was filled with the odor of incense, its sweet fragrance sharply contrasting with the horrible smell emerging from the staircase. He found himself in a darkened corridor with two rooms, one on the right of the entrance, the other facing it to the left. Smiling apologetically at his brother, Hussein said, "Have I come early? It's eleven o'clock."

Hassan yawned. "I usually get up in the afternoon. Singers work by night and sleep by day," he said, laughing. "But before anything else, tell me, how is our family?"

"Thanks to God, they are well. How is everything?"

Accompanying his brother to the room on the right, Hassan said, "Thanks to God, everything is all right."

They entered a small room, nearly partitioned into two halves, one containing a bed, the other a wardrobe, with a sofa between them next to the inside wall. Hanging above the sofa was a big photograph of Hassan with a very dark-skinned, fleshy woman leaning on his shoulder, her arms around his neck. As Hussein fixed his eyes on her, his astonishment caught his brother's attention.

"What are you thinking about?" Hassan asked, laughing.

"Have you married, my brother?" Hussein asked naively.

Asking Hussein to sit on the sofa, Hassan jumped on the bed and squatted there. "Almost," he answered.

"Are you engaged?"

"Neither married nor engaged."

"What do you mean?"

"I mean the third state!"

Dumbfounded, the young man raised his astonished eyes to Hassan. He smiled mechanically in spite of himself. A feeling akin to shyness appeared on his face. Hassan laughed aloud.

"Even without a marriage contract, she's my wife in every possible sense," he said lightly.

"Aren't you alone now?" Hussein asked fearfully.

Nodding his head affirmatively, he yawned aloud like a braying donkey. "Of course, you won't tell anybody about it," he cautioned.

"Of course."

"I don't want to hurt the family's feelings, that's all. By the way, have you had any experience with the female sex?" Hassan asked with a laugh.

Shyly, the young man shook his head no.

"Nor Hassanein?" Hassan continued.

Hussein's heart pounded with fear and pain for no obvious reason. "Nor Hassanein," he said.

Hassan became thoughtful. "That's better for you," he remarked. "If one day you intend to marry," he adding, laughing, "come to me and I'll supply you with wonderful bits of advice."

"I'm not thinking of marriage, as you know," Hussein said calmly.

"Is it possible that Hassanein will get married before you?"

His heart shook, but he said quietly, "This is certain, since he is bound by an old promise."

"Anyhow, when Hassanein finishes his studies, no obstacle will get in his way!" Hassan was moved. "Oh! By the way, what's the latest news about the job you are searching for?"

Hussein was delighted by the opportunity Hassan was affording him to bring up the subject.

"I've come to tell you that I've been appointed a clerk at the secondary school in Tanta, and I'll be starting my work on the first of October," he said.

"Will you travel to Tanta?" Hassan asked with astonishment. "What use, then, will it be to Mother if you live in Tanta?"

"Little use. But what's to be done?"

"This is really bad luck. This is the result of school education!"

To overcome his confusion, Hussein smiled. Summoning up his courage, he said, "I should be leaving by the end of September. As you know, government salaries are paid at the end of the month."

Hassan realized what his brother was driving at before Hussein finished speaking, and as he pondered it, he allowed no trace of his thoughts to appear on his face.

"How much of a salary do you expect?" he asked.

"Seven pounds."

"How foolish of Mother to have sent you to school! And, of course, you have not a millieme of the money needed to cover your travel and living expenses for the month of October?"

Hussein smiled resignedly, wondering at the embarrassment and confusion the situation had caused him; it was as if he were asking a stranger for help. His mind active, Hassan silently continued to stare at him. *Hussein comes to me at an inappropriate time. I'm expecting some money. But I'm not sure when it will come. Right now I'm empty-handed, entirely empty-handed. Damn him! I can't tell him the truth. Let hell destroy us all before I ever do. He has a pressing need for the money and he must obtain it. The future of the family depends on these few pounds. In fact, he doesn't need much, just the price of a few pounds of hashish. In one week's time, a reckless young man would spend such a sum of money on the women of Darb Tiab. Sana'a herself is hard up. I don't keep anything for her. I must help him. But how? Why did he wait until today to come see me? How long will my family remain a source of pain to me?* Silently, he continued to gaze at his brother, until the latter's heart was stricken with worry and fear. Suddenly Hassan moved away from the bed. Reaching the wardrobe, he opened a drawer. After fumbling in it for a few minutes, he returned to his place on the bed. Holding four gold bracelets in his hand, he stretched it out to his brother.

"Take these bracelets and sell them at once, for whatever you can get for them," he said hurriedly.

Hussein's hand failed to move as his eyes opened wide, disturbed and disapproving. "What's this? Whose bracelets are these?" he shouted in spite of himself.

Annoyed by his brother's disquiet, Hassan said simply, "They are Sana'a my wife bracelets!"

"By what right should I take them?"

"Your brother is giving them to you. You've nothing to do with their owner."

Deeply disturbed, Hussein wondered what sort of life his

brother lived. "I don't feel comfortable about taking them. Isn't there some other solution?"

This show of dignity made Hassan angry. "If you're this scrupulous, just leave them. I've nothing else to give you," he said dryly.

At first Hussein was skeptical. But after examining Hassan's face and realizing the genuineness of his expression, he felt annoyed and degraded. *A woman's bracelets! And what a woman!* he thought. *This is both impossible and unbelievable. I wouldn't have conceived of it, nor would I have believed this could happen to me even in a nightmare. How could I possibly respect myself afterward?! Should I refuse the bracelets? What's to be done if I do? He doesn't have any other money. I should believe him. I can't lose the job either! What would I do if I lost it? I can't refuse. Nor can I accept! I must refuse! But I cannot.* He kept wavering back and forth, unable to decide. *Only one thing deserves to be cursed,* he thought. *That's life. Yes, life and luck, and the two parents that have brought me into this world. Not caring a damn, my father used to play on his lute strings!* He started with alarm. *May I be destroyed! How dare I think so! The image of his corpse is indelibly imprinted on my memory. May God's mercy fall upon him. He was not the one to blame. We are all like chickens, scratching our food from the dirt. And Hassanein and Bahia meet in the chicken coop on the roof. How disgusting! Let me then refuse. But in order to survive we have to submit. Nobody would know anything about it. Still, I'll remember it as long as I live, and my shame will last for the rest of my life! He is waiting for me to decide. Either I submit or perish! I'll take them as a debt to be paid off when I have enough. No, I'm deceiving myself. No, I'm honest and I'll pay off my debt. If I don't refuse, I'll never be able to claim that I'm an honest man. I'm hungry. Honest but hungry. And I'll not refuse. Damn this life! Now I realize what drove my brother to live in this lair. Our family is lost and life is cruel. I must come to a decision before my head bursts. Like chickens . . .*

"What do you think?" came Hassan's voice.

Stunned, Hussein raised his eyes to him, his brother's voice fearful in its effect. Hassan was still holding the bracelets in his hand. Lowering his eyes, Hussein shyly said, "Thank you for your generosity, which I accept willingly. I beg you to consider this a debt, which I'll pay off when, by God's will, I have enough."

"Accept it as a present, if you like. And tell Mother that I borrowed the money from Mr. Ali Sabri."

Hassan's mention of his mother aroused his resentment and gave him acute pain. As he took the bracelets and put them in his pocket, his resentment doubled.

"Sorry to have disturbed you. I think I should be leaving so that you can get back to your nap," Hussein said.

Stretching out his hand in farewell, Hassan smiled and pressed his brother's hand. "May God give you safe conduct. My regards to everybody, and tell Mother that I'll visit her shortly," he said.

Disapproving and resentful, Hussein left the house. Climbing cautiously down the stairs with no handrail, he was so absorbed in his thoughts that he paid no attention to the putrefying odor.

FORTY-SEVEN

The members of the family were gathering in the brothers' room, which henceforth would become Hassanein's alone. As she cast a glance at Hussein's face, Nefisa's heart was pierced with pain.

"Oh, God! This will be the last night our family will be together!" she cried.

On hearing these words, their mother felt stabbed in the heart, despite the great patience life had taught her. Nevertheless, she smiled, or rather she forced a smile on her dry lips.

"Hussein is a mature man," she said. "He can manage to live by himself with no trouble or confusion. I'm completely certain that he won't forget us. He will always remember us as we shall always remember him. Don't be silly, darling, this is life. Painful though it is, the members of every family are eventually bound to part happily from one another, for each has his or her own role to perform in life."

Hussein knew his mother so well that he realized that she was hiding her sorrow under a cloak of wisdom and firmness, as she often did. So he decided to grapple firmly with his own sense of desolation. Like a child, he had wept bitterly. But he was determined not to weep again. Imitating his mother's smile, he murmured, "We shall meet during holidays. Perhaps I'll be transferred to Cairo one day."

"This is bound to happen one day," Hassanein remarked thoughtfully.

Hassanein felt melancholy and depressed. He had never been separated from his brother, not since he was born. He did not know how to face life without him. Hussein was a brother and friend to him. Though there were many occasions for dispute between them, and they sometimes even quarreled, they were indispensable to each other. Had Bahia been less stubborn, he would never have complained of loneliness. Yet he consoled himself in parting from his brother by the thought of writing letters to him every now and then. Perhaps during holidays he could travel to Tanta to see him. Could he hope to receive a monthly sum of money from Hussein, perhaps fifty or thirty piasters, especially since the fees he received from private lessons were discontinued at the end of the school year? How he wished he had enough nerve to confide his hopes to his brother. But he persuaded himself to be patient, postponing this matter until a more favorable occasion.

Samira's mind continued to churn. She was pleased that she had succeeded in maintaining an appearance of composure. However, this evening the agony in her heart reached its peak. She experienced a mysterious sense of remorse for the favoritism she had showed Hassanein and the sacrifice of the best part of herself for his sake. But what had things come to?! Hussein, her meek son, had accepted the sacrifice of his career and the suffering of loneliness for the sake of his family, and for Hassanein in particular. Her pain was intensified by the feeling that it was her duty to speak to Hussein, with detachment and no evidence of emotion, about a sore subject; she must disguise her actual purpose, the defense of family interests, by giving the impression that her real motive was love. Tenderly and compassionately, she looked at Hussein as she arranged his clothes in his father's suitcase.

"You're wise, and that gives me reassurance. Above all, I hope you will continue your gentlemanly conduct in your new surroundings and avoid evil company," she said.

"Mother, rest entirely assured about this," Hussein answered with a smile.

However, the reference to "evil company" evoked in his mind the image of Gandab alley, the stair without banisters, and the gold bracelets. Dispirited, his face lost its glowing smile. He bent over the suitcase to hide his sadness.

"Don't forget your family," his mother continued. "I know there is no need to remind you of this, but I must tell you that we shall need your help until Hassanein gets a job and Nefisa gets married."

"This was my only reason for accepting the job."

Horror-stricken, Nefisa shuddered. The word "marry" pierced her soul, and she imagined it disclosed her secret. Did her mother still have such hopes? Didn't she know that her daughter would rather die than marry? She cast a curious glance at Hussein's face. He was in the dark about what had happened. None of them could have possibly imagined it. Impossible! As the room swam before her eyes, she saw them gazing at her in demented fury, their fiery, bulging eyes flaming with anger and preying like monsters on her flesh. She shook her head to banish these horrible fantasies. Eventually she managed to recognize her surroundings for what they really were. But in spite of herself, she soon remembered the hours of her weakness when she had been seduced, overcome by the sexual urge brought about by her despair and poverty. In these hours of weakness, forgetting everything but her thirsty, unsatiated desire, she felt like mutilating herself. Now, struck dumb in the presence of her family, she remembered those awful hours; she was overwhelmed with painful shame and soundless fear. She kept looking curiously from her mother to her brothers. Though, of course, it was too late to repair the damage, she still saw a chance to retreat. But ... Oh, God! She did not know what to say. What use was it now? What hope did life hold out for her? She was doomed to self-destruction.

"Keep the money you need to meet your living expenses, and send us the rest of your salary," Samira went on. "You must do so, Hussein. We've nothing more in the house that is worth selling."

"I'll do my best."

Since their mother had asked for the rest of Hussein's salary, Hassanein almost lost hope of receiving an allowance from his brother. While Hussein's appointment might afford his family some relief, Hassanein would remain badly in need of money, especially during the long summer holidays. He wondered, once he had a job, whether his mother would have similar claims upon him! Impossible! By the time he finished his studies, his mother would be relieved of her most burdensome family duties. So it would be possible for him to marry and look after himself. Nefisa and Hussein being the victims of these difficult times, they had to face the storm at its most violent. He felt pity and sympathy for them, but he rejoiced that his prospects were more cheerful than theirs.

Without revealing all her thoughts, Samira wished to put Hussein on his guard against the snares of marriage. She was well aware that many parents easily laid traps for bachelors, away from their homes, to marry their daughters. But she was at a loss as to how to raise this point with Hussein, seeing that Hassanein, his younger brother, still a youngster in school, was already engaged and preparing to marry. Reluctantly she relinquished the idea of broaching this subject. However, she had confidence in Hussein's prudence and wise judgment.

The family conversation rambled on for a long time about various matters, and Farid Effendi and his family came to say goodbye to Hussein. They were, as usual, warmly welcomed. Their affection, generosity, and neighborliness were held in high esteem. Perhaps, since Hassanein's unofficial engagement to Bahia, a change of mood had come over some members of his family. Samira, for example, believed that they had used stratagems to capture her green young son and take from her the most dazzling of her family's hopes. Moreover, it was impossible for Nefisa to love anyone who aimed at possessing Hassanein. But these unspoken sentiments failed to weaken the ties of affection and brotherliness binding the two families. Samira could not possibly forget Farid Effendi's helpfulness and kindness, and Hussein was delighted by this farewell visit. He felt deeply grateful to this dear family, the Effendi, his wife, the girl Bahia, and his former pupil Salem. Gently and sincerely, they conversed about past memories and present hopes.

"Congratulations on the job," Hussein heard them say to him. "We've come to bid you goodbye and wish you a safe journey. We'll miss you a lot. It's a pity that Salem has lost an incomparable teacher."

Shy and reserved though she was, Bahia said to him gently, "You'll return to us shortly, by God's will."

With both tongue and heart he thanked her for her gentleness.

A really beautiful girl, he thought, *refined and decent. Hassanein is a splendid young man and he'll be a splendid husband. Has he kissed those charming lips? He has long complained and grumbled about her modesty. How wonderfully rare is this girl! But I leave tomorrow. These people will turn into mere images and memories. They'll get together often again as in the past, just as they are now. Yet they may remember me only a little, or perhaps not at all. But how shall I be? And where? In my loneliness, is there anything for me to do but remember them? The greater my misfortune, the stronger and more patient I become. And I'll remain so forever!*

FORTY-EIGHT

Hassanein's face disappeared amidst a crowd of people and their farewells. The pyramid-shaped ceiling of the Cairo railway station receded until the inside appeared obscure. Everything was receding faster and faster. Hussein bade Cairo goodbye. He withdrew his head inside the carriage, and sitting in a proper posture, he closed his eyes to hide a tear that had long contended with his self-composure. Quickly he winked, to shake it from his eyelashes. To his left sat an Effendi reading his newspaper, while in front of him two villagers were conversing. Though the carriage was only half full, the noise of the passengers was louder than the rattle of the train's wheels. His sadness had been tempered when he saw a tear in Hassanein's eyes. Conversing together on the platform, the two brothers had maintained their composure, but tears gushed to Hussein's eyes as the train started to move and he saw Hassanein waving to him. At home, Nefisa had wept so bitterly that her eyes became swollen. How pitifully and tenderly he recalled her ugly face! His mother, at whom he forced himself to smile, took him to her breast and kissed him on the cheeks. Perhaps she was doing this for the first time! At least he could not remember that she had ever kissed him before. By temperament, she was very firm with them. But this apparent firmness could not obliterate her deep tenderness. She believed farewell tears to be an ill omen, and preferred to keep her tears in check, but he realized that her convulsing lids foreshadowed the profuse tears that would soon gush from her eyes behind a closed door.

Perhaps she wept for a long time, he thought. *Perhaps she is still weeping.* At this thought he felt profoundly depressed. As he realized that he had never seen her weep before his father's death, his depression became more intense. *What a great woman she is! God has ordained that a mortal catastrophe would befall our family. Yet His Grace has also ordained this woman to be our mother. What might our fate have been without her? I wonder how she managed to feed and clothe us! How, too, could she have managed to control and direct us? How was it possible for her, under such cruel circumstances, to fulfill our family needs! This is a miracle that baffles the mind. But for my late father, she would even have made a different man of Hassan. I should speak of Hassan with more consideration. Without his help I would have lost my job. His money is all I have to live on until the end of the month! The bracelets! What a dreadful memory! Yet in order to live, I have to forget. One day I shall pay off the debt and draw the curtain on this most painful memory.*

To flee from his thoughts, he looked out the window. He saw the vast fields extending to meet the horizon, green, blooming, and delightful, the tops of their growing plants swaying in a constant gentle breeze. Here and there peasants and bulls and grazing cattle appeared like dummies swallowed up in the vast fields. An autumnal sky above, white and pale, was receding here and there into lakes of pure blue. The train hurried by a crystal-clear brook, the melting rays of the sun on its surface turning its waters into dazzling mercury. As though swimming in space with the monotonous sound of the throbbing engine as an accompaniment, the telegraph wires moved regularly in endless waves. Looking again at the endless flat earth, mute, patient, and good, he thought again of his mother. Like the green earth, she was as patient, as generous, and as exhausted by time. Poor woman! Her shabby clothes made it impossible for her to visit respectable people! His eyes filled with tears, and the scene lost its charm. He prayed to God to give him the wherewithal to relieve his stoical mother and patient family. *How curious that Egypt unmercifully devours its own offspring!* he thought. *Yet they say we are a contented people. Oh, God! This is the height of human misery! Nay, it is the height of human misery to be miserable and contented! This is death itself. But for our poverty, I would have continued my education. There is no doubt about it. In our country fortune and respectable professions are hereditary in certain families. I am not spiteful, but sad; sad for myself and for millions of others like myself. I am not just an oppressed individual, but a representative of an oppressed people. This is what generates in me the spirit of resistance, filling me with a kind of consoling happiness for which I know no name. No. I am neither spiteful nor desperate. Even though I have missed the opportunity of higher education, Hassanein, my brother, will not. Perhaps Nefisa will find a suitable husband. Once the soul returns to our family, we will remember the dark days with pride.*

Turning to his left, he saw that the Effendi, with a bored expression on his face, had folded his newspaper. As if he had been waiting for this casual turn of the head from Hussein, the Effendi, without any preliminaries, waved the folded newspaper and began to speak.

"But for the students, the leaders of this country would never have united. Who would ever have imagined that Sidki would agree to meet with Nahas? The Palace and the Wafdists at the same table!"

Hussein welcomed the conversation with relief. "That is true, sir," he said.

"Who could ever have believed the British would recognize Egypt as an independent, sovereign state and agree to abandon their four reservations. Do you really think the capitulations will be abolished?"

"I do."

"Nahas will remain in office forever," the man said jubilantly. "The time for coups is over now. Are you a Wafdist?"

"Yes."

"I thought so, from the good-natured expression on your face. A true patriot must be a Wafdist. Apart from the advantages of coalition, the Liberal Constitutionalists are Englishmen wearing tarbushes."

"True, indeed."

"Are you traveling to Alexandria?"

"No, just to Tanta."

"May the mercy of the saintly Sidi Badawi be upon us! I've spent some years in Tanta."

Hussein looked interested. "I'm a new employee. Could you direct me to a modest hotel?" he asked.

The man rubbed his chin with his hand as he tried to remember.

"Go to the Britannia Hotel on Al Amir Farouk Street, owned by Michel Kustandi," he said. "There you can have a room for one pound fifty a month."

Then they conversed for a long time, comparing life in hotels and flats.

FORTY-NINE

His room at the hotel was small, containing a single bed, a wardrobe, a wooden chair, and a peg. There was only one window, overlooking a narrow back alley and facing the wall of an old house that shut out the sun. The room's atmosphere betrayed a latent humidity. Other rooms in the hotel overlooked Al Amir Farouk Street, but since the price was exorbitant, he had chosen to live in this modest room.

It's only right that I should live at the same standard as my family in Nasr Allah alley, he thought, *with old houses on both sides.*

In his new lodging, the first thing he did was open the window. Driven by curiosity, he looked out. He saw a mean blind alley with old houses on both sides. He wondered at the vast difference between this and the street from which it branched off. Glancing at the wall of the house which shut out the open air, he felt annoyed. He was certain that his life, lonely as it was, would be devoid of entertainment, too. Turning from the window to the mirror in the wardrobe, he saw a bizarre reflection of his image. His face appeared long and his features distorted in the mirror's pale flyspecked surface. Laughing, he said to his own image, "With God's mercy and grace, I'm handsomer than you are."

He proceeded to take off his clothes and put on his gallabiya. Then he put his few clothes in order inside the wardrobe, which, small as it was, still looked nearly empty. In fact, he owned only one suit, two gallabiyas, and two pairs of flannels and pants. These were not only old but also darned and patched. For reassurance, he thrust his hand into the jacket pocket, taking out a packet of pound notes. After counting them, he returned the money to its place with painful memories.

He squatted on the bed, not knowing how to spend the rest of the day. With no one to talk to and nothing to do, he became totally absorbed in his thoughts and dreams. He felt lonely and surprised, realizing that he would suffer bitterly from the boredom of ample leisure time. He loved reading, but even if he were able to buy whatever books he liked, he would still find leisure time oppressive. He was not accustomed to heavy silence. In his mute loneliness he felt like a lost, trivial person for whom nobody cared or had the slightest consideration.

Where is Hassanein's sharp, hysterical voice, always bursting out laughing or complaining? he thought. *Where is Nefisa's thin one, and her daily satirical comments on neighbors and events?*

He refused to surrender to his feelings, and decided to work out his budget and calculate his expenses. His salary was only seven pounds. In his precarious circumstances, this sum would not have been inadequate. He would spend one pound and fifty piasters on the room, and not more than two pounds, under any circumstances, on his daily meals of beans for breakfast, a plateful of vegetables with meat, a plateful of rice and a loaf of bread for dinner, and Tahania sweets or cheese for supper. In emergencies, he could even forgo his supper, as he and his family often did during the past two years. Whatever his circumstances, he would never allow his stomach to give him trouble or play havoc with his budget. He should rise above such mundane matters. Now, immune from Hassanein's opposition, he could resolve this question. This austerity was not only tolerable but more satisfying than gluttony. He would also give two pounds to his mother. He was well aware that this was far too little and wished he could give her double the sum. But he could not help it, for after deducting the taxes due, only one pound and fifty piasters would remain of his salary to meet incidental and clothing expenses. Bewildered, he thought of saving up even a tiny sum. To him, life was unbearable without economizing, no matter how little. Reared by a mother such as his, he could not possibly conceive of living without economizing.

In fact, in political terms, his mother's position was analogous to that of Germany in relation to the other countries, in her ability to turn even garbage into grist for her mill. She would patch trousers; then despairing of patching them any more, she would turn them. Despairing again of turning, she would cut them up and use one part of the cloth as a skullcap and the rest as a cleaning cloth. Any remaining cloth was thrown away only when it was reduced to frayed tatters. And so he felt the need to economize. The cruelty of life, assaulting his family merci-lessly, made these thoughts a sort of creed. At this stage of his thinking, he became prey to the same poverty-generated fears that had hounded his family. Since occasions for extra expenses were innumerable, they always dreaded that they might exceed the limits of their income if one of them fell ill, or the school authorities asked them to pay fees for one reason or another, or if Nefisa should stop earning money for a period of time; the list of potential disasters was endless. In these ruminations, he experienced a gnawing pain, as he remembered his mother's dry face with its bulging veins, an incarnation of patience and sor-row. Miserable and ugly though it was, hers was of all faces the dearest to his heart. Curiously enough, now that he was con-scious of his ability to relieve his mother's burden, he felt a breeze blowing upon him. As of tomorrow he would be a gov-ernment employee. Sooner or later Hassanein, too, would be-come an employee of higher rank. All his life he would say with pride that he had been content with an intermediate certificate to help his brother obtain a higher one. Would Hassanein re-member this sacrifice? Hassanein seemed to be self-engrossed, though undoubtedly intelligent and industrious. But he ...! Away from home, Hussein felt he should not be critical of his brother. How great was his longing to see Hassanein! And how much greater was his longing to engage in argument with him.

The whistle of a train shattered the prevailing silence and interrupted his thoughts. His heart quivered. The hotel was not far from the railroad station, so every now and then the bustle of the trains was bound to remind him of Cairo and its people. Memories of the last farewells returned to him, and his aching heart overflowed with an intense yearning to see his family. A cloud of loneliness and melancholy darkened his heart.

Perhaps this is the price I have to pay for my first day of separation. However, gradually I shall get accustomed to it, he consoled himself. He was at a loss as to what to do. Should he spend most of the day in this room, or should he go out and have a look around this new town? The idea of writing a letter to his brother rescued him from these conflicting thoughts. He began writing, describing his journey, the hotel, Kustandi its owner, his room, and his longing for the family. He sent his regards to his mother and Nefisa. Then he paused, wondering whether it was good form to send his regards to Bahia, too. Here he felt uncertain. Should he mention her by name or refer to her as his brother's fiancée, or should he be content to send his general greetings to Farid Effendi's family. Finally, after much hesitation, he chose the latter course.

FIFTY

He left his room early in the morning. But he found Al Kha-
waga, the foreigner, Michel Kustandi, sitting at his old desk at
the bottom of the staircase. The hotel owner asked him if he
kept anything valuable in his room. Hussein smilingly said, "I
keep my valuables in my pocket." Then he hurried out into
the street and went to a restaurant that served beans, which
he had discovered the day before at the farthest end of town.
As he ate his breakfast, his attention was particularly drawn
by a salad of roasted peas, the likes of which did not exist in
Cairo.

He continued to walk around town until nine o'clock, when
he went to the secondary school to introduce himself to the chief
clerk and begin his official assignment. The sight of the school
filled him with agitation, and recent memories returned to him
as if in a dream.

Once Hussein had introduced himself at the gate, the porter
accompanied him to the chief clerk's office, asking him to wait
until the official arrived. Sitting in a chair close to the desk,
Hussein looked through the open door at the school playground, enveloped in heavy silence. In a week the scholastic
year would start, and the school would be teeming with life. He
remembered how only a few months earlier he had been spending his happiest hours at school in a similar playground, and
how the sight of any of the school employees had filled his heart
with awe. Now he had become one of these employees. Yet he
did not surrender to conceit. As a schoolboy, he might have
dreamt of becoming a counselor or a minister, but appointed to
the government service, he would not be more than an eighth-
grade employee. Before long, his ears were struck by a rough

cough and a deep clearing of the throat, followed by a vehement expectoration. Immediately he saw a short man with a delicate body, round-faced and bleary-eyed, his bald head shining as he swept hurriedly into the room. Seizing his tarbush with one hand, he used the other to dry his bald head with a handkerchief. No sooner did he see the young man than he shouted at him, "How, in the name of God, the Benevolent and Merciful, did you get here? Did you spend last night in my room? Are you a new pupil?"

Hussein stood up, embarrassed. "Sir, I'm the new clerk, Hussein Kamel Ali," he said.

The man burst out laughing. But soon the cough and the throat clearing returned. His mouth filled again with spittle. Looking around in perplexity, he rushed out of the room and was absent for half a minute, then returned, his condition improved.

"Damn this cold," he said apologetically. "I catch cold at the beginning of every season of the year. Thus you find me always torn between the seasons of the year and the seasons of the school. Excuse me, Hussein Effendi. I should have greeted you first. Peace be upon thee."

Smiling, Hussein extended his hand, greeting him more warmly. Sitting at his desk, the man asked him to have a seat. Hussein complied.

"My name is Hassan Hassan Hassan," the chief clerk began. "It is the custom in our family for the father to call his elder son by his own name. Haven't you heard of the Hassan family in Beheira province? You haven't? It doesn't matter. These curs of pupils call me Hassan cubed—see? Hassan³!"

Hussein laughed heartily. The man stared at him critically with bleary eyes.

"Why are you laughing?" he said. "Haven't you got rid of your schoolboy mentality? By the way, I should like to tell you something about myself. Though I'm a very nervous man, I'm very good-hearted. Many a time, without meaning any harm and being fully respectful, I curse people, no matter how high their position may be. Please understand me and don't forget I'm as old as your father!"

Hussein was very confused.

"By God's will, nothing will happen between us to make you angry."

"I hope so, by God's will. I just wanted to give you an idea about myself. That's all. Many a time I curse myself, too! Cursing is often a relief. But for that, many people would have suffocated to death in anger. Soon you'll learn what it means to work at a school." He sighed. "The ministerial letter concerning your appointment has arrived." He ruffled through his papers until he found it. "It's Number 1,175, dated September 26, 1936. You've come at the time when we need you most. For now, we shall start revising the lists of names and fees. The former clerk married the daughter of an inspector at the Ministry and all of a sudden was transferred to Cairo. Are you married, Hussein Effendi?"

"I was only a pupil last spring," Hussein answered with a smile.

"Do you think that being a pupil prevents one from getting married? I was married when I was a secondary school pupil. This is another custom in our family, like calling the elder son by his father's name. We also had other great customs, but they were uprooted by Sidki Pasha, may God forgive him."

Hussein glanced at him inquisitively.

"My father, Hassan Bey, was an outstanding Wafdist and a member of the higher circles of the Wafd party," the man added sorrowfully. "When Sidki Pasha came to his ill-omened office, he asked him to sever his relations with the Wafd. When he refused, as expected, Sidki Pasha deprived him of the assistance of the Loan Bank during the crisis. As a result, he was forced to sell his land and so lost his wealth."

"But Nahas was returned to office?" Hussein inquired.

"Yet the land was lost. Most ironically, Sidki went over to the patriots' side. At the beginning of this year, he gave an address at Disouk in which he conveyed the greetings of 'my leader Nahas,' as he then called him. Hassan Hassan Hassan, what a pity you have lost everything!"

Pretending to be moved, Hussein muttered, "May God compensate you for what you've lost!"

Shaking his head, the man remained silent for a while.

"You're lucky to be appointed at the school after the period of strikes was over. They almost burned us up inside the school during the latest demonstrations. May God curse the demonstrators, the students and Sidki Pasha. Hussein Effendi, where do you live?"

"In the Britannia Hotel."

"Hotel! May God disappoint you! Sorry. I mean may God forgive you. The hotel isn't a suitable place for a long stay. You must search for a small flat immediately."

"But I've no furniture."

With a sudden interest, Hassan Effendi thought the matter over, biting his fingernails.

"Furniture for a single room doesn't cost you much. With my guarantee, if you like, you can buy it in installment payments," he said.

He became thoughtful again, examining the young man's face. "There's a two-room flat on the roof of the house where I live," he added. "The rent won't be more than a pound. What do you think?"

After hearing the amount of the rent, Hussein's interest was piqued for the first time.

"I'll think it over seriously," he said.

"It's plain and axiomatic, just as one plus one equals two. Now let's start work. There are piles of papers left over since that son of a bitch got married and was transferred to Cairo."

FIFTY-ONE

Hussein decided to stay at the hotel until he received his salary. As time passed, he became convinced of the need to move into a private flat that would give him a greater sense of security and stability. Hassan Effendi was always underlining the advantages of living in a flat of his own. At the beginning of the month, Hussein bought a bed, a small wardrobe, and a chair for about two pounds, for which he agreed to pay in four installments, with Hassan as a guarantor. The flat rental being only one pound, moving in involved no extra expense. The new flat occupied half the roof of the house, on the middle story of which Hassan Effendi lived. In addition to the lavatory and kitchen, there were two rooms. Since one of these was superfluous, the young man locked it up, furnishing the other with new furniture. The one window in the room overlooked Walei al-Din Street, where the entrance to the house was situated. The rooftop flat was higher than the surrounding buildings, and the unrestricted open air in front of its only window gave the young man a sense of freshness and relief which he had been denied at the hotel, and he was thus very pleased. The day he moved in was a happy one indeed. For the first time in his life, he found himself the master of his own house and proud possessor of a salary and furniture. His sense of relief and delight when he had received his salary that morning still lingered in his memory. Nor did he forget how he shyly hid the smile on his lips, reflecting the delight in his heart, lest it be detected by the cashier. But this happiness dwindled to insignificance when compared with his joy in sending two pounds to his mother.

In this great moment he realized that his long patience was at last rewarded. As soon as he was settled in at his new quar-

ters, Hassan Effendi visited him to congratulate him. He assured
Hussein that he would feel at home among his family. Thanking
him, Hussein, always disposed to acknowledge the kindness of
others, felt grateful to him. He forgave Hassan's sharp temper
and his maladministration and confusion in carrying out his
functions at the school. In fact, he became accustomed to his
eccentricity, consoled by his good-heartedness and sense of humor. Refusing to leave him alone, Hassan invited him to spend
the evening on his balcony. Delighted at the invitation, Hussein
accompanied the man to his quarters. As he sat with his guest,
Hassan said, "You seem to dislike coffeehouses, so you can use
this balcony as a nightclub."

The balcony was adequately equipped. On the right were two
big chairs made of cane with a table between them; on the other
side was a big couch with a cushion at its back. On another
table in the corner was a tray with two water jugs and a ewer,
with several big lemons floating between them on the water gathered inside the tray. Hassan Effendi's tongue started to ramble
almost incessantly. In his loose garment, he appeared very tiny,
much smaller than in his suit, his tongue the only organ in his
body worth reckoning with. Bored with his leisure hours in the
past weeks, Hussein welcomed Hassan's company, for he did
not know how to spend his time. Reading was not the answer,
not because it bored him, but because with little money to spare
he could afford to buy only those books which appealed to him
most. Thus, in addition to his daily paper, he was compelled to
confine himself to one book. He tried to frequent coffeehouses,
but he found no pleasure in them and he was afraid they might
lead him to squander his money. Frugal by temperament, he
welcomed Hassan Effendi's invitation to spend his leisure time
at his home. Hussein was resolved, under whatever circumstances, to find pleasure in this man's company. Their conversation turned to the new flat.

"Don't worry about cleaning your flat," Hassan Effendi said.
"I've already instructed the servant to clean it every morning. I

shall also recommend a washerwoman, known to my family, to go to your place every Friday."

Touched, Hussein thanked him shyly. Yet he was somewhat annoyed because he could manage cleaning his room with his own hands and the servant's daily services would involve additional expenses which he would rather save.

"I've prepared a wonderful surprise for you," he said. "Here is a backgammon board. Do you play it well?"

"Somewhat." Hussein was pleased.

The man bounced up and left the balcony. Returning with a backgammon board, he put it on the table.

"Thanks be to God," he said, filled with childish pride, "I'm the best player in Lower Egypt, and perhaps in Upper Egypt, too."

Delighted with this unexpected entertainment, Hussein inquired, "Do you play it the usual way or the more restricted way?"

They started to play. It soon became obvious to Hussein that in talking Hassan Effendi tended to spray the face of a close listener with his saliva. He hoped to absorb this man in the game so as to divert him from conversation. But he continued to play and talk simultaneously. Since the game itself provided him with endless opportunities to chatter, he commented on whatever move was taken, proud of his own and critical of Hussein's. He beat the young man in the first round.

"Curse your bad luck that has made you fall into my hands," he cried. "You'll never enjoy the taste of victory as long as I live!"

Zealously they resumed the game. So absorbed was Hussein that he became aware of his surroundings only when he heard the sound of soft footsteps approaching the balcony. Turning his head back toward the door, he saw a girl carrying a tea tray. Realizing from the first glance that she could not be a servant, he immediately withdrew his eyes in shyness and confusion. As she bent down a bit to put the tray on a bamboo chair, he had a mysterious sense first of her presence and then of her departure. Though he had turned his eyes away, the image of her plump face, with its whitish complexion and two sweet-looking dark eyes—or maybe they were hazel, he was not quite sure—stuck in his memory. Confused, Hussein felt his face flush. All of a sudden Hassan stopped chattering.

"This is my daughter Ihsan. Since I consider you one of my children, I saw no harm in her bringing the tea to us," he said in a low voice.

Hussein moved his lips as if speaking, but did not utter a single word. Hassan Effendi poured the tea.

"A girl is a great blessing to the home," he said. "Her sisters are married, one in Cairo and two in Damanhour. She's the only one not yet married."

"May God give you joy in her marriage," Hussein muttered in confusion.

They continued to sip their tea in silence. Hussein's confusion was beginning to disappear, leaving behind it a sense of embarrassment which he could not clearly account for. Perhaps he was escaping the cause and deliberately ignoring it. Furthermore, he was conscious that he was still affected by the memory, vague though it was, of the girl's image. He knew this was typical of the effect a female presence had upon him. It had no particular significance; it was the usual reaction of chaste young men. This time, his excitement, occurring not as usual in the street or on a tramcar but in a home, had put him into a deep mood of perplexed delight. Away from Cairo, it was inevitable that he should think of matters more remote. Fear and weariness filled his heart. Hassan Effendi was watching him quietly, growing fed up with the young man's silence.

"Drink your tea," he ordered, "and get ready for the next round. You've fallen into my clutches and you have no chance of escaping."

FIFTY-TWO

She was pretty enough to stir his emotions. Later on he saw her in the street accompanied by her mother, and he observed her in her home more than once. Fortunately, she inherited only her father's protruding cheeks, which, however, instead of making her ugly, gave her a special attractiveness. He readily recognized that Hassan Effendi's flat was becoming a source of strong attraction to him, not to be explained merely by his desire for entertainment. He was full of youthful vigor and vitality. His heart seemed to be waiting to admit the first girl who would knock at its door. Soon a passion combining desire, admiration, and affection flared up in his breast. In her he sought a solace for his lonely life and a quenching of his thirst for companionship. From the very beginning, he was clearly aware of how critical his situation was. He understood his dilemma, and it never occurred to him to relax in carrying out his obligations to his family. Yet he was not firm enough with himself. This was beyond his control. He had to choose one of two alternatives: either to disregard his circumstances or to live a parched, lonely, and secluded life, cheerless and barren. As his perplexity increased, he thought several times of inventing some pretext or other to return to the hotel. But he remained where he was. Surrendering to fate, he allowed matters to take their natural course. Life continued its march without producing any novelty. Though he seldom saw the girl, her image was indelibly imprinted on his mind. Hassan Effendi kept on chattering as usual, ignoring the whole matter.

In the meantime, Hassanein's meticulously detailed letters kept Hussein as well informed about his family as if he were still living among them and sharing all their feelings. Hassanein told him that their mother had decided to use the money he was sending them to buy clothes, that he himself had managed to wring a new jacket from her to wear over his old trousers, and that their mother, so that she could do without woolen clothes and still keep warm, had bought herself a new dressing gown to wear over her light dresses. The allocation of Hussein's money to clothing, though necessary, made it impossible for the family to make use of it to improve their diet, which continued to be bad. As for Nefisa, Hassanein said that she was making only little progress and that their mother had ceased to take the bulk of her earnings as she had done before Hussein began sending them money. Thus Nefisa spent what little money she could spare on her clothes to keep up an appearance appropriate to the family's reputation. It seemed that there was no room in Hassan's mind for his family, since his new life absorbed him totally. Or perhaps he thought that with Hussein's appointment to the government service they were no longer in need of him. In any case, he had completely ceased paying visits to his family. Hassanein informed his brother about his own preparation for the baccalaureate exams at the end of the year, telling him how he was striving to pass them, knowing what it meant to fail.

Seeking in his last letter to ingratiate himself more firmly with his brother, Hassanein mentioned at the close that his new jacket lost its attractiveness when worn with his thin, shabby trousers. Would it be possible, he inquired, for Hussein to come up with the price of new trousers over the next three months? Hussein paused thoughtfully, uncertain as to whether he could comply with his brother's request without jeopardizing his own savings. Yet he already knew that hesitation was futile, for he could not fail to respond to any appeal from Hassanein. Had he been at home with his brother he might have scolded him. But the distance separating them softened his heart and made his longing for his family irresistible. His devotion to careful economizing made him dislike squandering his money. But in the interest of sacrifices for his family, he found it only a little difficult to relax his carefulness. To please Hassanein, it would do him no serious harm if he tightened his belt for another three months. Knowing his brother well, Hussein realized that Hassanein thought that the others had an obligation to be kind and helpful to him, and that if Hussein failed to buy him the trousers, he would indignantly forget the real favor of buying him the jacket. Furthermore, he was driven by a mysterious urge to shower his brother with favors and good turns, for he believed there was a dazzling future in store for this young man. He had sacrificed his own career for the sake of Hassanein and his sacrifice should be complete. Again, with a mixture of sadness and delight, he saw himself as a sacrificial goat, patient and stoical in facing the grim fate of his family, shielding them from its blows. This feeling gave him strength and pleasure and lent a superb moral significance to his life.

Then the unexpected happened, or so he thought, since he was not quite frank with himself. One day as he sat conversing with Hassan Effendi, the man asked him, "Haven't you thought of marriage?"

The young man became confused and a bit frightened. "No," he muttered.

The man raised his eyebrows in disapproval. "Then what are you thinking of?" he asked. "Why do you live? Do you think that a man, especially after securing a job, has any end in life other than marriage?"

Hussein hesitated for a moment. "I have other responsibilities which demand priority," he said.

He proceeded to confide to the man the difficult circumstances of his family, sometimes exaggerating them to strengthen his position. The man listened with interest until he finished, but he did not appear to be convinced. He was not prepared to be convinced of anything that got in the way of realizing his hopes. He shook his bald head with indifference.

"I see that you are exaggerating the seriousness of the situation," he said. "Just be patient until your brother obtains the baccalaureate. Then you'll be free from your obligations, and he, in turn, will have to find a job for himself. Nahas Pasha himself got married. Do you think that your responsibilities outweigh his?"

Confused, Hussein laughed. "But my brother is determined to continue his education," he said.

"Listen," the man continued. "If you have goals in life such as the restoration of the 1923 Constitution, for example, it would be better for you to put off your marriage! You must marry at the end of this year, as soon as your brother finds a job. But if he insists on completing his education, your mother, who approves his plan, has no right to object to your marriage. She has no right to pamper one son if it means depriving the other of his elemental rights in life."

Hussein was affected but not convinced by the man's remarks. Because he wanted to maintain their friendly relations, Hussein did not contradict him. "I believe it should be possible to realize my hopes without destroying those of my brother," he said.

On the surface, this conversation about marriage appeared to be rambling and haphazard. Yet there was a tacit agreement between them about its purpose, for it had been preceded by earlier hints in their conversations every evening. As if dissatisfied with this implicit degree of agreement, Hussein, with much shyness, said frankly, "I think Miss Ihsan is still young."

The man laughed aloud. "Ihsan is young, of course," he said. "But marriage isn't meant just for adults."

Hussein's situation remained unchanged in the days that followed, until Hassan Effendi offered to introduce him to some of his relatives at a family party, and he readily accepted. He was ashamed to appear in his shabby clothes before the girl's relatives. Something akin to madness, as he would call it later, seized him. Driven by this capricious passion, he ordered a new tailored suit, to be paid for in installments, and bought a new pair of shoes and a tarbush. On the first day of the month, he realized that it was impossible to send any money to his mother.

Instead of the money, he sent her false excuses. He told her that he had fallen ill and that the price of the medicines he had bought was beyond his limited means. He wrote the letter with a lifeless hand and depressed heart, convinced at the bottom of his soul that he was making a series of blunders and that they had deprived him of mental balance and sound judgment; so much so that he failed to fabricate a more adequate excuse.

FIFTY-THREE

It was Thursday. Hussein was lying in bed reading the morning paper, which he usually laid aside until the afternoon. Hearing a knock on the door, he thought it was Hassan Effendi's servant. Going to the door to open it, he found himself face to face with his mother! His mouth agape, he took her hand between his.

"Mother, in Tanta! I can hardly believe my eyes!" he exclaimed.

Pressing his mother's hands, he kissed her cheeks; or rather, they exchanged a kiss. Turning back into the room, he asked her with surprise, "Why didn't Hassanein tell me you were coming so that I could meet you at the station?"

She took the chair he offered her.

"I found little difficulty finding where you live," the mother said with a smile. "It's much more difficult to find the way to a house in Shubra itself! Hassanein suggested that I wait until he could write and tell you of my coming. But I saw no reason to disturb you in your illness. In the meantime, I couldn't stay in Cairo knowing that you are here both lonely and ill."

At the sound of the word "ill," he awoke from the ecstasy of their meeting, a depressing fear gripping his heart. But with his potent fear came a similarly potent power to combat it.

"Mother," he said, "I'm sorry I've disturbed you. But I didn't expect this happy result, your coming in person."

Her face overflowing with kindness and compassion, she examined him carefully. "What's wrong with you, my son?" she asked. "How are you now? Tell me about your illness."

He exerted his utmost to hide his confusion so that it would leave no traces on his face. He was sure he didn't look like a sick man. In fact, with a better diet, his health had improved since his appointment to government service.

"Nothing serious," he said simply. "I had a bad intestinal upset. It only lasted one day and part of another."

"We were all very worried about you, especially as you had reassured us about your health in your previous letter," she said, fixing her eyes on him. She paused. "Good God!" she continued. "We thought there must be something seriously wrong with you if you weren't able to send us any money this month."

He felt her words pricking him like a sharp needle. With a faint smile on his face, he hurried to say, "I had to spend more than two pounds for a doctor and some medicines. And as you know, I don't have any reserve for such emergencies!"

"Never mind. I'm delighted to see you in good health. Now you must send a letter at once to your brother to reassure him and Nefisa, who were extremely worried when I left."

Then she cast a scrutinizing glance about his room. In fear and anxiety, his attention fixed on the new suit hanging on the peg. He was mentally preparing himself to invent a new lie. But she only commented. "Your room is clean and its furniture is good. Come on and show me your flat."

"My flat only consists of this room," Hussein said, laughing. "There's an extra room which I lock up because I don't need it."

"This means that for one room you pay the rent on a whole flat? Wasn't the hotel cheaper?"

"On the contrary, the flat's rent is fifty piasters less than the hotel."

"You've told us that you don't need a servant to clean the flat. Doesn't the cleaning give you trouble?"

"No. It's easy for me, as you know."

She smiled gently. "My son, you seem happy and comfortable, which pleases me."

The crisis now apparently over, he said with genuine relief,

"It's I who am happy, Mother. I'll have your company for a whole month."

She could not help laughing. "Only this night," she said. "There is no room for me to sleep in. Besides, I shall be too much of a burden to you, since you buy your food from the market."

Before he could open his mouth, there was a knock on the door. He went to open it. Samira heard a voice speaking with a countryside accent: "My master Hassan is asking why you're late today."

Then she heard Hussein excusing himself, telling of his mother's arrival from Cairo. Closing the door and returning to sit on the bed, he saw his mother looking at him with inquiring eyes.

"That was the servant of my neighbor Hassan Effendi, the chief clerk of the school," he said.

She knew from her son's letters that this was the man who had persuaded him to rent a flat and served as guarantor so that he could buy his new furniture.

"From what the servant said, it seems to me that you spend your leisure time at his place," she remarked.

Imagining for a moment that she could read all his secret thoughts, he avoided her eyes; he felt the sting of fear creeping into his mouth and obstructing his throat.

"I often do," he said. "He's a good-natured man, and besides, he's my boss. I've found his company a substitute for coffeehouses and their corruptions. One has to entertain oneself in one's leisure time."

Samira rose. She went to the bathroom to wash her face. Removing her overcoat, Hussein took it and brushed it with his own brush, praying to God that her visit would end peaceably. He was worried and afraid his secret might be discovered. His mother's presence here where his secret lay agitated him. He cursed the stupid circumstances which made him fail to send her the money. Returning to her place, the woman began inquiring about his life. But their conversation was soon interrupted by a

245

second knock on the door. Rather indignantly Hussein went to open it. The same servant had returned.

"My elder mistress," she said aloud, "wishes to greet Madam, your mother."

Samira hurried into the hall to speak to the servant.

"There's no room here to receive her. I shall visit her myself."

The servant went away. Samira and her son returned to the room.

"There's no need for this visit," Hussein said. "Since you can't stay here very long, we shouldn't part even for one minute."

"These are customary courtesies," she sighed. "Obviously, I'm concerned about courtesy to your boss's family."

They resumed their conversation until the brightness of the daylight faded away. When twilight came, Samira rose and put on her overcoat.

"It's time for me to visit your neighbor's wife," she said.

With gloomy eyes, the young man watched her until she left the flat. Heaving a deep sigh, he wondered if she had any doubts about him and how this trip would end!

FIFTY-FOUR

Worried and depressed, he remained alone; his worry increased as time went by. He no longer entertained any doubt that his secret had been discovered. In his attempt at reassuring himself, he wondered why his imagination was running wild. He hoped that his mother's visit would end in peace. Surely they would not hint at anything. Yet would she fail to discover the truth if she saw Ihsan? In the gathering darkness, he rose and lit a kerosene lamp. Then, hearing a knock on the door, his heart beat violently. He opened it for his mother to enter.

"I don't think I was away for long," she said.

They both entered the room. He stood leaning on the windowsill. Silently she started to take off her overcoat and shoes.

I know it, he thought. *Her face is hiding something, many things. I'll bet she didn't go to the trouble of traveling to Tanta just to be reassured about my health. My mother is not that weak. She is kind indeed, but unquestionably strong. When will this dreadful silence end?*

"How did you find them?" he asked with pretended indifference.

Climbing onto his bed, she sat cross-legged.

"I don't know why, but my heart didn't feel at home with them," she said curtly.

But he knew the reason. His secret had been discovered, much to his dismay.

"The truth is that Hassan Effendi is a good-hearted man," he said.

"Perhaps! I haven't met him, of course."

He would not inquire what caused her uneasiness with them. Better ignore it. But he couldn't ignore it for long. He saw her looking at her hands, lying clasped in her lap. She was thinking of what she should say. What a serious blunder he'd made! He should not have yielded to the circumstances that tempted him not to send any money to them this month. He, the head of the family, and how far he'd gone astray! He saw his mother looking sullenly at him.

"Now that I'm reassured about your health," he heard her say, "I don't think it shameful to tell you frankly that we were frightened when you stopped sending us the money. Excuse me, my son, if I confess to you that I had some doubts that your illness might be a mere pretext!"

"Mother!" he cried in spite of himself.

"Forgive me, my son; sometimes it's sinful to doubt. But for a long time I've been pondering the temptations that beset a lonely young man like you in a strange town. Yes, I trust your wisdom. But Satan is clever, and I was afraid that he might have led you astray. Since you know that my dependence on you is next to my dependence on God, you can easily imagine the extent of my grief. Your brother Hassan is no longer a member of our family. Nefisa is an unfortunate girl. And Hassanein is only a student and will remain so for a long time to come. You know him better than we do. We lead a starving, miserable life to overcome our bad luck. Besides, we've lost your share of your late father's pension, and shortly we'll lose that of your brother."

"I need no reminder, Mother," Hussein said passionately. "It was a mistake. I was forced not to send you the money. I'm really sorry, Mother."

She spoke tenderly as if in a soliloquy. "It's I who am sorry." Then, after a pause, she added, "I'm sorry that I often give the impression of getting in the way of my sons' happiness."

"You're doing yourself great injustice," he said with concern. "As a mother, you're the model of clemency."

"I'm glad you understand me." Looking into his eyes, she sighed. "Nothing preoccupies my mind so much as the future of your sister, Nefisa. I wish to see her married. But how? We don't possess a single millieme for her trousseau. It disturbs me deeply to think that I may die before getting her married. You're men, but she's a helpless woman with no support."

"As long as we're alive, she won't be without support," Hussein replied disapprovingly.

"May God prolong your life," she said, sighing again. "But a girl finds no happiness under a married brother's roof!"

A knowing look appeared in his eyes. He understood the implication of his mother's words. Since a girl found no happiness in her married brother's house, and since Hassanein was almost married, it followed that Hussein should remain single! Sound logic! And compassionate, too! Yet it entailed his death sentence. What could he say? Now he was no longer afraid of her blows, such as she sometimes used to deal to him. But he could not take advantage of this sense of safety to anger her. On the contrary, he would turn it into an innocent incentive to treat her with exaggerated generosity.

"Rest assured, Mother! I hope Nefisa won't find herself one day in this impasse!"

Intimating that he should put equivocation aside and speak frankly, she shook her head. "In fact, certain lingering thoughts still preoccupy me," she said. "Despite the trouble and expense of travel, I couldn't rest until I came to you."

He smiled. "This means that you didn't come just to reassure yourself about my health?" The words came forth almost unconsciously, and no sooner had he uttered them than be regretted that they had escaped his lips.

She smiled at him sadly. "Listen to me, Hussein. Do you want to marry?" she asked.

To hide his agitation, he pretended to be upset. "I wonder what makes you think so!" he said.

"Nothing would be dearer to me than to see my sons happily married, but do you want to rush into marriage before your family is able to get on its feet?"

"I've never thought of this."

"Are you annoyed by my intrusion?"

"Never."

"If I suggested that you postpone any thoughts of marriage, wouldn't you consider it unfair?"

"This would be fairness and charity in themselves."

She lowered her eyes. "My real misery," she said sadly, "doesn't lie in the catastrophe that has befallen us, but in what I see to be our duty, which might seem cruel and selfish to any person who has only a superficial view of our situation."

"I'm not such a person, anyhow."

After a moment of hesitation, she said, "Seeing that you are sympathetic with what I say encourages me to advise you to leave this flat and go back to your room at the hotel."

His secret was now unearthed. He was stunned.

"The hotel?" he inquired with a murmur.

"You're ignorant of people," she said firmly. "Perhaps your neighbors are good folk. But they care only for their own interests. Your neighborly relations with them will turn you against us without your realizing it."

FIFTY-FIVE

They did not speak of this subject again. Unlike many of her sex, Samira was not a chatterbox. They had spent Friday morning in complete happiness, partly in Hussein's flat before setting out for the town on a visit to the tomb of the saintly al-Sayed al-Badawi. But as she was determined to go to the railway station that morning, he was forced to acquiesce. On reaching the station, he bought a ticket for his mother. While they waited for the train, he said to her, "I'll remain in the flat until the end of this month, because, as you know, I've already paid the rent."

In answer, she prayed for him to do the right thing. When the train arrived, she said goodbye. Boarding a third-class carriage, she was squeezed in with a throng of villagers of both sexes. At this first experience in his life of seeing her off, a heavy depression came over him. The sight of the departing train and the lonely figure of his mother, surrounded by misery in a mean third-class carriage, cut him to the heart. Depressed and absorbed in thought, he returned home.

I'm to blame, he thought. *I'm paying the price of my folly. What devil is singling me out for his temptation? This is the second time for me. Failure always chooses me. No escape.*

Hassan Effendi's servant came to invite his mother to dinner, and Hussein told him she had left for Cairo. Later, when the servant returned to invite him as usual to spend the evening in Hassan Effendi's house, he accepted at once.

The balcony window being tightly closed because it was winter, the two men sat around the backgammon table inside the room.

"Why did your mother return so quickly?" Hassan Effendi asked.

"Our home can't spare her for more than a day," Hussein answered, smiling.

"She arrived on Thursday and departed on Friday. It's a journey that's not worth the trouble of traveling by train."

"But this journey accomplished what she wanted. She reassured herself about me, and she paid a visit to al-Sayed's tomb and invoked his blessings!"

The man pointed toward the interior of the flat. "They've told me she is a very good-natured lady," he said. "Your good-naturedness outweighs hers." His bleary eyes blinking, the man added, "We hoped she would visit us before she left!"

"She was in such a hurry," Hussein said. "I tried to persuade her to postpone her departure till the afternoon. But she excused herself, saying that her family needed her."

"We had prepared a good dinner for her, for which I myself had selected three fat chickens," the man said with regret.

Confused, Hussein smiled. "I hope you enjoyed eating them," he muttered.

The man laughed, and opened the backgammon table. But instead of arranging the counters to start the game, he inquired with interest, "Didn't you tell her of our agreement?"

Hussein felt embarrassed. "No," he said.

"Why not?"

"How is it possible for me to broach this subject with her while she considers me responsible for the family?"

The man seized the die in his hand, rattled and cast it. Then he added, "You're too apprehensive. Your mother would have been happy to hear this piece of news."

"It would make her happy only if it came at the right time."

The man laughed aloud. "I've my own special philosophy, which is to throw oneself fearlessly into the surge of life. Have you ever heard of anyone starving in Egypt?" he said slowly.

"That's because our people are accustomed to hunger!"

Laughing, Hassan Effendi continued. "All people survive. In the twinkling of an eye, people change. Children grow up, the pupils become employees, and the celibate get to be married men. The only losers are those who are full of fear as you are. This is life."

Full of fear? Annoyed at the words, he revolted inwardly against them. This was not fear, but an adequate awareness of the situation. Would he be courageous if he let this woman down, left her in the lurch?! This was not fear. Only foolish men misunderstood him. Disappointed in his hopes, he found no one who would show him mercy or understand him. As his thoughts reached this stage, he suddenly detected in them a strange flavor. Though people might misunderstand him, the feeling that he was in the right delighted him. Moreover, his delight resulted from a sense of being always misunderstood although always in the right. It was a mysterious delight similar to that which people experience when they resign themselves to the harsh verdict of fate.

"Hassan Effendi," he said with a smile, "since your family was a large one, it's impossible for you to understand the troubles of a family like ours."

The man hid an arrogant smile under a façade of pretended grimness. "Deal with your problems as you like," he said. "But don't forget yourself. God said, 'Don't forget your share of this world.' Things are destined to ripen. In another few months, your brother will obtain the baccalaureate, which will change the situation. Throw the die and see who will begin the game."

FIFTY-SIX

Two weeks later he received a letter from Hassanein telling him that he had paid the examination fees and was constantly studying, determined to succeed. Confident of his brother's intelligence and ability, Hussein had no doubt he would pass. Though it was not in his nature to yield to the enchantment of dreams, he tended these days to entertain them. However, although he did not believe in these fantasies, Hussein imagined in his reverie that once his brother had obtained his certificate, he would get a job to relieve Hussein's burden. Thus he could visualize himself embarking on a new, happy life with an easy conscience. He did not hope for more than a secure married life. His lonely days in his barren flat taught him the value of having a family, for which he was as eager as a homeless person for a shelter to protect him from the pouring rain. He could not bear to frequent restaurants to take his meals. He seemed afraid to remain alone in his room even for a short time. He was at once fatigued and fed up with his bachelor's life, which required continuous attention to his flat, furniture, and clothes. And this itself dwindled into insignificance in comparison with the hunger and yearning in his heart. He was not in love with this particular girl so much as he was with the femaleness and conjugal life she represented. As the tangible ideal of his dreams, his heart yearned for her, becoming the more attached to her since he saw very little of her except on certain rare, happy occasions. At first Hussein thought that they were hiding her from him. But later it became clear to him that Hassan Effendi was a genuinely conservative man, tolerant up to a point but not beyond the limits of decency. If Hassanein agreed to get a job, this would make it possible for Hussein to go directly to his girl, marry her, and lead a true life. This was his dream. But realizing it was merely a dream, he did not know when it would come true. Hassanein would continue his education, and he himself should accept this without resentment. He must wait for life to run its course as God ordained.

But one evening an unexpected event made it clear to him that he would not enjoy this interval of waiting in peace and security. Immediately after he finished having tea with Hassan Effendi, the latter said to him, "An important matter, worth discussing with you, has recently come up."

Inquiring, Hussein raised his eyes. The man said seriously, "Ihsan's cousin, a merchant and farmer in Beheira province, wants to ask for her hand. But before deciding this matter, I thought I'd better ask your opinion."

So shocking was this inauspicious surprise that it left the young man incredulous, dumbfounded, defeated, and bewildered. In fact, although he had some doubt as to how true it was, he found himself at an impasse, which his suspicions failed to overcome. He felt the resentment of a man whose circumstances forced him to waver and reduced him to a state of speechlessness. What should he say to the man?! If he agreed to marry, he would betray his family; and if he refused, all connections between him and Hassan Effendi would be severed. In spite of his agitation and bewilderment, he pictured the face of the girl on whom he had pinned his hopes, feeling the grip of despair closing about his neck. Disguising his increasing resentment, the young man cast a cold look on his tormentor; the man patiently scrutinized his face.

To break the long silence, the man inquired, "Hussein Effendi, what do you have to say about this?"

Knowing that he must speak, Hussein replied beseechingly, "There is nothing I can add to the detailed account I've already given you of our family circumstances."

Sounding bored, the man said, "Your brother will be finishing his studies at the beginning of next summer."

"But as far as I can see, he is determined to continue his education."

The man became annoyed. "This is a silly idea to which you must not submit and you must not bear responsibility for it," he said.

Seeking to avert this danger, Hussein was as evasive as a mouse hiding itself uselessly behind the leg of a chair.

"I can announce the engagement right now on condition that I can wait for a period of time before I marry," he said.

"For how many years?" Hassan Effendi asked warmly.

Oh! The man thought that he was concerned only for his brother; he was almost unaware of Nefisa and her problem. Hussein genuinely wished he could blurt out the whole truth to him. Extremely fearful, he answered, "Four years." Hussein looked at him to see the effect of this declaration. "Waiting will do us no harm. Don't you trust me?" he said hurriedly.

Making a wry face, the man shook his head. "Four years!" he said with dreadful calm. "Who knows whether by then we'll be alive? Do you want me to tell her mother that I've refused her cousin, who wants to marry her now, to keep her waiting four years more? Hussein Effendi, it seems to me you weren't serious about your desire!"

Shaking in his agony, Hussein shouted, "May God forgive you, Hassan Effendi! I'm a faithful man and I still stick to my honest purpose. I see no reason why any obstacle should get in our way."

"You simply don't see the reason because you're in the position of neither a father nor a mother. Now, put all arguments aside. Can't you get married this year?"

A long silence prevailed. But Hussein uttered not a word. He had nothing to say. For a long time he remained both thoughtful and perplexed. Desperate and defeated, he pressed his lips. Hassan Effendi smiled faintly, compressing his lips in turn, his small oval face anguished and immobile. A long, strained silence fell upon them, and an odor of unfriendliness, intolerable to their nerves, spread like the hot dust carried by the winds of the khamsin, which blew up off the desert. However, Hussein, not bearing to take the first step in cutting off relations, asked dejectedly, as though predicting the answer, "Can't you wait?"

"No," the man nervously replied.

Embarrassed and pained, Hussein remained for a while. Then, taking his leave, he rose and departed. So intense was his sadness and despair that he left the flat with unseeing eyes, knowing that never again would he return to it. Back in his room, he lit the kerosene lamp and flung himself on the bed. He viewed everything around him with discontent and hostility. At this moment he hated not only himself but humanity at large. *Am I weak or strong?* he thought. *What have I done with myself? Is it daring and courage or just contemptible flight? Everything appears detestable to me; I'll be leaving this room, with the lonely room at the hotel waiting to engulf me. Perhaps the man imagines that he can annoy me in my work at school! Damn him; he will find me tougher than he thinks. But of what use is it all? Death is more merciful than hope itself! There is nothing surprising in this, for death is divinely appointed, while hope is the creation of human folly. Both end in frustration. Am I destined to lead a life of endless frustration? Why doesn't Hassanein get a job on the baccalaureate? Why doesn't he want for me what he wants for himself?*

He became extremely vexed. Finding his loneliness intolerable, he took his suit from the peg, dressed, and left the house. The night was cold. He continued to roam the streets until he tired of walking, and finally went to a coffeehouse. Unexpectedly invigorated by the walk and the cold air, and calmer than before, he took a seat in the café. To pass the time, he watched the people sitting in the coffeehouse, listening to whatever scraps of their conversations reached his ears. These were not devoid of amusing remarks that made him smile. His mad fury subsided, leaving him in deep but mute sorrow, tinged with remorse. He wondered whether he should have agreed with the man. But would this man have been pleased if he had left his own family to the mercy of fate?! He realized his own folly, that he had a right to be sorrowful but no right to feel so furiously angry. Besides, it was foolish to surrender to sorrow. He knew that as long as he allowed irrationality to sway him he could not banish sorrow from his life, not for a long time to come. All the same, he believed that ultimately everything would come to an end. Even this choking sorrow would eventually be relieved. Like a person attempting to shake off a nightmare, he awaited this relief. Life's miseries had taught him that one day it was bound to come. And when it came, he would experience no regret, but would have every reason for pride and the peace of an easy conscience. His sense of duty outweighed all his other emotions. How wide of the mark was Hassan's accusation that he was fearful! To him it was enough that his mother understood him and considered him her hope and her consolation. Suffering in the pain of his present grief, he smiled at the prospect of hope.

FIFTY-SEVEN

Along about midsummer there came a happy day in the life of the family inhabiting Nasr Allah alley. Hassanein had passed the baccalaureate examinations. Calm and serene, Samira, Nefisa, and Hassanein gathered to spend a peaceful hour, their tired hearts overflowing with joy. Farid Effendi Mohammed and his family came to congratulate Hassanein on his success. In his fiancée's presence, Hassanein experienced a complacent feeling of innocent pride, as though the baccalaureate had lent him further manliness, deserving both her respect and sympathy. Merry and pleasant as usual, he spoke with animation, ecstatically triumphant, and volleys of laughter rocketed from his mouth. The sight of Bahia filled his heart with a mixture of happiness and sorrow. It delighted him furtively to meet her clear, serene eyes and to read in them evidence of profound and refined love. However, the serenity he derived from her glances was slight, for it soon gave way to the flames of passion flaring up in his heart. When these arose, he grew indignant as he remembered his long deprivation and looked back with regret and sorrow over the past two years. Casting surreptitious glances at her during the conversation, his amorous eyes fixed intently on her moonlike face and plump body. As was his frequent custom, he formed a mental picture of her completely naked, with only her hair flowing down her back. As he pictured her thus, he felt his boiling saliva scorching his mouth. Mutely he wondered whether her attitude toward him could possibly change now that he had obtained the baccalaureate! Would it not be fair to grant him a kiss by way of congratulation? As his thoughts shifted from one object to another, his mind flitted from the girl to his mental image of her naked body, then to the people gathering around. Though the general atmosphere was pervaded with complete happiness, his own was tainted with the relentless torture imposed by her presence.

The guests departed. Left to themselves, the mood of pure delight now was gone, and the family was assaulted by a new sense of responsibility. Life had taught them that obtaining the baccalaureate was a source of transient happiness to be followed by troubled reflection. They were already agreed that Hassanein should continue onto higher education, but they were still undecided about the kind of education he should pursue.

"Now you have to choose the profession you want for yourself," Nefisa said.

Hassanein had thoroughly probed this matter. "Higher education," he said, "is a long, arduous process, and its prospects are vague."

The two women eyed him with surprise.

"I've thought this matter over for a long time," he added. "I have come to the conclusion that I should choose either the Police College or the War College."

"How wonderful!" Nefisa exclaimed happily.

Preoccupied with the obstacles standing in the way of his hopes, he paid no attention to Nefisa's delight. "After only two years of study, I'll become an officer," he said. "Since the course of study is like playing games, success is almost certain. Eventually there will be a secure job waiting for me. These are advantages to be reckoned with."

"A two-year study after which you become an officer!" Nefisa exclaimed with the same enthusiasm. "How dreamlike this is!"

"What about the fees?" his mother inquired fearfully.

Rather bewildered, he stared at her. "The Police College is very expensive," he replied. "But the fees of the War College are reasonable, only thirty-seven pounds."

Stunned, the two women stared at him.

"There is some possibility of exemption from paying the fees," he hurried to say, "or at least half the fees. In this case, we have to appeal to Ahmad Bey Yousri, whose intercession will carry a great deal of weight."

In her anxiety his mother still looked stunned.

"Farid Effendi Mohammed told me about the Primary Education Training Institute," she said. "I find that it has certain advantages worth considering. No fees, and after finishing the three-year course, you get a teaching job."

"I would hate working as a teacher and I would hate even more to enroll in a free institute," the young man said resentfully.

"But you don't object to joining the War College gratis."

"There is a vast difference between an institute designed to be free and another which exempts me from all the fees or half of them. If I joined the former institute, people would say that I received my education gratis. But if I joined the latter, nobody would ever know about it except the college clerk."

Unconvinced, the mother shook her head. "Our situation," she muttered, "is too grave to consider such a thing."

"Nothing can be more grave than this. Not only do I loathe poverty but I hate the mere mention of it. I can't bear to walk with my head lowered among people with their heads raised."

This was not his only reason for preferring an officer's career. In fact, his motive in joining the War College was a thirst for domination, power, and a dazzling appearance. His mother remained anxious, unconvinced.

"And if you are unable to obtain an exemption from the fees?" she inquired.

He became grimly thoughtful. "As a start, I need the first installment of the fees, which I hope to get from Hassan," he said. "I don't think he will let me down, since he didn't let Hussein down. As for the rest of the fees, these can be managed if you give me the money Hussein sends, plus whatever Nefisa will be generous enough to offer." He looked at his sister. "I don't think she will be miserly with me, especially because her earnings are good enough."

He looked from his mother to his sister to observe the effect of his words. Seeing no sign of encouragement, he continued tenderly: "We'll have two more lean years, after which there'll be comfort and happiness!"

He directed his hopeful glances from one to the other, and added cajolingly, "You'll become the mother and sister of an officer! Imagine it! Imagine that we'll leave this alley for a respectable flat on the main street!"

Touched by his entreating glances, Nefisa was overcome by a generous, altruistic impulse.

"Don't worry as far as I'm concerned. I'll give you whatever I can," she said.

There was a look of gratitude in his eyes. "Thank you, Nefisa," he said. "Mother won't be less generous than you are. Thus everything will be all right."

His mother wished him good luck. She had no great expectations from him. Her maximum hope was that after getting a job, he would postpone his marriage for two years to give her the opportunity to get her family back on its feet. However, she gave him the rescue money provided by Hussein, wishing him the best of luck from the bottom of her heart. Still under the sway of her generosity and altruism, Nefisa had reached the lofty peak of eagerness, peace, and happiness. Only for a few precious moments did she enjoy real delight, for assailed by a cloud of dark memories, her happiness soon disappeared. No longer did it flow abundantly; instead, it was strangled and smeared with the mire of those memories. Her enthusiasm subsiding, she lowered her eyes, dispirited and feeling that she had no right to unalloyed joy. Anyhow, what could happiness do to console a miserable, disfigured, tainted soul?

FIFTY-EIGHT

As he left Al Khazindar Square for Clot Bey Street, it occurred to Hassanein that Hassan would mention that they visited him only when they needed money. Though the thought distressed him, he tried to alleviate his discomfort by arguing that it was Hassan who did not want any of his family to visit him at home. Inquisitive, he started to wonder what he might find in this forbidden place! Sensing something unnatural about it, he thought it was perfectly in keeping with Hassan's character.

Remembering the money he needed, he felt appalled. He wondered what would happen if Hassan was unable to help him. He felt as though cold fingers gripped his heart, ready to crush his hopes. Finally he found his way to Gandab alley. He walked up the filthy incline in search of house number seventeen. Reaching it, he saw a sweet potato seller close by, squatting on the earth in front of his cart. Pointing to the house, Hassanein asked the hawker, "Does Hassan Effendi Kamel live here?"

The man asked in his turn, "You mean Hassan the Head?"

"I mean Hassan Kamel Ali, the singer," Hassanein said.

"This is the house of Hassan the Head, who works in Ali Sabri's coffeehouse in Darb Tiab," the man replied.

Shamefully lowering his head, Hassanein became terribly upset. When he heard the mention of Ali Sabri, he was sure that he was approaching his brother's house. But he could not have imagined his brother working in such a *darb*, the name fulminating against his ears like a charge of explosives. Hassanein also wondered at the epithet "the Head" attached to his brother's name and what it meant. Extremely reluctantly, he entered the house. The putrefying smell of the staircase filling his nostrils as he climbed the spiral stairs, he experienced a feeling that he was descending into a bottomless abyss. When he knocked on the door, a woman's voice reached him, shouting vulgarly, "Who is it?" As the door opened, he saw a short, plump, dark-complexioned woman whose features exhibited an insolent sort of beauty. Casting a piercing look at him, she inquired, "What do you want?"

Hassanein was so confused that he answered in a low voice, "Hassan Kamel."

"Who are you?"

"His brother."

The woman smiled. Standing aside, she asked, "Are you Master Hussein?"

"No. Hassanein," he muttered with amazement.

Embarrassed and awe-stricken, he entered. Who was the woman and how did she know their names? Was Hassan married? He felt a shudder passing down his spine. Was it possible for his brother to marry such a woman? And for his mother to be her mother-in-law? He desperately wished her to be a mere mistress. The woman walked up to a door at the end of the corridor and knocked on it. When it opened after a while, Hassan appeared on the threshold. As though sensing his presence, Hassan's eyes were riveted on his brother, and he exclaimed with astonishment and delight, "Hassanein!"

With welcome and solicitude Hassan hurried toward his brother and shook hands with him. Before either opened his mouth, a number of men stealthily streamed out of the room in succession, casually glancing at Hassanein. Before departing some of them said to Hassan, "This afternoon, by God's will, we'll leave for Suez, and you'll catch up with us tomorrow."

Then they left the flat. All wore gallabiyas, and their strange features drew one's attention. Almost all their faces were disfigured. Hassanein grew anxious.

Who are these men? he wondered. *The members of the band? Impossible!* Their features reminded him of the gangsters who appeared on the cinema screen. An appalling idea dawned on him; his brother's flat was the lair of some outlaws. Casting a suspicious glance at Hassan, he saw that he was wearing a loose, lined garment. Hassan appeared vigorous and in good health, but there were two scars, as of two piercing stabs, above his left eyelid and on the left side of his neck. Good God! His brother, too, bore the marks of injuries received in criminal activities! Now perhaps it was possible to understand the real causes that kept his brother away from the family. Nodding to the room at the corridor's end, Hassan said to the woman, "Put the room in order and collect the things that are scattered about."

Taking Hassanein's arm, he went toward the bedroom. They entered. Closing the door behind them, Hassan seated his brother beside him on the sofa.

"How are you?" he inquired. "How is Mother? How is Nefisa? What's Hussein doing?"

Absently, Hassanein told him the family news, adding whatever he knew about Hussein. Then, gently reproachful, he said, "You've stopped coming to see us as if we were strangers to you, which distresses my mother a great deal."

Shaking his head sadly, Hassan said, "I'm up to my ears in my life. But I'm reassured now that Hussein's secured a job."

Affected by the changes he saw in his brother's appearance, Hassanein wondered whether he was still attached to his family. Instinctively, he started to ingratiate himself with his brother before discussing the reason for his visit. Anxiously, he inquired about the scars. "What is this, brother?"

"Traces of fights," Hassan said, laughing. "My life was never free from fights. As a matter of fact, fighting has become one of my main duties in my new life."

Hassanein wanted to ask him about this new life. But again, instinctively, he avoided the subject. Life, which drove him to this forbidden house, had also driven Hassan to take up fighting as a means of making a living. How horribly humiliating their life had been! *When we were playful children, who would have ever dreamt that such would be our fate?* he thought. *Hassan was a clever child. My father loved him more than any other living soul. Then my father changed, and it seemed as if he were Hassan's enemy. But anyhow, nobody would have imagined that Hassan would end up in such a house as this. No doubt Hussein had realized the truth on his visit to this place last September. I wonder whether Mother knows everything!*

He could not possibly summon up the courage to pose this question frankly to his brother. Instead, he inquired cunningly, "What's the connection between singing and fighting?"

Hassan burst out laughing. "To many people, they're the same thing," he answered.

At that moment, the voice of the woman reached them. "I'm going out. Do you want anything?"

"Goodbye," he responded curtly.

Unable to contain his curiosity, Hassanein asked anxiously, "Have you married, brother?"

"No."

Hassanein's face exhibited obvious relief.

"Does this please you?" Hassan inquired.

"Yes."

"Why?"

"I prefer that you choose your wife from our milieu," the young man said.

Hassan frowned in disapproval. "She's much better than many ladies; she loves me devotedly and gives me whatever money I ask her for," he said.

He was on the point of making a slip of the tongue, adding, "And from her own money I gave Hussein the funds he needed." But out of mercy for his brother he stopped. In spite of the changes that had occurred in his character, Hassan's sympathetic feelings toward his brother remained the same. Not even his resentment against him would change them. When he saw remorse and anxiety appear in the young man's eyes, he said tenderly, "A wife's devotion to her husband is, in one sense or another, utilitarian. But this woman's devotion is pure and untainted. Life will teach you so many things which you now know nothing about."

Shaking his head, Hassanein pretended to be convinced. Ingratiatingly, he gave his brother a tender smile. Remembering what he had nearly forgotten, he addressed Hassan warmly, believing this would impart congeniality to the almost strained atmosphere. Laughing, he asked his brother, "When I was inquiring about your house, I learned that they call you the Head. What does this mean?"

Hassan gave a loud laugh that restored his brother's reassurance.

"They call me that because of this," Hassan said, pointing to his head. "Somehow, I sweat to earn my living." Stretching out his hand, he butted it with his head. Then, casting a meaningful look at his brother, he laughed. "Or rather, I earned it by the blood of my forehead. We all have to sweat in order to live. But different organs sweat in different people."

Hassanein felt estranged from his brother. Pondering, he said sadly, "There are people who earn money without sweating at all!"

Hassan, appearing not to comprehend the real meaning of his brother's words, said enthusiastically, "It's very clever, to earn one's living with other people's sweat!"

Bored with this rambling conversation, Hassanein decided to discuss the reason for his visit. After remaining silent for a while, he said in a low voice, "I think you'll be pleased to know that I've passed the baccalaureate exams."

"Congratulations. Of course, I'm pleased at whatever pleases you and Mother," he shouted with delight. Scrutinizing the young man's face, Hassan continued in a tone containing both irony and compassion: "You get a job. Then you go to Tanta or Zagazig. Isn't that right?"

Seizing the opportunity, the young man took a further step toward discussing the reason for his visit. "No. I intend to join the War College."

"The War College! Splendid! Thank God you haven't decided on the Police College!"

"The fees are too high."

"I don't mean that. I mean I don't like police officers!"

Curious, the younger man stared at his brother.

"Army officers are only meant for festivities," Hassan said with a smile. "You see them marching before the *Mahmal*, and in big ceremonies, while the police officers are only interested in bringing about the destruction of people's homes."

There was silence. The two brothers exchanged glances, Hassanein anxious and embarrassed, Hassan smiling knowingly. For a long time they remained in this posture until Hassan burst out laughing, followed by his brother, who lowered his eyes shyly. They went on laughing until both of them were tired.

Then Hassan came right out and asked him, "How much?"

Again, Hassanein laughed, his face flushing with embarrassment.

"You mean the first installment of the fees," he said. "I'm sorry to tell you that it's a considerable sum of money. But from Hussein's money and what Nefisa promised to give me, I'll manage to pay the second installment and the fees for next year as well."

As he recalled how the family used to consider him its black sheep, and how they now considered him their resort in time of distress, Hassan's heart was filled with pride. However, this did not change his cordial feelings for his family; perhaps it intensified them.

"How much is this considerable sum of money?" Hassan asked, smiling.

"Twenty pounds," Hassanein said fearfully.

Despite himself, Hassan couldn't keep the worry from his

eyes. "Twenty pounds!" he exclaimed. "Our whole army isn't worth that much money. Do you intend to join a college for field marshals?"

Worried and confused, Hassanein waited. He kept silent until his brother resumed the conversation on a more serious plane. "This is a really big sum. Today, I can't give you more than ten pounds."

A painful period of silence prevailed. Hassan snorted with annoyance.

"I wish you had come to me a week earlier!" he exclaimed. "However, tomorrow I leave for Suez. Perhaps I'll come back with what you need."

He was absorbed in his thoughts. Hassanein said in a low voice, "I'm sorry I've disturbed you."

Laughingly pinching him on the nose, Hassan teased him, "I know you've got a long tongue, so I'm surprised to find that you've learned to be so polite. Don't worry. I'll bring you what you want even if I have to murder a man and steal his wallet!"

Hassan gave him the ten pounds, and asked him to convey his regards to his mother and sister, and to be wise enough not to disclose to them what he had seen in the alley. Thankfully pressing Hassan's hand, Hassanein left the flat. As soon as he was alone, he said to himself in a heavy, melancholy voice, "Hassan's life is a scandal we should conceal. Perhaps what's hidden is worse and even more hideous."

Walking along the street absorbed in his depression, he felt nauseous and fearful. He could not help remembering his brother's favors and kindness to him. Yet he could not forget the woman, the disfigured men, and Hassan's two appalling scars; all this had been horrifyingly inscribed on the young man's heart. Good heavens! How different from other human beings Hassan had become! He was no longer one of them or of the community in which they moved. Hassanein staggered as if a terrible blow had fallen on his head and knocked him unconscious. Walking rapidly, he was beset by a sense of catastrophe. His need for money, which had caused him to seek his brother's assistance, accentuated his nausea and resentment.

Desperate and defeated, he cursed his need from the bottom of his heart. More painful to him was the fact that he still needed his brother; after a few days he would return, begging for his help. Hassanein wondered how his brother would get the money in Suez. His heart did not lie to him. What he had already seen furnished enough evidence. In spite of all this, he would return to him, asking him to fulfill his agreement. Should he allow his anger to replace wounded pride? Would he actually return these pounds to his brother, shouting in his face that he disapproved of his filthy life?! He laughed hoarsely, realizing that he was foolishly daydreaming. He knew as well as Hassan that he would return of his own accord to accept the money with thanks and gratitude from him if he was kind enough to offer it. He could not help wishing his brother the best of luck, even though he knew he was going to steal it. As if to appease his gnawing conscience, Hassanein thought: *To us, at any rate, he is a virtuous and generous brother!*

FIFTY-NINE

That afternoon, Hassanein paid a visit to Ahmad Bey Yousri's villa in Taher Street. He was, in fact, vigorously heading for the realization of his life's dream, to join the War College or perish. He had climbed the stairs and now sat waiting in the drawing room, glancing absentmindedly about the garden. He saw it enveloped in mystery. His eyes moved among the elegant palm trees growing amidst tastefully arranged circlets of grass interspersed with rosebuds and surrounded by hedges of camomile. To relieve himself for a while of worry and preoccupation, he focused his attention on a wide circle of grass in the center of the garden between the entrance to the villa and the drawing room. In the middle of this circle stood a short, young palm tree, with a white trunk, rosebushes profusely covering the top, their branches touching it and the intertwining roses merging in a vast halo, whose red, green, and yellow hues blended in peace and harmony. He smiled without realizing it. An evening shadow crept over the garden area and part of the road behind it. Traces of the setting sun fell on the top story on the other side of the road, and the warm air was filled with the fragrance of the jasmine which mounted the fence. He wondered whether it would be possible one day for him to own such a villa! He imagined life there, the bedroom and the garden, the car and the respectable family that living in such a place usually involved. This was his second visit to Ahmad Bey Yousri's villa, and in both cases the lava of frustrated ambition, discontent, and desire for life's clean and respectable pleasures erupted from his volcanic breast. Most of all, he feared that his life would be as confined as that of his brother Hussein, and that, lacking any flowery prospect, he would spend the rest of his life striving for

menial promotions from the eighth to the sixth grade. He felt
he must have his full share of the world's pure air and higher
pleasures. Suddenly his thoughts were interrupted by the sight
of a girl riding a bicycle through the left side of the garden. The
girl was so absorbed in warily weaving her way on the mosaic
paths between the circular flower beds that she paid no attention
to anything around her. She was sixteen years old, slender, with
a pure complexion and a blossoming bosom. She wore a long
white dress, her head demurely bound with a small kerchief.
Hassanein was so attracted to the movements of her legs pedaling up and down under the cover of her dress that he hardly
made out her face. She disappeared behind the right wing of the
villa before he could see what she looked like. His eyes glowed
in watchful interest. He wondered who this girl might be, if she
were not Ahmad Bey's daughter. The image of Bahia with her
soft, plump body and moonlike face came to him, beautiful and
delicious but with nothing approaching this girl's elegance. Remembering his sister, Nefisa, he wondered at the vast differences between creatures of the same species. The compassionate
ache in his heart brought him back to himself with the realization that the sight of the cycling girl, the garden, the villa, and
the chandelier of the reception room combined to stir in him
ambition, revolt, and discontent.

How wonderful it would be to possess this villa and lie with this girl!
he thought. *It's not mere lust. It would be a symbol of power and
glory to have this girl of good birth lying in my arms naked and surrendering, her eyelids closed, as though all the organs of her passionate
body were clamoring, "My master." This is life. Mount it, and you'll
mount a whole class!*

Again recalling Bahia, his pain intensified, mingled with
something akin to remorse and shame. Then his thoughts were
interrupted by the sound of footsteps from the direction of the
stairs. Turning, he saw Ahmad Bey Yousri approaching in a
white silk suit, a red rose in the lapel of his jacket. Hassanein
stood up, went politely up to him, and bowed, greeting him

with veneration. Smiling, the Bey welcomed him. He inquired, as they took their seats, "How is your family, my son?"

"Remembering your favors, they kiss your generous hand," Hassanein answered ingratiatingly.

"You need not mention it," the Bey murmured.

The Bey was certain that shortly this young man would beg him to find him a job or transfer his brother to Cairo. This was the routine of his life every day. Though such requests irritated him, he actually liked them, and could not bear to see his house empty of people seeking his help.

"What's the matter, my son?" he said.

"Your Excellency, I'm appealing to you for help, to intercede for me in joining the War College."

Astonished, the Bey seemed to have expected anything but this aristocratic request. Without hiding his surprise, he inquired, "But what made you choose this narrow gate?"

Distressed at the Bey's astonishment, the young man at this moment developed a blind hatred for him, yet continued to address him in the same polite and ingratiating manner. "Your Excellency, the government's decision to enlarge the army affords me a golden opportunity this year that had never presented itself before. Furthermore, your intercession will be more important than anything else."

"What about the fees?" the Bey asked curtly.

Once more he felt detestation for the Bey. He soon forgot about his request for exemption from the fees, or decided instead to put it off until some other time.

"I'm ready to pay the entire fee," he said, confident and reassured.

The Bey pondered the matter.

"The Under Secretary of State for the Ministry of War is an old friend. I'll talk to him about it," he said.

Hurrying forward, Hassanein took the Bey's hand to kiss it to express his gratitude. Withdrawing his hand, the Bey stood up, perhaps to end the interview. Hassanein bowed low over the man's hand, saluted, repeated his thanks, and left the room, full of cheer and hope. Crossing the garden, he remembered the cycling girl. As he looked at the traces of the wheels on the path, her image flashed before his mind, but absorbed as he was in his hopes for the future, the vision soon passed away.

SIXTY

At the same hour, Nefisa was in Station Square. In supplication, the sky waited for the darkness of evening to fall, while the square bustled with hurrying human beings, animals, trams, and motorcars. On the pavement next to the statue of the Renaissance of Egypt, the girl stood waiting for a break in the traffic so that she could cross the street to the tram stop. She observed a man standing a few arm's lengths away, looking curiously at her. She had learned to understand the real import of such looks. But overcome with astonishment, she wondered: *Even this man!*

He was sixty, age lending to his body a sagging yet dignified appearance. In spite of the hot weather he wore a woolen suit; he carried an elegant fly whisk with an ivory handle, and his eyes were shielded by blue spectacles. His tarbush, slanting backward, revealed a broad forehead, the lower part of which was scorched by the sun, while above the marks left by the fringes of the tarbush, his skin was a brilliant white. His whiskers and the hair at the back of his head were likewise pure white. Held by curiosity and greed, she remained where she was, although the traffic had stopped. Turning her eyes, she found him still gazing at her. As though encouraged by her glances, he walked toward her with heavy steps. As he passed her, he whispered, "Follow me to my car."

He walked to a car as old and dignified as himself, parked very close to the pavement. The step was almost two inches above the level of the pavement; at the door stood a driver, motionless as a statue. He climbed into the car without closing the door behind him; on instruction the driver immediately took his place behind the steering wheel. Thinking that she was lagging behind, the old man took off his spectacles and motioned to her with his hand. She could hardly restrain a smile. Then casting a scrutinizing look around her, urged for the first time in her life by sheer greed, she walked to the car. He moved a bit to give her room, and she sat down beside him. But anxiety soon overcame her when her nostrils filled with the strong smell of liquor on his breath.

"I can't be late," she said.

"Nor can I," he said, his tongue thick with intoxication.

He gave his instructions to the driver, and the car started off at high speed. A sense of alienation came over her. Sorrow and fear struck her heart, in a feeling of absolute degeneration. It was the first time in her life that she had gone with a man without any preliminary acquaintance, whether brief or protracted. Urged on partly by her sexual appetite, she had previously accompanied men she had met only once, twice, or three times. But this time, out of pure greed, and feeling no desire at all, she surrendered to a passerby. How complete was her degeneration! And how dreadful her end! She wondered how the man could single her out as a bed companion. Did her face, ugly though it was, betray her degeneration? Torn now by her old confusion, she was uncertain whether to keep her seductive makeup or to abandon makeup altogether, thus revealing her ugliness.

He placed his palm on her hand. "You're as beautiful as the moon," he stammered.

"I'm not at all beautiful," she said.

"No woman is devoid of some sort of beauty!" he replied disapprovingly.

Was this man a liar or a fool? She marveled how lechery blinded men's eyes. "Except me," she said simply.

Rapping his fingers on her bosom, he said, "But for your beauty, I wouldn't have felt this desire!"

She would have liked to believe him, but she knew it was a lie. No man's love for her lasted more than a few hours. Perhaps he was dissipated, or, like her, suffering from bitter despair. Men had given her enough pain to make her spiteful. Nevertheless, the flames of desire which engulfed her body were never extinguished. Her body degraded her so much that she came to hate it as bitterly as she hated poverty. A captive of her body and her poverty, she knew no way to rescue herself. Swept away in the current of life and bruised on its rocks, naked, injured, unprotected and unpitied, she realized the futility of searching for a safe refuge. She heard him say with a sigh, "We've arrived." Looking out, she watched the car move around a circular road with huge trees, like the shapes of giants, on one side. On the other the Nile ran its course through a vast area shrouded in darkness, decked with flickering lamplight at its remote fringes.

"Is this the island of Gezira?"

"You know it of course!"

Waiting until the driver left his seat and disappeared in the dark, he took off his glasses. "Now," he said, "show me your skill, for everything depends on it."

He was a decayed maniac, soaked with liquor. He thrust his body upon hers, roughly petting her, biting her brutally and pinching her until she was about to scream. The whole business was about to end in a pathetic fiasco. He soon became exhausted. His bizarre, fruitless exertions were almost laughable. At last, lying back drunkenly, he said to her coarsely, "Reach over to the driver's seat and get me the bottle."

Uncorking it, he took several gulps. Then as he leaned back against the seat, his breathing became rough and heavy. Unable to bear waiting any longer, but having learned from experience that nothing more was to be feared, she entreated him ingratiatingly, "It's time for us to return."

As if soliloquizing, he said, "I wish I would never return."

She did not grasp the meaning of his words, but summoning up her courage, she murmured, "Please!"

Putting his hand in his pocket, he sluggishly took out a twenty-piaster piece, letting it fall in her lap. As she picked up the money, she stared at him in disapproval.

"What is this?" she asked, infuriated.

Suddenly aggressive, his eyes glistening with intoxication, the old man said, "It's plenty! If you refuse it, I'll put it back in my pocket."

"I think you're a man of too high a position for this," she said resentfully.

He took another big swig from the bottle and smacked his lips, frowning. "True enough," he replied. "But a twenty-piaster piece is too much for a person like you. I'll bet no woman with a nose like yours would hope to get this sum!"

This wounding insult pierced her breast. Allowing her fear to overcome her anger, she said, "Why do you speak to me in this way?"

"First, because you're greedy, and second, because the female sex is responsible for what happens to me. For your information, I only keep change on me. When I return home, my wife questions me even about this change. So I prefer to beat you rather than be beaten by her!"

Shaking with anger, she kept silent.

"One day," he continued, "I was pestered by a woman in a similar situation. I slapped her on the face and threw her half naked out of the car. What do you think she did? Nothing. Sure, she knew that a policeman would do her more harm than I. I know she's unjustly treated. So are you. But so am I. The real oppressor in this case is my wife."

Sighing resentfully, she muttered, "Please, let's go back."

"It's up to you," he said with a yawn. "Open the window and call the driver."

The car sped on its way back. Her eyes dim as she huddled absentmindedly in a corner of the car, she stared out into the darkness.

SIXTY-ONE

Hassanein's admission to the War College was the happiest event of his life. As he always took the fulfillment of his wishes for granted, he had mistakenly imagined that his enrollment would be rather easy. But later he realized how extremely difficult it was, so much so that eventually he became convinced that, of all his troubles, his arrangement for obtaining the first installment of the fees was the easiest. He paid frequent visits to the villa of Ahmad Bey Yousri, who, almost despairing of his admission to the War College, advised him to turn his attention elsewhere. But the "miracle" of acceptance (as the difficulties of enrollment caused the young man to call it) occurred, thanks to his determination, an advanced place on the list of applicants, his good appearance, his outstanding ability in football and running sports, and above all to the intercession of Ahmad Bey. He was nearly put out of his mind with joy. In fact, he had pinned his hopes so much on his admission that had he failed to get into the War College, he would have been incapable either of doing anything else or of turning his attention elsewhere. His ambition to join this college burst from the depths of his soul, for he was desperate to climb out of his miserable, humble life.

The College seemed like a magic wand, capable of transforming him from a feeble, obscure nonentity into a highly envied officer in only two years' time and with hardly any effort. A friend of his had once observed, "Army officers are pompous and highly paid, and their work, like play, is good for nothing." This description had turned Hassanein's head and intensified his dream of becoming such an officer. When he learned he had been admitted, he refused to acknowledge the great importance of the role played by Ahmad Bey Yousri; it was primarily due, he told his mother, to his physical fitness and distinction in sports. *As of this moment I can consider myself an officer,* he thought proudly. In the fancy of his conceit, he happily began to form a mental picture of the people on whom his military uniform would exert its magical effects: soldiers, girls, the rank and file, even Ahmad Bey Yousri himself. Hassanein in person broke the pleasant news to the family of Farid Effendi Mohammed, and they welcomed it enthusiastically. Farid Effendi saluted him. "We're honored by your visit, young officer," he said with a laugh.

For Bahia's benefit, Hassanein remarked, "I'll have to stay away from you for forty days, until we're permitted to leave the College once a week." At the moment, he hoped to get what he had been deprived of for two years. But there was opportunity to be alone with the girl for only a few minutes; had she acquiesced, this would have been enough. But the girl insisted on chastity. Overcome by her usual shyness, she shrank at bidding him farewell, her heart throbbing with pain and anxiety. Almost inaudibly he said to her hurriedly, "I want a hot kiss from your lips!" But her shyness and immobility persisted.

"Even at a moment like this," he said, "you deny me. I can't imagine that you love me."

Breaking her silence, the girl replied, "I refuse because I do."

He mused inquiringly, "I don't understand you."

With touching courage, she spoke more frankly, "I refuse you because I love you."

This was the first time he had heard her open and candid confession, and he was so deeply moved that he was about to come too close to her. But nodding her head toward the open door of the room, she signaled a warning.

Farid Effendi and his wife soon returned, and he spent the rest of the time torn between mixed feelings of ecstasy, anxious longing, and torment. Bidding Farid Effendi's family goodbye, he went down to his flat.

This is wise love, he thought. *Love governed by firmness and foresight, as if she had devised a careful plan to make sure that I will marry her. But does true love know this kind of frigid logic?*

But these thoughts were, in effect, provoked by his overwhelming feeling of irritation and regret. He considered the farewell scene the worst a lover could ever have experienced. He spent part of the night with his mother and sister. Unable to control her feelings, Nefisa as usual shed tears. Depressed, she said, "We're doomed to live alone."

Hassanein himself experienced the sinking feeling of a person parting from his family for the first time in his life. But his yearning to lead an independent life in a different place and milieu alleviated his depression. As for Samira, she preserved her apparent calm, bidding Nefisa not to allow grief to carry her away. Sharply she said to her daughter, "Don't cry like a child. We'll see him frequently. It gives us happiness enough to see that he has realized his hopes."

But her heart actually spoke a different language. The imminent parting from her son evoked her sorrow and brought back to her mind memories of grief long past. She remembered Hussein's farewell scene. She imagined what her home would be like when her last son was gone. In spite of herself, the memory of her departed husband was revived; she wondered at her own life, which would not allow her any measure of happiness unless it was associated with the pains of partings and farewells. Was she doomed to remain alone for the rest of her life? And was it for such an end that she had patiently and stoically suffered and struggled?

But summoning up her latent strength, she prevented herself from being carried away by grief. She drew on the success of her son to dispel the melancholy that beset her. However, she now believed that her patience and strivings had not been in vain, and that the tossing ship of her life was heading for a secure harbor. She felt she had the right to rejoice, for she had sacrificed every drop of her heart's blood to cause the fruits of her family life to bloom and flourish.

Next morning, Hassanein bade his mother and sister farewell and went off to his college.

SIXTY-TWO

Hassanein found himself among the freshmen in the College court. To escape loneliness his eyes searched, to no avail, for an old friend from the Tawfikiyah School. Although this annoyed him, he felt proud that he was the only one from his school admitted to the War College. As eager as he was for conversation, it was no use waiting for someone to address him first, and his sense of pride stopped him from taking the first step. So he contented himself with the sights of the College, the extensive court, with its superb, massive buildings, and the statues of the two guns erected at the entrance, which engaged his attention for a long time. The qualities of the College which he admired not only thrilled him but turned his head. At the beginning he was confident of his physical superiority: his tall stature, erect carriage, and handsome figure. But much of his self-admiration was deflated when he examined his classmates, among whom he saw young men in the prime of their youth, of blooming vitality and splendid good looks. Moreover, some of these young men were aristocratic in appearance. Hassanein's eyes fell upon a man coming out of a room overlooking the court; he recognized him as an old schoolmate at the Tawfikiyah School, perhaps his senior by a year or more at the War College. He wore short khaki trousers and a shirt with four stripes on his left arm. He was not a friend but merely an acquaintance to whom he had been introduced in the court of the school. Although he remembered him only as Irfan, and since under normal circumstances he would have been reluctant to speak to him, yet at that moment he warmly welcomed a conversation with him to show the other freshmen his friendship with this upperclassman.

Hassanein walked up to stand face to face with the young man. He stretched out his hand with a smile. "How are you, Irfan?" he said with familiarity.

But a rigid glance from the grim, conceited countenance of his colleague caused his smile quickly to die out. Examining his interlocutor with arrogance and something akin to anger, Irfan uttered not a word. He merely touched Hassanein's hand and withdrew it quickly as though he were afraid a hideous disease might contaminate it. Dumbfounded, Hassanein thought the young man might have forgotten or misunderstood him.

"Don't you remember me? I'm Hassanein Kamel Ali," he cried plaintively.

Unimpressed, Irfan remained as rigidly recalcitrant as before. Finally breaking the silence, he said gruffly, "There's no friendship here. You're a freshman and I'm a sergeant major."

With these words, Irfan moved off. Finding himself in an embarrassing situation which he had never before experienced, Hassanein felt his limbs go numb and his lips twitch. He imagined the others laughing and winking sarcastically at him; to avoid their glances he stood aside. Why, he wondered, did the fool behave in this way? Was it possible that he had gone out of his mind or had he insulted him out of sheer spite? Was this the customary College procedure? Absorbed in his thoughts, he became blind to everything around him, and he came to himself only when the freshmen were called for the first time to line up in their civilian clothes.

As instructed by the sergeant major, Mohammed Irfan, and several soldiers, they formed two parallel lines. Hassanein avoided looking at his old schoolmate, to whose cutting authority he had to submit. He controlled his fury lest it betray him. Surrounded by a group of junior officers, a high-ranking officer approached. He cast a penetrating glance at the freshmen, then delivered a speech on the military life which they had chosen for a career. Addressing them in colloquial language and with a gruff voice reflected in his fierce, stern features, he punctuated

several of his sentences with repeated references to "strict punishment" which, recurring like rhythmic beats, struck awe into
their hearts. Immediately after this speech, the first day of their
new military life began. This was Hassanein's initiation into the
new life to which he was to become accustomed. Like all days,
the first was long and arduous, beginning with cold showers in
the early morning, followed by the lineups and the lessons. So
continuous were their labors, and so coarse their food, clothes,
and treatment, that when bedtime came they slept like logs.
Harsh treatment, considered mandatory by the authorities, was
the worst aspect of this life. A cadet had only to earn a stripe
for seniority to feel it his right to treat his subordinates roughly
and exercise his authority tyrannically and without mercy, in
what almost amounted to insults and deliberate effrontery. Since
the cherished motto of the College was blind obedience, objection and protest were out of the question. Hassanein found his
only solace from such a terrifying atmosphere in the hope that
one day he would become a corporal and later a sergeant major.
Then, at one stroke, he would be able to pay it all back!

With fondness he recalled his days at the Tawfikiyah School,
which he had once described as instilling "stark fear." He sometimes became so annoyed with this harsh discipline that he regretted his choice of such an infernal college, wishing that he
had guts enough to leave it. Many of his classmates shared the
same sentiments, especially in their first days at the College.
The discipline sapped their energy and left them weak. Indeed,
Hassanein might perhaps have been the only cadet immune to
the baneful effects of this unnatural mode of life. Unlike the
others, his body seemed to have been unexpectedly replenished.
Coarse as the food at the College was, it provided him with
regular meals, so infrequent during his previous, troubled years.
But on Fridays, when parents were customarily permitted to
visit, he underwent unusual psychic suffering. Such days were
delightful occasions; the outer court of the College was filled
with parents and relatives, and the cadets returned afterward to

their rooms laden with presents of sweets, fruits and delicious food. Since even the cadets from the countryside had relatives in Cairo, none spent this happy day alone except for Hassanein; nobody visited him, nor did he expect anybody to visit him. Before he left home, his mother had told him that she could not possibly visit him because, as he knew, she was unable to afford a new, decent overcoat to wear before his fellow cadets. As for Nefisa, she had said to him in her usual joking manner, "I don't think it would do you honor if I put in an appearance before your classmates with a face like mine." Since Bahia was shy and unaccustomed to appearing among strangers, he had no hope that she would come. The only possibility was Farid Effendi, but he was lazy by nature and refused to leave his house except in matters of urgency. However, Farid Effendi once did pay him a visit and brought a present of biscuits. On visiting days, Hassanein used to choose a place at the entrance to the interior court, watching the visitors with melancholy eyes and enjoying the sight of the women and girls, their captivatingly beautiful faces and their superbly elegant dresses. He wondered at the class differences that segregated human beings, and he was perplexed and disturbed. Boiling inside with discontent, anger, and revolt, he could give vent to such passions only in questioning God's ways toward man, wondering defiantly about His wisdom in making the world what it was. One of his classmates once asked him why he kept himself aloof. "My father is dead," Hassanein replied without hesitation, "and my brother is a teacher in Tanta. My family is conservative, and we're not accustomed to appearing here in society as you are."

Yet Hassanein's depressing thoughts had little opportunity to flourish under the rigorous discipline of military life, which made him forget these thoughts most of the time. As the days passed, he adapted himself to the rigor of this stifling atmosphere, and he found life much more tolerable than before. Moreover, new friendships relieved his loneliness. Thus, in spite of everything, he could once again laugh. And so passed forty days.

SIXTY-THREE

As he departed from the College in his military uniform, it occurred to him that facing the world in this colorful garb was in itself a splendid achievement. He started off as erect as a pillar, self-admiring as a peacock, glancing foppishly at his own image reflected in the windows of shops and coffeehouses. Pleased with the red stripe on his uniform, the long tarbush, and the glistening shoes, he waved his short baton with its silver handle and held his gloves as if to defy the whole world. As he approached Nasr Allah from a distance, he was moved by mixed feelings of sympathy and revulsion. Since he had not revealed his home address to any of his classmates, he was sure that no one whom he did not desire to see the place would encounter him. At the same time, he hoped that only those he wanted to would set eyes upon him. All of them, the shoemaker, the blacksmith, the tobacconist, and Gaber Soliman the grocer, greeted him, waving their hands and staring at him. He raised his eyes to Farid Effendi's balcony. Noting that it was closed, he was pleased at the happy surprise his unexpected appearance would afford him. Crossing the courtyard, he knocked at the door, and waited with a smile on his face. Nefisa's voice struck his ears, shouting, "Who is it?" She opened the door. She had barely seen him when she exclaimed, "Hassanein!"

Excited, she pressed his hand, shaking it with force and pleasure. At the sound of her daughter's voice, Samira came hurrying. He let her embrace him with her emaciated hands and take him to her breast. He kissed her forehead in happiness mixed with concern for his jacket as her arms encircled it. Surrounded by his mother and sister, he walked to his old room, which, strange though it seemed now, stirred nostalgic memories.

The three stood together, the two women looking at him with love and admiration. Samira prayed to God to make her son prosperous, briefly expressed her delight, then took refuge in silence. But the talkative Nefisa said, "We missed you very much. Without you the house is like a tomb. Since you were away, I've had to answer Hussein's letters, and my handwriting is uglier than my face. Hussein couldn't take his vacation this year because of his colleague's illness; it made us almost mad with grief. Did you really exchange letters? He told me about it ten days ago. What did you learn at the College? Can you now fire a gun?" Jokingly he answered her questions as he took off his tarbush and put his baton and gloves on the desk. He remained standing, carefully examining his jacket for any damage from the embraces. His mother sat on the bed. "Sit down, my son," she said.

"I'm afraid my trousers might get wrinkled," he replied after a moment of hesitation.

"Will you keep standing as long as you have your uniform on?" the woman inquired with astonishment.

Confused, he smiled, then sat down warily on the chair, stretching out his legs and carefully inspecting his trousers. "A wrinkle in my trousers," he said, "means strict punishment, no less than a month's detention at College."

Watching his mother's countenance to observe the effect of these remarks, he realized that she was disturbed. "Our life is terribly hard," he continued in a bored voice. "We spend all day and part of the night in the open amidst guns, bombs, and bullets. The slightest mistake might cost a man his life."

Terrified, Nefisa's eyes opened wide. Worried, his mother queried, "How can they endanger the lives of our dear sons?"

"Why did you choose the College?" Nefisa exclaimed passionately.

"Have no fears for me," he replied, shaking his head with confidence. "I can manage the firearms skillfully, and I've won the praise of all the officers."

"What good is praise if, God forbid, you're injured?" Samira sighed.

"Then what will you do if tomorrow we're called upon to fight?" Hassanein spoke with inward pleasure. "Haven't you heard that Hitler is preparing for war? If war breaks out, Mussolini will attack Egypt, and all of us will be recruited to fight."

Horror-stricken, Samira stared at him. "Is it true, my son?" she asked earnestly.

"This is what some people say," he said, retreating a bit.

"But what do you yourself think?"

Before he could reply, Nefisa cried, "If it's true, leave the College at once!"

The young man burst out laughing. Afraid he might spoil their pleasant reunion, he said, "Don't take what I said seriously; I just wanted to scare you." Then, changing his tone, he added, "Let's put joking aside. Tell me, *Lady* Nefisa, what will you prepare for my dinner tomorrow?"

Smiling, the girl realized that her brother would be her guest Thursday afternoon and during the day on Friday, and that she was obligated to treat him most generously.

"I'll buy two chickens for you," she said, "and Mother will cook them, and make green soup."

"Splendid! And the desserts?!"

"Oranges?"

"How about some sweets—some *kunafa*? I've seen those Friday presents to my colleagues so often that I drool at the thought!"

Nefisa was concerned less for the *kunafa* than for the shortening required for this kind of dessert, but overcome with generosity, she did not balk at the request.

"And you'll have *kunafa*," she said, "for dessert, as you wish."

"I could have been greedy and asked you to stuff it with nuts and pistachios," the young man said hesitantly. She dismissed the question with a joke. Realizing that this was the limit of her generosity, Hassanein laughed. "If you'd only seen the presents

my colleagues received! Once, a friend of mine offered me
something called pudding."

"Pudding?"

"Yes, pudding."

"Don't blame me, but I might have said pudding was a fire-
arm!" Nefisa said with a laugh.

"Why don't you take off your uniform?" his mother asked.

"No, I'm going to the cinema," he said shyly.

Noting the resentment in his mother's eyes, he hurried to say,
"I'll come back early so that we can sit up together tonight.
We'll spend tomorrow together, too."

They resumed their conversation and reminiscences at length.
Unable to restrain his fancies longer, his heart was attracted to
the flat upstairs. It was difficult to interrupt the conversation to
say that he wanted to visit their neighbor Farid Effendi.

"It's time to go to the cinema," he said indifferently. "Perhaps
I can take a few moments to visit Farid Effendi."

SIXTY-FOUR

He wished he could, somehow, be alone with his girl. But how? Her parents had received him in the sitting room. Joining in the customary lengthy conversation, he waited impatiently for her to come. Shyly she entered the room, wearing a long pink dressing gown that revealed only her limbs. She greeted Hassanein formally, her father looking at her with laughing and admiring eyes. She sat beside her mother. The conversation dragged on. But her presence absorbed all of his attention, and he found it difficult to follow their chatter, and even more so to take part in it. Overcome with boredom, he looked at her furtively, forming a mental picture of her plump, naked body. The blood boiled in his veins, and he felt resentment against the group for restricting his liberty. He noted the confidence and serenity in Bahia's eyes, her statuesque appearance, her reassurance as she sat at home under the comforting protection of her parents, listening to their conversation, safe in this refuge from Hassanein's caprices. Although sometimes her attitude angered him, he could not ignore the sense of confidence and trust which she managed to inspire in him, lending an unshakable sense of security and constancy to his profound feeling for her. The conversation went on. Lacking sufficient courage to take part in it, she merely responded with a nod of the head or a smile on her lips, and his annoyance reached a climax. As he sought for a way out of the dilemma, a bold idea occurred to him, and with his characteristic audacity he put it into action at once. He said to Farid Effendi, "Would you allow me to take Bahia to the cinema?"

Bahia's face flushed and she lowered her eyes, while her parents exchanged glances.

"I think in these modern times, this should be permissible for an engaged couple," Farid Effendi replied. But his wife disagreed. "I'm afraid this might not appeal to Madam, your mother," she said to Hassanein.

To prevent his stratagem from being wrecked, Hassanein lied unscrupulously. "I've already asked her permission," he said, "and she agreed with pleasure."

A smile appeared on the woman's face. She looked at her husband. "I've no objection," she said, "since her father agrees."

Farid Effendi asked his daughter to get ready to accompany the young man to the cinema, and shyly she stumbled out of the room. A few minutes later, the couple left. Approaching his flat, Bahia noticed Hassanein's cautious steps, as if he feared they might attract his family's attention. She was worried.

"You lied to my mother," she whispered, "pretending that you had your mother's permission. And Nefisa will get angry because you didn't invite her to go with us to the cinema!"

He motioned to her to keep silent, took her hand, and led her across the courtyard to the alley. They walked side by side, Bahia's parents watching them from the balcony. Her red overcoat brought her pure, white complexion into relief; she was as pretty as a kitten. But in her lingering worry she said accusingly, "Sooner or later your family will know about our outing."

His pleasurable sense of triumph dismissed all concern. "We've committed no sin," he said with a laugh, "nor will the world fall apart!"

"Wouldn't it have been better to invite Nefisa to come with us?"

"But I want to be alone with you!"

She feared Nefisa more than anyone else. "You don't care about anything at all," she said with concern, "and it's a pity."

He reacted with frank, sometimes even offensive words, attacking her reserve and frigidity. "I wish I had committed a sin with you," he said, "to deserve your accusations!"

Her face turned red, and she frowned with resentment. She kept silent now as they mingled with the people standing on the platform of the tram stop. With inward satisfaction he gazed upon her angry face. "I mean a minor sin," he whispered with a smile.

She turned her face away until the tram arrived. They climbed into a first-class compartment. Finding it occupied by a foreign lady, Hassanein felt relieved. Sitting close to Bahia, he said teasingly, "Did you miss me much while I was away?"

"I never thought of you," she said, as if in anger.

Pretending to be sad, he shook his head. "Nothing," he said, "hurt me more than my feeling that you were anxious to see me."

"To be frank with you, your new college has made you more unpleasant than before," she said coldly, hiding a smile.

Involuntarily he recalled Nefisa's indictment of Bahia as not being sweet-tempered, and he looked closely at the girl. He found her superbly beautiful, yet his sister had described her as not having a sweet temper. He was aware that being head over heels in love with her made him adore even this defect in his beloved's character. He decided to stop teasing her.

"While I was away," he said warmly, "I never forgot you for a single moment. Eventually I realized that while it's torture to be near one you love and she won't give in, it's heaven on earth not to be tragically separated from her."

Lowering her eyes, she remained speechless. Yet, scenting the fragrance of mute passion in her absentminded surrender, he was profoundly relieved. He spoke ramblingly until the tram reached Station Square; they got off the tramcar and walked toward Imad al-Din Street. He asked her to take his arm, and she did so hesitantly.

Walking for the first time beside a person other than her mother, she was overwhelmed with shyness and confusion. Feeling his elbow touch her breast, deliberately or accidentally, she withdrew her arm from his.

"What have I done?" he protested.

"I like it better this way."

He was indignant at missing this opportunity. "It'll take a miracle to change you into a real wife," he said. "I mean a wife who embraces and hugs her husband and . . ."

Soon afterward, they were seated side by side in the cinema. His feeling of conceit and arrogance returned. This time he had two assets, his uniform and his beloved. When some of his classmates, passing by, cast appraising glances at his girl, this made his heart swell with further pleasure. Leaning toward her, he whispered, "Have you noticed that your beauty attracts attention?"

Noting a shy smile on her lips, he continued to be merry. "My heart tells me," he whispered again, "that tonight I'll get the kiss I've long desired."

She threw him a threatening glance, then looked straight ahead. In the dark he tried to touch her with his elbow or foot, but she did not encourage him. Finally, under his persistent pressure, she allowed him to take the palm of her hand into his, both resting on the chair arm separating their two seats. Time passed in total happiness.

SIXTY-FIVE

On Friday evening, he stood in Queen Farida Square, waiting for the No. 10 bus to take him to the College. He had spent a happy day with his family and had a delicious dinner. Nefisa was merry as usual, but within hearing distance of her mother, she said to him sarcastically, "I wish I'd seen you escorting the 'lady' to the cinema!"

Realizing that his secret was known when his sister opened fire on him, he gave a loud laugh. He glanced at his mother; she was silent, with something like a smile on her face. He was grateful for his military uniform, which had rescued him from her blows forever.

"What a lovely couple you are!" Nefisa began again with sarcasm. "You with a figure like a lamppost, and your 'lady' only a few inches tall, her sour temper announcing the presence of both of you!"

"With your defects," her mother scolded, "you're in no position to find fault."

"Anyhow, at least I've got a sweet temper," the girl replied with a laugh. "But you're excused, Master Hassanein, since my face isn't made for the cinema!"

Now he experienced remorse, and Hassanein very warmly apologized to her. What harm would there have been if he had invited her to go with them to the cinema? While he stood waiting for the bus, the memories of the day passed through his mind. After a while many of his classmates appeared and the bus arrived. Jostling, they all rushed into it. Other classmates, some of whom he had seen the day before at the cinema, climbed aboard. Hassanein was pleased at the thought that, as was customary under such circumstances, they would probably comment on his girl. He eagerly awaited their observations on his adventures as a Don Juan. He had not long to wait, since more than one of his classmates seemed to be on the alert. Pointing to him, one of them said, "Guess what. Yesterday this hero was seen with a girl on his arm."

Hassanein hoped that all his classmates heard this remark and would devote their conversation to him alone.

"What type was she?" another inquired.

"The homely type."

"Beautiful?"

Focusing all his attention on their remarks, Hassanein's awareness intensified.

"She had blue eyes," the first one said, "but she had a crudely native look."

The blood rushed to Hassanein's face. His high elation vanished; his ecstatic enthusiasm was extinguished. The others continued their commentary in boisterous hilarity.

"Too short and too plump."

"As sour-tempered as a field marshal."

"Old-fashioned, on the whole. Where did you find her?"

Returning to his senses, Hassanein realized that this last question was directed to him, but he remained silent. Pretending indifference, he kept laughing, despite his wounded feelings of shame and defeat. One young man said, "I hope she's not your fiancée."

Almost unaware of what he was saying, Hassanein exclaimed, "Of course not!"

"A mistress?"

Feelings of pain and frustration upsurging within him, he answered, "It's only for fun!"

"In that case, she's good enough. A virgin?"

"Yes," he said, extremely perturbed.

"May God disappoint your hopes! Why do you waste your time with virgins? Don't you understand that it's our College tradition to spend Thursday night with a mistress and Friday with a fiancée, or a substitute for one?"

Hassanein forced a laugh. "Hereafter," he said, "I'll straighten out my schedule of appointments with women!"

They all laughed, and the drift of their conversation changed. Suffering the anguish of defeat, he became absorbed in his dejection. Unwittingly, he had denied his girl. *Ah! If they knew she was my fiancée,* he thought, *and that even after two years of perseverance she still refuses to allow me to kiss her! A crudely native look . . . too short and too plump . . . as sour-tempered as a field marshal. Is this true of Bahia? Sure, she's old-fashioned; there's some truth in the description. She doesn't know how to appear with me in public. She lacks a sense of humor and doesn't know how to converse with people. She only grumbles and finds fault.* He wondered how he could possibly appear with her in public! People would say all these things and even more about her. He was depressed and resentful. Totally absorbed in these thoughts, he realized that the bus had stopped in front of the College only when his classmates left their seats.

SIXTY-SIX

The next week, at the usual time, he paid Farid Effendi a visit. Since Farid Effendi and Salem, the youngster, were not at home, he was alone with Bahia and her mother, and the father's absence afforded him an unusual degree of liberty. Bahia appeared in a brown dress, with a decorative fanlike silk frill attached by means of a clip to the lower part of the collar, the wings spreading out upon her bosom. Once invited, she had only to put on her overcoat to be ready to go with him to the cinema. But today he had absolutely no intention of inviting her. Nefisa's voice still echoed in his ears. After giving him a ten-piaster piece, she had warned, "This is for your outing alone!"

But Nefisa was not the only reason. In fact, he lacked the guts to appear again with Bahia in front of his classmates. He had thought she was the most beautiful girl. But then, his eyes were not open, and the sarcastic remarks of his classmates testified to his blindness. As he looked closely at her, their eyes met, and his dark thoughts disappeared. Blood boiled in his veins and a reckless desire surged up in his chest. There was no doubt she was at once beautiful and luscious. But how could he possibly disregard the appalling fact that he must avoid appearing with her in public? As Bahia's mother continued to converse with him, she noticed his absentmindedness and curt replies.

"Master Hassanein," she wondered, "what's the matter with you? You look worried!"

Disconcerted, he became aware of his surroundings and said, as if apologetically, "Our training last week was so strenuous that we left the College almost dead."

More attentive, he took an active part in the conversation,

until the mother excused herself to perform the prayers, leaving him alone with the girl.

"What's wrong with you?" the girl asked.

"Nothing!" he said, smiling to dispel her doubts.

"But you're not normal today."

Alone with the girl and under the sway of his surging passions, a cunning idea suggested itself to him. Pretending to be sad, he said, "I can't forget your reserve toward me."

"Again, the same old subject?"

"Of course! It's my right and I won't give it up as long as I live."

"I thought we'd finished with this," the girl said beseechingly.

"You baffle me. All my classmates have fiancées, but, unlike you, they don't deny them their right to kisses and embraces."

Her face flushed; she murmured, "They are different from me, and I'm different from them."

That was true. Perhaps his classmates emphasized it too much. Ironically, he thought, she was unaware of the implication of her words! But before he could reply, she quickly changed the drift of the conversation. "Are you going to the cinema?" she asked.

He understood that she was paving the way for an invitation. He was filled with annoyance and embarrassment. But as concern outweighed embarrassment, he said, "No. I've an appointment with some of my classmates."

Shyly, she lowered her eyes. A painful silence prevailed.

"What was your family's reaction to our going to the cinema together?" she asked him.

Taking advantage of her question as a convenient pretext to avoid speaking of such matters, he said, "Nothing worth mentioning—except that my mother was upset because I asked you to violate the tradition of your respectable family!"

"There's nothing indecent about respectable families allowing their daughters to go to the cinema," she said coldly.

"Likewise, there's nothing indecent in embraces and kisses. But, like my mother, you don't believe in it!"

Ignoring his insinuation, she inquired, "Did she tell you not to take me to the cinema again?"

"No! But she's afraid I might unintentionally offend your respectable family."

"Didn't you tell her of my parents' approval?"

"Yes, I did. But she believed they approved out of embarrassment."

"Should I understand from this," Bahia inquired, "that we won't go out together after today?"

Incapable of confronting her with his innermost thoughts, he said, "No. We'll go out whenever we like."

No sooner had he uttered these words than he regretted them. Shyly smiling, she said in a low voice, "I thought we'd go today to the cinema."

He thought about inviting her. Although it softened his feelings, he refused to surrender to them. "But for this appointment I told you about . . ." he said.

"Ah! Of course, your appointment is more important than taking me to the cinema!"

"That isn't true, but I'm bound by my previous appointment. Besides . . . besides, it might not be advisable within such a short time to do again what my mother considers a violation of traditions."

Shaking her head, she said with a sad smile, "Then it's not the appointment that stops you!"

"No. For both reasons," he answered with resignation. "Excuse the old-fashioned mentality of my mother."

For the first time, unable to contain her emotions, she said, "Why, then, do you allow Nefisa to go out every day?"

Resenting her tone and offended by the implication of her words, he retorted rather sharply, "Nefisa goes out for work; otherwise she would stay at home."

"I didn't mean to offend anybody," she said to him tenderly. "I just wanted to say that going out doesn't shame anyone."

Silence prevailed until they heard the returning footsteps of Bahia's mother. "Hassanein, are you angry?" Bahia asked worriedly.

Because of her mother's arrival, he could not answer her, but his tender smile restored her confidence. Hassanein remained with them for an hour; then, bidding them goodbye, he went away.

SIXTY-SEVEN

He had no appointment with his classmates as he had pretended. He entered the cinema alone a few minutes after the beginning of the show. He was shown to his seat in the darkness. Half attentive, half reminiscing about Bahia and his fraudulent departure, he watched the newsreel. He remembered how Bahia tenderly pressed his hand as she bade him farewell. It was a pleasurable pressure which caused a quiver in his heart and made him forget whatever offenses she might have committed! *Now,* he thought, *my dream can come true. I'd have realized my cherished desire a long time ago if, instead of humble entreaties, I'd shown some self-restraint. She wouldn't have refused if I'd repeatedly frowned upon her. How foolish of me! Then I'll not be content with just a kiss. I'll crush her to my breast until her bones snap under my arms, but far from the critical eyes of those who admire a girl for her good looks, elegance, and fashion. But even after marrying her, should I hide her away from the public view? Why pay attention to other people and their critical remarks? No. This is an evil thing which I can't possibly put aside. It's my nature.* He found relief from his thoughts as he focused his attention on the screen to watch Hitler receiving the ambassadors on his birthday. A cartoon followed, then an intermission, and the lights went on. Turning his head, he examined the faces around him. His eyes were arrested by a colossal, disgustingly obese woman conversing with her husband beside her. He could not help admiring this man's courage and complete indifference to society in escorting such a woman.

A glimpse to his left revealed a charming girl in a gray jacket and skirt occupying the next seat. It occurred to him that he had seen this face before. He searched deep in the recesses of his memory to identify her. Meanwhile, his eyes fell on a woman next to her, then on a man at the sight of whom his heart beat violently. Springing to his feet, Hassanein courteously extended his hand in greeting. "Good evening, Your Excellency."

The man, no less than Ahmad Bey Yousri himself, looked at him and greeted him with a smile. He introduced the young man to his wife and daughter as "the son of the late Kamel Effendi Ali." Having saluted them most politely, Hassanein withdrew to his seat, still feeling the touch of the girl's hand. The Bey asked him about his progress at the College and he offered his thanks as he answered. Then silence fell between the two men, each keeping to himself. Staring straight ahead, Hassanein was relieved to have been able to maintain his composure when he was introduced for the first time in his life to two distinguished ladies of the upper classes. A waiter passed by carrying a variety of chocolates and refreshments. He wished he had enough money to order some of these for the Bey's family. But with only a few piasters in his pocket, he became indignant at missing such an opportunity, detesting his poverty more than ever before. The lights went down and the cinema screen came back to life. Absorbed in his thoughts and giving rein to his heated imagination, Hassanein was unable to concentrate on the film. Now he was convinced it was not the first time he had seen this charming face. He remembered the naked leg revealed by the pedaling of a bicycle in the garden of the Bey's villa. He wondered what impression he had left upon her, what impression, too, had been made by Ahmad Bey's words of introduction, "the son of the late Kamel Effendi Ali."

Obviously, his father had been a minor employee. Moreover, the two women undoubtedly knew of the Bey's efforts to help his family, first by interceding to find a job for Hussein, later by assisting Hassanein to enroll in the War College. Again, it was impossible that they were unaware of his true social status. Perhaps the girl considered his career the result of her father's benefaction. Perhaps she thought that without her father he would not be wearing this red-striped uniform. All this was quite possible, even certain. Hassanein's forehead was hot with shame and discontent.

I've seen your leg on the bicycle, he thought, *lovely and ivory-colored, but not miraculous. There are no miracles in this world. Don't you go to bed the same way any other girl does? Don't you fly into raptures in sexual intercourse like any other woman? And become pregnant like the servant we dismissed because of our poverty, and, like a bitch, groan when overcome by the pangs of childbirth?* Suddenly he rubbed his nose with his forefinger, which still bore traces of the lovely perfume on her hand. It had an exciting, almost magical effect on him and penetrated his heart. Quieting, contenting, and intoxicating, its fragrance purged his breast of the impurities of anger and pain. Observing her lovely, fairylike figure, he guessed that her arms were folded on her breast. He wished that, placing her hand on the arm of the seat, she would casually touch his. He formed a mental image of her face, the face of which he had had a glimpse when he had shaken hands with her: long and full, with two black eyes expressing vitality and vivacity, a circle of deep black hair and a mole on her left cheek which added beauty to her white complexion. Conjuring up Bahia's image and comparing the two, he became convinced that this girl was no more beautiful than his girl. But at the same time he found Bahia's beauty cold, like a statue's, while that of the other girl was full of blood, inflaming the imagination and infusing warmth into the soul. Furthermore, to his ambitious spirit she appeared as a living symbol of the socially privileged, to which he desperately looked forward to joining. He regarded her not so much as a girl as a representative of a certain class and a certain mode of life. But his momentary ecstasy did not blind him to his true feelings, and he did not delude himself that she penetrated his heart as Bahia did. Totally passive though she was, Bahia was in possession of the very roots of his instincts and nerves, while the other appealed to his unlimited ambition. Perhaps this other girl enabled him to discover an enigmatic part of himself, his heart's basic preference for ambition over happiness and security. Suddenly his passions cooled down.

I'm swept away by foolish dreams, he thought. *But don't I have the right to resort to dreams for relief? Don't we all dream what we dream? Yes, but our dreams are disturbed only by the illusion that they are real.* Some time passed before he could concentrate his attention again on the cinema screen. But, his energy exhausted by thought, the scenes of the film bored and tired him, and he sat through them by an effort of will until the lights were turned on. As his eyes met those of Ahmad Bey's family, he greeted them with a nod before he dissolved into the crowd streaming out of the cinema. At last, separating himself from the crowd, he wandered for an hour in the streets before he took the tram for Shubra.

As he approached the quarter where he lived, Nasr Allah alley appeared to him more sordid than ever. As he crossed it, grudgingly and with downcast eyes, his nostrils were filled with the smell of dust mingled with smoke and grease.

SIXTY-EIGHT

The days passed and the scholastic year came almost to an end. During the third quarter of the year, Hassanein learned that, so as to increase the size of the Egyptian army after the ratification of the Anglo-Egyptian Treaty, the Minister of War had decided to graduate a group of officers after only one year, and that these new graduates would complete their training after joining their regiments. The students received double work assignments, but they welcomed this additional work with enthusiasm. In fact, the whole business appeared so incredible that it seemed stranger than fiction. None of the students, least of all Hassanein himself, would have imagined that he would become an officer after only one scholastic year, but when the year came to an end, Hassanein graduated.

His mother's heart filled with delight and she felt secure, like a lost sailor, his food run out and sails torn, finally emerging from an engulfing mist into a safe, clear harbor. She thought: *Oh, God! You alone have helped me out of my troubles. Who could compare our situation yesterday, when we were groping in the dark, with our promising, hopeful situation today, without recognizing Your justice and mercy!* For the first time in her life she felt contented and happy. To her fading eyes, the long-drawn-out dilemma of her life now appeared in a halo of pleasurable pride as though it had been no more than a casual, forced frown on the forehead of Merciful Fate.

Thus she gave thanks to God and shed tears of joy. She had saved enough from Hussein's and Nefisa's money to pay the college fees of the next year. With these savings, Hassanein had an officer's uniform tailored, which kept him busy until the graduates were assigned to the various regiments. High on the list of successful cadets, he was appointed to the cavalry in Cairo, a piece of good fortune the family would never have dreamt of. Hassanein's uniform symbolized the fulfillment of his old dreams. As she looked at him with amazement and happiness in her eyes, Samira abandoned her usual taciturnity and solemnity. This was her beloved son, the blossom and cherished dream of her life.

"During the *Mahmal* ceremony," he had once said to her, "you and Nefisa will have an excellent opportunity to see me on horseback at the head of the cavalry band!"

"I'll be there," she could not help answering, "only if you buy me a decent overcoat to wear before the multitudes crowding the street!"

"Have patience until I receive my salary!" the young man said with a laugh.

These were days of unadulterated happiness and pleasure, although Hassanein had many things to be concerned about. Hoping to establish his happiness on solid, unshakable foundations, when he was alone with his mother in the house he said to her with unusual gravity, "Mother, Nefisa must stop her shameful work at once. It doesn't become an officer's sister to work as a dressmaker."

His mother smiled. "My son, she'd welcome this from the bottom of her heart," she said simply.

Although he had anticipated these words, they failed to wipe out the thoughts which preoccupied him. "I wish we could erase the past out of existence," he continued with a melancholy sigh. "I'm afraid some people might bring it up to hurt us. You know how people are! If my colleagues ever heard of it, my prestige would suffer."

His concern partly infecting her, she smiled and patted his shoulder to banish his worries. "We were poor, and most people are poor," she said. "There's nothing in that to be ashamed of."

He shook his head in protest. He said with sorrow, "This is more idle talk. You know people better than I do."

"My son, I don't want you to poison your peace of mind with such thoughts!"

As if deaf to her words, he added, "This alley knows the humble circumstances of our life. So I can't bear to stay in it."

Fearing that her happiness might be totally destroyed, she begged him. "Don't you worry. Time will straighten out these matters."

Staring curiously at his mother, he envied her self-control. But soon he became angry at her indifference to the dangers, which were exaggerated in his imagination. "True," he said sharply, "time will straighten matters out, but only after destroying me."

A look of terror appeared in the woman's eyes. Gently reproachful, she replied, "I see you're impatient and anticipating trouble as usual. My advice to you is not to get your actual happiness mixed up with insignificant sorrows, which are only imaginary."

"Insignificant!" he exclaimed.

"Yes, insignificant."

"You consider insignificant Nefisa's past and the things the inhabitants of this quarter know about us?"

"Unless you have faith in God, you'll never know real happiness."

"I wish I could drop a heavy curtain on our past," Hassanein sighed.

"Have patience and it will happen."

Inflamed with anger, the young man grew impatient. "I fear nothing," he said, "more than this patience you're asking me to have. Look at this mean alley and this house, which is bare of furniture. Do you think I can hide them forever from my colleagues?"

Feeling miserable, the woman realized that her life was

doomed to anguish. "Do things gradually!" she said bitterly. "We had no food to eat, but look where we are now!"

Shaking his head with sorrow, he said, "Mother, I didn't mean to make you angry. But these days I think very much of the troubles that threaten us. I've only mentioned some of them, and perhaps those I've not mentioned are much graver. Look, for example, at my brother Hassan and his way of life. Surrounded by these troubles, how can we possibly lead a quiet life?!"

She studied his face, astonished by his ability to fish for worries. Desperately, she murmured, "Leave God's creatures to their Creator. We have always been so. Yet we neither perished nor were we destroyed."

"I wasn't an officer then," Hassanein protested. "But now that I've become one, my reputation is in jeopardy."

Frowning, the mother took refuge in anguished silence.

"Everything must change," Hassanein sighed. "Even my father's grave, out in the open amidst charity burial places, must change. Imagine what my colleagues would think of me if they knew where he is buried!"

She concealed her feelings beneath a smile. "I hope for these things as much as you do. But I advise you to be patient and I warn you against the sad consequences of your futile revolt. You desire to wipe out the past, change the house, build a tomb, and reform your brother. Yet it's impossible for you to achieve these things for a long time to come. What will you do then? It was the hope of my life that you be happy with us as well as make us happy. But if you don't acquire patience and resign yourself to reality, you'll be miserable and will make us miserable, too."

He fell silent, fed up with the conversation and his own troubles. His rebellious nature refused to be persuaded by her arguments; to him, she seemed unsympathetic to his hopes and feelings and he felt alone in the battle of life and death. He yearned for a cleaner, more decent life, and he would never deviate from this goal. Let him then defend his hopes and happiness with whatever power and enthusiasm he could muster.

He heard a knock on the door. Evening was spreading its wings. Surmising that it was Nefisa returning from her work, he hurried with fresh determination to open the door.

SIXTY-NINE

Smiling, Nefisa entered the flat. These days she seemed to be always smiling, always cheerful. Observing that her mother was absorbed in her thoughts, she approached her and said jokingly, "Mother, now that our troubles are over, you don't need to worry anymore."

Depressed, Hassanein mentally echoed his sister's words. But had their troubles really come to an end? It occurred to him that the entire budget of the army was not enough to resolve their problems. He raised his eyes toward Nefisa. He said to her, "It's time that you took a rest!"

"Do you mean that I should give up my work?"

"Yes."

"I'll give it up with absolutely no regrets. I'll stay at home as ladies do. I'll be the lady sister of an officer!"

He could not help saying sarcastically, "And the sister of Master Hassan, too."

She looked in astonishment from him to her mother, wondering why he referred to his brother with such sarcasm.

"Doesn't this please you?" he continued.

With tenderness and compassion, the girl replied, "Whatever Hassan may be, his kindness in undeniable."

"I don't need to be reminded of that," the young man added. "God knows that I love him. But I can't help saying that his way of life is disgraceful."

This last sentence pierced her heart, and she averted her eyes. As she recalled her own loose behavior, her limbs went cold and she shuddered with horror. Obviously, she thought, he is referring to me and nobody else. The silence made her nervous, and she murmured, "It happens in every family!"

"But not in respectable families," Hassanein said resentfully.

Overcome with suffocating anxiety, she would have liked to vanish into thin air. Pretending to laugh, she said with affected merriment, "It's quite possible to have in the same family two brothers, one of them a minister and the other a thief. For God's sake, don't disturb our peace. Guess what—I've prepared a platterful of *kunafa* for you. Let's warm it up and eat it in peace!"

Leaving the room, she headed for the kitchen, her face troubled, her soul disturbed, and her heart fluttering with fear and worry. He had asked her to stay at home as respectable ladies do, and she certainly welcomed this. But what was done could not be undone. She could easily make excuses for her loose behavior, pretending that her object was to earn money to support her starving family. True enough, but only part of the truth. There was the tormenting mortal despair of resisting her sexual urge. How much she wanted to extinguish it, even if it involved her own extinction! Yet this sexual urge, flaring up more desperately and degenerately than before, had become almost uncontrollable. Her sense of guilt caused her great suffering. Her only consolation, if it was any consolation at all, was that fate held no better prospects for her. And she became torn between a wretched past and an irrepressible thirst for sexual gratification. Realizing how impossible it was to ignore this thirst, she was incapable of predicting whether she could adapt to her new way of life at home. Could she possibly be content to wait monotonously, indefinitely, for death to come upon her? She was not quite sure that she could accept this new life faithfully, or that, having lost everything, she could resolutely face up to the torture of sexual deprivation. She loathed and feared the past, but she was bound to it by a demonic force and would cleave to it desperately, stricken with guilt and horror, like a man falling from a mountaintop in a nightmare he was unable to shake off. Absently, she gazed at the slightly burnt surface of the rose-colored *kunafa* until she imagined her own skin burning black inside the platter. Life at the moment seemed so ruthless, so absurd; ruthlessly absurd. She wondered why God had created her. Yet she had an undeniable gusto for life, and her despair, torture, and fear were merely its manifestations. In spite of it all, she had an appointment with a man and did not want to miss it.

Carrying the platter with a cloth, she entered the room and placed it on the desk. As if she had forgotten her fearful thoughts, she said merrily to Hassanein, "I offer you this *kunafa* by the sweat of my brow. From now on, it's your turn to provide our tongues with sweets."

Putting their worries aside, the family devoured the *kunafa*. "I wish Hussein were with us," Samira said as she took a piece from the platter. Waving his finger at her, Hassanein swallowed a mouthful. "It's high time," he said, "that we get him transferred to Cairo. Ahmad Bey Yousri had promised to transfer him after a year or so. And now almost two years have passed since his appointment at Tanta."

He wished to enjoy the company of his brother as he had in the past, and hoped to appeal to Hussein for help in overcoming his troubles. Moreover, he had his personal reasons for paying a visit to Ahmad Bey's villa.

SEVENTY

At sunset the next day he went to the villa of Ahmad Bey Yousri to thank him on the occasion of his graduation from the College and to beg him to intercede to get his brother transferred to a school in Cairo. The porter stood up respectfully for the visiting officer, led him to the sitting room, then disappeared to inform the Bey of his presence. Hassanein sat on the same chair he had occupied more than once before, under different circumstances. Looking out over the garden, his eyes traced the long zigzagging path on which the girl had ridden her bicycle slowly and warily more than a year earlier. He wondered whether she was still interested in this exercise. For a while, his memories made him smile. Once more he wondered whether he had come, really, for the sake of thanking the Bey and begging him to intercede on behalf of his brother. He smiled again, still perplexed, uncertain of his goals and uneasy about his motives. He felt reluctant to offend his fiancée. He recalled his latest visit to Farid Effendi's flat immediately after graduation and how, spending his time there in tedious conversations, he was overcome with painful feelings of deprivation, for he couldn't be alone with his girl even for a short while. The memory left him with a fuming resentment that submerged the guilt he felt about these other pleasurable memories, which Ahmad Bey's villa revived. Shunning his remorse, he was swayed by ambition which the surrounding magnificence of the villa set aglow in his heart. His imagination was kindled by dreams of eradicating his past, of having a new house, a new tomb, new relatives, prosperity, and a dazzling life. Though he had attained the enviable position of an officer, yet he was conscious of a burning desire for a clean, luxurious life. His heart's innermost feelings made him miserable and discontented. He was still immersed in his dreams when the porter returned from the interior of the villa, courteously bowed, and whispered, "His Excellency the Bey is coming." Hassanein rose when the Bey appeared in a white suit, a red rose in his lapel. Casting an all-encompassing glance at the young man's uniform, the Bey said with a laugh, "Welcome to the officer."

Bowing, Hassanein shook hands with him. But before he could open his mouth to speak, the young man saw the Bey's wife coming from the inside, followed by the girl. Since the family was obviously preparing to go out, he realized he had come at the wrong moment, particularly when he noticed the car turn on the wide path and stop at the entrance hall. Hassanein shook hands with the two ladies, retreated two steps, and said, "Your Excellency, I've come to thank you on the occasion of my graduation. Excuse me for leaving now. I'm afraid I may delay you."

"No," the Bey answered. "We'll sit down for a drink of lemonade. We still have enough time."

When the members of the family took their seats, Hassanein also found a chair, trying his utmost to control his nerves, for he loathed the thought of panicking in the presence of the Bey and these ladies of the upper class. The porter went off to get the lemonade.

"Where have you been appointed?" the Bey gently inquired.

"To the cavalry in Cairo," Hassanein answered with barely concealed pride.

"You seem to have been high up on the list of the graduates?"

"I came in eighth."

The man congratulated him. A silence prevailed. Had he met the Bey alone, he would, as intended, have gratefully enumerated this man's favors to his family, his kindly intercessions for himself and his brother, and then proceeded to request Hussein's transfer. But determined to preserve his dignity in front of the two women, especially the girl, he changed his mind. He saw no harm in postponing discussion of his brother's problem until some time the next day or the day after, when he could raise it with the Bey in his office at the Ministry.

A Nubian servant entered with the lemonade and served it to them. As he lifted his glass to his lips, Hassanein glanced furtively across the rim at the girl. He watched her gently and quietly sipping the lemonade, too much the true lady to take the drink in noisy, vulgar gulps. Relishing the taste slowly and delicately, she took the drink softly and shyly into her mouth, her face wreathed in splendid quietude and dreamy relaxation as if she were surrendering to the numbing touches of slumber. He replaced his glass on the tray, his head turning at the fascinating sight of her grace, elegance, and obvious aristocratic breeding. Suddenly he started as he imagined the girl lying meekly and submissively in his arms. *What madness comes over me!* he wondered. *It's not only lust. Perhaps it's not lust at all. Though it shames me to appear with Bahia in public, yet she is more attractive than this girl. To lie on top of this girl is not a sexual act, but a triumph, a conquest. That's it.*

He became aware of the external world when Ahmad Bey asked him, "How is the family?"

An idea occurred to him, inflating his conceit. It was his nature to lie sometimes. "Thanks be to God," he said without hesitation. "Our troubles came to an end after winning the lawsuit."

"What lawsuit?" the Bey inquired.

"An old lawsuit between my mother and uncles over some entailed property," Hassanein said with steady confidence. "The court handed down a decision giving Mother her full share!"

"Congratulations! Congratulations!" the man replied.

Proud and relieved, Hassanein rose to his feet. "Your Excellency," he said, smiling, "I'm sorry I've delayed you."

They all rose and went down the stairs to the parked car. Hassanein hoped they might offer him a lift. But the Bey merely gave him his hand, bidding him goodbye. The young man bowed to the two ladies and hurried off. Apparently the visit was a failure since he hadn't accomplished his purpose. But he considered himself lucky for this unexpected meeting with the girl, and he thought that his spontaneous happy lie was more significant. The real purpose could wait for a few days.

SEVENTY-ONE

Before leaving Taher Street, Hassanein lifted his face to the sky. Looking at the pale sunset, he wondered whether he would find his brother Hassan at home if he ventured to pay him a visit. Though Hassanein had faint hopes of reforming his brother, he was determined to confront him. He was engrossed in thoughts about his own and his family's future, and his meeting with Hassan was his main preoccupation. Though he proceeded with unbending determination, his heart was heavily laden with worry and doubt. He took the tram to Al Khazindar Square, then walked toward Clot Bey Street.

Now Hassanein's attention was diverted to his uniform. He reflected that it had been purchased, in part, with the money his mother received from selling his old clothes. He was concerned that circumstances forced him to appear in a suspect area. But he had no alternative. He saw in Hassan the family's most serious, thorny problem. Nefisa had abandoned her dressmaking business, and soon he would be leaving Nasr Allah alley, even the entire district of Shubra. Probably a curtain of oblivion would fall on his family's whole detestable past. Yet the problem of Hassan would remain unsolved. And as long as this brother continued his evil life, security would be impossible. Approaching Gandab alley, he headed for his brother's house, avoiding the people's astonished and searching glances, hurriedly crossing the alley like a fugitive.

His nostrils offended by the putrefying smell, he disgustedly climbed the spiral stairs, remembering with both annoyance and embarrassment his first visit to this house a year ago. Halting on the darkened threshold of his brother's flat, he knocked. A strange man opened the door, one of the disfigured faces indel-

THE BEGINNING AND THE END

ibly imprinted on his memory from his first visit. No sooner did he see Hassanein than the man slammed the door shut with a loud cry: "The Police!"

Surmising what had happened, ashamed, pained, and disturbed, Hassanein thought of withdrawing. But filled with an obstinate determination to carry out his objective at whatever cost, he stood his ground. To him, this was no insignificant question but a matter of life or death; he would be unable to make progress in the world as long as this house haunted him. He knocked on the door again and waited, realizing how useless it was. He knocked again, violently. Perhaps, he wondered, they might have escaped from the flat through one of the windows. Perhaps his brother would recognize his voice if he called his name aloud. But he was too ashamed to reveal his identity; to reassure his frightened companions, Hassan might tell them of their relationship—which Hassanein would rather bury forever. Yet how could he be sure that Hassan, to show off, had not already told someone or other who his brother was? As he gnashed his teeth, shame and despair made him all the more obstinate, and he violently hammered on the door with his fist, shouting, "Hassan, Hassan, it's Hassanein!" Soon the door was opened. Appearing behind it, Hassan stared at him in amazement. As though recovering from shock, Hassan, motionless, fixed his eyes for a while upon him. Finally, he came alive, smiling. "Hassanein an officer!" he exclaimed. "I can't believe my eyes!"

Pressing Hassanein's hand with one of his and patting his arm with the other, he pulled him inside the flat with a loud, nervous laugh. Hassan walked by his side to the bedroom. "An officer! What a surprise! Congratulations! Congratulations! This is a happy day!"

Hassanein sat on the sofa. Hassan closed the door and sat by his side. Trying hard to overcome his confusion and excitement, the young officer smiled at his brother. "I deserve to be congratulated," he said, "but you deserve to be thanked."

319

Hassan laughed with pleasure, pleasure doubled by a sense of relief following the flurry. "Why should I deserve thanks?" he asked. "I've only given part of what's due to you. But forget about that and tell me about our family. How are Mother and Nefisa? And how is Hussein?"

Pretending to be interested, Hassanein kept the conversation going. Their rambling talk brought Hassanein to the point of asking Hassan why he had stopped coming to see the family. But then he remembered that the ending of his brother's visits afforded an unintended benefit; under the present circumstances, any continued relations would be most disastrous. Thus at the last moment he refrained from asking him.

"In fact," Hassan said, "I miss the family very much. But my kind of life no longer allows me to satisfy my longing for them. True, we live in the same city. Yet I feel, indeed, that I'm the inhabitant of a remote place cut off from the rest of the world. Perhaps I worry less about them since I know that they no longer need my help and that I've performed part of my duty to them. Besides, I'm not always prosperous. Though my pockets may bulge with cash for several days, they soon become empty for several weeks. And when my pockets are full, I'm compelled to spend extravagantly whatever money I have. But never mind. Now that you've become an officer, I should congratulate you on your good fortune and keep my happiness for it pure. Congratulations to our respected officer!"

As he listened attentively to his brother, Hassanein studied his face. He was appalled at the disfigurement and the strange changes in it; it was as though Hassan in one year of his precarious life had gone through what would normally have been many years. Hassan had already stopped talking. Depressed and pessimistic, Hassanein realized the heavy weight of the task he had come to perform, but not for a moment did it occur to him to abandon what seemed to be his sense of duty. Determined to approach the purpose of his visit gently, he said, "I'm afraid my visit may have upset you."

"Spit those words out of your mouth! What's that I'm hearing from our respected officer?"

Pretending astonishment, Hassanein pointed to the exterior of the flat. "A strange man opened the door for me. Horrified, he cried, 'The Police!' and shut the door in my face!"

"An unfortunate misunderstanding," Hassan said, laughing aloud. "But when I recognized your voice, everything ended up all right."

Finding himself in difficulty, Hassanein hesitated before asking him, "But why was he so scared?"

Hassan looked at his brother inquisitively. Was he really ignorant or just playing the fool? "There are people, you know," he replied indifferently, "who have a phobia about the police."

"Isn't it dangerous for you," Hassanein asked, "to shelter such people under your roof?"

"Yes, it is," Hassan said after a pause. "But a man isn't free to choose his companions."

"How is this, brother?" Hassanein inquired with astonishment. "Certainly a man is free to choose his companions!"

"Forget about it. Let's change the subject."

"I can't, until I'm reassured about you."

"Then be reassured and don't worry about me," Hassan answered with a laugh.

"I wonder what makes you befriend such evil people. You're a respectable artist and you can choose your friends from your fellow artists."

Hassan lowered his eyes to hide the grim look that appeared in them. He was infuriated, and had his anger been aroused by anyone other than Hassanein, he would have exploded. He was hurt that Hassanein knew more than he pretended to know about him and that he treated him like a child. Had Hassanein spoken his mind, had he described him as being as evil as his companions, he would not have felt angry as he did now. Determined to tear off the mask which concealed the true drift of their conversation, Hassan, still restraining his anger, spoke curtly in a tone different from before. "I'm one of these evil people!"

Hassanein was astounded.

"Hassanein! Stop pretending to be astonished," Hassan said roughly. "You're not a fool. Neither am I. You'd better speak to me as frankly as you always used to. What's so strange about my being a black sheep? Haven't I always been one, all my life?"

Sullen and ashamed, Hassanein lowered his eyes. His thoughts shattered, he fell speechless. Relieved by his brother's confusion, Hassan's merriment returned. Desiring to put an end to this painful conversation, he said, "Let's forget about the whole thing. Damn the coward! But for his childish panic, our conversation wouldn't have taken this foolish course. Now let's discuss more important matters. I've no doubt," he said, laughing, "that you've come to talk to me about a more important subject!"

Hassanein collected his thoughts. "I have, in fact," he said with a sigh, "come only to discuss this matter with you."

Hassan's face clouded with resentment. "I thought," he said ironically, "you'd come to ask for money."

Although he knew how angry his brother was, Hassanein did not waver. Ingratiating himself with his brother, he said gently, "Thank you for your previous kindness. But I'm no longer in need of money. I've come to discuss a matter much more serious than money. I want to reassure myself about you."

Hassan cast a piercing look at his brother. "I still demand that you be more frank with me!" he said in an ironical tone. "My respected officer, you want to get reassured about yourself and not about me!"

In defeat and indignation, Hassanein answered, "They are one and the same."

"Really? I see things differently. Why didn't you give me this piece of advice before? A year ago, for example?"

Having inadvertently said that he had come only to discuss

this matter, it was impossible for him to pretend that he had known nothing about it. Annoyed, he posed this question to avoid answering his brother: "Don't you see that I'm interested in your own good?"

Hassan ignored the question. "A year ago," he continued in the same ironical tone, "you were in desperate need of money. So you didn't care then to give me advice. Now that you've become an officer, your sole concern is to protect this shining star on your shoulder."

Hassanein's face remained unchanged, but his heart palpitated with anger and irritation. He seemed shaken by the fact that Hassan was able to penetrate the depths of his soul with such ease and accuracy. "Brother," he said softly. Hassan motioned to him to keep silent.

"I'll be entirely frank with you," Hassan added recklessly. "If you really want to know what my work is, I'll tell you that I'm a bouncer for a coffeehouse in Darb Tiab." He pointed to the photograph above his head. "I also keep this mistress and deal in narcotics."

"I don't believe you," Hassanein exclaimed, worried.

"Yes, you'd better believe me. Perhaps you guessed it earlier and now you're sure of it. Now what do you think?"

In silent pain and compassion, the young man looked at Hassan. But as the silence weighed heavily upon him, he said sadly, "Nothing would make me happier than to see you start a new, honorable life."

With a loud laugh, Hassan said sarcastically, "By virtue of my dishonorable life, I was able to protect our family from starvation, provide your brother Hussein with the money he needed to start his government job, and to provide you as well with the installment of the College fee which, thank God, has made you an officer."

Hassan's words, as sharp as a needle, pierced Hassanein to the marrow. Life seemed about to suffocate him. But a strong desire to defend himself prevented him from accepting defeat.

"All of this has come about," he said, "only by virtue of your nobility of character, not because of such a dangerous life as this!"

"Don't deceive yourself. They call me Mr. Head, not Mr. Noble. Besides, what do you mean by a dishonorable life? Or an honorable one? There's only one life, in which we all strive to make a living, each in his or her own way."

"But there is a secure life and another kind of life that flies into panic at the mere mention of the police."

"This is due to the arbitrary actions of the police and we're not to blame. For heaven's sake, what do you want me to do?"

Hassanein's enthusiasm returned in what he thought might be a ray of hope. "Abandon this life and take an honest job as before."

Bursting into laughter, the man said with astonishment, "A mechanic's apprentice? Asking me this is like asking a man to resign from the army to start school life at Tawfikiyah."

Once more the blood in Hassanein's veins boiled with anger. Composing himself, he asked with a smile, "Don't you realize how such a life must inevitably end?"

"Either I'm imprisoned or killed!" Hassan answered in ironic simplicity. "And if it's my fate to be killed, then, naturally, I'll be saved from imprisonment."

Hassanein pretended to laugh, but his anger increased, especially at his brother's recklessness. Almost desperate though he was to change Hassan, he replied gently, "Obviously, you realize the danger, so you don't need me to remind you of the disastrous consequences of your kind of life. For God's sake, be wise enough to take care of yourself."

Hassan cast a prolonged, smiling glance at his brother, as if saying to him, "Don't try to deceive me with your softness."

"Don't worry about me," he said. "May God forgive me; but I should rather say, don't be worried about yourself and your reputation. My advice to you is, don't burden yourself with unnecessary worries and shut me entirely out of your life. Don't worry about what people may say about you because of me. Despite what people say, you can lead the life that appeals to you."

Desperate and exasperated, Hassanein sighed. He was filled at this moment with black anger toward his brother, and actually wished he didn't exist. But the fact remained that he did exist and his existence, hanging like a sword over his head, was a perpetual threat to him. What should he do? Sighing again, he inquired, "Isn't there a gleam of hope that you'll return to an honorable life? Is this your final word?"

Hassan became furious. As if afraid of what he might do to his brother in his fury, he leapt to his feet and walked back and forth across the room, thus giving vent to his pent-up anger in his violent strides. He leaned on the edge of the bed, his arms crossed against his chest. "An honorable life!" he shouted impatiently. "An honorable life! Don't let me hear such words from you again. You make me sick. A mechanic earning a few piasters a day. Is this the honorable life you're talking about? I'd rather spend my life in prison. If I'd followed your honorable life all along, that star would not be decorating your shoulder. Is it only my life that isn't honorable? Young officer, you're laboring under a delusion. Your life is no more honorable, since mine is its origin." He pointed again to the photograph. "I've made an officer of you with illegal money obtained from this woman and from traffic in narcotics. So you're indebted for your uniform to narcotics and this prostitute. Fair enough; if you really want me to abandon my tainted life, then you, too, must abandon yours. Go ahead, take off your uniform and let's start a new honorable life together."

Hassanein's face turned pale. Dumbfounded and desperate, he cast down his eyes, his heart seething with anger. Again and again, his lips twitched as if he would speak, but overwhelmed with mounting despair, he soon closed them. Sullen and miserable as Hassanein was, Hassan had no mercy.

"Don't you see," he persisted, "that you prefer the star on

your uniform to an honorable life? I don't blame you. Like you, I prefer my earnings to an honorable life." He laughed. "We're brothers and the same blood runs in our veins."

Frowning, Hassanein stood up. "Don't mock me for the advice I've given you. Farewell," he added as he walked to the door. But he paused, his hand on the knob.

Hassan spoke to him with unexpected tenderness. "Before you go, don't you want to shake hands with me?"

Hassanein turned, stretched out his hand. Hassan pressed it for a while in his. "I'm sorry I've made you angry," he said with a laugh. "Forget what has happened and let's keep, even at a distance, the same old mutual feelings. You'll always find me the same Mr. Head you know quite well. And please convey my regards to Mother and Nefisa. Goodbye."

SEVENTY-TWO

Intolerably miserable and preoccupied, Hassanein gave his mother a clear picture of Hassan's life. Heavy in heart, sullen, rancorous, and hopeless, he listened to her advice and consolation. With still a few days left before he had to join his regiment, he thought of leaving for Tanta to visit Hussein. The same old urge to consult with his brother in time of distress! He hesitated, but did not carry out his plan. Instead, it was consolation, not longing for the girl, that drove him to visit Farid Effendi. Conscious of this change, Hassanein attributed it to his melancholy, although he realized it was more than casual or temporary. On the third morning after his visit to Hassan, he wondered, baffled, if he had stopped loving Bahia. He sat alone with her in the sitting room, while her mother was busy in the kitchen, and continued to wonder if he was still in love with her. She was his girl, body and soul, and sure enough, she stimulated his desire. Yet he felt inclined to break with her as part of the process of breaking with his past. Yes, he desired her, but he was torn by a perplexing conflict between desire and uncertainty whether he still loved her! How was it possible, he wondered, to desire her and stop loving her at the same time? But despite the strong physical attraction, he wished to break their engagement as much as he wished to break with the alley and his brother's life. She was no longer his ideal girl. He came to think of his attachment to her as a symptom of a kind of lunacy of which he must be cured. As he gazed at her fine, quiet face, an incarnate torment, his heart pinched in pain. Undecided, he tried to dismiss his thoughts.

"Don't stare at me like that!" he heard her say.

If only he could take her to his breast and press a thousand kisses on her! In the future his attitude toward her might change, but he regretted this period of protracted deprivation. "I'd like to give you a kiss. With this we could start a new life!" He smiled.

"That's all you think about!"

"Is there anything more pleasurable?"

She lowered her eyes. "There are more important matters," she said hesitantly.

He guessed her meaning at once. Dismissing his worries, he inquired, "What's more important than a kiss?"

"For once in your life, would you speak to me seriously?"

"But, seriously, I want to kiss you."

Somewhat perplexed, as if deliberately to oppose threatening danger, once she gained control she continued: "Don't you know what Mother says?"

He guessed right, it was bound to come. "What did she say?" he asked stupidly.

Shyly, she answered with difficulty in a low voice. "She says we've been waiting too long, now that you're an officer!"

Her presumptuous statement angered him in the extreme; although he realized that there was no reason for anger, at this moment his heart filled with hate for her mother.

"Does she want to hasten our marriage?"

"No," she murmured, flushing, "but she thinks it's about time we announced our engagement."

"Hasn't it already been announced?"

Embarrassed, she felt the ring finger of her right hand. "Certain formalities are still incomplete," she said.

He got the point, and was overcome with an unaccountable resentment. The request was reasonable enough, but, like a hunted animal at the approach of danger, he developed an aversion to the girl's family. As he studied her face, he remembered what his classmates on the bus had said about her. *She's a good-hearted girl,* he thought, *but she doesn't deserve to be the wife of an officer like me. And if this marriage takes place, it would be the first of its kind.*

"These things aren't important," he said calmly, with a smile.

"But to other people they are extremely important. Our relatives have been asking about the engagement ring for a long time."

If only, he wondered, she could show the same enthusiasm for making love. *She wants to marry me, not love me,* he thought. *That's why she's so frigid and reserved. Why would I marry her if I didn't love her passionately?*

"No need to hurry," he said. "We'll realize our hopes in due time."

"But when is 'due time'?"

"I think," he said, knitting his brows as if in deliberation, "I will be able both to support our own home and to help my family—who need me, as you know—when I'm promoted to the rank of lieutenant."

Downcast, dumbfounded, and dim-eyed, she bit her fingernails. While his words afforded him relief and a sense of liberty, yet her misery touched his heart. His heart beat violently as he looked at her body. Forgetting his anger and fears, he arose and sat beside her on the sofa. But she moved away from him to the farthest end, holding him back with her arms, resisting him, with a lingering, sad look in her eyes. He seized her arms and imprinted kisses on her palms. She arose and left him. "Let go of me," she exclaimed. "Let go of me. You've changed."

Out of his mind with excitement, he rose and followed her. Embracing her, his limbs quivered. She pushed him away, but he thrust his mouth violently on her lips. She leaned her head back, and he missed her mouth, his lips touching her chin. She wrested herself from his grasp, and they stood, panting, face to face.

"Don't use force with me," she sobbed.

As his lust turned to anger, he thought of leaving the room. He took two steps toward the door, then turned suddenly to her. Anger giving way to mad desire, he pounced upon her, determined to satiate it. Her hands resisted, but he embraced her, took her to his breast with brutal violence, and pressed a kiss on her lips. It was no use turning her face away to escape him. His mouth persistently searching for hers, he struggled against her resistance with brutal force until he crushed her to him. She almost fainted in his arms. Paying no attention, he kept pressing her to his chest until he sensed the softness of her plump body on his abdomen and thighs, and a profound sensation of satisfaction arose in him as though he were exploring the pleasures of life for the first time. She put up a feeble, token resistance as short-lived as the moments of wakefulness that precede death. But as he crushed her resistance, he became mad with desire, and yearned for further satisfaction. A sweeping, melting pleasure ran through every one of his nerves, inconceivable pleasure; then he collapsed in sudden surrender. When he came to, he found the girl in his arms, his lips on her cheek. As his arms relaxed, she retreated with a push on his chest. "I'll never forgive you," she said.

Her words had no effect at all; he ignored her existence and was indifferent to them. He felt triumphant and relieved. As his senses cooled, he retreated in astonishment to his former seat. Wavering, she stood motionless, then resentfully returned to her chair, scolding his deaf ears. He looked at her curiously. He wondered: *Is it she? Is it I? Where are we?* An intolerable sense of coolness weighed heavily upon him.

He listened to her without taking the trouble to apologize. Her mother came in; taking advantage of the latter's presence, he sat for a while with her, then excused himself. As he left the flat he felt a strong desire to escape, and at that moment the thought of traveling to Tanta returned. He smiled, welcoming the idea with enthusiasm.

SEVENTY-THREE

It was about five o'clock in the afternoon when he reached the Britannia Hotel on Al Amir Farouk Street in Tanta. A boy showed him the way to his brother's room, and he knocked on the door and stood smiling, waiting for the pleasant surprise. The door opened and Hussein appeared in a gallabiya. At once his eyes opened wide with astonishment and, welcoming his brother, he exclaimed, "Hassanein! I don't believe my eyes!"

The two brothers embraced warmly. As they entered the small room, Hussein, with love and admiration, cast a scrutinizing glance at his brother. "What a happy surprise!" he exclaimed with delight. "Do military men thus attack without an ultimatum? Congratulations. I sent you a cable of congratulations."

"I received it and thought of coming in person to thank you."

"How are Mother and Nefisa?"

"Very well. With still a few days' leave before starting my assignment, I thought of spending them with you."

"Well done. What about Hassan? Do you have any news about him?"

Hassanein's face darkened. But so as not to spoil the pleasure of their meeting, he said, "For now, at least, let's forget about him."

Hussein guessed the reason for his brother's sadness. No less eager than his brother to avoid spoiling their meeting, he invited Hassanein to sit on the only chair, while he himself sat on the bed. They looked at each other carefully, each observing the signs of health and vigor in the other. Hussein had put on more weight than his brother might have expected. His new mustache, as broad as his lips, lent him a dignified, manly appearance, making him look older than his years. "You're born to be a good father," Hassanein remarked.

His brother's words stirred sad memories, but Hussein made no reply. "I'm proud of you," he said, pointing to the star on Hassanein's shoulder.

Hassanein was touched. "I'm indebted to your noble sacrifice," he said.

Soothed by these words, Hussein murmured, "Don't mention it. You deserve it."

There's nothing about this brother to be ashamed of, Hassanein thought. *But for Nefisa's past and Hassan's present, I'd have been the happiest man on earth.*

"Cheer up," he said to his brother, with a feeling of delight. "I've begged Ahmad Bey Yousri to try to get you transferred to Cairo, and he promised me he'd do something about it."

"Splendid! By the way, I have my annual leave now, so I'll go back with you to Cairo." He got off the bed. "Now go wash your face," he said, "and brush off your suit; it's covered with dust from the train. Why stay in this room? Let's go into town."

Hussein dressed in his suit and the two brothers set out for the streets of the town. They continued their conversation in a coffeehouse. Speaking at length of his life in Tanta, Hussein complained of his loneliness, how it had brought him to frequent this place, to spend no less than two hours on backgammon or conversation, before he returned to his room to read for an hour or so before falling asleep. The last book he had bought, he told Hassanein, was *Socialism,* by Ramsay MacDonald, translated into Arabic from the English, in which the author claimed that the socialist system did not run counter to religion, family, or morality.

Lonely and bored, he found pleasure, he said, in dreams of social reform, imagining the emergence of a better society than the present one and improvement in living conditions. The prospect of realizing his dreams without jeopardizing the religious creed he had imbibed early in childhood made his heart overflow with exuberance.

Hussein wondered whether his mother had divulged to his brother the secret that had driven her to pay him a visit nearly a year and a half ago, but since Hassanein made no mention of the matter, Hussein was confirmed in his early conclusion that his mother had said nothing about it. The thought, now reminding his calm and peaceful heart of past suffering, would have entirely ceased to trouble him but for a general feeling of longing for love and companionship. When he asked his brother about his fiancée, Hassanein answered vaguely. "She's well, thanks be to God." Hassanein wondered whether he should speak frankly to his brother about his change in attitude toward Bahia. Shying away from the revelation, he postponed it for some future time, for he knew in advance that Hussein would never approve of his motives and intentions. But their amiable, lengthy tête-à-tête induced him to broach the grave subject which preoccupied him most.

"Imagine how marvelous our life would have been," Hassanein sighed, "but for Hassan and our family's past."

Hussein understood the sorrow and discontent underlying his brother's sigh. "I believe our troubles are over now," he said simply. "Besides, there's nothing to be ashamed of in our family's past. As for Hassan, it's a pity, but he can do harm only to himself."

Hassanein shook his head in disapproval. "I've learned that, as time went on, Hassan degenerated into a thug and a dealer in narcotics."

Although Hussein's view of his brother was negative, indeed, he could not possibly have imagined this fall into such an abyss. "No! Don't say it!" he exclaimed in horror.

Disregarding the shock to his brother, Hassanein related what he had seen and heard on his latest visit to Hassan. Silent and sullen, Hussein listened. To break his brother's protracted silence, Hassanein inquired, "What do you think?"

Hussein extended the palms of his hands as if to say, "What can we do about it?" "Alas!" he muttered. "Hassan was the victim of our father, and our father was the victim of his own empty pockets."

"Can't you persuade him to renounce his way of living?" Hassanein asked in fright.

"Whatever we do or say, he'll never change it," Hussein sighed. "The only possibility would be to provide him with enough money to start a new life. Can we afford it? That's the question."

The answer being too obvious, the two brothers exchanged despondent glances.

"Should we," Hassanein asked sharply, "allow him to destroy our hopes by his wicked behavior?"

"He's destroyed only himself."

"And destroyed us, too. With a brother like him, how can we face the world? One day our names will appear in newspaper stories about arrests and crimes."

Hussein sighed sorrowfully. His brother's words revived thoughts that had often tormented him in his loneliness. "We aren't to blame," he said. "And we shouldn't allow exaggerated fears to fill our hearts. Sooner or later we may be exposed to the slanders. But we won't be able to face life unless we develop a measure of indifference."

To Hassanein, his brother was either unaware of what he was saying or indifferent to the family's good reputation, which he considered the foundation of all his hopes in life. But Hussein's circumstances were different. He knew none of the friends of Hassanein, whose discovery of the family secrets his younger brother dreaded. Moreover, Hussein, not being ambitious, did not fear people who told tales. Offended at this lack of a sympathetic hearing from his brother, Hassanein regretted that he had confided his fears. At the moment, he was not only indignant toward his brother; he despised his calm resignation.

"Do we have the right to consider ourselves honorable people?" he exclaimed in a flash of anger.

"Why not?" Hussein inquired with surprise.

"Because we've straightened out the difficulties of our lives with tainted money!"

His eyes emitting sudden sparks of fury, Hussein silently stared at his brother's face. Grief, long buried, surfaced in his consciousness, evoking with it the most somber memories.

"We had to defend ourselves," he said sharply. "And even murder is justified in self-defense."

Secretly relieved at his brother's anger, Hassanein began to wonder at his own motive in confronting him with this painful revelation. Now they were separated by a wide gulf of silence; as the two brothers tired of it, their conversation drifted to other matters. But it took some time before the strain wore off and amiability was restored.

SEVENTY-FOUR

The two brothers returned together to Cairo a few days later for an unforgettable day in the life of the family. Samira gave Hussein a long kiss and Nefisa embraced him warmly. In the afternoon Hussein talked for an hour about Tanta and his life there as the two women listened attentively. Gazing at his mustache and his growing obesity, Nefisa was surprised by the changes that had taken place in him.

"Why do you imitate men while you're still a child?" she said disapprovingly.

"I'm no longer a child." Hussein grinned.

"We're men and you're our elder sister," Hassanein said, laughing.

"In the past," the girl said sharply, "I was your elder sister but from now on you look older. Do you understand?"

Turning to her mother, she inquired, "How do you like his mustache, which makes him appear older than he actually is and, for no reason, makes us age, too."

It was noon. Hussein took off his clothes. Strange though the house appeared to him, it aroused feelings of deep attachment to home and family, his heart overflowing with tenderness and total relief: shelter at last in a safe harbor after sailing on uncharted seas. His eyes searched the study: the same old desk, the same few chairs, the same windowpane, the sheet of newspaper replacing the broken glass, all stirred dear memories. His bed had disappeared; evidently it had been sold, as if, like Hassan, he had ceased to be a member of the family. He understood, yet he could not help feeling melancholy and depressed. At this moment he was awakened from his thoughts when Nefisa said, as she left the room, "Give me two hours to prepare a good meal for you."

Hussein smiled with satisfaction. He had not tasted sumptuous food for a long time, probably since his father's death. While it was obvious from his physical appearance that, compared with his days as a pupil, his diet had improved, the mere act of eating failed to excite him. His happiness in returning to the scenes of his early life far outweighed any joy in food itself. His longing for the atmosphere of his early boyhood days pervaded his senses with a strange sweetness—even the familiar, unhygienic air of the alley now seemed invigorating. As he conversed with his mother, his eyes wandered about the small room, resting finally on the star fixed on Hassanein's jacket, which hung on a peg. Year after year Hassanein would be promoted to a higher rank, while throughout his own period of service, he would remain a mere clerk in the seventh or, at best, the sixth grade. Yet he was entirely free of rancor and jealousy toward Hassanein; on the contrary, his brother's success filled his heart with great happiness. But in silent sadness, as he contemplated the vast distinction that segregated the different categories of employees, unconsciously he began to think of distinction in society at large. Once he was transferred to Cairo, he wondered if he could enroll in an evening institute so as to improve his social status. Inwardly smiling at this happy thought, he cherished it as a recourse to rescue himself from the fate of Hassan Effendi Hassan, who would not have been promoted to the sixth grade but for the minister of the Wafds! Recalling conversations in Tanta, he asked his brother, "Is it true what we hear of a cabinet change?"

"Officers aren't allowed to mix in politics," Hassanein said with a laugh.

"Why should there be a cabinet change," Hussein replied good-humoredly, "since the British have stopped interfering with our internal politics?"

"Will we have demonstrations again?" their mother asked.

"Who knows?"

"Doesn't the army have something to do with demonstrations?" she inquired again, this time with concern.

"If a revolution breaks out," Hassanein said quietly, "the army must take action."

Hussein laughed. Understanding the insinuation in this laughter, their mother looked askance at Hassanein, and shrugged her shoulders indifferently. Nefisa returned to report that a delicious dinner was in preparation and to ask them what they wanted for a salad. Then, her forehead covered with perspiration and her sleeves rolled up, she left the room. In the ensuing silence Hussein became absorbed in thoughts about how he would spend his vacation. His colleagues in Tanta called him the Jew because he neither gambled, drank, nor spent more than one piaster in a coffeehouse. But they were ignorant of his circumstances. True, he was frugal by temperament, but his many responsibilities left him with nothing.

His mother soon brought him out of his reverie as she revived the conversation. It struck him that she looked at him with an unusual tenderness which she rarely showed. Did she remember, he wondered, how cruel she had been to him one day? True, she had been cruel, but certainly fate itself had treated them all with even greater cruelty. How would she deal with Hassanein and his lack of enthusiasm about his marriage? Why did Hassanein avoid speaking about it?

At two o'clock, Nefisa brought in the dinner tray and put it on the desk. "Today," she said, "we'll take our meal at the desk, as it does not become government employees to have their dinner on the floor!"

For the first time in two years the family was reassembled for dinner; later they would retire to their seats on the bed and resume their conversation. At about half past three there was a knock on the door, and Nefisa went to open it. A strange idea occurred to Hussein: was Farid Effendi's family paying them a visit on the occasion of his return from Tanta? But wasn't this unusual at this time of day? Nefisa returned on the run, stopping to stare at them with wide, worried, and astonished eyes.

"An officer and policemen!" she exclaimed.

SEVENTY-FIVE

Astonished, the two brothers rose to their feet. Hurriedly, Hassanein put on his jacket.

"What do they want?" he inquired.

Nefisa turned her eyes from the members of her family to the newcomers. Fear-stricken, she blurted out, "Oh, God! They've entered the hall."

Rushing out of the room, the two young men encountered an officer, two policemen, and another man, apparently an informer. Hassanein advanced to the officer.

"May I respectfully ask what you want?" he inquired.

"Excuse me," the officer said. "We've orders to search this flat."

The officer produced a search warrant. Hassanein looked at it with unbelieving eyes.

"Perhaps there's a mistake about the flat," Hussein asked. "Why our flat?"

"We're searching," the officer answered, "for a man by the name of Hassan Kamel, commonly known as Mr. Head."

Dumbfounded, the two young men cast desperate, worried glances at the officer; terror-stricken, they stood transfixed at the entrance of the room.

"We've already arrested some of his accomplices," the officer continued, "but he disappeared before we could catch him. Certain persons informed us of his former residence, and this information was confirmed by Sheikh al-Hara. He's well informed about every quarter, and operates as a link between the residents and the government."

"But he doesn't live here," Hassanein said in an agitated

voice. "He left our house many years ago, and we know nothing of his whereabouts."

"At any rate," the officer replied, shaking his head, "I'll carry out my orders and search the flat."

The search began. One of the two policemen withdrew to the door, while the officer and the two other men swept into the rooms. *Never in my life,* Hassanein thought, *shall I forget this moment!* He mentally followed the officer as he searched one bare room after another, turning their contemptible, decaying furniture inside out. It was not merely a search for Hassan, since he could not possibly conceal himself in the drawer of a desk or inside the intestines of the bedclothes. The scandal seemed hideous beyond description. The officer's searching eyes exposed the humbleness and destitution of the flat, which in this terrifying moment gave Hassanein a profound sense of social shame and degradation. Stunned though he was, Nefisa's sobs struck his ears. He raised his head. "Shut up!" he shouted madly at her in a shrill voice.

The search was over and the officer ordered his men to leave the flat. Approaching Hassanein, he said gently, "Again, I'm sorry. I'm glad we've found nothing that could cause you trouble."

Raising his hand in salutation, the officer departed, leaving a depressing silence behind him. In the silence of the room, the brothers looked absently at each other. Pale as death, the two women approached them. Suddenly recovering from the shock, with a sigh Hassanein leaped to the door and, craning his neck, glanced around the courtyard of the house: at the farthest end, the policemen were carving their way with difficulty through a crowd of men and children, including the grocer, the blacksmith, and the tobacconist. Beating his chest with his fist, he exclaimed, "The whole neighborhood is witnessing our scandal. We've been exposed, and now we're finished!"

Nefisa continued to weep. Their mother turned to Hussein as

if for help. But he did not know what to say and seemed shattered by the blow. Still violently beating his chest, Hassanein stamped back and forth across the hall. "I feel like murdering somebody," he exclaimed. "Nothing less than murder would get this out of my system!"

His mother was disturbed at her son's violent self-torture. "Calm down, my son," she muttered. "What good is it to beat your chest?"

"Let me kill myself since I can't find anyone else to kill," he cried with fury.

Hussein broke his silence. "Let's think this over calmly," he said in a strange voice.

With feverish eyes, Hassanein cast a fiery glance at his brother. "What is there to be thought over?" he demanded. "We've been exposed, and now we're finished."

"This disaster is beyond our power," Hussein replied, "but we're not finished. Let's think the matter over."

Finding this conversation intolerable, Hassanein retired to his room and flung himself on the bed. Choked by shame and burnt by fury, he loathed his guilty brother from the darkest recesses of his heart. He wished Hassan were dead. His mind wild with hallucinations, he surrendered to his thoughts. Hussein followed him into the bedroom and sat silently on the chair, waiting for his brother to respond. For his own part, Hussein was in a pitiable condition. Never before in his whole life had he felt so saddened. He was fully aware of the seriousness of this blow to their reputation, the troubles awaiting them now and in the future, and the consequences of this final blow to Hassan, his elder brother. What had his family done to deserve this fate? Accumulated memories of past sorrows were linked in his mind to those of the present; together they suddenly assumed the appearance of a poisonous abscess, developing serious complications at the very time he thought it was cured. As usual, associating his family's misfortunes with those of other people, he found himself contemplating the universality of human sorrow. Sad though his contemplation was, it frequently inspired him with a measure of patience and consolation. Searching for a gleam of hope in the surrounding darkness, he looked furtively at the angry face of his brother, waiting for an opportunity to speak to him.

Samira and her daughter remained motionless. Nefisa's tears continued to flow. Overcome by a sense of defeat, despite her long experience, the mother felt at a loss as to what to do. Crushed by sorrow, her heart carried all the misfortunes life had piled up for her children, and in addition a personal, deep-buried, terrifying grief that frightened her as much as it tormented her—her compassionate sorrow over Hassan himself, which she feared most to reveal.

Where had he gone? What would they do to him if they arrested him? What did fate hold in store for him? In spite of everything, she must not forget his good nature and kindness; she must not forget that he had given them generously whatever he could, and that he was their refuge in time of distress. What a miserable, friendless outcast he was! This must have been the work of somebody's envious, evil eye. They envied her for her son who had become a government employee and for the other who had become an officer, and in their envy they had forgotten that her painful struggles had reduced her to an absolute wreck. Unable to bear Nefisa's weeping, she sighed nervously and scolded her. "Stop weeping," she said. "Nobody has pity for me. I beg you, have mercy upon me."

But Nefisa could not help weeping. In her hysterical state, she had no idea how very painful their situation was. She was overwhelmed with a curious fear that made her limbs shudder. Her tears were stirred by neither pity nor sorrow nor anger; they were hysterical tears, an attempt to overcome an unconquerable fear that grew out of her and made her identify herself with the hunted. Her heart was filled with sinister forebodings, more dreadful than the present. She turned around in fright, as if she feared someone might suddenly attack her. "Let's go to them," she heard her mother say in a feeble voice. She welcomed this opportunity to escape from her tortured feelings, and with heavy steps she followed her mother to the room. But as she crossed the threshold, her heart quivered in dread at meeting her brothers.

SEVENTY-SIX

Hassanein turned to Hussein. "Where do you think he escaped to?" he asked with ferocity.

Sufficient time had passed to restore Hussein to something like his normal condition. But he was disturbed by the harshness of his brother's tone. "How could I possibly know?" he replied reproachfully. "Don't forget that after all he's our brother."

"Even after all that's happened."

"Yes, even after all that's happened."

These words were uttered from his very depths, as consolation to his mutely suffering heart, which he knew was badly in need of consolation. But Hassanein, bursting out in anger, shouted at him, "We're as good as lost!"

"Now the whole quarter is talking about our scandal."

"We can leave the whole quarter," Hussein said calmly.

Hassanein stared at him, a gleam of hope appearing in his eyes as he sat there gloomy and perplexed. Hussein's suggestion struck a chord in his heart.

"What did you say?" he responded at once.

"Why not? Cairo is vast and boundless, and in less than a week our shame will be forgotten."

Somewhat relieved, Hassanein sighed. "We'll never wipe out the past," he said.

"Let's think of the future."

"But the past will pursue the future forever."

"Let's think seriously of moving to another place," Hussein said. "Let's get it over with before the end of my vacation."

"We should seriously think about it," Samira said hopefully.

Baffled, Hassanein looked from the one to the other. The police might or might not arrest his brother, but in either case,

Hassan would pursue and threaten them. Their lives would be in danger as long as he remained alive.

"Where do you suggest we go?" he queried, dispirited.

"Away from here ... to Shubra Street." There was hope in their mother's voice.

He made a gesture expressing fright and dissatisfaction. "Farther away than that," he said. "We'll go to Heliopolis."

"As you like." Hussein was rather relieved.

For a moment, Hassanein appeared to waver. He said with a sigh, "But we're badly in need of new furniture!"

"Don't complicate matters," Samira said, annoyed. "How important is furniture if nobody else sees it?"

"I can't hide our home from my friends forever!"

"That's another question," Hussein said. "You can buy a sofa, two big chairs, and an Assiut carpet to serve as sitting-room furniture. We can go out today, if you like, and look for a new flat."

The tension relaxed slightly, but they all surrendered in silence to the melancholy that engulfed the place. There was a knock on the door: Farid Effendi, accompanied by his family, paying an unexpected visit at the most inopportune time. How was it, Hussein wondered, that a few hours ago he had dreamt of Bahia's visit, while now he received her with an uninterested heart. For no apparent reason, Hassanein was filled with anger. If Farid Effendi had not seen him when Nefisa showed the way to the sitting room, he would have taken to his heels. They all assembled in the sitting room. Farid Effendi's family warmly welcomed Hussein back to Cairo, and the conversation rambled from past to present. Apparently, the visitors were ignorant of the arrival of the police and the search; but perhaps they deliberately did not mention it. Their apparent disregard for the matter failed to diminish Hassanein's anger; rather, it intensified his inner revolt and deeply injured his pride. As his eyes occasionally met Bahia's she seemed sorrowful and perplexed, wearing the same worrisome look she had borne ever since his sudden departure to Tanta. Let her feel the way she did. He had grown sick of it all. Now, in his state of fuming anger and irritation, he would face up to his innermost thoughts with candor and courage. This woman would never become his mother-in-law, nor this man his father-in-law, nor this girl his wife! All of them painfully reminded him of Nasr Allah alley. Like all the other neighbors, Farid Effendi's family knew that the police had come. But they wanted to give the impression of being too magnanimous to refer to it. Perhaps this was another act of charity added to their previous ones. Damn it all! How sick he had grown of their favors, past and present! He looked forward to new people who had done him no favors that would strain his relations with them, new people who were in no way connected with his sordid past. *Look as sad and confused as you wish,* he thought. *But I'll never be your husband! Never! Everything must change. What was so attractive about her body? Was it her soft flesh? The markets were full of soft flesh. How hideous this atmosphere is! If I stay here any longer, I'll come to hate my family itself.*

The visit was protracted and he had to endure it patiently until the visitors left, a short while before sunset. As she shook hands with him, the girl slipped a folded paper into his hand. Once he was alone, he unfolded it. "Meet me on the roof," it said, the first message she had ever sent him. Carefully examining her handwriting, he was surprised to find that it was like a child's, but at once he remembered that she had only a primary school education! Brief as the message was, it sounded profoundly like a cry for help. Undoubtedly, before their visit she had secretly written the message in her flat, all of which suggested a foreboding in her heart that he would continue his flight from her, already begun with his journey to Tanta. His heart ached with pain. He was disturbed, discontented with everything around him. But why discontented? Wasn't it better to acquaint her with the changes that had come over him? Could he possibly imagine that she hadn't begun to suspect him after his sudden departure? Come what may, he would never yield

347

to the pressure of circumstances, even if it involved his self-destruction. Moreover, he would never sacrifice his career and happiness for the sake of an old, infantile passion or promise. He could stand loneliness no longer and went to his room. "Let's get out," he suggested to his brother.

Hussein agreed and they left the room. But now Hassanein began to regret his proposal; he wished Hussein hadn't responded so readily, for he wanted to be alone with his thoughts. Although he could still change his mind, he continued to walk along in silence with his brother. At the thought that Bahia might now be waiting for him in front of the chicken coop, his heart beat violently. How curious that he should keep her waiting hopelessly at the very spot that had witnessed his plaintive passion and confession of love! With firm determination, he tried to dismiss the picture from his mind. The voice of his brother reached him, saying, "We'll waste no time. Before the end of this month, we'll move to a new house."

SEVENTY-SEVEN

The search for a new flat consumed considerable time, but finally they were able to find a reasonably priced one in a charming location on Al Zagazig Street in Heliopolis. Having agreed to bring their furniture surreptitiously during the evening, so as to conceal it from curious eyes, they moved in on the appointed day. Hassanein remained in the new flat with the heaps of furniture, while Hussein returned to the alley to accompany his mother and sister to their new home. With hope and no regrets, they bade farewell in the dark to their old quarter. Reaching the new quarter, they stood in surprised admiration for its enormous size, its quiet, the fine, dry air, and the sight of blocks of flats and villas on both sides. Despite sad, lingering memories, Nefisa, in this new atmosphere, could not help saying with a smile, "We're now part of the upper class."

The flat was located in a two-story house surrounded by a small garden. They climbed the seven steps to find Hassanein waiting for them, the kerosene lamp already aglow. Assisted by the two brothers, Samira and Nefisa arranged their few pieces of furniture in the three small rooms in less than an hour, including a brief break. The shabby chairs, sofas, and beds seemed out of place in these elegant rooms. It was to be expected that Hassanein would comment resentfully about this discrepancy, but the sight of the sitting room afforded him a measure of comfort. Entering from outside, a visitor could be shown into it without having to cross the interior hall. They discussed their new surroundings at length, the buildings, the streets, and what they imagined their neighbors must be like. Hassanein discussed the necessities of their new life as he saw them.

"We must have two things at once: electricity and a girl servant. Without these, we've no business staying here for even a day."

Since it was understood that it was he who would supply these requirements, no one objected. But as he considered his surroundings from a new angle, Hassanein wondered whether his mother and sister would fit in with them. Mentally, he could hear women's insulting comments after visiting their flat, and his boiling blood rushed to his brain.

"We mustn't," he warned his mother, "mix with anyone in this new quarter. We shall neither visit nor be visited."

"I have no desire to mix with anyone," his mother said indifferently.

"We've got no friends here that we'd be sorry to avoid," Nefisa said.

"It'll be better, too, if you don't see your old female friends," the young man said with concern.

The girl was disturbed. It was true that she wanted to sever her contacts with the outside world, but impelled by a repulsive urge to seek outside contacts, inevitably she failed to obey her wishes. "Am I doomed," she asked fearfully, "to be a prisoner for the rest of my life?"

Taking his sister's side, Hussein intervened. "Brother," he urged, "don't ask too much!"

"I don't want anyone from our quarter to visit us," Hassanein answered sharply.

"Except for Farid Effendi and his family, no one will take the trouble."

Repressing his discontent, Hassanein kept silent. He remembered yesterday's farewell visit from Farid Effendi's family and how they got the new address. If only right now, he thought, at this moment in the twinkling of an eye, the entire past would cease to exist! Had the girl confided his recent lack of interest to her parents? he wondered. Could he arrange to slip easily out of this relationship or might he encounter unforeseen troubles? He would fight it out at whatever cost. His liberty and prestige were more important than the problems which faced him. If he could manage to recover from the past, a bright life full of peace and security would be assured.

Hassanein took his brother aside to straighten out their budget, with its extra expenses for transport, the purchase of the furniture for their sitting room, and the further anticipated expenses of the servant and electricity. Nefisa arose to look out of the windows at her new surroundings. In her loneliness, Samira summoned up memories of the recent events, ending with their arrival in this new quarter. Her thoughts revolved around only one subject: her son Hassan. Where was he now, she wondered, and what was he doing? Whenever she was alone, her memory of him always returned, stirring long-buried grief and remorse.

Thus they spent their first night in Heliopolis.

SEVENTY-EIGHT

"We've come to congratulate you on the new flat," Bahia's mother said. "May God make it a happy home for you!"

Bahia and her mother sat on the new sofa. It was afternoon. All the members of the Kamel family were present except Nefisa, who had left an hour before the two visitors arrived.

They had high praise for the new flat and the luxurious quarter, but Bahia's mother complained of the loneliness her family suffered after the Kamels' departure. She apologized for the absence of her husband, Farid Effendi, who was busy at the Ministry in the afternoons, so many of his colleagues being on vacation. They talked about familiar affairs, and Hassanein as usual took part in their conversation. But he was anxious and painfully embarrassed, and his tension increased as Bahia threw furtive, sad, and silently expressive glances at him. When Bahia's mother suddenly expressed her wish to be alone with Hassanein's mother, his uneasiness was accentuated. The two mothers left the sitting room; embarrassed in the presence of the engaged couple, Hussein made a pretext to leave. Hassanein realized that the decisive hour in his life was at hand; he would either perish or remain safe. Bahia and Hassanein exchanged prolonged glances, she disapproving and inquisitive, he with a faint, meaningless smile.

"Why did you stop visiting us?" she asked disapprovingly.

"You know, for reasons that prevent me from appearing in our old quarter," he said, taken aback.

"Why didn't you meet me on the roof after I left the paper in your hand?" she asked again.

"My brother and I had an important appointment."

"And what about your sudden departure to Tanta without telling me?" she asked him sadly.

"I had to get away at once," he said, avoiding her eyes.

"You don't even try to make up reasonable excuses," she exclaimed in anger.

As delicate and painful as the situation was, Hassanein realized that any wavering on his part would be fatal. As far as his liberty and career were concerned, he would make no concessions. Pretending sadness, he murmured, "My situation is too complicated for you to understand."

"That you've changed is the only thing I can understand. You've become a different person. I'm neither foolish nor stupid. You don't want to see me."

"May God forgive you."

Although she had originally been less communicative, her awareness of their limited time together loosened her tongue.

"Don't be so equivocal," she said, obviously pained. "I want to understand everything. What's wrong with you? Why have you changed so much? Tell me!"

In his concern for his own salvation and escape, he failed to sense the pain and despair in her words. "I didn't change, but my situation did," he said.

"Yes, your situation did change, but for the better."

"Only on the surface. Actually, I'm beginning to realize that my responsibilities are heavy indeed."

"Weren't you aware of them before?" she asked, her anger seeping into her voice. "All your responsibilities put together won't stop you from doing whatever you want if you really want it."

"I want but I can't."

Looking closely at him, her face pale, she murmured, "No. You can but you don't want."

How tormented he was, for he knew he had no answer. He grew more recalcitrant. "You're mistaken," he murmured.

Seeking to penetrate his innermost thoughts, she looked him up and down in fear and desperation. "No," she replied, "I'm not mistaken. If you really wanted it, you would stop saying that you couldn't. These are only pretexts." She sighed in spite of herself. "You're no longer in love with me and you want to get rid of me. Is there any other reason?"

Although he inwardly admitted this was the truth, yet it appalled and pained him to hear her say it.

"You're most unjust to me," he said, raising his eyebrows in contradiction.

Far from calming her, this made her even more desperate. Pressed for time, in her increasing anxiety she cast off her characteristic shyness. "It's you who are unjust," she exclaimed. "You're thinking of getting rid of me after three years of engagement!"

He avoided her eyes. Pained and embarrassed, he was still determined not to retreat. "My situation," he said, "is too difficult for you to understand. I've got to struggle on, come what may."

Suddenly her tone became soft. Flushing, she said to him beseechingly, "If this is the only reason, I'm ready to share your struggle."

This new approach made him ill at ease. "The struggle will be long, hard to endure."

Continuing in the same tone, she said, "Never mind. But I beg you to declare our engagement in the usual way."

This sudden drift in the conversation after it had almost come to an end caught him unawares; he was overcome by fear, irritation, and worry. "No!" he exclaimed involuntarily.

Stunned, she stared at him. She lowered her eyes desperately, her face flushed. She opened and closed her lips again and again as if she wanted to speak but could not.

"Don't you see?" she murmured. "I was right when I said you wanted to get rid of me."

Overtaken by a kind of confusion he had never experienced

before, he fell into deep silence. Then, as if apologetically, he said, "I'm very, very sorry. Perhaps someday you will be able to forgive me."

"That's enough," she said, fatigued and defeated. "I don't want to hear another word."

A deep silence fell on the room as if infesting it with an incurable, suffocating disease. Despite his anguish and embarrassment, the young man found solace in this silence, confident that eventually, no matter how long it took, his pain was bound to end. And when it did, he would feel free. He cast a secretive glance at her. What, he wondered, was passing through her mind? Did she still want him? Or did she hate him? Or did she want to avenge herself upon him? What were their mothers speaking about, and how would their long conversation end?

Only I, he thought, *and nobody else, can determine my destiny*. He heard the voices of the two women approaching. In sudden anxiety, his heart beat fast, accelerating as they returned contentedly to their places. There was a knock on the door. Nefisa entered and Hussein returned to the room; this diversion restored part of his calm. Despite Bahia's obviously sullen mood, the conversation took the usual course until the visit ended.

SEVENTY-NINE

Hassanein looked anxiously and inquiringly at his mother. She understood that he wanted to know about her conversation with Bahia's mother. Her glance was cool.

"Bahia's mother spoke to me," she said, "about the need for an official declaration of the engagement, and I ultimately approved."

Frowning angrily, the young man struck the palm of one hand against the other. "Mother, you were too hasty!"

Seeing that his words astonished his mother, he added, "Of course, I don't blame you. But I've broken off the engagement."

All eyes stared incredulously at him.

"What are you saying?" his mother inquired.

Stressing each word as it came out of his mouth, he answered, "Today, right now, I've broken off the engagement. When they left us, Bahia knew that everything between us was over."

"Brother, what is this you're saying?" Hussein worriedly exclaimed. "How did it happen?"

"I'm amazed at your words," his mother said. "I understand nothing. Did any misunderstanding flare up between you and Bahia? When? How?"

Nefisa stopped in the middle of taking off her shoes. "Speak, Hassanein," she said. "This news is most surprising, to say the least."

"Yes, and it wasn't just a short time ago that I decided to break off the engagement," the young man said grimly. "But I didn't want to tell anybody about it. Today, alone with her in this room, I found it imperative to tell her. So everything is over now. Please, all of you, don't ask me about what we said. This concerns nobody but us."

"This must have been a cruel shock to the poor girl," Hussein said. "I hope you have good reasons to justify this dreadful decision."

"What a scandal!" the worried mother declared. "I reached an agreement with the girl's mother at the very moment you annulled it. What will the woman think of me? Will she suspect that I knew your intentions and that I was deceiving her all along? What did you do, my son? What is the reason for all this? And what's wrong with the girl?"

Annoyed at the conversation, Nefisa cried sharply, "Let's hear what the young man concerned has to say."

"Bahia is a faultless girl," Hassanein said to his mother. "But I realized quite clearly that she couldn't be the ideal wife for me."

"You've been engaged for three years," his mother said. "How can you possibly desert her without good reason?"

Shaking his head, Hussein supported his mother. "That's right," he said. "Breaking off an engagement is a dreadful thing. It shouldn't happen without good reason!"

"What made you think she's not the ideal wife for you?" Nefisa asked.

"Bahia just isn't fit to be my wife," Hassanein said with annoyance. "Sure, I chose her myself. But at that time I didn't know she wasn't for me."

"Bahia is a polite, beautiful girl," the worried mother replied. "Besides, we can never forget her father's help to us."

"Your judgment surprises me," Hussein said disapprovingly. "What is your idea of a good wife?"

"I want a wife from a higher class, cultured and reasonably wealthy," Hassanein said after a pause.

"So these are your reasons for breaking your promises?" Hussein inquired in the same tone.

"We're poor and Bahia is almost as poor as we are," Hassanein sighed. "If I should die as my father did, before my time,

I'm afraid I'd leave my sons, as my father left us, to the same cruel poverty."

"You're right," Nefisa said with enthusiasm.

Hussein was angered by his sister's enthusiasm. "Have you considered the serious consequences of the step you're taking?" he demanded.

"I'm extremely sorry about this," Hassanein replied. "But I don't approve of wasting my life."

"All the same, you approve of wasting hers?"

"Her life won't be wasted. She's still in the prime of her youth, and she's got a brilliant future ahead of her."

"Would you allow me," Hussein said angrily, "to describe your behavior for what it really is?"

Hassanein looked at him sullenly.

Hussein shook his head, disturbed. "I wonder," he said, "how you can condemn Hassan's behavior when there's no justification for yours?"

The young man turned pale. "No doubt," he answered sharply, "my behavior is not without its cruelty. But it will all end well for both parties. Anyhow, this is far better than an unsuccessful marriage."

Hussein turned his face away in desperation.

Striking the palm of one hand against the other, their mother murmured, "What a terrible offense to this most good-hearted family! Oh, God! How can I hide my shame?"

Her words were sincere, but actually she felt a deep inner relief. She was afraid that Hassanein's precipitous marriage would reduce the family to its former state of worry and insecurity. Wondering about Nefisa's future, she invariably became fearful and sad. But despite her sense of inner relief, she thought of Farid Effendi's family with pain and shame.

Unable to conceal her real feelings, Nefisa said, "Don't worry about Bahia. She'll soon find a husband."

"The same generally applies to every girl," Hussein said. "But it's no defense for our mistakes."

"It doesn't apply to every girl," Nefisa said, "and the proof is that it doesn't apply to me, your sister."

Her irony relieved the pervading tension. Hassanein seized the opportunity to exclaim enthusiastically, "Isn't it better to choose a special kind of wife, such as Ahmad Bey Yousri's daughter, for example?"

"God has the power to grant the wishes of His creatures," Nefisa said gaily. "Who knows? Perhaps one day you'll be living in a respectable villa and we'll continue to have your help and kindness."

Hussein paid no attention to the remarks of his brother and sister. Their mother said, as if to herself, "This evening Farid Effendi will know everything. What will he say about us? I wish I could muster up enough courage to visit them and apologize to them!"

Pondering at length, Hussein murmured calmly but firmly, "I've got that kind of courage."

All were interested.

"Would you really go?" Nefisa asked him. "And what would you say to them?"

"God will inspire me on the spur of the moment with something suitable to say," the young man answered with a frown. "Oh, God! Surely there's some impurity in our blood."

He put on his clothes and left the flat.

EIGHTY

Hussein did not go directly to his destination, but went first to a coffeehouse in Heliopolis, where he sat for an hour thinking the matter over. His thoughts wandered from the memories of the past to the events of the present. For a long time, he probed his mind and heart, then came to a decision. Putting aside all doubts and fears that caused him to waver, he became unusually bold, firm, and decisive, so much so that he marveled at his speed in reaching the decision. Did he arrive at this decision on the spur of the moment or did it result from an accumulation of his own deep sentiments over a period of three years? Somewhat confused, he reviewed all the various perspectives. Now, nothing could deter him from his determined course. He rose and left his place with mixed feelings, vacillating from an expansive kind of pleasure to a gripping worry to a bountiful spirit of adventure. Proceeding to the alley, he easily reached it by the evening. Now, as he approached their old house, he realized how difficult and embarrassing his mission was. Yet he advanced with steady steps and an unflinching determination. With a beating heart, he knocked on the door. The astonished glance of the servant who opened it for him irritated him. She showed him to the sitting room. Farid Effendi entered, his body sagging, his face sad for the first time, his eyes burning with anger. No sooner did the host finish with the customary complimentary salutations on receiving a guest than he exclaimed in a paroxysm of passion, "Our lifelong friendship, our lifelong neighborliness, and our lifelong companionship! In one moment you've torn all these to shreds!"

Confounded, Hussein looked at the table in front of him. "Our old mutual feelings of affection can never change," he murmured in a low voice. "Nor can we forget as long as we live your splendid character and your assistance to us."

Paying no attention, Farid Effendi continued, striking one palm against the other. "When they told me about it, I couldn't believe my ears. My heart refuses to believe that such disgraceful treachery is possible."

"Sir, what you say is justified. But believe me, we found it just as hard to believe as you. My mother is deeply upset."

Still paying no heed, Farid Effendi went on. "I noticed that he didn't visit us as frequently as before. And to explain this change of attitude, they put forward childish excuses, which made me more pessimistic. This evening I learned that he had openly breached his promise. How amazing! Does he imagine that girls of good families are mere toys in his hands, to be disposed of any way he likes? So he gets engaged as he pleases and breaks engagements as he pleases! I have always treated him like a son, and it never occurred to me that he could be so wicked and so treacherous!"

Acutely embarrassed, Hussein began to advance whatever came to his mind in defense of his brother: "My brother is a rash young man, and this business of Hassan made him go out of his mind."

"But are we at fault?" the man asked. "This is an incomprehensible excuse!"

"What I mean is, the disaster so shook his nerves and impaired his judgment that he was sick of the whole world."

Violently waving his hand, the man said indignantly, "What you say is unconvincing. I'm a man of some experience, and I know that a man does not desert his fiancée for such a reason. Tell me a different story if you want me to believe you. Say now that he's an officer he wants to marry a different sort of girl."

"With all my heart I wish I could repair the damage," Hussein said sadly.

"The damage is beyond repair. What has happened doesn't

become honorable people. Had I been a different man I would have chastised him. But thank God that, after his deceiving me for so long, I've discovered what kind of person he is. He's only a mean and cowardly young man. Excuse me for blurting out the truth so bluntly."

Pained by the man's words, Hussein kept his eyes lowered for a long time. "I'm extremely sorry," he said in a feeble voice. "We're all sorry. Our only wish is to preserve our old affections."

Silence prevailed, until Farid Effendi murmured coolly, "You were never deceptive in your dealings with us."

Still tense and worried, Hussein recalled with an agitated heart the decision he had made before his arrival. He wondered whether now was the right time to declare it. Although Farid Effendi's attitude was not encouraging, Hussein refused to put it off any longer. Looking at the man with searching eyes, he inquired, "May I see Miss Bahia?"

The man violently waved his hand. "What for?" he queried. "Leave her alone. Under the circumstances, this is the only thing to do."

Moved, Hussein wondered what the poor girl might be doing and how her tender nature would receive the shock. What should he do himself? Should he proceed or withdraw? Wouldn't his words sound ridiculous in this electrified atmosphere? But he had a deep-seated feeling that if, at this particular moment, he allowed himself to retreat, he would never carry out his plan. Dispelling his hesitation with a deep sigh, he attempted to conceal his confusion.

"Sir," he said with apparent calm, "I don't know how to express my feelings. Nor do I pretend that I've chosen a suitable time for expressing them. But I can't help saying a final word in this matter; that is, I hope one day you'll bless my honest desire to ask for your daughter Bahia's hand."

Astonished, the man's eyes opened wide. He appeared to have expected anything but this proposal. He seemed anxious, but unable to speak, whereas Hussein, having survived the climax of his confusion, recovered a degree of his calm.

"Don't imagine," he said, "that my request results from a feeling of guilt over my brother's behavior. Nor is it from pity for Miss Bahia. No. I swear this isn't the case. My own, my independent, unconditional desire grows out of my esteem for your daughter and yourself."

Farid Effendi's astonishment continued. Hussein found courage and warmth in his silence as well as in his own volubility.

"Only one thing disturbs me about this request," Hussein went on. "Perhaps I'm not her equal."

Breaking his silence for the first time, the man murmured, "Don't belittle yourself, Hussein Effendi. You're like a son to me."

"Thank you," Hussein said, flushing.

Perplexed, the man pondered for a while. "I should thank you for this request," he said. "God only knows how much it would please me to see it fulfilled. But, you know, this isn't the proper time to discuss it."

"Sir, this is quite natural," Hussein said with enthusiasm. "I can wait until the proper time comes."

With this remark, their conversation came to an end.

EIGHTY-ONE

Deeply absorbed in his thoughts, Hussein returned to Heliopolis. On his journey from Farid Effendi's flat, he reviewed once more a long stretch of his forgotten past as he had in the coffeehouse. Despite his perplexity, Hussein experienced hope and pleasure he had never known before. Formerly, he had been in love with Bahia. But this love was nipped in the bud and nothing remained of it in his prudent, faithful heart except an image of her as the ideal of the good wife. He remembered how much he had patiently suffered. From his frustrated love, he had learned that, with a measure of wisdom, it was possible to derive lofty, sublime pleasures even from pain itself. He came out of this experience with a tranquil heart and a serene smile on his face. He was consoled and his suffering relieved by the thought that confronting the misfortunes of life with patience and forbearance was a golden road to good fortune. Now his old, buried love had revived in his heart as if it had never died out for a single moment. Thus he set out in a kind of ecstasy, and finally reached home. He found them all waiting for him. At once they exclaimed, "What happened?"

To prepare them for his strange piece of news, he thought it best to exaggerate the gravity of the situation. Sorrowfully wringing his hands, he said, "They were so distressed that, in shame, I kept to myself. And for the first time in my life I saw the peaceful, meek Farid Effendi in a rage of blind fury."

"Tell me everything that happened," the mother said sorrowfully. "Did you meet Bahia's mother?"

"No, I only met the man. Before I opened my mouth, he lashed out at me with a storm of reproofs."

Hussein repeated the man's words, omitting his biting accusations but adding all the paraphernalia of pathos to stir their sorrow and sympathy. Except for Nefisa, all were moved, sullen, and ashamed. "You shouldn't have gone to see them tonight," Nefisa said. "Anyhow, the responsibility for the first mistake lies with the man who accepted a schoolboy as his daughter's fiancée. Then all his guile in bringing the engagement about. As I see it, Hassanein isn't to blame. As I said, he was only an inexperienced schoolboy, ignorant of the ways of the world."

Determined to finish what he had to say, Hussein spoke calmly to his sister. "Please speak kindly of the girl. She might be your other brother's fiancée."

Astounded, they all stared at him. Nefisa gave a quick sigh and Hassanein inquired, "What are you talking about?"

Exerting all his willpower to control his confusion, Hussein said, "She may be my fiancée."

"Yours!"

"Yes, mine."

"Nonsense!" Nefisa cried.

"But it's the truth, pure and simple."

"Did you really ask for her hand?" his mother asked, studying his face.

"Yes, I did," the young man said, lowering his eyes. "I told him it would please me greatly if he would approve my request for her hand."

"Did you do this to repair the damage?" Hassanein asked with worry in his voice.

Hussein hesitated briefly. "Partly so. But I have a deep appreciation for the girl, and since marriage is inevitable, I believe she is the right wife for me."

"Who told you that marriage is inevitable?" Nefisa asked sarcastically.

"What did Farid Effendi say?" the mother interrupted.

Answering on Hussein's behalf, Nefisa said, "He said, 'You're most welcome.'"

Indifferent to her, Hussein replied, "He thanked me but said he was sorry he couldn't approach the girl at this moment. So he asked me to give him time."

"Did you mean to do this when you left us?" Hassanein asked.

"No," Hussein said.

"I'm afraid," the other young man said, "that you may discover later on that you don't really want to marry her."

"May this come true!" Nefisa said with a sigh.

"Nefisa!" her mother shouted at her angrily.

Speaking to his brother, Hussein said, "By temperament, I'm inclined to the stable life."

"I wish happiness to you both," Hassanein said with relief. After a pause, he added in a low voice, "I have my hopes, too; that is, to marry the daughter of Ahmad Bey Yousri. Brother, do you think that's foolish?"

"Why not?" Hussein said with a smile. "You're her equal."

Somewhat excited, Nefisa said with a laugh, "May God help us. We wanted to get back one of you two, but most probably we shall lose you both. What is happening to us is the mischief of an evil eye."

"May God bless you," the mother murmured calmly. "I'm confident my sons will not forget me."

"Then you're quite ignorant of marriage and its secret distractions," Nefisa said to her mother. "I know all about it."

"Mother knows more about it than you do," Hassanein said, laughing.

Silence fell upon them. Glancing surreptitiously at his brother, Hassanein suspected that his engagement had been planned beforehand.

EIGHTY-TWO

Perhaps it was wise to wait. Yet Hassanein wondered angrily what use there was in waiting. Suppose his bird flew away and he missed the chance to catch it? For nearly a month, his mind dwelled on this matter. All his family, especially Hussein, advised him to wait until he could amass a small fortune before asking for the girl's hand. Hassanein thought they were probably right. But afraid that the girl might not wait for him that long, he was persuaded to renounce this wiser course of action. Eminent as Ahmad Bey Yousri was, the fact that old ties had always linked him to the Kamel family encouraged Hassanein to hope the Bey would be patient and tolerant with him and lend a sympathetic ear. Hassanein realized that if he missed this wonderful opportunity he might wait a long time before another appeared. Why not ask for the girl's hand, and then ask the Bey to give him time to complete his preparations for marriage? This was quite possible, but even if impossible, his rejection should not stop him from persisting. He was too bold to let anything stand in his way, for whatever reason. Moreover, he found the so-called virtue of patience intolerable. Come what may, now and without fear he would pursue his objective.

Approaching Ahmad Bey Yousri's villa in Taher Street, the young man was absorbed in these thoughts. Having decided upon a definite course of action, Hassanein proceeded to carry it out with no second thoughts. This was the life for which his soul yearned. Now that Hassan had disappeared, Nefisa had become a respectable lady, and the past had almost vanished, he felt secure. He hoped that he and his family would lead a happy, decent, and comfortable life. He was especially careful about his appearance, for in him, youthfulness was combined with manly virility. When he reached the villa, he was shown into the sitting room, where he sat thinking with an anxious, beating heart. *Curious, isn't it, that I, who have nothing but what's left of my salary, should propose to a girl who owns such a villa as this! Besides, there's the useless, fictitious story of the entailed Wafd property case which I told the Bey about. Why Mother isn't actually in possession of the property is another question. Had we been property owners, our past and present would have been entirely different! Come what may, I won't retreat. Anyhow, I won't be beheaded for this proposal. At best I've everything to win and at worst almost nothing to lose. In the latter event, the worst that can happen is that the Bey will say to me, "I'm sorry, my son," and bidding him farewell, I'll answer, "Goodbye, Your Excellency." I'm sure I'm her equal. What does she want from me that I don't have? Money? She already possesses a fabulous amount of money! How foolish it would be of her to reject my proposal! Here in this place I saw her for the first time riding her bicycle. How beautiful her leg, how lovely her thigh! Poor Nefisa.*

I wonder where Hassan is now! I hope he's escaped to some other place and disappeared from my life for good. The memory of him disturbs and haunts me. When will I be reprieved from all this awful past?

I won't retreat. Right over there, she was about to fall off her bicycle.

I hear the Bey's approaching footsteps!

Hassanein sprang to his feet respectfully when he saw the Bey drawing near. He shook his hands with reverence.

"Welcome to our respected officer," the Bey said. "How are you and your family?"

Keeping his purpose firmly in mind, the young man replied, "Thank you, Your Excellency."

Laughing, the Bey inquired, "Is your brother still in Tanta?"

Welcoming any conversation that would allow more time for preparation, Hassanein said with ostensible interest, "Yes, sir."

They sat down. "It isn't possible to get him transferred during this vacation," the Bey said. "But I've been given a definite promise that he'll be transferred during the next vacation."

Although Hassanein already knew about it, he expressed his gratitude. "This is another favor, after all your previous kindness."

As silence fell upon them, the young man realized that he was approaching an extremely critical moment in his life and that there was no room for wavering or retreat. He summoned up his courage, and said in some confusion, "Your Excellency, I've come to you about a personal matter."

The Bey raised his eyes. "What can I do for you?"

The young man sat erect, as if he found strength in a formal posture. "I beg Your Excellency to help me attain a difficult objective, which is above my ambition."

The Bey stroked his coarse, dyed mustache with his fingers. "Do you want to be promoted to the rank of field marshal?"

The young man gave a nervous laugh, which soon died out. Then he said in a low voice, "Dearer than that. I want to have the honor of being your son-in-law."

The Bey's smile disappeared in a contemplative stare. Despite his assumed solemnity and self-control, he seemed to be overcome with astonishment. *Why?* Hassanein wondered. *Was it surprise or annoyance?* His heart beat violently as he sensed the profound gravity of the moment. After a period of silence and contemplation the man said, "I must thank you for your confidence."

Hassanein was touched by the man's gentle words. Yet he experienced a vague pain. "I hope I've not stepped out of line," he said.

"God forbid," the Bey said with a smile. "Thank you again. But I'll postpone my answer until I consult with those directly concerned."

Hassanein was relieved by this proposed respite, which he welcomed as a fighter on the defensive welcomes the advent of a truce.

"Naturally, Your Excellency. But I sincerely hope that I'm not out of order."

"I don't want to hear you say this again," the Bey said with a smile.

Hassanein took his leave and left the villa. On the way home he recalled every word of his conversation with the Bey, all the gestures, the signs, the intimations, the motives behind them all. While he interpreted everything with optimism and a bold and ambitious imagination, yet he felt anxious and depressed. Ultimately shrugging his shoulders indifferently, he thought: *I've got everything to win and almost nothing to lose.*

EIGHTY-THREE

As though he wanted to give Farid Effendi time enough to think the matter over and come to a final decision, Hussein desisted from paying another visit until his vacation was about to end. During this period Hussein never stopped consulting his mother. While she did not object to his marriage, she advised him to postpone it for one more year until he could complete his marriage preparations. Curiously enough, the hasty Hassanein lent deaf ears to similar advice. Hussein did not approve of his brother's haste, which he described as rash; for it was obvious that if Hassanein succeeded in his fantastic plan to marry Ahmad Bey Yousri's daughter, and if he himself got married after one year, both his mother and his sister would find themselves alone without support. Consequently, he brought peace to his mother's mind by reassuring her that he was determined to keep his wife under the same roof with her mother-in-law and Nefisa. Satisfied with the proposal, he went to Farid Effendi's house. The man's welcome revived his hopes. Although the visit had just one meaning that was clear to everybody, yet Hussein said to him, a bit confused, "I came to say goodbye before returning to Tanta tomorrow."

Farid Effendi smiled in his characteristically gentle fashion. "May God give you safety, and by God's will we'll very soon hear of your transfer to Cairo."

"I hope this will take place during the next vacation," Hussein said.

He wondered whether he should bring up the subject or wait until Farid Effendi broached it. Having consulted his mother, Hussein took his marriage for granted. Yet how could he possibly know what Farid Effendi's family really thought? Waiting for their approval, he became increasingly worried. When Bahia's mother entered, he rose to receive her courteously, warmly pressing her hand. He considered her coming a good omen. Taking a seat, she said, "I'm delighted to see you, my son. How is your mother?"

"All right, madam," Hussein said warmly. "She sends her regards."

Glancing toward his wife, Farid Effendi said to her, "Hussein Effendi has come to say goodbye to us before leaving tomorrow, and I think now is the proper time to tell him of our decision."

He turned to the young man. "As for your proposal, it gives me pleasure, Hussein Effendi, to tell you that we agree to it."

Hussein followed the man's words with a rapidly beating heart that gave him a sharp ache at the utterance of certain words. When Farid Effendi had finished speaking, Hussein leapt to his feet with joy.

"Thank you, sir," he said with a sob in his voice. "One thousand thanks. I'm tremendously happy."

"He'll be transferred to Cairo during the next vacation," the man said, smiling, to his wife.

"This is good news," the woman said, laughing.

"Naturally, we want all of you to be near us."

Flushing, the young man said in a voice expressing pleasure, "By God's will, so it shall be!"

"We'd better wait a reasonable period of time before announcing the engagement," Farid Effendi suggested, then added with a confused laugh, "So that there will be a decent period of time between the two engagements."

Lowering his eyes, Hussein murmured, "I entirely agree."

Farid Effendi rose and left the room, to return minutes later followed by Bahia. Though Hussein knew instinctively that she would appear, yet her actual arrival came as such a shocking surprise that he sprang to his feet, exerting his utmost in self-control. Silently he stretched out his hand to her. As their hands met, he felt the softness, the cool delicacy of hers. His breast was heaving, his heart overflowing with grateful tenderness. He felt strongly that he must say something, but his mind was a blank. Mentally paralyzed by her presence, he was speechless. But soon his senses were submerged in happiness and satisfaction; he had no regrets for his speechlessness; he felt the kind of gentle peacefulness that follows therapy after a bout of pain. *How lovely,* he thought. *How could anybody be blind to her accomplishments? She has been an embodiment of virtue and meekness that quenches my burning thirst for a happy domestic life. She doesn't excite, but infuses the heart with peace and serenity. He said that they agreed and he brought the girl in person as tangible evidence of this agreement.*

Hussein wanted to probe Bahia's thoughts. Had she already recovered from the shock? Was her heart cured? Had she really begun to develop an interest in him? As they resumed their conversation, which he now considered intrusive and unnecessary, the girl's parents put an end to his self-absorption. Might they, Hussein wondered, possibly, by a miracle, leave them alone? He remembered, when his eyes had once met hers, how he had become ecstatically absorbed in their pure blue serenity. Surely, he had so many things to say to her. Anyhow, he had ample time ahead of him to reveal his thoughts and feelings to her, no matter how insignificant they were. During pauses in the conversation, there came to him a tender sensation that there was enough pure, sublime happiness in this world to obliterate its misery. He wished this happiness would last, and that he could remain sitting with her forever in the same room. He wanted these sentiments of the moment to be life-embracing and continue as long as he lived.

The conversation went on, but a gesture or a murmur was her only contribution to it. It was time for him to leave. Excusing himself, he shook hands with her and left the flat, feeling for the first time that the luscious fruits of life were awaiting him, ready to be plucked.

EIGHTY-FOUR

Hussein had departed. Part of the period of waiting for the Bey's answer, which Hassanein called the probationary period, had passed. Wavering between hope and despair, he was forced to endure it stoically. Hassanein was unhappy that his brother was gone. He wished to have him by his side for advice when he received Ahmad Bey Yousri's answer. Willful and tyrannical though Hussein was, Hassanein always listened to his advice. The fact that Hussein had embarked on his marriage project was a source of relief to Hassanein, who was actually uneasy about marrying before his neglected brother, who had denied himself all the pleasures of life and borne the brunt of it. This did not mean that he was uninterested in the future of his family. In fact, he expected much good, both for himself and for his family, to emerge from his prosperous marriage. With this logic, he dismissed his family's troubles; now he was free to seek his own fortune with an easy conscience. This was his state of mind when a friend and colleague asked him to meet him at Luna Park Casino in Heliopolis. Ali al-Bardisi was his favorite friend. Their friendship started and flourished while they were cadets at the College and it was continued in spite of the fact that Hassanein joined the cavalry and Ali al-Bardisi the air force.

Hassanein found his friend waiting for him, and they sat in the Casino garden. His friend ordered two glasses of beer. From the first moment, Hassanein sensed that his friend had a serious matter to discuss with him. Despite his apparent joviality, al-Bardisi struck him as unusually grave and pensive. After a while he asked Hassanein, "Do you remember Lieutenant Ahmad Rafat?"

"Of course," Hassanein said with indifference. "He graduated with us in the same year. An artillery officer, isn't he?"

His friend nodded affirmatively, then proceeded with bitterness and annoyance, "Yesterday I heard him speak about you to a group of friends in a way that angered and offended me."

Astonished, Hassanein stared at him. This was most unexpected. "What are you saying?" he inquired.

"Some friends and I were playing cards in his house in Ma'adi," Ali al-Bardisi said somberly.

"So?"

"I don't remember how the subject came up. We were drunk, and I heard him say things that were offensive to you personally. First of all, tell me, did you really ask for the hand of the daughter of a man called Ahmad Bey Yousri?"

The name shook the young man like an earthquake and his heart beat violently. He suddenly remembered that Ahmad Rafat was closely connected with some of Ahmad Bey Yousri's relatives. He tried hard to compose himself. A coarse feeling of fear and pessimism came over him.

"Perhaps," he answered curtly.

"Do you know that Ahmad Rafat is a friend of this family?"

"Possibly. But tell me what he said."

For a while, al-Bardisi hesitated and kept silent. "I understood, from his conversation," he murmured in a low, obviously embarrassed voice, "that the family did not approve. I'm sorry to tell you."

This piece of news weighed heavily upon him, making him feel small, shattering his sense of dignity and manhood. Boiling with anger, he was about to surrender to his flaming fury, but at the last moment he managed to subdue his passion. He pretended indifference.

"Was this what you found offensive, my friend?" he asked with a laugh.

"No, this sort of thing happens every day," his friend said, gloomy and disconcerted. "But he indiscreetly mentioned the reasons for the family's disapproval. Though they are trivial reasons that don't degrade a man, yet I was very much offended to hear them repeated in a crowd of drunkards."

Hassanein had always felt that his past constituted a constant threat, like a heavy hammer suspended over his head. Now it fell with full force on his brain, smashing it into scattered pieces. This was strikingly obvious. But could he possibly ignore it? He raised his eyes to the gloomy face of his friend.

"Tell me what he said," Hassanein asked mechanically.

His friend made a wry face. "It was something negligible," he went on, annoyed and irritated. "But to be fair, you should know about it. I don't need to tell you that I was so angry that I silenced their wagging tongues."

So he was the object of their drunken slanders! What did they say? He should have taken all this into consideration when he had proposed to the Bey's daughter. Smiling faintly at his friend, he said, "I believe you, and I appreciate your sincerity. But I beg you to repeat to me everything that was said, word for word."

Ali al-Bardisi looked disgusted. With extreme distaste, he replied curtly, "He said many things about one of your brothers. I was so indignant that I told him about a highwayman in our village whose brother is a minister in Cairo!"

Hassanein's face turned pale. His friend's defense offended him as much as the charge itself. Yet he said with a desperate laugh, "Usually, a friendly eye sees the minister, while an unfriendly eye only sees . . . Anyhow, forget about it. What else?"

"Foolish talk of this sort," the friend said evasively.

Hassanein was suddenly overcome with annoyance and impatience. "Please!" he exclaimed. "Don't hide anything from me, please!"

Embarrassed, Ali al-Bardisi said, "I loathe speaking about a lady's honor."

"You mean my sister?"

"He said that she worked to earn her living. And I angrily gave him to understand that there's nothing to be ashamed of in any honorable work. Poverty isn't a crime."

Shaking his head, Hassanein reiterated his friend's words with painful irony. " 'Poverty isn't a crime.' Splendid! What else did he say?"

"Nothing."

That's enough! Hassanein thought. *A brother who is a highwayman and a sister who is a dressmaker, a mere worker. How could I dare to propose to the daughter of an illustrious Bey?*

"I believe," al-Bardisi said, "you made a mistake in proposing to the daughter of such a faultfinding family."

"You're right," Hassanein murmured with a sickly smile. *I'm up to my ears in the mud*, he thought. *My only way out is to smash the head of Ahmad Rafat. But will it actually change my circumstances? No. It's useless to defend myself in this way. Yet I should always remember an important fact: that is, with a strong blow a man can compel people to respect him. Thank God, I lack neither courage nor strength, and I'm capable of dealing such a blow. Hassan was the lowest of our family but he was the most feared and respected: a useful lesson I should not forget.*

Then he heard his friend consoling him: "You shouldn't care too much."

Shrugging his shoulders, Hassanein pretended indifference. "This is well-reasoned advice," he said. "There's nothing in our family to be ashamed of. One day we were rich. Then poverty struck us. We faced it with courage, and we managed to overcome it. There's nothing shameful in this."

"On the contrary, one should be proud of it."

Hassanein suddenly stamped the ground with his foot, his eyes bloodshot with anger. "But I know how to deal with anyone who insults me."

"Of course you do."

In the ensuing painful silence, for lack of anything better to do al-Bardisi ordered two more glasses of beer.

"You can find a better girl," he murmured with a smile.

"Oh! Girls in this country are more plentiful than air and cheaper than dust."

To quench his thirst, he swallowed gulps of beer, while his friend stared into his drink. Silence fell upon them again.

Ah! Hassanein thought. *I wish I could be born all over again, in a new family and with a new past. But why should I torment myself with futile hopes? This is me and this is my life, and I won't allow anyone to destroy it. The battle is not over yet.*

EIGHTY-FIVE

Al-Bardisi bade him goodbye. As he left the Casino, the combined effect of the shock and the beer almost unhinged Hassanein's mind. Above all, he desired, at whatever cost, to give vent to his pent-up feelings. Yet he knew that a confrontation with Ahmad Rafat would be foolish indeed. Anger made him think of more serious plans. *It's useless to be angry with this conceited young man,* Hassanein thought. *He heard something nasty and only repeated it. If in the future I have any opportunity to provoke him, I won't pass it by. But I shall put off the idea of punishing him until the opportunity arises. My real target is the Bey himself with his dyed mustache. I shall tell him that the least he should have done was to preserve the dignity of a man who asked for his daughter's hand, especially the son of an old friend. If he denies my charge I'll confront him with conclusive evidence, pointing out to him that poverty is no disgrace, while slandering people is mean and shameful. And if he becomes offended, which in his illustrious position he is bound to be, I won't be sparing in giving expression to my anger until I've got it out of my system.* Under the influence of beer and bitter feelings, he flung himself inside the first tram to arrive and rode as far as Station Square. There he boarded another which took him to Taher Street.

When he saw Ahmad Bey Yousri's villa, his footsteps became heavy, as if he desired to have more time to think over what he intended to do. From the depths of his mind, voices clamored for his withdrawal. But these were silenced by the heat of the passion that kept driving him to the villa until he found himself in front of the porter. The latter rose respectfully. Without asking permission, he forced his way toward the interior of the villa. Though he was aware of the foolishness of his behavior,

379

he did not stop. The rose and camomile bushes seemed to be slumbering in the slanting rays of the sun. In the middle path he saw the traces of the motorcar wheels in the form of two broad, curving lines. He advanced toward the entrance hall, the vacillation and uncertainty which punctuated his determination showing that he was not entirely convinced of the soundness of his motives. Nevertheless, he climbed the stairs with unexpected determination. On reaching the veranda, a sudden surprise, which his delirious mind had never anticipated, caused him to halt in his tracks. There he saw the Bey's daughter in flesh and blood sitting in a big chair. Lifting her eyes from a book, she looked inquiringly at the newcomer. Immobile in his amazement, he focused his eyes on her. A profoundly withering sense of shame struck him to his very roots. He realized that he faced a situation in which any shameful surrender to weakness would mean subjection to new humiliation, more degrading than all that had gone before. Encouraged anew by his fears, he got control of himself, determined to find a courageous and dignified way out of this dilemma. Bowing his head respectfully, he said with a gentle smile, "Good evening, miss. Excuse me for this unintended disturbance. May I see the Bey?"

It was the first time he heard her voice. With complete self-composure she said gently, "Sorry, my father is indisposed today."

He bowed his head again, relieved by this unexpected way out. On the point of leaving, he said, "Farewell." He had already turned on his heels and taken two steps away from her. Then he halted with sudden determination. His passivity had disappeared, giving way to irresponsible anger. The strange state of emotion that drove him from Heliopolis to the Bey's villa returned to him.

Turning around, he faced the girl once more with an audacity disrespectful to her proud eyes. He said in too loud a voice, which the situation did not require, "Sorry. It pains me to say farewell to this house without expressing my thoughts."

Not uttering a single word, she looked at him inquiringly.

"I think you were told that I had asked for your hand?" he asked.

Lowering her eyes, she said, "I'm not accustomed to having my father's visitors speak to me."

"I thought it quite normal in high-class society," he said, rather surprised.

"Not always."

"Nevertheless, allow me to speak," he continued. "I wanted to see the Bey to speak to him about this very matter. I've been told that my proposal was considered unpardonable impertinence."

"It's better to postpone discussing this subject until you meet the Bey," she said, still casting down her eyes.

Fixing his eyes on the girl's face, Hassanein said, "But I must speak, since I've been lucky enough to meet you, who are primarily concerned. It's important for me to know your opinion. Is my proposal really an impertinence?"

"Please postpone discussing this matter until the right time," she said with annoyance.

Although he had anticipated her annoyance, it pained and irritated him. "A man who proposes to a girl," he went on, "usually offers the best of himself. Unfortunately, it happens sometimes that people only see the worst side of him, such as certain things connected with his family background."

Frowning, she rose. "I must go," she said.

She walked toward the entrance of the hall. He said in a loud voice that followed her in her flight, "I wanted your opinion. But that's enough. I'm sorry. Please convey my regards to the Bey."

Hurriedly turning on his heels, he climbed down the stairs and walked toward the door. A jumble of distant, scattered scenes swiftly rushed to his mind. He remembered his treatment of Bahia in their new flat, al-Bardisi's conversation in the Casino, and this recent scene with the Bey's daughter.

Thanks be to God, I'm not a failure as a lover; I was about to be one, but God has saved me. Yet I'm a failure as a man, which is even worse. I need to think about all these conversations. I feel I'm suffering from a new disease. What is it? What's wrong with me? And what's the remedy?

As he came out into the street, he was sure he had committed an absurd, foolish mistake.

EIGHTY-SIX

Despite the sorrowful look in her eyes, Samira could still smile. "It's strange," she said, "how you thrust yourself into serious trouble without being prepared. Suppose they had approved your marriage, what would you have done? Didn't you think of this? Didn't we all warn you of its consequences?"

About ten days had passed since Hassanein's conversation with his friend al-Bardisi. Whenever Samira observed Hassanein's absentmindedness as they sat together in the afternoons on the balcony overlooking the road, she started talking to console his sad heart. Nefisa joined in with mingled levity and seriousness.

"Tomorrow doesn't seem much better than today," Hassanein said in a bored voice.

"Rubbish," Nefisa said, and Samira added, "In time you'll discover that it is mere nonsense, and you'll find a better wife."

He wondered why he seemed to be the only pessimist in the family. Was it he or they who were stupid? Wasn't the role the devil played in this world more serious than the roles of all angels combined? Why didn't they see this? He had sent Hussein a letter, telling him the news of his rejected engagement. His brother's reaction had been similar to that of his mother and sister. Were they all as they appeared? Alive—or dead? Had the idea of a decent, luxurious life ceased to have any meaning for them?

His train of thought was suddenly interrupted by the continuous ringing of the doorbell and by screams of "Master . . . mistress," uttered by the agitated servant who opened the door. Hassanein, followed by Samira and Nefisa, rushed into the hall to find out what the matter was. In the open doorway he saw two strangers supporting a third man, whose neck reclined on one of their shoulders. That he was injured was clear from the dirty bandage on his head, dripping with blood. Stunned and uncomprehending, Hassanein approached the two newcomers until he was only a few steps away. He fixed his eyes on the wounded face under the receding bandage; its pale white complexion was tinged with a blueness that suggested death. The face, covered with hair, bore marks of swelling and inflammation. The closed, tired eyes blinked. Through the eyelashes appeared a wan, familiar glance which shocked Hassanein's memory suddenly back to life like an exploding bomb. Before Hassanein could speak, his mother's voice behind him confirmed his growing suspicions, as suddenly she cried, in a voice full of fear and compassion, "Hassan! It's Hassan!"

"Hassan!" Hassanein repeated in amazement.

Supporting Hassan's neck with his shoulder, one of the men who helped carry him growled, "We must put him to bed at once."

Astounded, Hassanein advanced toward them. Bending over his brother's feet, he grasped and gently raised his legs and helped the two men carry Hassan to his bedroom. There they laid him on the only bed in the flat. Followed by Hassanein, the two men hurried out of the room, while Samira and Nefisa rushed in indescribable fear toward the bed. On reaching the hall, one of the men, in gallabiya and skullcap, was the first to speak.

"Excuse me," he said, pointing to the other, who was dressed as an Effendi, "this is the taxi driver."

Realizing that he was hinting at the unpaid taxi fare, Hassanein walked out with him to the taxi. He paid the driver and dismissed him, but he held the other man.

"What happened?" he asked in fear and confusion.

"Master Hassan is my brother and friend," the man said. "Perhaps you know he's a fugitive from the police. Seizing this opportunity, some of his enemies hid themselves in a spot they knew he was accustomed to pass, treacherously ambushed him, robbed him of his money, and fled. Suffering from his injuries, the poor man arrived at my house and begged me to take him to his family. We took a taxi to Nasr Allah alley, and the neighbors told us you had moved to this flat. So we came here immediately."

Hassanein listened absentmindedly. Though his heart was charged with emotions, fear and worry predominated. When the stranger finished his story, Hassanein muttered, "Thank you, sir, for your kindness. Would you be so good as to stay with him for an hour until he gets some rest?"

But raising his hand to his head in an expression of thanks for the invitation, the man said, "I must go at once. I've got to tell you something more before I go. You must take care of this wound at once. But I warn you, don't call the police or take him to the hospital, as this will lead to an investigation and the meddling of the police."

The man saluted and departed. As if he were groping his way through the murky dark on shaky ground, Hassanein returned to the room where Hassan had been placed. He found his brother lying senseless, as before. Obviously worried, the women bent over him, and at the sound of Hassanein's approach, they turned to him for help. For a long time, he looked closely at his brother.

"Didn't he speak?" he inquired in a strange voice.

Swallowing hard, the mother said, "He muttered a few meaningless words before he fainted. Go get a doctor!"

The injured man moved his hand with a strenuous effort. When there was need for it, he seemed able to overcome his weakness. With a feeble voice, devoid of its usual vigor, he said, "No doctor. The doctor ... informs ... the police."

Hassanein studied his brother. The bloodstained bandage covered his head, his forehead, and parts of his cheeks; beneath it nothing appeared except his wan, tired eyes and an unshaven chin. His mouth was agape, his breathing heavy and rattling.

His necktie and jacket pocket were torn. He moaned from time to time, and his right hand kept opening and closing. Stunned at the sight, Hassanein forgot his fears in a powerful upsurge of pain and compassion. For a moment he forgot everything; he had to do something for his prostrate brother, something to save him at whatever cost. But the feeling of fear and anxiety which had pursued him in recent days emerged from his depths and floated on his consciousness, threatening his career and reputation. Shame for such sentiments and remorse for entertaining them now cut him to the heart. Talking offered an escape from this heavy weight upon his conscience, and Hassanein spoke gently to the wounded man. "Let me get you a doctor. Your life is much more important than anything else."

"Yes, Hassan," Samira and Nefisa entreated him. "Let's get a doctor."

Raising his heavy eyelids, Hassan said in a tired, muffled tone, "No. Don't be scared. This is a trifling wound."

When he tried to take a deep breath, he had to rest for a while. With his eyes closed, he said, "They betrayed me and I'll punish them. If I survive, I'll punish them. But don't call a doctor; a doctor will inform the police."

Conflict still stirring within him, Hassanein replied, "We must get a doctor. It won't be difficult to persuade him to keep quiet."

"Hassan, have mercy upon me and allow us to get a doctor," his mother begged him.

Snorting, Hassan murmured impatiently, "Have mercy upon me and leave me in peace! Oh!"

Their mother kept turning her eyes from Hassan to Hassanein in his inner struggle. All ambivalence resolved, Hassanein became aware of his true feelings. He realized that his sympathy for his brother was nothing compared with the fear that weighed heavily upon him. *We're done for,* he thought. *My heart tells me no lies, at least not when I expect evil to occur. Now we're done for in Heliopolis as we were done for in Shubra. The police will pursue us all like criminals. I can almost see the officer searching the rooms and arresting this fleeing culprit. Is there no way out? But should I deny my brother? Despite everything, he's still my brother. But he is trampling down my life while he moves on his own thorny way. Oh! How sick I am of this!*

He heard his mother shouting at him, "Help me, Hassanein! Can't you see that he's dying?"

No, he won't die, Hassanein thought. *It is I who will die a slow, cruel death. My dignity is mortally wounded. Now, if he dies here, a doctor will come to examine his body. Soon the police and prosecutor will follow. While they can't hurt him after he's dead, the rotten stench from his decaying corpse spreading throughout the place will be scandalous in itself.*

Suddenly he turned to his mother; her frightened, distracted eyes moved from the prostrate man to Hassanein. Silent though she was, her glances seemed to him as vocal as heartrending screams. He wondered about himself. At first he had hated his mother; then, attacked by quick, vague flashes of memory, he softened and his attitude changed abruptly. As once more he focused his attention on the bloodstained bandage, he recovered his vigor of mind. A bright idea dawned on him. "Why didn't I think of this before?" he murmured. He spoke hurriedly to his mother. "I'll go get a friend of mine," he said, "a doctor at the Army Hospital. Wait, I won't be long."

He rushed to his clothes, dressed quickly, and having determined on a course of action, left the house.

EIGHTY-SEVEN

Hassanein leaned on the windowsill, watching the doctor as he carefully went about his delicate work. Samira and Nefisa had left the room, their breathing almost audible from behind the closed door. At first frightened and deeply agitated, Hassanein gradually calmed and became self-absorbed. In a fight with a member of the family, he had told the doctor, his brother received an injury in the head. He begged him to aid his wounded brother and keep silent about the incident so as to spare the family a public scandal. With some reservations, the doctor accompanied him. After a preliminary examination of Hassan's injured head, he said, "It's a deep fracture with profuse bleeding. I don't understand why you refuse to inform the police."

"We've got to avoid that," Hassanein entreated.

"You don't seem to understand the gravity of the situation," the doctor replied as he prepared himself for the operation. "However, for the time being, let's postpone any discussion."

During the surgical operation Hassanein was neither calm nor reassured. The doctor's last words had uprooted all his tender emotions. This mission of mercy when he went to the hospital to get the doctor aroused in him deep feelings of compassion for his brother, stirring up memories of the days when Hassan had been their sole haven from misery and their only resort in time of need. But fear and anxiety soon hardened his heart toward Hassan, driving out all compassion. Now, in the image of the wounded man he saw instead an evil portent that threatened both his career and his reputation. Here Hassan lay, completely unconscious, unaware of the delicate surgical tools that cut into his flesh. All his life he had been insensitive to pain; a deep cut that would have shattered the nerves of others, bothered him far less. Hassanein remembered his own tears and entreaties, begging Hassan to change his way of life. And Hassan's only response had been bitter sarcasm. If only he had died in a foreign land!

Fixing his eyes on the face as it began to disappear under the bandages, Hassanein shuddered in gloom and despair. At last he heard the doctor address him: "I've done all that I can possibly do now. Come out with me."

He waited for the doctor to wash his hands and put on his jacket before showing him to the sitting room. In deep thought the men remained standing.

"I don't think his case is very serious," he said with unexpected calm. "But he'll need treatment for a long time. What a brutal attack! Why don't you inform the police?"

Though the doctor's words helped to restore some of his power to reason, Hassanein remained stricken with fear. "To avoid a scandal. After all, we're members of the same family."

Disapprovingly, the doctor shook his head. "Tomorrow morning I'll come to see him," he said firmly. "If he's O.K., I'll forget about it. But if he isn't, I'll be compelled to inform the police."

"I hope this won't happen," Hassanein replied as if, overcome with worry, he was talking to himself. Then addressing the doctor, he added, "Thank you for your help and all the trouble you've taken."

Hassanein accompanied the doctor to the door and gratefully shook his hand. But before departing, the doctor repeated emphatically, "I'll be back in the morning."

Hassanein watched him get into his car and zoom off with a roar. He sighed as if to clear away an immovable weight from his chest, and then, with heavy, melancholy steps, he returned to the room. At once his worried mother rushed up to him.

"What did the doctor say?" she asked him anxiously.

He loathed her worry and anxiety, but he answered her calmly. "He's optimistic about the case and will be back in the morning. How is Hassan now?"

"He hasn't recovered consciousness yet," Nefisa replied.

Flinging himself into the only chair in the room, he closed his eyes. *I'm the one who's really injured,* he thought. *As for him, he's sound asleep in a happy state of unconsciousness, which I wish would overtake me. "I don't think the case is very serious." That's what the stupid doctor says. No, it's very serious; recovery would be more serious than death. If his condition becomes worse, the police will be informed. And if it improves, his existence will continue to weigh heavily upon me until his enemies inform the police. So scandal is inevitable. Is there no escape? I loathe this wounded man, I loathe myself and even life itself. Isn't there a better life, aren't there better creatures?*

As he thought, his features contracted with agony and resentment. Deeply moved, his mother turned to him.

"Get over it," she said gently. "Your brother is all right. May God preserve him and us!"

Astonished, he looked at her curiously.

EIGHTY-EIGHT

The next morning the doctor left the house, declaring himself reassured about his patient. Although now he was safe from impending danger, worries continued to torture Hassanein's mind day and night. Yet for a brief period, the family enjoyed relative peace. Gradually the wounded man recovered his consciousness and vitality and, with his restoration to life, became preoccupied with certain thoughts of the past which soon infected the rest of the family. At first he smiled sadly with unusual resignation. "I've given you a lot of trouble," he said somewhat apologetically. "It seems that God has created me for trouble. May God forgive me!"

The pleasant and affectionate smiles of his family flashed about him, but he was not deceived. "Sure, you're angry," he said, turning his eyes to Hassanein. "Perhaps you'd like to remind me of your previous sermons."

"I only want to see you safe," Hassanein murmured.

At first a mysterious smile crossed the wounded face, but soon it grew grim, overpowered by his thoughts. The calmness disappeared from his voice. "They robbed me of my money. I'll get even with them. I intend to escape, and I must escape."

He felt his head with his hand, and closed his eyes. As if speaking to himself, he murmured, "What has God done to Sana'a? Will they leave her alone? She won't surrender to any of my enemies. But she can't escape with me. It's too late now. Besides, we've lost our money."

Hassanein listened in silence to his brother's delirium. Looking furtively at his mother and sister, Hassanein saw them exchanging anxious glances.

"I must disappear," Hassan continued, with the same agitation. "The man who brought me here is a faithful friend. But he's not smart enough to keep a secret. He'll get a lot of satisfaction out of telling his mistress all about his kindness. Then she'll have to tell it to someone else, until it finally reaches those who wish me ill. Then without warning the police will come sweeping into this house."

Hassanein sighed in despair. Turning to his mother, his eyes met hers briefly before she lowered them. Fired with indignation, he mentally placed the blame on her. *Why did you bring us into this world?* he thought. *Why did you commit this heinous crime?* Then he heard his brother shouting violently.

"I must disappear. I'll leave this house as soon as I'm able to walk. Perhaps I'll leave the country entirely."

For the first time since this man of evil destiny had been carried into the house, a glimmer of hope struck Hassanein, as refreshing as a soft breeze. *Could this possibly happen, before the catastrophe occurs?* he thought. *Could he really disappear into some unknown land without leaving a single trace behind? In that case, let him stay here and get well. Then my life will be secure.*

As time passed, they became used to the melancholy atmosphere of the house. Almost recovered, Hassan began to think seriously of leaving the flat and escaping from the country. In continuous, silent meditation, he worked out plans to achieve his purpose. Nefisa no longer stayed at home; she resumed her regular daily visits. Returning to normal life, Hassanein spent his time in his office, his home, and his club. But he continued to worry about his brother's presence and its threat to their reputation. He hesitated to discuss this delicate point with his mother. He said to her one day with concern, "It's a divine miracle that the police haven't yet discovered where he is, and the miracle can't last forever!"

In response she threw him a glance which, at first, he couldn't interpret. Was it mute reproach? Or was it helpless resignation to fate? Or was it a sort of disapproval which she couldn't express? Perhaps it was all of these combined. But the mystery was unraveled when he saw a slow, shy tear that painfully wavered before it glistened in her eyes. This was disturbing in the extreme, for in spite of all their frequent predicaments and misfortunes, he found it difficult to remember ever having seen his mother in tears. The thought vanished as in pain and astonishment a stream of images of her stoicism and self-control passed through his mind. Now, he thought, she's like a ferocious lioness in the pangs of death. But once alone, Hassanein was concerned only for his own pains and fears; the others didn't matter. As his anger increased, he cursed both himself and his mother.

The following afternoon he received a further shock. He was sitting on the bed conversing with his mother and brother. Nefisa was out. Suddenly the bell rang and the servant went to the door. Returning in obvious confusion, she addressed Hassanein.

"Master, a policeman wants to speak to you!"

EIGHTY-NINE

At the sound of the word "policeman," their souls burst apart like shrapnel. Hassanein leapt to his feet, staring at the servant. Hassan flung one of his feet from the bed to the floor. With a gruesome glance at the window, he muttered, "Escape!" Their mother looked dazedly from one son to the other, her throat so dry that she was unable to utter a word. Hassanein remained momentarily immobile. Realizing how stupid it was just to stand there doing nothing, he shrugged his shoulders in despair and went to the policeman at the door. They exchanged salutes.

"Yes?" Hassanein inquired.

"Am I addressing the respected officer Hassanein Kamel Ali?" the man asked gruffly.

"You are."

"The respected officer of Al Sakakini police station wants to see you at once."

Looking beyond the policeman as far as the road, Hassanein was reassured when he saw none of the faces he might have expected. Uncertain, he inquired, "What does he want me for?"

"He ordered me only to inform you that he wanted to see you."

Hassanein hesitated a little. Then he went to the room to put on his clothes. He found his brother eavesdropping behind the door. At once Hassan asked anxiously, "Have they come?" In a sickly, feeble voice his mother repeated the question. As he dressed, Hassanein recounted the conversation with the policeman.

"Perhaps," Hassan spoke up immediately, "this officer is one of your acquaintances. Maybe he wants to alert you before they ambush the house. This is clear enough. Listen to me. If he asks you about me, tell him you haven't seen me for ages. Don't hesitate and don't be afraid about lying to them, for they'll never be able to trace me. As soon as you leave, I'll disappear. So have no scruples about what you tell them. May God protect you!"

Hassanein hid his eyes from his brother lest they reveal the gleam of an emerging hope. "Are you strong enough to make your escape?" he asked.

Hassan snatched his suit from the peg. "I'm all right," he said. "Goodbye!"

Hassanein went off with the policeman. The first thing to occur to him was to ask the officer's name. Maybe he actually was one of his acquaintances. But he was once more in the dark when the policeman gave him a name he had never heard before. Now matters were complicated indeed. However, Hassanein was relieved and reassured at Hassan's decision to disappear. They reached the police station a little before sunset, and the policeman led him to the officer, stopped, and saluted.

"Lieutenant Hassanein Kamel Ali," he said.

At arm's length from the officer as he sat at his desk stood two lower-class men and a woman, the marks of a recent fight on their faces. The officer rose, stretched out his hand.

"Welcome!" he said. He ordered the policeman to leave the room and close the door. He waved the young man to a chair in front of the desk.

What does it all mean? Hassanein thought as he sat down. *Welcome and compliments. What next?*

The officer rose, and leaning with his right hand on the edge of the desk, stood facing Hassanein, carefully studying his face; a curious, perplexed sort of glance, as if he didn't quite know how to begin the conversation. Hassanein found this short interval of silence coarse and intolerable. An abhorrent feeling of awe, worry, and annoyance had come over him from the very moment he stepped into the station.

Maybe he's a refined officer and is too embarrassed to fling the charge in my face, he thought. *This is curious in itself. Speak out and take the burden off my chest. How much I've dreaded this nightmarish moment. I already know what you want to say. Speak.*

"The policeman said you wanted to see me," he said, losing his patience.

"Sorry to bother you," the officer apologized. "I'd have preferred to meet you under better circumstances. But you know what duty dictates sometimes!"

Breathing out his last hope of safety, Hassanein replied gloomily, "Thank you for your kindness. I'm listening."

"I hope you'll take what I have to say with courage," the officer said earnestly and gently, "and behave in a manner that suits an officer who respects the law."

Hassanein was wan and almost fainting. "Naturally," he said.

The officer clenched his teeth, his cheeks contracting. "This," he said curtly, "has to do with your sister."

Hassanein raised his eyebows in surprise. "You mean my brother?" he said.

"I mean Madam, your sister. But excuse me. First I should like to ask you: Do you have a sister by the name of Nefisa?"

"Yes. Has she had an accident?" Hassanein asked.

"I'm sorry to tell you this," the man said, lowering his eyes, "but she was arrested in a certain house in Al Sakakini."

Hassanein rose to his feet. Frightened, rigid, and pale, he stared at the officer. "What are you saying?" he asked, out of breath.

The officer patted his shoulder sympathetically. "Get hold of yourself," he said. "This has to be handled with reason and calm judgment. I hope you'll help me do my duty without making me regret the measures I've taken to protect your reputation."

Staggered, Hassanein stared at the officer, listened vaguely to his voice. As if in a dream, the voice would vanish, the face remain; the face vanished, the voice remained, sometimes only two lips spewing forth a stream of frightful, disconnected, incomprehensible words. Despairing, Hassanein glanced nervously around the room, his eyes blinking: a gun fixed on the wall here, a row of rifles there, an inkstand, and the strange odors, the dead smell of old tobacco, the strange scent of leather. In a kind of receding consciousness, his mind harked back to memories which had no connection with the present. The old alley floated in his mind's eye; now he was again a boy playing with marbles with his brother Hussein.

She was arrested in a certain house, he thought. *What house? Surely one of us has lost his mind! But which one of us? First, I've got to be sure that I've not gone crazy.*

Resigned, Hassanein sighed weakly. "What did you say, sir?" he asked the officer.

"A Greek woman has a house in this quarter," the officer continued. "She rents rooms to lovers at so much per hour. This afternoon, we raided the house, and found Madam ... with a young man. We arrested her, of course, and I proceeded with the customary cold-blooded formalities, of which, of course, she was frightened, you know, and in the hope that I would release her, she confided that her brother was an officer."

"My own sister? Are you sure? Let me see her."

"Please control yourself. Had I been sure she was your sister, I'd have released her. But I was afraid she was lying. So I referred the matter to my boss, the *Mamur*. He approved of suspending legal action on condition that we could prove the truth of what she was saying."

Curiously enough, Hassanein entertained no doubt about the identity of the arrested girl. Yes, his pessimistic heart told him, it's got to be Nefisa. Was this the end of his journey in life? In his state of shock, he felt like some ancient relic of the past, of no relevance to the present. He was eager to get it all over with.

"Where is she?" he said in a lifeless voice. "Please let me see her."

The officer pointed to a closed door. "She fainted when she knew I'd sent for you instead of setting her free, so we left her in this room. Conduct yourself like a man with respect for law and remember I'm responsible for security. You're a decent, respectable man. So use your head. Nobody in this police station needs to know anything about it. But don't forget, everything depends on you."

"Please let me see her," Hassanein repeated in the same lifeless voice.

With heavy steps, the officer walked to the door and opened it. Like a sleepwalker Hassanein approached, casting a glance over the officer's shoulder like a man entering a morgue to identify a corpse. Close to the wall facing the door, a girl huddled against a sofa, her head flung back, her eyes half closed, dim, unseeing. She was either unconscious or had just recovered. Her face was as pale as death, and a few wet strands of hair stuck to her forehead. It was unmistakably Nefisa.

When it comes to disaster, he thought, *my heart never lies to me. If she was dead, I'd disown her without hesitation.* Unaware of their presence, she remained motionless, perhaps too exhausted to move. The officer looked inquiringly at him. But Hassanein's eyes became glazed as he stared at his sister. Surprisingly, in the deathlike silence, he found a temporary escape from his agony. Oblivious of the passage of time, he seemed to hear a terrible inner voice shattering the silence: *Everything is finished!* it proclaimed. He recalled the scene at home before he had left, an hour earlier, his mother desperate and perplexed, standing between him and Hassan, who was then preparing to escape. His mind filled with blasphemous imprecations, Hassanein wished he might die.

What does the officer expect me to do? he thought. *What should I do? Oh, God! How can I leave this place?* He heard the man address him. "I've done my duty. The rest is up to you."

"Where is the other?" Hassanein asked, avoiding the officer's eyes.

Understanding his meaning at once, the officer replied rather sternly, "After the usual legal routine, I released him."

"Thanks," Hassanein murmured. "Let's get out of here."

NINETY

In the dark outside, a cold breeze was blowing. With heavy steps, he walked out of the police station, followed at arm's length by his sister, her face cast down. The two walked along the tram tracks. Since this was his first visit to this quarter, he did not know where he was going. The street was deserted, although it was still early in the evening. *Where does this street go?* he wondered, surprised at the nature of his own thoughts. Where the street went was without significance for him. What to do with her was the main thing. He had thought of doing something as soon as they came out of the police station, and this was exactly what she expected. But he did nothing, and they continued to walk. He felt her intolerable presence behind him, the sound of her footsteps like bullets shot into his back, crushing every desire to look back at her over his shoulders. The terrible silence estranged them; he appeared absorbed in deep thought, but in reality his mind was utterly, terrifyingly, involuntarily blank. His self-control had vanished, all power of will was gone. Helpless, he yearned to recover his customary authority. When his foot collided with a small stone in his path, a flash of anger burst in his chest, as if attracted by his wandering thoughts in the dark. Should he strangle her, he wondered suddenly, or smash her head with his shoe? His pent-up feelings demanded some kind of relief. The infernal silence which separated them still prevailed. He was mustering all his willpower to break through this barrier when, to his surprise, she did it herself. He heard her murmur in a quaking, sobbing voice, "I'm a criminal, I know. I won't ask for forgiveness. I don't deserve it."

How, he wondered, *could she have the courage to speak? How devilish!* Her feeble voice stirred up in his breast a blind tyrannical storm of agitation that poured anger into his limbs and caused him to stop in his tracks. Turning to her with surprising swiftness, he raised his hand and with full force slapped her on the face. Mutely she staggered backward and fell, the back of her head crashing to the ground. Momentarily speechless, she quickly sat up. Summoning all her strength, she rose to her feet, withdrawing from him, until her back touched the wall of a house. She leaned against it. As he approached her, she could see the determination in his glances, despite the darkness which engulfed his face. She motioned with her hand as if pleading with him to stop.

"Stop!" she begged him hurriedly. "Don't! I'm not afraid for myself but for you. I don't want any harm to come to you because of me."

Increasingly infuriated by her gentle words, he bellowed, "You don't want any harm to come to me because of you! You filthy prostitute! You've already done me incalculable harm!"

"But," she passionately entreated him again, "if anything should happen to me, I can't bear the thought of their harming you."

"This kind of sly deceit won't help you to save your rotten life. No harm will come to me for killing you."

"I don't want you to be punished in any way," she exclaimed with the same passion. "What will you say when they ask you why you killed me? Let me do the job myself so that no harm will come to you and nobody will know anything about it."

"You'd kill yourself?" he inquired, astounded.

"Yes," she said breathlessly.

As he sought to control himself, suddenly a heavy weight seemed to lift from his chest. Burning with anger and tormented by his sense of duty, he had constantly considered the consequences of the spread of the scandal and the punishment involved. But now that she had cast the verdict on herself, his breath came more easily and he began to distinguish a ray of light in the suffocating darkness.

"How?" he asked, still absorbed.

"By any means whatever," she answered, hardly able to swallow.

He thought about it for a while, then cast a cruel glance at her. "Drown yourself in the Nile," he said bluntly.

"All right," she agreed calmly.

Snorting with fury, he withdrew. "Come on!" he muttered. He walked off. She left the wall with heavy steps and continued to follow him as before. He experienced a momentary feeling of relief which was as suddenly spoiled by the realization that he had lost his sense of personal dignity, of which he had been so proud as long as he was determined to kill her himself. Now he had changed from a man who prized his personal dignity to one who wanted only to save his own skin. Her proposed suicide choked him with a sense of defeat. But he was not strong enough to sacrifice safety on the altar of dignity, or weak enough to submit entirely to his urge for safety.

"How could you do such a thing?" he said roughly to give vent to his feelings. "You! Who would have imagined it!"

"It's God's decree," she sighed, surrendering to despair.

"No! Satan's!" he roared.

"True," she sighed as before.

"Who is it?" he asked after a moment's hesitation.

"Don't torture yourself and me," she said, shuddering. "Everything will be over in a few moments."

"Did he know me?"

"No," was her quick, emphatic answer.

Further hesitation doubled his torture. "Was it the first time?" he inquired.

She quaked again. "Yes," she said in the same voice.

Stamping his foot on the ground, he cried, "How could you surrender to temptation?"

"This is the decree of Satan," she murmured.

"You're Satan incarnate. We're destroyed."

"No. No," she exclaimed hopefully. "Now everything will be over, and nobody will ever know."

"Do you mean what you say?"

"Of course."

"And if you get scared?"

"No. My life is more dreadful than death itself."

Exhausted, both fell silent again. Confused, he looked ahead, along the tram rails.

"Where are we going?" he asked her sarcastically. "Probably you know this quarter better than I do."

She made no reply, her features contracting with pain. Now Daher Square came into view, teeming with life, buildings, and human voices. Absently he focused his eyes on a row of waiting taxis, headed for the first one, and opened the door for her. He followed her inside, temporarily absorbed in his thoughts while the driver waited for his instructions.

"The Imbaba Bridge, please," Hassanein said in a low voice.

NINETY-ONE

The taxi sped swiftly to Farouk Street, Ataba Square, then Imbaba.

Like strangers they sat inside the taxi. Half of his back to her, he looked out of the window at the road; Nefisa, her head bowed, was dazed and self-absorbed. Nothing significant passed through her mind. She was quietly immobile, like the silence in the wake of a storm, the motionlessness of death after the last painful breath. Before she fainted in the street, she had already reached the apex of insane paroxysm. As she returned to consciousness she was assaulted anew by her train of fearful thoughts. In infernal horror, her life passed before her, until the weight of her sorrows caused her to bow her head over her chest, as if desperately doomed under the weight of a collapsing wall. Now, she realized, it was all over, after her complete collapse, the appearance of Hassanein, and their conversation in the street. Horror left her mind in a mute vacuum, save for some distant memory of the days of her childhood, or some trifling aspect of the taxi floor. Yet she was undergoing an experience hitherto unknown to her. Life was worthless; death would rescue her from its painful humiliation. True, she had long resented her past life and sometimes dreamt of death. But she had not considered suicide, for always a gleam of hope lay hidden at the bottom of her heart. Now all connections with her life had been severed. Gone were the roots tying her to existence. Profound despair gave way to relief from the burden of living.

Now in her resignation, the death she hurried to meet became a soothing drug. As the speeding taxi suddenly swerved at a corner, Nefisa almost fell off the seat and became fearfully aware of her surroundings. Though her head was bowed, she felt his presence by her side. At the glimpse of his suffocating shape enveloped in a mysterious mist, her heart ached with pain and shame. *What could he be thinking of?* she wondered. *When will he feel anything but anger? When will it all be over? This will only be the end. Will Mother guess the truth? I shouldn't think of it. I'm doomed to die.*

Hassanein was strained and agitated, overcome with awe, anger, and despair. *How will this ordeal end?* he wondered. *And how will I come out of it? Will the curtain really fall on this affair, will no rank smell rise from it to make all this labor futile? I feel as if I'm being choked. One can never wipe out the past; it goes on with the future. Why can't we be different? Everything is finished and there is no need to think about it, no need at all. Such torment! How to overcome my misery? Wait. I'm driving her to her death, and she knows it. Will she have enough courage to do it? Sure, she's absorbed in her thoughts. But what is she thinking about? I shouldn't think of her. Death is the right end for her. Our eyes shouldn't meet; it would be too intolerable for both of us.*

"This has to do with your sister." Oh! Damn the officer. *"I'm sorry to tell you this, but she was arrested in a certain house in Al Sakakini."*

Who would ever have dreamed of this? Death is not an end but the beginning of further misery that awaits me at home. When shall I free myself from such thoughts?

What chimney is this? Perhaps a factory chimney. We're approaching Abu al-Ila Bridge. The chimney sends forth black, thick smoke. Were my thoughts or my breath to fume, I would send forth much filthier smoke. "I don't want any harm to come to you because of me." *Right you are. You must perish alone. When will we come to the end of the road?*

The taxi crossed the bridge. Strong gusts of cold, humid air, full of the fragrance of the Nile, gushed inside the taxi. Like a man scorched in a blazing fire, the young man welcomed the breeze, but it sent a shudder down Nefisa's spine, arousing a mysterious fear in her heart, until she finally gave way to her former state of resignation, immobility, and despair. The taxi doubled its speed. As it reached the neighborhood of the Imbaba Bridge, it gradually slowed down. As the driver turned inquiringly to Hassanein, he ordered him in a low voice to stop, paid the fare, and got out. She left by the opposite door, and the taxi departed.

Now brother and sister were alone, close to the entrance of the bridge. Lamps on either side of the bridge pierced the darkness with a strong light, and distant lamps twinkled faintly along the banks of the Nile, engulfed as it was north and south in the gloom, the rows of trees on either side of the river appearing like gigantic apparitions. The place was almost deserted, with only an occasional passerby. The branches moaned against the cold wind; the trees whispered when the breeze fell. Shocked into immobility, they stood quietly. He glanced secretly at her, and saw that her head was lowered and her back a little hunched, but the sight of her stirred no feelings of pity in his hardened, merciless heart. Suddenly exasperated by his own inaction, he spoke to her roughly. "Are you ready?"

"Yes," she answered in a strangely curious voice.

Her simple answer cut deep into his soul. He could stand still no longer and moved off with a heavy step. Before he had gone an arm's length from her, he heard her beg him, "Don't remember the harm I've done."

Taking wide strides like a fugitive, he replied in a gruff voice, "May God have mercy on all of us."

He left her alone in front of the bridge and walked toward the pavement extending to the right along the bank of the Nile. He quickened his pace. He felt an urge to escape, but an all-encompassing power held him back. His resistance collapsed near the huge trunk of a willow tree about thirty meters off the beginning of the pavement. Overcome with fatigue, he hid behind it. Like a monster sinking its teeth into the flesh of its prey, the bridge appeared to him as a solid mass, sparkling in the light of its lamps, obstinate and determined to link both sides of the Nile. At the entrance of the bridge facing him, he watched her move with unusual heaviness and rigidity, her head cast down as if she were walking in her sleep. Observing her clearly under the bright lights, his eyes were fixed on the illuminated side of her face, as she continued step by step to the middle of the bridge, where she halted. She raised her head and cast her eyes about her. Turning to the rail, she looked down at the swift, tumultuous water underneath. Breathless, he continued to watch her. At this moment, two men appeared at the farther end of the bridge. Busily conversing, they crossed the bridge quickly. The tram from Imbaba, shattering the silence with its noise, turned toward the bridge. The young man briefly recovered his breath, but soon became worried and depressed. Surely others must hear the violent beating of his heart. Several moments elapsed. He thought of himself as a detached observer of a scene in no way related to himself, but only after his sense of awe had displaced his anger and exasperation. In a turmoil of conflicting thoughts, he felt perplexed, like a man faced with an abstruse, mysterious problem who finds he cannot solve it or has no time to think about it. Now he was baffled and lost. Meanwhile, the two men crossed the bridge, the tram preceding them. The girl still stared at the water. Looking around, he saw no trace of a human being. All his senses crystallized in a fixed, terrified moment of expectation. He saw her turn her head to the right, then to the left. Suddenly she swiftly climbed the rail. Watching her movements, his heart quaked and his eyes protruded. *Impossible! Not this* . . . he thought. She had thrown herself into the water. Rather, she did nothing to stop herself from falling. Her protracted scream sounded like a groan, conjuring up the image of death for anyone unlucky enough to hear it. His own cry of terror was submerged in her last, piercing scream. As he watched her drown, he felt he could find the

solution to the abstruse problem which perplexed him, a solution different from the one she had chosen. *There might have
been another solution,* he thought. His cry sounded like an attempt
to redress his mistake, but the cry vanished. As he heard her
body tumble into the water, he gave another cry.

NINETY-TWO

He leapt to the sloping bank, his eyes staring at the spot under the bridge where her body had disappeared. Uncertain what to do, or what he wanted, he remained transfixed, staring. In a few moments, he thought that perhaps her body would float up to the surface of the water, but then he realized that the rushing current under the bridge must have carried her away. Perhaps her body was being tossed under the bridge; perhaps it was sinking in the river beyond the bridge. Although the thought occurred to him to take off his clothes and jump into the water in an attempt to save her life, he remained motionless. More immobile than before, he thought how bitterly ironic it was. Had his reason ceased to control his mind? He was taken aback by a voice behind him.

"Did you hear a scream?" someone shouted wildly.

Turning around, he saw a policeman, obviously concerned.

"Yes," he answered in surprise. "Perhaps someone is drowning."

In the darkness, the policeman gazed at the surface of the river, then walked quickly toward the bridge. His presence brought Hassanein back to an awareness of where he was, and he withdrew to his place behind the tree. But he was unable for long to control himself, and rushed toward the bridge, crossed it, and reached the rail overlooking the other side of the river. He glanced down at the swift current. Others were aware of the accident. A swift boat was moving from the left bank to the middle of the river. He heard screams and cries for help from the farther bank. Beyond the bridge the surface of the river was illuminated by the reflected images of the lamps. His eyes searching the surface, he failed to see anything.

Carried by the current, the boat left the illuminated area, headed into the darkness. *Could the boat win this race against death?* he wondered. Either he couldn't recognize his true feelings or perhaps his concentration on the boat was an attempt to escape from his thoughts. The boat stopped, and amid the noisy voices of the occupants, someone jumped into the water. This was the decisive moment. His heart quaked and his mouth was dry. In the darkness that enveloped the boat, he tried in vain to distinguish any object or make out a word in the tumult of different voices. His eyes were as tired as a blind man's; he could no longer see anything. He became aware that a crowd of people had gathered around him.

"The boat is returning," he heard one of them say. "Maybe they've rescued whoever it was."

A shudder passed down his spine. *Did she survive or perish? Should I stay or get out of here?* The desire to torture himself to the utmost proved irresistible; he walked toward the bank which the boat was heading for. Then, too frightened to trust to walking, he began to run as fast as he could to the place on the bank where a crowd gathered. He reached it just as the boat landed, and with shaking legs approached the crowd. His limbs trembling in spite of himself, he joined it stealthily, casting dazed glances at the boat in its thin veil of darkness. Not far away, the officer of the police station, together with some policemen, stood facing the bank. Now the shapes of men appeared carrying the drowned body, as they moved from the boat to the bank.

"Did they save him from drowning?" a bystander exclaimed.

Hassanein pricked up his ears for the answer, but none of the men uttered a single word. With an effort, they climbed the sloping bank, all eyes centered upon them.

"Oh, dear!" someone cried in horror. "It's a woman!"

"How'd she drown?" another inquired.

"She jumped from the bridge," a boy exclaimed. "The boatman's wife saw it and urged her husband to save her."

Hassanein's dazed, uncertain eyes followed them. He found it difficult to persuade himself that this was actually his sister; since no one else knew about it, he merely stood in the crowd like any curious stranger. When they reached the pavement, the men immediately attempted to revive her and emptied the water from her lungs. The officer ordered the policemen to disperse the crowd. But since none of them attempted to dismiss him, Hassanein remained standing in his place, staring fixedly at the hunchbacked body handled indelicately by these coarse men. Aware of his presence, the officer approached and greeted him with a nod.

"Did you witness the accident?"

Deeply disturbed, the young man came to his senses. "No," he hurriedly answered.

The men laid the girl's body on the ground. Kneeling down by her side, one of them felt for her pulse. He put his ear to her chest, listened for a heartbeat, then raised his head.

"The divine secret," he said, "has risen to its Creator. It's the will of God."

An overpowering feeling of alienation, neither sadness nor relief, returned to Hassanein. His mind became stagnant, his dreadful feeling of emptiness intolerable. He stared again at the girl's prostrate corpse not far from his feet, her hair scattered, a few plaits sticking to her cheek and forehead, her face mute and terrifyingly blue with no signs of recovering consciousness. Deep furrows around her gaping mouth and eyes suggested her last tortured convulsions in this world. Soaking wet, her dress clung to her body, the hem muddy and soiled with the dust from the ground. Her shoes had disappeared; one foot still retained a stocking. As he continued to look at her face, his chest, turbulent with agitation, swelled with emotion.

Why am I so agitated? he thought. *Wasn't I really convinced this was the best end? Didn't I drive her to kill herself? My soul must find rest. What were her thoughts when she fell into the water? What shock to her emaciated body? What went through her mind while she was tossed by the waves? What a struggle when the mud choked off her breathing! What terrible torture when, fighting her instinctive desire for survival, the river dragged her floating body down into the depths! The desperate attempts of a drowning woman to rescue herself are as futile as a poor man's dream of happiness. Can she see me now from the other world? Is she content, angry, or sardonic? What does she think of my situation now? Why did all this happen?*

As his thoughts suddenly flashed back to his mother, the image blanked out his view of the corpse. He shook his head, determined to banish the picture of his mother from his mind. His feverish attention returned to the corpse. In spite of himself, he remembered the girl's kindness to him, how she loved him, how generously she treated him. She would never have imagined losing her life at his hands. Desperately tired, he wondered again, fearfully: *Why did all this happen?* Unable to bear the sight of the corpse any longer, he closed his eyes. His head was feverish. Sorrow crushed his interest in life. The world seemed as void as her blue face. *God, I'm finished!* he thought with a deep sigh.

He heard the officer instructing the witnesses to accompany him to the police station, as the corpse was carried to the other side of the street. His eyes followed the group until they disappeared in the darkness. Less than two minutes later, he found himself alone, amid the rustling trees whose twisted, coarse branches almost covered the whole area. His limbs hanging loose, he staggered backward. Leaning against a tree trunk, he fell into a kind of somnolence, as if he were falling into a dim, hopeless abyss. *I'm finished,* he thought. *Since misery plagues us all, none of us has the right to make his brother miserable. What have I done? In despair, I did what I did, imposed my stern punishment upon her. What right did I have to do it? Was I really avenging the honor of our family? But I'm the worst of them all, as everybody knows. And if this world is ugly, I'm the ugliest part of it. I've always wished to destroy those around me. How then, as the worst of the culprits, could I appoint myself a judge to pass verdicts on others? I'm finished!*

He looked around in fear and perplexity. *Where can I go? Can*

I survive this ordeal as I've survived so many others? Hopes and delusions be damned! What do I care! Well, how can I help it? Rather, being what I am, I should go away, seek happiness in oblivion. He laughed bitterly. *How mercilessly I torture myself. But the dreadful past has devoured the present, and the past was nothing but myself. Burdened as I am, can I carry on with life? I can't. I could have loved life until the very end, regardless of the circumstances. But I don't understand what it is that is so essentially wrong with our nature. I'm done for.*

He stood erect, tired of leaning against the trunk, perhaps impelled by a fresh motive. Sick at heart and wanting only to escape, he walked off with a farewell glance at the spot where she had drowned herself. He remembered their words: "I don't want any harm to come to you because of me." "This is God's will." "The decree of Satan." "The Nile." "All right." "And if you get scared—" "No, life to me is more dreadful than death." "Are you ready?"

What was the officer thinking about him now? Where was Lieutenant Hassanein when it happened? Did he send an apology, make any excuses? I saw his face immediately after we took the corpse out of the water. I asked him if he saw the accident, but he was too astounded to reply.

Hassanein reached the same place on the bridge. He climbed the rail, looking down into the turbulent waters. Driving all other thoughts from his mind, he made his decision.

If this is what you want, so be it! I won't scream. For once, let me be courageous. May God have mercy upon us.